A Veil of Frost and Flame

K. D. MILLER

To Tess.

Thank you for being my favorite (ok, only) superfan. It's a very questionable life choice, honestly, but I fully support it - and there are no takesie-backsies! You are stuck with me forever.

Killian now belongs to you - treat him well 😉

Also, I am still very sorry that I inadvertently named the twat waffle of a twin after you. I swear she existed years before I met you and it was completely coincidental 😅

Copyright © 2026 by K.D. Miller

All rights reserved.

No part of this book may be reproduced in any form or by any electronic or mechanical means, including information storage and retrieval systems, without written permission from the author, except for the use of brief quotations in a book review.

ISBN: 979-8-9991824-6-3

Cover by Y'll That Graphic

CONTENTS

Chapter 1	1
Chapter 2	11
Chapter 3	21
Chapter 4	35
Chapter 5	53
Chapter 6	63
Chapter 7	73
Chapter 8	83
Chapter 9	91
Chapter 10	105
Chapter 11	127
Chapter 12	135
Chapter 13	147
Chapter 14	167
Chapter 15	197
Chapter 16	209
Chapter 17	227
Chapter 18	235
Chapter 19	245
Chapter 20	253
Chapter 21	265
Chapter 22	279
Chapter 23	293
Chapter 24	299
Chapter 25	317
Chapter 26	325
Chapter 27	337
Chapter 28	345
Chapter 29	351
Chapter 30	357
Chapter 31	365
Chapter 32	379
Chapter 33	387
Chapter 34	393

Chapter 35	405
Chapter 36	407
Chapter 37	415
Chapter 38	417
Chapter 39	423

Some say the world will end in fire,
Some say in ice.
From what I've tasted of desire
I hold with those who favor fire.
But if it had to perish twice,
I think I know enough of hate
To say that for destruction ice
Is also great
And would suffice.

-ROBERT FROST

CHAPTER ONE

"Great Makers, who died?" Matthais jokes as he enters the tavern and eyes me where I sit frozen at one of the long tables near the mostly unused fireplace, parchment in hand and shock on my face. We live in the southern-most port on Hypathia, as far away as I could possibly get without actually leaving the empire, so fires are rarely needed, but the stone hearth does have a certain aesthetic quality that gives the tavern a homey feel. I miss the true winters of the North. I miss the ice and the snow, the beauty and stillness of the earth when it's wrapped in a blanket of white. But no matter how much I might miss it, I swore that I would never, ever go back there.

But now...

I raise my eyes from the parchment to meet his gaze. His smile immediately fades, his dimples disappearing and his eyes growing stark. "Oh, Great Makers, who died?" he asks again, serious this time.

"My sister..." I croak.

"Your sister died?" Math echoes, confusion furrowing his pale blonde brows. I rarely speak of my sister, and Math and Cece are the only two people in the world who even know she exists. Cece emerges from behind the long, polished bar with two tankards of sweet ale in her hand, just arrived this morning on a ship from Sol, the big island to the south. She rolls her eyes and kicks out at Math's rump as she walks by.

"No, you daft idiot. Her sister sent a letter."

"Well, how was I to know that?" he grumbles, coming to join us at the table and stealing a sip of ale from Cece's cup. She swats at his hand, but grins fondly at her husband. "She sent you a letter? After all these years?"

I nod numbly, staring at the elegantly written letter before me. *Of course Tesni's penmanship would be impeccable*, I think savagely. Tesni had been given every luxury, been raised in a castle, tutored by the best scholars, dressed by the finest seamstresses. She'd never wanted for anything in her life. *She'd* never been cold and starving. *She'd* never thought she might die or be taken by Hunters at any moment. *She'd* never slept in the rain, been bitten by rats, or had to beg for food—and fight back against men who thought to take something in return for the scraps they threw her way.

I clench my teeth, bitterness clawing inside of me like a living thing, a beast with razor sharp claws and a hunger for vengeance. I grab my ale and drain the entire cup in three long gulps. It's sweet and crisp, spreading a delicious warmth through my belly. Randolph knows this is one of my favorites and makes a point to bring a cask or two anytime he returns from Sol. *Perhaps I'll sooth my frustrations with him tonight, thank him properly.* My lips curl slightly at the thought, but even the temptations of losing myself with Randolph for a few hours can't assuage my anxiety over the letter.

I glance to the parchment, trying to push past all of my feelings about it and think logically, not emotionally. Why the letter now? I've heard from my sister only once before this in nearly fifteen years. About a year after we'd opened the tavern, a missive had arrived for me. It had been a simple letter, just a few sentences, but still it made me nearly vomit from fear:

> *I know where you are. Barony believes you to be dead, thanks to me. Stay away and live your own life, and I'll let that lie be a secret kept between sisters. If you try to come back or interfere, I'll make the lie an absolute truth.*
> *Live well...*
> *-T*

The threat had been clear as glass, and I'd been all too happy to oblige. I wanted nothing more than to forget my sister, forget King Barony and Lyanna and everything my life used to be. I never knew how she found me, but I knew without a doubt she spoke true. Even then, her reputation had traveled throughout the continent. She was cold and ruthless and wouldn't bat an eye to choose violence before all else.

So, I never thought I'd hear from Tesni again since I kept up my side of our silent bargain. I stayed away. I stayed hidden as far from her as I could get, never interfering, never stepping foot anywhere near Lyanna again, doing my best to pretend that she didn't exist and that I wasn't who I was.

But now, this damned letter arrives. I grit my teeth, fingers flexing on the parchment. I just stop myself from balling it up and throwing it across the room. Instead, I close my eyes and pinch the bridge of my nose, taking slow, deliberate breaths. When I open them again, Math and Cece are both staring with a mixture of concern and curiosity.

"She says she wants me to come to Lyanna. She says she needs my help and she wants to...make amends." The words taste like acid on my tongue, and my own shock and confusion give way to anger. I loathe my sister with a fire that could thaw even my cold heart. Why the fuck would I care if she needs help? Why would I want to make amends? I know without a doubt that she doesn't actually think I'll care—she knows she has leverage over me and is just pretending to let the decision be my own. My location. My identity. Still, I'm going to pretend as if I have a choice here for as long as I can.

Cece and Math share a look, one of those looks that two people who are so connected and in love can share and words somehow pass between them without speaking. I've sure as hells never shared such a look with anyone before. I've had bedmates, of course—some that I've cared about, some that I couldn't even tell you their names—but everyone in town likes to joke that my heart truly is made of ice. It doesn't stop most of the men from trying desperately to thaw it, or to at the very least chip away enough that I might agree to one of their marriage proposals. I always smile slyly at them, hold my hand over my chest, and frown, quipping, "Sorry, lads, still cold as winter. Perhaps next time..."

"Could it be true, you think?" Cece asks gently. She knows the story of the fallout between Tesni and me, knows the depth of my twin's betrayal, yet she still has a glimmer of hope in her eyes. Cecelia is all warmth compared to my cold. She sees the good in every person and in every situation, never met a stranger, is truly good and bright. *No wonder Math loves her so much*, I think as I watch him absently brush a wayward chestnut curl from her forehead. The touch is so tender, so unthinking, it makes my chest clench. *To be loved like that...*

I shake myself. I can never be loved like that because I can never let anyone *truly* know me. Without truth and honesty, love can't exist. Everyone jokes about my cold heart, but the truth is that I desperately *want* it to thaw. I want someone to share my life with, my*self* with. But it can never happen.

I roll Cece's question around in my head. Could it be true? I can't imagine how or why Tesni could possibly want to make amends after all this time. She has plenty to atone for, there's no doubt of that, but why now? There are rumblings even this far south, disturbing rumblings about war brewing between the northern kingdoms. Helios mostly remains out of empire business and gossip, feeling almost like we're an island like Sol to our south, separated from the rest of the continent by two rivers called The Vines. We're welcoming of any who wish to come here, of course, but we're a peaceful kingdom, more keen to revelry and drink than war and destruction.

But...could Tesni really need my help? Is that why she sent the letter requesting my aid, instead of having guards arrive on my doorstep simply demanding it? Maybe she really does want to try to make things right between us...

"What if..." Math chews his lip. "Well, what if she's sick? Dying even? I've heard plenty of tales of folks changing their tune about their lives when they don't think they have much life left. My own grandpa begged my pa's forgiveness for being a right ass his entire life as the fever took him"

"That's a good point," Cece agrees.

A loud *caw!* echoes through the room, making Math jump and spill his ale down his front.

"Bloody ruddy fucking fuck! What *is* that!?" he sputters, shoving his chair back and staring at his now damp chest. Cece snorts and hands him a rag, shaking her head, clearly saying *what am I to do with him?* I feel my lips twitch, despite everything. Math has always had quite a gift when it comes to cursing.

"That is one of the King's personal winter ravens," I say, waving negligently at the bird sitting on the windowsill. He's beautiful, with his snow-white feathers and midnight eyes, twice the size of a normal raven and three times as smart, but his presence sends a cold shiver up my spine. It brings King Barony into my life here, and that's the last thing I've ever wanted. Not to mention, it brings back too many memories that I'd rather leave forgotten. I'd had a winter raven of my own before I'd been forced to flee all those years ago. I'd loved the bird fiercely and it had broken my heart to leave her behind. I hope Tesni at least had the decency to see her taken care of.

"I'm to have him return with my answer," I say with a roll of my eyes, motioning between the parchment and the bird. I should refuse it, obviously. I want to, but...well, some small, very stupid and naive part of me just can't. Despite everything, a tiny, secret part of my heart aches for it to be true, aches to have my sister fix the rift between us.

Plus, I remind myself scornfully, *she's not truly going to accept no for an answer*. So, my choices are to say yes, or to run, leaving my life and the only people I care about in this world behind. And running is no guarantee of my safety—if she found me once, she can surely find me again. And I would never, ever risk leaving Math and Cece here to get caught in the crossfire.

I exhale roughly and press away from the table to pace. My worn leather boots are silent against the pale beachwood floor as I walk, back and forth, back and forth. I twirl a lock of black hair around my finger and then scowl at it, tossing it back with a huff of annoyance. My sister has taken *everything* from me. I pay an alchemist monthly for a tonic that changes my eyes from their natural deep green to a muddy brown, and my hair to this ink black. It also has an interesting side effect of making hair on the rest of my body disappear entirely. Donovan believes that to be permanent, but interestingly enough, men seem to *adore* it. He's assured me many times that the other changes can most certainly be reversed, so perhaps one day, I can be myself once more.

Looking in the mirror is still a shock sometimes, even after all these years, a stranger staring back at me. I wonder if I would even recognize my true self anymore. My chest aches at the thought, but icy fire fills my veins, fury and rage at all my sister has taken from me rising. I know that it had to be done if I wanted any chance at a real life. I needed to be sure that I bore no resemblance to my former self, to look *nothing* like the King of Lyanna's precious Gifted. If they realized who my sister was, they would have known that I, too, have powers beyond imagining. Being a Gifted without the protection of someone like Barony was far too dangerous in Hypathia. Gifteds were enslaved every day.

Being a slave at all is a terrifying thought, but for years most Gifteds ended up in Duskthorne, and *that's* a fate worse than death. King Dorian employs hundreds of Hunters to track down as many Gifteds as possible and bring them back to his kingdom. They're enslaved, used for their powers, kept in cages and forced to perform like animals for travelers from all across the continent for a price. Well, that used to be the case before he dropped farther and farther into his madness and became a recluse, shutting the gates of his kingdom to outsiders. Makers know what goes on behind those impenetrable walls now, but I'm sure the atrocities have far from ended. Rumors still swirl that he keeps the female Gifteds for himself to...*breed*. Even now, I shiver with fear at the thought of ending up there. I would choose death a thousand times over.

Most Gifts aren't particularly noteworthy or powerful, nothing that could be used in any offensive or violent way: the ability to light candles without match or flint; coaxing crops to grow or flowers to bloom; traces of telekinesis; the ability to breathe under water like a sea creature. There are legends of a time when Gifteds bonded with great beasts—bears and lions and even dragons—and drew even more strength from their familiars, resulting in powers that could move mountains and turn entire armies to ash on the winds, but there's been no record of a bonded Gifted in almost a century as far as I know, familiars are truly only myths these days.

But even the smallest Gifts are enough to catch the attention of the greedy. No Gifted is safe within the empire anymore, not really, especially with some of the gossip I've heard the sailors bring from the northern ports, gossip I pray to all the Makers is simply that. The alternative is almost too horrible to imagine.

I shiver and keep pacing, watching Cece take up the parchment, dark eyes darting over the elegant script, widening before eventually meeting mine again.

"She's *begging* you, Thea. She says it's a matter of life and death."

"Ah, see! Death! I was right," Math says with a smug grin, tossing the rag down onto the table with a soggy *plop*. Cece gives him a level look, and he ducks his head sheepishly. "Sorry. Sorry. Not something to celebrate. Right." He holds his hands up in surrender.

"It seems truly important." After a heartbeat of silence, she adds softly, "Perhaps this is your chance to heal old wounds, to finally truly move on."

I narrow my eyes and stop my pacing, putting my hands on my hips indignantly.

"I am perfectly healed, thank you very much." Math snorts but quickly covers it with a cough. "Ok, fine, I'm not *healed*, exactly, but I'm fine." At their unconvinced looks, I throw my hands up in the air. "Alright, fucking hells, I'm..." I trail off, not knowing what word to use. I'm mostly content in my life here with Math and Cece. I love the two of them more than anything else in this world. I love the tavern. I love the raucous sailors and the ever-present noise from the docks. I definitely love my time with Randolph when he's in port and some of the other fellows around town when he isn't...But am I happy? Am I whole?

I'm not sure that I ever can be, really. Tesni broke a fundamental part of me and I'm not sure that those jagged pieces can ever truly be put back together again.

"Look, I don't know if those wounds can be healed, even with an apology or whatever it is Tesni is planning to do or say."

"It could be worth a try though, right?" Cece says. She has seven sisters and loves them all dearly. I envy that, but I know it makes it nearly impossible for my friend to comprehend how sisters could be torn apart as Tesni and I had been, to have hatred between us instead of love and adoration. She'd been angry at Tesni on my behalf after I'd told her and Math my story all those years ago, but she's always held onto the notion that perhaps it was a misunderstanding of some kind. *She'd been young, she'd been afraid, she hadn't understood what she was doing*—Cece had given a thousand explanations in her attempt to dull the razor-sharp edge of my rage and hurt.

"And she says she needs your help. You can't really ignore that, can you?"

I give her a look that says I most certainly fucking *can*, but she shoots me one back that makes me press my lips into a hard line. Cece is sweet and bright, but she can also be unyielding and brutal when she needs to be. *She is going to make a brilliant mother one day*, I think, knowing that she and Math have been trying for a child for a few months now.

I exhale roughly and stare at the empty hearth as if it holds all the answers.

After a minute or an hour, Math asks softly, "So...will you go then?"

Will I go? I twirl a lock of hair around my finger once more. It's an absent-minded gesture that I've always done. When we'd been young, it was the only way King Barony had been able to tell Tesni and I apart. If he watched long enough, I would always give myself away with my hair twirling.

I take a deep breath and force myself to think through everything again.

When I'd had to flee the north, I'd been a terrified child of only twelve, without the power to fight back. All I'd known was that I wanted to live, and at the time, that had meant running from everything I'd ever known and fighting tooth and nail in a world that wasn't kind to young girls. Now, I'm a woman of twenty-seven with too much knowledge of the world and a heart made of ice. Now, I *burn* to make my sister answer for her crimes. I will not forgive, nor will I forget...but perhaps I'll allow my sister to *try*, to beg for mercy. *And then I'll laugh as I deny it, deny whatever help she's requesting.* My power stirs at the thought, my palms tingling. Once upon a time, the power would have overtaken me completely as my emotions roiled, but I'm stronger now. I know how to handle myself.

And if my sister wants a fight, I'll be ready for it.

I turn back to Cece and Math, the best people I've ever met, the only two people I can ever truly love and who, by some miracle, love me in return. They know my past and my true identity, and welcomed me into their fold without question or hesitation, saving my life years ago. They aren't my blood, but they're my family.

If they think I should do this, maybe I should.

I press my shoulders back and give them a hard nod.

"I'm going."

CHAPTER TWO

I sit inside the carriage that had been waiting for me when my ship pulled into Aldmoor Harbor on Lyanna's western coast. I'd nearly forgotten how different the northern seas were from those off Helios, and as the gray, stormy waves tossed our ship around like a child's toy, I'd missed my home with a pang that seemed to shudder down to my soul. The journey north had taken almost two weeks because of violent storms—perhaps I should have taken that as a sign that I shouldn't have come, that Raya, Maker of the sea, was trying to steer me away—and while I'd enjoyed the time with Randolph and his crew, had enjoyed drinking their rum and beating them at quills and using Randolph's company to keep my thoughts from what was to come, I'm ready to be done with this and get back to my life.

And yet, I can't force myself to leave this carriage. I hate to admit it, but a part of me is terrified to be back in this place...and I hate even more that a part of me longs to see my sister again so badly my heart aches for it. Maybe not the sister that exists here, in reality, but the one that still exists in my mind. The twin that had been my best friend, other half, and protector when we were girls. I've missed that connection almost as much as I've missed the snow, though I know that connection is gone forever. *At least the snow never fails to fall,* I think with a bittersweet twist of my lips. I'd spied a few flakes as I'd left the Wave Dancer, and could feel it in my bones, calling to me, welcoming me back.

"Do you require assistance, miss?" one of the footmen asks from just outside the door, looking at me quizzically. I don't know how long he's been standing there, waiting for me to exit.

"N-no," I stammer, barely a whisper. I inhale deeply and try to calm the power that's seething inside me, swirling like a tempest of Raya's making. "No," I say again, more firmly, curling my fingers into fists. "I'm fine."

I step out of the carriage and stare up at the imposing castle. The entire structure had been carved of white moonstone, each turret and tower tipped in shimmering gold, each balcony and statue gilded. It simply oozes opulence and wealth. *This had been my home,* I think with an unexpected twist in my chest. King Barony had never been particularly warm or fatherly to us, but he was the only family we'd ever known, and I'd been safe within these walls—until I hadn't been.

I steel myself to take the first step up the wide staircase leading to the towering golden doors, the kingdom of Lyanna's crest stamped within the gleaming metal: a lion rearing up on its hind legs, wings flaring from its back, claws and fangs bared. These were the stairs I'd run down all those years ago, fleeing for my life with nothing but the clothes on my back and terror in my broken heart. Memories assault me without warning, and suddenly I'm back to that day.

The day that changed everything.

"My girls," King Barony said when we entered his grand study. We'd never been allowed in this room before, and I stared, wide-eyed, taking in the enormous room. Shelves lined the walls, filled with all sorts of strange objects: crowns and scepters, leather-bound books, swords and shields and daggers with ruby-studded hilts, other things that I had no names for, but

knew must be extremely important to be stored here in the King's personal study. I'd heard tales of an evil king in the northern mountains who collected people the way King Barony collected things, and the thought made me shiver in fear. My gaze shifted to King Barony's desk and I gasped in horror, recoiling. The heads of slain animals covered the wall behind him, lips curled up in terrifying silent snarls. Tears sprang to my eyes at the thought of all of them dying, of their possible suffering. I thought of the animals in the menagerie, the horses in the stables, my own beloved winter raven, Midnight. I'd giggled for hours over naming the snow-white bird after the deepest dark of night. The thought of any of them being harmed made me feel sick. I'd glanced to my sister, and an odd feeling settled in my belly: Tess looked...enthralled with the violence, eyes wide—not in shock, but in excitement. I pushed the unease away, knowing I must be mistaken.

We stopped before the King's desk. He wasn't very old, not like some of the members of court who we'd seen from afar, spying from the hidden alcove in the throne room that Barony doesn't know about. We're never allowed to see them, always kept hidden. He says it's for our safety—people try to take Gifteds away from their homes and use them, but he won't let that happen to us. So, it's better no one knows we're here. His smile seemed more bemused today than usual, his black eyes gleaming with a dark glee that I didn't really understand, but that made the hairs on the back of my neck stand on end. I wanted to reach out for Tess, but something stopped me.

"We're going to play a bit of a game, my dears." He eyed us both, looking between us over and over, eyes narrowing slightly as he tried to tell us apart. After a few moments, my finger snaked into my hair, twirling a strand around and around like a fiery snake. King Barony's grin widened and he steepled his fingers beneath his chin, studying us.

"What kind of game?" Tess asked, not sounding like she shared my unease at all.

"You know how much I care for you both." The King had never been very warm or loving towards us, never laughed or played, but he did care for us in his way, I thought. He'd taken us in when our mother had died, *fed us and clothed us, given us toys and pets and books, and protected us by keeping us within the palace. But even at only twelve, I knew that what he cared about most, were our Gifts. If that kept us safe, then that was ok by me. "But I have received an offer that I simply cannot ignore."*

"Offer?" I asked, voice small, as it always was around the King. Unease and cold began to unfurl in my chest.

"Simply put: I am going to keep one of you, and the other will be sold to the King of Enola."

"Sold?" Tess asked, brows drawn down. We shared a confused look.

"Sold, yes. For an outrageous amount of gold, actually." King Barony smirked and my stomach knotted.

"You can't...you can't sell a person," I said, incredulous, wondering if this conversation were even actually happening. Had I fallen asleep inside the hedge maze again? Was this a nightmare?

"Oh, my dear, I think you'll find that I certainly can. It happens all the time, in fact, especially for ones such as yourselves. Gifteds," he clarified at my confused look. The evil king in the mountains, *I thought with a gasp.* He bought people. *King Barony's grin widened, reminding me of the evil snake in one of my favorite books from when we were younger.*

"Now, for the game: I'm going to let the two of you decide who stays, and who goes. I would caution you to choose wisely. King Morthan is far less...gentle than I."

I swallowed hard, not fully understanding his words in the moment, but instincts deep inside were roaring to life, telling me that I did not want to go to King Morthan. Even still, my mind couldn't quite catch up to what my gut was trying to tell me. This simply couldn't be real. We couldn't be split up. One of us couldn't be sold *like an animal. This had to be some kind of strange joke that I didn't understand.*

As if reading my mind, King Barony said, "I'm afraid this is very real, my dears. You will choose, or you will be punished until you do." I shuddered and ran my fingers unconsciously over the faint scars across my knuckles. The King's punishments were...severe.

Tess took my hand and squeezed, giving me a reassuring look, though there was something...off. I ignored the uneasy feeling and breathed a sigh of relief. Even if Barony believed this was real, there was no way that either of us would play into this game. Never! We would endure his punishment and then run away together, leave Lyanna and the King behind forever. We were sisters. We were twins. We were each other's whole worlds.

Just before I could voice my thought, put my foot down and refuse to let this happen with a courage I rarely felt and never demonstrated, Tess released my hand. Everything seemed to happen slowly then, as if in a dream. Tess stepped forward, towards King Barony's desk and away from me, and though I couldn't say why, it felt as if that small step put miles between us.

"Pick me, Your Majesty," Tess said in a strong, clear voice, and my heart splintered, my breath rushing from my lungs so quickly they burned. "I'm much stronger than Tee. Her Gift hardly works at all and mine is growing every day." To demonstrate, she held her palm out, and a small flame danced in the center. "Fire is much more impressive than ice, don't you think?" Her voice was sweet but cold in a way I'd never heard, a sharp edge that made me recoil and Barony smile. I suddenly saw that they were a pair, matching snakes.

I took a step backward, my entire heart freezing in my chest and thundering so loudly I thought that surely the whole kingdom could hear it. No, this couldn't be happening. Tess couldn't be betraying me this way. This had to be some kind of trick. She had a plan and she had to pretend to play along with the King for it to work. It had to be...Please...

Tess glanced my direction and I searched my sister's gaze, looking for some sign that this was, in fact, all a cunning ploy. She'd always been cunning, even when we were younger. She could manipulate our nannies, weave tales and make them believe anything she said, could get anything she wanted.

But all I saw in my sister's eyes was a wicked gleam that had never been there before. No, it's always been there, it was just hidden below the surface, *a part of my mind whispered. Hadn't I always been afraid that Tess had darkness in her, had seen small glimpses over the years as we'd gotten older? Those same manipulations that had seemed funny and innocent when we were young turned darker. Cruel. Yet I'd always pushed* the unease or unkind thoughts aside, refused to acknowledge them, even to myself. Now, I understood that I'd been right all along. My sister wasn't who I'd always believed her to be.

And now, it would be my undoing.

Tess turned back to King Barony.

"I'm the better choice, Your Majesty. She's weaker, will always be weaker. I understand the world better than she does."

My sister faded away in that moment, a ruthless, terrifying stranger taking her place.

"Tess," I whispered, a cold shiver working its way up my spine and radiating outward, filling every inch of my body. A thin, pathetic sheen of frost coated my palms and extended to my fingertips. Tess was right, of course: she had far more control over her power than I did. I was honestly surprised that the King didn't simply choose her, but he'd always eyed me with interest, knowing that my power could be great if I ever learned to channel it properly, so I suppose he was willing to see how this played out instead of choosing himself. I think he simply enjoyed the pain he knew this game would cause as well.

Tess met my gaze again, a mirror image staring back at me. There was the tiniest bit of regret there, but mostly a terrifying cold calculation that made her green eyes look like true emeralds: Hard. Unforgiving. Beautiful in a fierce, cold way.

"I'm sorry, Tee, but I belong here."

It felt as if I'd been kicked in the chest by one of the Northland horses, bigger than their southern counterparts and far stronger, built to withstand the harshness of the winters. We didn't really need them here in Lyanna, but Barony had several simply to say that he did. I'd seen one kick right through a stall door once, turning it to splinters with ease. That's what happened to my heart in that moment: it was ground to splinters. Destroyed.

Tess moved to stand behind the desk next to King Barony. He beamed, staring at her like the prize she apparently was.

"But...I..."

"I'm sorry, Thea, but you must go now. I promised delivery within the month, and it is a long journey." He beckoned at the door with two fingers and two of his guards came forward, each seizing one of my arms.

"No! No, stop this! Please!" They dragged me away as I fought and screamed. Tears streamed down my face, my chest constricting painfully. "Tess! Tess!!" I screeched as they yanked me through the doorway. The last thing I saw was my sister's cold gaze and her look of disgusted pity. That was when I knew that my sister was gone. The sister I thought I'd had, the one who had held me when I'd cried and promised to keep the monsters away, was dead. Maybe she'd never truly existed at all.

The guards dragged me through the palace, the hallways where I'd run and laughed and played, to the grand entrance. I couldn't believe it was truly happening, but I felt the truth in every breaking piece of my heart, every terrifying drum of my pulse. They were taking me away from my home, taking me to be a slave of a ruler of a faraway kingdom to do Makers knew what. He would use me for my Gifts, make me do whatever he pleased. He would find a way to force my Gifts to cooperate from the way King Barony spoke of him. I didn't know much about King Morthan, but it didn't matter who he was: he believed he could own people, which meant he was evil, just like the terrible king in the mountains.

Desperation clawed at my stomach and chest and I dragged my feet, trying to fight the guards, but they were too strong.

Weak, weak, weak. Tesni's words echoed through my mind, and something shifted inside my chest, resolve I didn't know I had buoying me in the storm. My heart was shattered, but I thrust the jagged shards back into the forge. I let it burn, hotter and hotter, until the pieces melted together, becoming something new, something harder than before. I covered it in impenetrable ice, vowing to never let it be broken again.

I felt my Gift surge within me, the cold radiating through my body once more, but this time, it wasn't just the barest frost. My skin turned to ice, so cold it burned the guards' hands. They both gasped and released me long enough that I could stumble a few steps away.

"Grab her!" the taller guard yelled.

He clenched his hand into a fist as he lurched towards me, looking like he planned to pay me back for the pain I'd just caused. I raised my hands to ward him off and spikes of ice shot forward from my palms. The man screamed in agony, covering his face with his hands and staggering sideways as blood streamed between his fingers. He tripped and smashed his skull on one of the gilded lion statues set in a semicircle around the foyer, guarding the front door with watchful eyes. My own went wide, unbelieving that I'd just hurt someone. I'd never so much as stepped on an insect in my life. I'd once accidentally given one of our nannies a bruised eye when we'd been playing silly games outside and though Marisol told me over and over that it was fine, that it had been an accident, I'd cried for days over it. I'd always loathed violence and causing others pain. Tess had always teased me, saying I was too soft hearted for this world.

Not anymore, *I thought*. You saw to that, Tess.

I stared in shock, willing the man to rise, terrified that he never would. I blinked tears away, believing that if I just stared hard enough, his chest would rise. I waited another endless heartbeat and then white-hot pain laced through my right shoulder. I stumbled backwards, hitting the marble floor so hard my teeth clattered. I looked up to find the other guard towering above me, a bloody blade in his hand. I clamped my hand over the wound, blinking around tears and black spots. I'd never been truly hurt before. A scratched knee from climbing trees, a bump on the head, a bruise here and there, but nothing like this. I felt bile rise in my throat, but I desperately tried to keep it away as blood oozed between my fingers.

"Easy now, little one. We can do this easy, or hard, but make no mistake, you will be coming with us."

Panic and pain fought for dominance inside my body and mind, and without thought, I threw my bloody hand out towards the second guard. Ice flew once more, even thicker than before, the spikes more like small daggers. One caught the guard right in the throat, and crimson sprayed in a wide arc as he collapsed to his knees. I turned my head away but felt the blood coat my neck and chest, sticky and hot.

His hands flew to his ruined throat, trying to staunch the life flowing from his gaping wound. He tried to speak, but only sickening gurgling sounds escaped his lips. He fell forward onto the gleaming white floor with a thud and didn't move again.

"Oh, Great Makers," I whispered in horror, staggering away from the man until I hit the front door of the palace. Blood pooled outward from beneath his body, as if it was reaching for me. Slow, accusing fingers. Monster. Murderer.

I did vomit then, barely holding myself upright and leaving a smear of my own blood across the golden metal. The first guard groaned quietly, and though part of me was happy that I hadn't killed him too, I knew that he would raise the alarm—that was if other guards weren't already on their way, having heard the shouts.

So, I did the only thing I could: I tore open the door and fled.

And I never looked back.

CHAPTER
THREE

My throat goes dry at the memories, ice coating my hands, my chest burning as my Gift rises. *No. I'm not that little girl anymore. I'm not afraid.* I clench and unclench my fists over and over, refusing to let memories overwhelm me. I take deep, controlled breaths the way Tobias taught me all those years ago when fear would take my breath out of nowhere, for seemingly no reason.

Focus on things you can see and hear and feel. Breathe in as you count to three, hold it as you count to five, and then exhale slowly as you count to three again.

As it so often does, his voice in my mind helps to ground me. I take one more breath and shift my shoulders back. I march up the stairs, ready to be done with this.

Two guards pull the doors open for me and servants within bow their heads respectfully as I enter. I take in the four-story foyer, craning my head back to study the soaring ceiling. I'd always loved the gold-dusted chandelier that dangles high above. As a child, I'd thought it resembled a giant golden spider, and I'd imagine that it would come to life and have adventures with me all around the castle. I shake my head now, feeling silly for remembering such things. I tell myself not to, but glance to my right all the same, staring at the spot on the floor a few feet away. I can still see the guard's lifeless body lying in a pool of blood, those crimson fingers reaching towards me...

"Tee," a soft voice breathes from the top of the grand staircase. My eyes snap upward, colliding with my twin's. Tesni's lips part, a smile spreading over her face. I inhale sharply at the sight. Tesni looks just as I *should*—red hair flowing down her back in soft curls, those emerald eyes wide and gleaming. My skin is more sun-kissed than Tesni's fair coloring thanks to so much time spent outside at the docks and splashing in the bay in Helios, but there's no denying that Tesni is even more beautiful because of it. She looks like a porcelain doll, delicate and exquisitely made.

Tee. I wince at the nickname from so long ago. A flash of a memory sears my eyes, nearly making me stumble: the pair of us, lying beneath the huge canopy that covered my bed, making up stories about the stars embroidered there. "See, Tee! The jester is just there, with his funny hat." A peel of giggles. "No, Tess! That's the queen with her crown!"

"Thea," I respond cooly. "My name is Thea." Tesni looks hurt for a brief moment, but then inclines her head as if to say she understands that though Tee and Tess had been sisters, Thea and Tesni are simply two strangers who have agreed to a meeting.

"You came." Her voice sounds tight, as if she's truly surprised to see me. I narrow my eyes, wondering what game she's playing, my defenses up and ready. She breezes down the stairs, looking every bit the King's treasured Gifted, the spoiled princess. She's in a stunning midnight blue gown that seems to flow like water behind her as she descends step after step. I glance down at my own clothing: leather riding pants and matching boots, a white linen tunic with a worn leather vest that cinches my waist and ties across my breasts. I'd worn a coat on the ship to keep up appearances once we crossed into the northern seas, though the cold doesn't affect me as it does most people, but I'd discarded it in the carriage. Anyone here would already know exactly who I am, so there was no reason to pretend or hide. Though I hate being back here, I can't deny that the relief of being myself is intoxicating. *I've been hiding for so long...*

I shake myself, clearing my throat and throwing my shoulders back. The longer I looked at Tesni—and that is who she is now. She'll never be my Tess again—the angrier I become. My rage burns low, just below the surface, like embers in a fire. They need only be stoked just right to bring the fire to roaring once more. *And if anyone can stoke that fire in me, it's my sister.*

I clench and unclench my fists as I watch my sister like a hawk. Tesni's eyes are glassy when she finally reaches me, but when she steps forward and extends her arms, as if to embrace me, I flinch away, taking a step back to keep space between us. It's taking every ounce of control just to be in the same room with her. There's no way in all seven hells that I'll ever be ready to hug her like nothing is wrong between us. Tesni drops her arms.

"I-I'm sorry. I know you hate me, Tee—Thea," she corrects quickly at my glare. She studies me. "You changed your hair. And your eyes." She says it with a bit of a smile, as if we're just old friends commenting on how we've changed as we've gotten older—*oh goodness, look how tall you've gotten! You've lost your chubby cheeks! I love the new haircut*—but there's something else there, some kind of calculation in her eyes. I'm not gullible or delusional. I know that Tesni must have some kind of ulterior motive in this meeting, but no matter what's to come, I'm fully prepared to protect myself. I'm not afraid to hurt people like I'd been all those years ago, and my power is no longer weak and unreliable.

"What do you want, Tesni?" I ask, keeping my voice cool. I notice with some satisfaction that I'm taller than she is by an inch or so. It's a stupid thing to be smug about, but I'm smug all the same. "You said it was a matter of life and death, so I imagine the conversation should get underway as soon as possible."

Tesni's lips thin and I don't miss the flash of anger before she quickly covers it with what looks like sadness and regret. She's gotten even better with her performances since we were young.

"Yes, you're right. Thank you for coming. I know I had no right to ask, not after...well, everything, but you're the only one who can help me. And...and I know that I owe you an apology. Not that it will help or that you want it, I'm sure, but...I *am* sorry for how things transpired all those years ago." How things *transpired?* As if she'd played no role? As if she hadn't sentenced her own twin to life as a slave—or death, when I'd been forced to flee. Twelve years old. Alone. Afraid. Completely unprepared for the real world outside the gilded walls of the palace.

I inhale sharply, grinding my teeth as my power flares in my palms and a deep chill settles in the air around us. Tesni's eyes widened when her breath frosts the air before her, goosebumps erupting along her pale skin.

"You've gotten strong after all," she whispers, looking intrigued. Tesni had always been intrigued by power, had always hungered for it. It's why she'd betrayed me all those years ago. Her love of power had been far greater than her love for me, I just never wanted to see it until it was too late. I suppose that's why she and Barony have gotten on so well all these years. He, too, has an insatiable hunger for power. He hadn't been born a king—he'd taken the title by force.

"I've had to be," I snap.

Tesni at least has the decency to look away at that, shame coloring her cheeks. After a moment, she meets my eyes once more.

"Well, as you said, we should get on with it. Over wine?"

Alcohol sounds like a fantastic fucking idea, so I give her one sharp nod.

"Lead the way."

We sit in one of the large sitting rooms that we'd played Hidden Fairies in once upon a time, the two of us hiding away until the nannies came to search for us. We'd barely been able to keep our giggling under control. The furnishings have been updated over the years, but it's still much the same: rich wood floors, thick curtains over the towering windows to keep out the winter drafts, oversized fireplace, a winged lion rearing up on each side, their paws arching over the center.

Tesni pours us each a goblet of wine nearly the color of blood. She offers me one and I eye it suspiciously. She rolls her eyes.

"Do you really think that I would ask you to come back here after all these years simply to poison you?" The arch of my brow gives her answer enough and her lips actually curl upwards at the corners. "Alright, I deserve that."

She takes a long drink of her own wine as she settles down into the chair opposite me, and I shrug. If she'll drink it, I suppose it must be fine.

"Where is King Barony?" I ask, motioning towards one of the lions with my goblet. Crystal of course. Everywhere I look, I see wealth. I'm comfortable in my life now, but it hadn't always been that way. I'd been poor and starving for *years* before I'd met Math and Cece, before the three of us had settled in Helios and scraped up enough money to buy the building where the tavern now teems with sailors and pirates and merchants, earning us a decent living. Something tickles the back of my mind, something from those first awful days after my escape, running and hiding through the city outside the palace walls...but I can't quite grasp onto the memory and fades away like smoke.

In her letter, Tesni had promised that the King wouldn't be anywhere near the castle or grounds when I arrived, but I trust Tesni's promises as much as I trust the local drunk to abstain from a pint at the tavern. I barely fight the urge to glance over my shoulder, as if the bastard might be lurking in some darkened corner, waiting to attack. *Let him try*, I think with a savagery that surprises me. My hatred for the King is almost as strong as my hatred for my sister, but really, he owed me nothing. I was his ward, nothing more. Tesni, on the other hand...

Tesni's eyes darken at the mention of the King.

"He's away on kingdom business." She sounds bitter. I keep my expression blank, but I *am* curious about this hostility. King Barony had made Tesni's life practically perfect. She was fawned over as a Gifted and protected by the King's wealth and status. Even as far south as Helios, there was talk of Lyanna's stunning Gifted. The Flame of Lyanna. The Burning Beauty. The Fire Bitch. Tesni was infamous, though she hadn't exactly endeared herself to the people of Lyanna or any other kingdom—she was rumored to be cold and arrogant, refusing to lift a finger to help anyone unless she (or more accurately, King Barony) was paid handsomely for it.

But pay they did. Her Gifts of fire came in great use across the north when deep winter can bring twenty feet of snow over the course of one night, and her ability to raze cadres to ash had been instrumental in helping Barony to keep his throne when there was an uprising several years back. I never quite gathered the reason for the uprising in the gossip about the tavern from sailors and peddlers. Some claimed other kingdoms thought to take over Lyanna, others that Lyanna's own people rose up against their king. But why would they do that? Lyanna was one of the most prosperous in all of Hypathia thanks to its gold mines.

No matter the reason for it, all of the stories of that fight ended the same: Tesni burning them where they stood and leaving nothing but smoking embers behind. I can't imagine such destruction, but I have no doubt that Tesni felt no guilt for what she'd done, all those lives lost. Her power had only grown over the years, and I have to admit that she's...formidable.

Well, so am I. And a Gifted can bleed just like anyone else...

I merely nod and sip my wine. It's sweet, but there's a tangy undercurrent that I don't enjoy. I know it's probably obscenely expensive as everything in Barony's palace is, but perhaps that's why I don't enjoy it. The refined pallet I'd had for the first twelve years of my life living within this castle and being fed delicacies for every meal, only the finest meats and cheeses and fruits brought from all over the continent and shipped from the surrounding islands, had been lost long ago. Out on my own with not a coin to my name, I'd had to resort to eating out of trash bins to avoid starvation. I'd even made meals of worms and grubs when I'd been hiding within the woods along the roads, stomach cramping horribly from hunger. I'd sobbed for hours the first time I'd killed a hare in my desperate desire for meat—and had nearly vomited up my spoils afterwards.

"How did you find me?" I ask, unable to keep the question at bay any longer.

Her lips curl into a smug smile. "I'd been studying the books in the library on alchemy for years before you...left." Left. As if that's what I fucking did. Just decided to take a nice little stroll through the continent. I clench my jaw but hold my tongue, my desire to know the story outweighing my fury. Barely. "I knew that blood could be instrumental in myriad things, so when we saw the aftermath in the grand entrance, I collected what I knew to be yours and kept it, just in case..."

I inhale sharply and take another sip of wine, clenching the goblet so tightly I feel the crystal creak beneath my fingers.

"I brought one of Barony's alchemists into my confidences and he was able to use old, nearly forgotten ways to track you using your blood."

I frown. "Barony's alchemists?"

She blinks and for a moment I can tell that she's said something she didn't mean to, but she recovers quickly, putting on that perfect mask and waving it away.

"He's had a team of them for ages, working on all manner of things: ways to manipulate and replicate the gold stores, that kind of thing." She gives me an admonishing look then. "You don't remember? The building near the conservatory?"

My brow furrows as I try to recall ever seeing this place or these people, not having any memories of such a thing, but I start to get a headache and decide it's better to avoid thoughts of the past altogether.

"And why did Barony believe I was dead?" I remember the words sending shivers up my spine when I'd read them in that first ominous letter she'd sent. *Barony believes you to be dead, thanks to me.*

"Because we showed him your body, of course." I blanch at that and it only makes her smile. "He was relentless in his search for you, and it was taking attention from me. So, I made it stop." She shrugs as if this makes perfect sense and it strikes me how truly spoiled and petulant and fucking heartless she's become. Always has been, I suppose. "We found a beggar girl that no one would miss. She was on the brink of death anyway, so really, we were doing her a favor, in the end." My stomach roils and I look at the monster that was my sister, completely aghast. "We altered her appearance to look enough like you that Barony would never know the difference and that was the end of the search. Very few knew you existed at all, it turns out—Barony kept us cooped up inside these grounds for a reason. He wanted no one to know what he had in his possession lest they try to take it. Well, at least until one of us was powerful enough to put fear into his enemies and coin into his pocket, that is. He only told King Morthan about us at all because he needed more troops to bolster his army and Enola was willing to give them in exchange for a Gifted. Plus, they were of some relation. Third or fourth cousins, perhaps, I can't recall the particulars."

It takes me a few moments before I can speak again.

"So, you…you killed an innocent girl and somehow made her look like me?"

She tilts her head, brow furrowing as if she can't understand my indignation.

"Yes. It was the simplest way to end the search and let you live your life far, far away from here and for me to become what I was meant to become. You should be thanking me, really."

"Why not just kill me?" I spit. She studies me for a moment

before answering, and that cool calculation flashes in her eyes once more.

"I know you think I'm heartless, but I don't want you dead, Thea. You're still my twin."

I get the feeling that there's more to that sentence that she's not saying, but before I can press, the door opens and a man enters. He's young and good looking enough, though I would call his features a bit bland. Brown hair, brown eyes, average height, average build. He isn't ugly, but he's not anyone I would look at twice. I prefer men who are a bit more...rough-hewn. Men who have a rugged air about them. Men who look like they can fight off bandits or dragons alike, drain a tankard of ale, and snatch me against them for a deep kiss afterwards before carting me off to the bedroom over their shoulder. I like rough palms and rougher cheeks. This man looks as if he's never done any work for himself in his life. If he's ever raised a hand, it was only to ring a bell for a servant.

"Thea, this is Hastings, the King's High Advisor." *That explains the soft look of him.* The man nods in greeting.

"I trust you had a good journey?"

"It was...pleasant enough," I say, lips curling ever so slightly at the memories in Randolph's cabin. Hastings blinks as he studies me.

"Great Makers, even with the differing hair and eyes, the resemblance between you is uncanny," he says, looking between me and Tesni, his eyes alight with excitement. I press my lips into a hard line in response. Tesni smiles and gestures towards my now empty goblet.

"Another?" she asks, taking another sip of her own wine. I nod. The unease of not knowing why the fuck I'm here grows with every second that passes. Maybe more wine will help calm my rattling nerves. Tesni is at least doing me the honor of pretending she can't force me to cooperate with whatever she's requesting—or so she thinks, anyway. She may have leverage over me, but I decided on the journey here that if I have to kill my sister to be rid of her shadow over my life, I will. I'm prepared to do what needs to be done. I'm... eighty percent sure I could go through with it.

"Please, allow me," Hastings says, taking my goblet with a small bow. Tesni holds hers out to him as well in a haughty way that just screams *princess*. She isn't one, technically, but she may as well be growing up here and with Barony having no children and never marrying. Hastings refills them both from the carafe and hands them back to each of us, a genial smile to me, a doting one to Tesni. She smiles back, her features softening for a moment. Does she... care for him? He steps away, moving to stoke the fire in the hearth. I take another long sip of wine to give me what Math calls liquid bravery.

"Why am I here, Tesni? What's so important that you demanded I come?"

"I didn't demand..." I press my lips into a hard line, giving her a cold look, and a genuine smile spreads across her face. She huffs out a laugh, and for just the briefest moment, I get a glimpse of the twin I lost all those years ago. "Alright, alright. Yes, I demanded. I tend to do that, truth be told." Hastings laughs as he straightens, placing the iron poker back onto the rack. Another fond look from Tesni.

"So?" I wave a hand, asking her to get on with it. My head is starting to pound, and I think that skipping lunch was perhaps a mistake. I just want to finish this conversation and go to bed. Tesni sighs, eyes darkening.

"Barony has *sold* me," she says, voice sharp and brittle. She reaches for the gold chain at her throat, and I nearly spit out my wine. What I'd thought was a simple piece of jewelry is in fact a *collar*. It's what slavers use to control Gifteds, to make sure the Gifted's powers aren't turned against them. Of course, most Gifteds wouldn't be able to do much harm anyway, but Hunters and slavers don't take chances. I barely stop myself from laughing in her face, the glorious irony making me want to sing.

And then I realize that she's powerless. Completely and utterly defenseless. I should kill her right here, right now. I could do it so easily, take care of Hastings too, and escape before anyone was the wiser. I could go back to my life and finally be truly free.

Do it. Come on, just fucking do it. My palms tingle and my skin goes cold, a thin sheen of frost coating my fingertips. I grit my teeth and curse silently as the cold begins to recede and I know damn well I won't. I should. She deserves it and more.

And yet I can't bring myself to. I've taken lives before, it's true, but it was always in self-defense and always accidental. This would be deliberate and cold and just...not me. As much as I hate the woman in front of me, as much as she deserves to be punished not just for her betrayal of me, but for all of the things I know that she's done in the years since, I won't let her change who I am.

Tesni goes on, completely oblivious to my internal debate of the merits of her murder.

"He has promised me to the King of Marrowood to solidify the alliance between them. Six of the nine kingdoms have allied now, if you didn't know. Helios, of course, hasn't declared because they never do much of anything that has to do with the rest of the fucking continent—" she rolls her eyes "—and Tithmoore remains neutral as well."

"Allied for what?" I'd heard a bit about a supposed allying of the kingdoms but I paid no real mind. As she said, the people of Helios keep out of empire business, and me more so than the rest.

"They plan to take Duskthorne. Barony wants to take their Gifteds and add them to his—"

"Tesni," Hastings interrupts hastily, the two of them sharing a meaningful look.

"It doesn't matter," Tesni finally says when she meets my gaze again. "Regardless, I have been sold as part of this ridiculous alliance and that simply won't do."

I mean to say something scathing but before I can open my mouth, the entire room seems to sway before me. I blink to clear my vision and mind, shaking myself. *Makers, how strong is this wine?* I peer into the glass, as if it will somehow give me answers. Tesni sips her own, watching me over the rim of her glass, a gleam of...something in her eyes.

"As you can imagine, it will be highly dangerous for me to be on the road as I travel to Marrowood. Any number of unsavory parties would wish to ambush my carriage and take me for ransom, despite the threat of my power." It's true that she's beyond powerful, but she's not immune to poisons or physical harm should someone get close enough. *And now that she's collared...*

"Both King Barony and King Tybalt would pay handsomely to get me back. All of the Alliance, really," she muses.

"Why...why are you telling me this?" My stomach clenches painfully and dark spots dart across my vision. I force my eyes wide and turn to glare at my sister. Tesni smirks, that same smirk King Barony had given me all those years ago, the same wicked smirk as the snake from the storybook. My stomach hollows and I try to pull up my power again, but I can barely seem to find it now, only the faintest stirring in my chest.

"Wh-what did you do, Tesni?" I try again to call my Gift, but I can't make it respond. I can't make any part of my body cooperate, actually. *Oh, Great Makers.* Poison. There are poisons that can block a Gifted's powers. It's how Hunters often capture Gifteds to begin with until they can get close enough to slap a collar around their throats. *Fuck, fuck, fuck.*

I pull up all of my strength and somehow stand, but I'm only able to lurch a few steps before falling to my knees. Tesni rises from her chair gracefully and strides forward, a wickedly satisfied look on her face.

"You bitch," I spit, glaring with all the hatred I can muster.

"Just so," she agrees breezily, not concerned with the insult. "Now, Hastings and I have come up with a brilliant plan." She looks adoringly at the man before he swoops in and kisses her, the noises alone making me want to vomit. They finally pull apart and she pats his cheek before turning back to me, and I would swear I catch a flash of disgust in her eyes.

"The details of my journey to Marrowood have been kept entirely secret. Only the King's most trusted staff know when I am leaving, which path we are taking, and which carriage I'll be in."

"I don't...understand," I bite out before my body goes rigid and I collapse to the floor, landing with a resounding—and painful—thud.

Tesni leans down and puts her face directly above mine. She reaches out and I try to flinch away from her touch, but I'm now completely frozen. I could almost laugh. *The Gifted with powers of ice is now frozen on the floor*. Tesni raises a lock of my hair to her eyes, studying it as she rolls it between her fingers. She *tsks*, sounding annoyed, and turns to Hastings.

"We'll need Klaus. Have Greta fetch him immediately; we have little time." I want to ask what the fuck she's talking about, but my lips won't move, and my thoughts are growing warped and fuzzy around the edges.

"You see, Tee, we've made sure to leak the details of my trip to certain...individuals. The unscrupulous sort," she clarifies with a sly grin and a knowing glance at Hastings. "They will attack the carriage, a kidnapping will take place, a ransom will be demanded. Of course, King Barony will pay it in order to get his prize back and to keep in good graces with his newest ally. They need Marrowood's ironworkers for this little war of theirs." Something dark flashes across her face but she continues on. "As High Advisor, Hastings will be entrusted with the most important duty of delivering the ransom himself. They'll want to keep the kidnapping as quiet as possible, lest rumors begin to spread that both Lyanna and Marrowood are weak and have been robbed. The entire Alliance could crumble with a blow like that. It's all resting on thin ice as it is." She laughs then, eyes alighting with actual joy. "Ha! Thin ice." She gestures to me and waggles her brows as if it's the funniest joke she's ever told. Though I can barely move, I manage to narrow my eyes, telling her that it is in no way amusing. She rolls her eyes.

"Anyway. After the ransom has been negotiated and sent off with Hastings, he'll be free to take all that money for himself."

I try desperately to speak, but only wheezing gasps come out. Understanding what I'm asking, Tesni smiles.

"Oh, don't you understand, Tee? When they attack the carriage, *I* won't be inside." My entire body goes cold in a way that has nothing to do with my power because I know what she's going to say a heartbeat before the words leave her tongue.

"*You* will."

CHAPTER FOUR

I feel as if I'm back on the ship again, a gentle swaying beneath me keeping me lulled in that place just between sleep and waking. I try to remember what happened, but admittedly can't recall much... but I certainly don't think I ended up back at the docks? I slowly try to swim up from the darkness, but it feels as if I'm clawing through mud. A muted voice inside my mind is screaming that something is very, very wrong, so I scrape and pull as hard as I can, and finally, I find the light. My eyes flutter open and I immediately squeeze them shut again as a wave of nausea roils through me. My head is absolutely pounding, the light far too bright. *How much did I drink?*

I press the heels of my hands into my eyes, breathing in deeply to settle my stomach and clear my head. After a moment, I pry my lids open once more and take in my surroundings, confusion immediately furrowing my brow. I'm sitting on a cushioned bench, covered in thick, luxurious velvet of the deepest sapphire blue, another identical one opposite me in the small space. Gold silk lines the walls and golden lace curtains cover windows on either side. I lurch a bit again and realize that I'm not on a ship at all. *A carriage. I'm inside of a carriage.*

I glance down and frown, hands flying to my stomach and rubbing down to my thighs. My worn leathers and high riding boots are gone. Now I'm in a *dress*. It's not that I mind dresses—I wear them often at the Port, but those are made of thin, wispy material that moves like air around my bare legs as I dance or lounge by the water, much to the sailors' delights.

This dress, however, is made of heavy velvet, with long sleeves that bell outward at my wrists. It flows down to my toes and when I lift the hem, I find that I do have boots of a sort on, though they are a far cry from my beloved riding boots. These only come to my ankles, are lined with fur, and have *heels* for fuck's sake. I nearly growl at the fucking audacity.

The dress is a deep sapphire, matching the cushion below me almost exactly, with golden embroidery along the hem and the edges of the sleeves, delicate lace adorning the low neckline. Already I feel too constricted, too contained. I try to run my hands through my hair only to find that it's been pinned up into intricate braids atop my head, like some sort of crown.

"What in the Great fucking Makers...?" I narrow my eyes when I finally notice a letter lying on the other bench, the Kingdom of Lyanna's seal adorning the front in thick, crimson wax, reminding me of dried blood. I snatch it off the bench and rip it open, only to frown: the page is empty. I let out a rough exhale of annoyance and letters began to appear on the parchment, unfurling slowly like the petals of a flower.

Tee,

Believe it or not, I am sorry that I've now betrayed you twice in this lifetime, but I am not sorry enough to change my plans. There will be no winners in this war for our kind, dear sister, and you know better than anyone that I will always do what is necessary to ensure my own survival.

You will be taken not long after you wake and read this—if the alchemist is correct on how long the drugs will keep you asleep that is. I'm already well hidden away by now, waiting for the ransom to arrive. If you are thinking of revealing your true identity once your captors have you, I would advise against it: after all, why would they keep you alive if they don't think you're worth anything?

I feel sick as the memories come flooding back: the strange taste of the wine, the feeling of being trapped within my own body, all that Tesni had revealed about her twisted plan to let me be kidnapped in her place. I put the rest together on my own: Tesni left Lyanna at the same time as her caravan, heading the opposite direction. She'll hide away until Hastings steals the ransom and joins her, and the two of them will leave Hypathia, probably travel to one of the islands off of the coast and I'll...I have no fucking idea what will happen to me in the end.

"That fucking bitch," I whisper to no one. I knew she was cold and cruel, that I couldn't trust her, but *this*? This is far beyond what I thought her capable of. I wonder what she means about the war having no happy endings for our kind, but when the carriage lurches again, I push that aside and focus on the more pressing issues.

Like how the hells I'm going to get out of this.

The letters begin to fade and I almost laugh, remembering this ink from when we were young. It only reacts to a specific person's breath. King Barony had brought some back for us from a trip to Enola, one of the few times he seemed to care about us. You had to mix a bit of the person's blood with the ink, but it was worth the price for all the fun we had, leaving secret notes to each other all over the castle that only we could read.

Clever. Tesni wouldn't want anyone else to read these words, to have any other witnesses to her crimes. *No, not clever. Cunning*, I amend. You call ruthless, vicious people cunning.

My thoughts begin to run wild, trying to come up with a plan. Tesni was right: I have to pretend to be her if I want any chance of getting out of this alive. If the Hunters find out that I'm not Barony's Gifted, but a Gifted nonetheless, I'll be taken to the highest bidder—and the highest bidder when it comes to Gifteds is almost always King Dorian. Being taken to him would be worse than death.

"So, I can't fight back with my Gifts when they come for me," I whisper to myself, dread settling in my belly like a cannonball. Not unless I'm prepared to kill every single person who attacks. If I can't and I'm captured, they'll know the truth and that lands me on Dorian's doorstep. So, no. I can't use my Gifts at all. I have to keep my power in check and hidden, no matter what. I take a deep breath and force myself to think clearly. I'd survived the unsurvivable for years as a helpless child. I can survive anything. I just need to stay calm and think, like Tobias always taught me. He saved my life when I fled all those years ago, and he's still managing to do it now. A part of me smiles, my chest aching with missing him, but the rest of me is trying very hard to stay calm and find a way the fuck out of this.

"Alright, so I'll just have to escape *before* they come for me." If Tesni's letter is to be believed, that will be happening any moment now. If I can get away before they even find me, then I can hide, get lost in a snowstorm of my own making until I can make a new plan, find a way back to Helios. Just as I call out to the driver to demand that he stop, I hear a soft, muffled grunt and then a low thump against the front of the carriage.

"Hello?" I call cautiously. No answer. "Fuck, fuck, fuck." They're already here.

The horses slow without someone to drive them onward, and eventually we stop. My heart thunders loudly in my ears as I wait, bracing myself in the corner of the carriage away from the door, preparing to attack whoever the hells comes through it first. But the door stays shut. *What are they playing at?* A moment later, I understand, shrieking as the glass of the window shatters and some kind of smoking pouch sails inside, attached to the end of an arrow that plugs itself into the door on the other side. I begin to cough as the smoke fills the space, thick and acrid. Already I can feel the drugs in the smoke beginning to dim my Gift and make my eyelids heavy. With no other choice, I freeze the smoke, then quickly melt the ice, soaking the bottom of the carriage, effectively neutralizing the poison. I know they'll be approaching soon, assuming that I'm knocked out. I only have moments to act, to try to flee and take my chances on the run. I take one deep breath and throw the carriage door open.

I jump out and run—where, I have no fucking idea, but running is better than sitting here just waiting to be taken. I hear shouts of surprise and glance back to see several cloaked men on horseback in the trees lining the path. Thankfully they were on the opposite side of the carriage when they approached and shot that arrow, so I'm already heading away from them. I curse these damned boots as I slip time and time again on the snow and ice. It's not a thick covering, but it's enough to make the trek difficult. These boots were made with fashion in mind, not function, and the dress is making it hard as hells to run.

"Damn Tesni to the pits of the seventh fucking hell!" I spit through gritted teeth as I continue to run as best I can like my life depends on it. It fucking *does* depend on it. The men draw nearer, but the trees start to grow closer together the farther from the path I get, and the horses can't maneuver between them as quickly as I can. As if realizing the same thing at the same moment I do, several of the men dismount and begin to give chase on foot. I dart to my right, changing directions to try to throw off my pursuers. My power roils within my chest, burning in my palms, begging to be used. I clench my jaw, knowing I can't do anything with my Gift right now...but then a thought sparks to life.

I can't send ice daggers soaring at them from my fingertips without giving myself away, but I *can* make it snow without it looking suspicious. I glance up and smile: snow's already in the air, thick and heavy in the gray clouds overhead. I call to the flakes, willing them to fall, and soon the sky opens open, raining a thick blanket of white all around me. I hear the men curse and I grin, breathing in deeply as the cold and bite in the air settle my beating heart the tiniest bit. I keep running, clearing a small path before me through the snow as it continues to rain down all around, making the men slow.

I cut back to the left again, but slip when the earth dips sharply. I scream as I fall, desperately trying to grasp a tree or dig my fingers into the ground to stop my descent. Pain erupts in my shoulder when I strike a boulder hidden beneath the snow and I bite my lip as I continue to topple. I finally come to a stop and roll onto my back, groaning and gasping in pain. I feel blood trickling down my forehead and lip, and can barely move my shoulder. I don't think it's dislocated, but it was a close call. Still hurts like fucking hells though.

One sleeve of my dress has been torn in half, and I see that I have a large, bloody gash on my forearm as well. I wince as I gingerly poked at it, but then I glance up and see three of the men following my path down the hill and know I don't have time to worry about my injuries. *Survive first. Tend to wounds later.*

"Ruddy fuck," I moan as I make myself rise and continue onward, just to have the skirt of my dress snag on a branch a few seconds later. "Oh, fuck this!" I form a dagger of ice and slice at the dress, hacking until my legs are able to move freely, sawing at the material until the bottom half of the skirt falls away. It's an uneven cut, angling down from my mid-thigh one side to just past my knee on the other, but it'll do. I start running again, faster now that I can actually fucking move, and will the snow to fall harder. But it's not enough to stop the men. They're determined, I'll give them that, but then again, I can only imagine the bounty on Tesni's head. I'd bet these men would be willing to do just about anything to catch me.

I turn to my right, sprinting along a wide creek, but my heart sinks and I skid to a stop when I find a solid rockface rising before me, a small waterfall feeding the creek from a crack within the stone about ten yards above my head. The creek blocks my path on the left, and the earth rises in a sharp incline on my right. I whirl to go back the way I'd come, but two men are there blocking my escape. They toss back the hoods of their worn, patched cloaks as they stalk forward. The stockier of the two smiles, taking in my bare thighs, the heaving of my chest, and my power surges inside my body, my palms burning with the cold.

I've seen that look.

I know that look

I will cut that look off of his fucking face if he tries.

I steel myself, preparing to fight as Tobias taught me all those years ago. The thought of him fills my heart with bittersweet warmth. He's the only reason I survived my first few years after fleeing Lyanna. He found me on the road a few months after I'd run, dirty and bleeding and nearly starved to death, and gave me shelter in his wagon. He didn't pry into who I was or how I'd come to be there, just let me ride beside him—or hide when we passed any other travelers, but especially soldiers. He noticed, I know he did, but he never said a word. He'd just smile and hand me a piece of bread or dried meat when I got up enough courage to crawl back up onto the seat again.

"I know you've got a story, little sparrow, but I'll not push to hear it. You tell me when you're ready. Until then, the only thing you need to know is that you are safe."

I probably shouldn't have believed him so easily, but the kindness in his chocolate eyes shone so brightly it was impossible not to trust in him.

"Sparrow?" I'd asked quietly a few minutes later, my voice meek and hoarse from disuse. I hadn't spoken to another soul in weeks at that point, save screaming at those men to stop...

"You have a scrape just there," he said, pointing to the torn shoulder of my dress, "looks a bit like a sparrow to me. So that's what I'll call you, shall I?"

I nodded and for a long time, I was simply Sparrow. I wasn't an orphan running for her life. I wasn't a Gifted whose sister broke her heart and betrayed her as easily as breathing. I wasn't a coinless beggar who had already had to fight for her life more times than any child of nearly thirteen should. I was just Sparrow, the girl who liked to feed the horses sugar cubes and who sometimes had nightmares so terrible that they woke her, screaming and shaking, in the night.

He bought me clothes at the first town we came to, and, noticing how I worried I seemed to be about my hair, a hat to go with. I'd loved that damned hat with its floppy brim, the kind fishermen wore on boats in pictures I'd seen in our storybooks.

So, the two of us traveled together for years. He became the father I never had, and I the daughter he'd always dreamed of. His wife had died years back and when I asked if he ever thought to marry again, he told me that his heart had already been given away to his dear Mary—there was nothing left to offer anyone else. We healed each other, I think, as much as two broken souls could be healed at least. He taught me so many things: how to live in the world; how to tend to horses; plants that could be eaten safely out in the woods and which ones to avoid; how to haggle for a good deal from the stalls at the markets; how to play quills like a fiend. Too many things to count.

But one of the most important was how to defend myself when I couldn't use my Gift.

I briefly touch the scar on my shoulder, the one in the shape of a sparrow, and hear his words echo through my mind now: *Anything can be made into a weapon. Use your surroundings.* I glance around and take up a sharp-edged rock from the ground, brandishing it at the men. The taller of the two approaches first while the stockier one remains behind, muttering curses and wiping snow and mud from his trousers. He must have fallen a few times in their pursuit.

The first man is reed-thin, with rust-colored hair, bushy eyebrows, and pock marks covering his long face. He doesn't even pull a weapon as he nears, assuming I'm completely harmless. *His mistake.*

"Oh, fucking hells, what are *you* doing here, Blackheart?" the stocky man says, a note of...something in his voice. Fear maybe? The tall man stops, turning back to his companion. I follow his gaze and see that another man has joined us now, but based on the stocky man's reaction, he's not exactly welcome.

"The same reason as you, Ennis," the new man—Blackheart—says, as if Ennis is a fool.

"But...but you came *yourself?*" I don't know who this man is or why it's a marvel that he's come to collect a bounty himself, but I make a note to stay away from him at all costs. He's tall, almost seven feet if I had to guess, absolutely towering over Ennis. He's broad shouldered and looks as if he could fling Ennis across this creek with the tiniest bit of effort. His black hair is windswept, his beard and mustache a bit unkempt as if he hasn't trimmed them in at least a week, and ferocity seems to radiate from him in cold, dark pulses. A black fur cloak is draped over his shoulders, a silver broach pinning it in place, and he rests a hand casually on the hilt of a massive sword at his hip.

"A prize this big? Of course I came to collect it myself." His voice is low and smooth, sounding nonchalant but there's a fierce coldness beneath the surface. Velvet over steel.

I swallow hard and take a small step towards the creek while the men are distracted, wondering if I can possibly make it across. Though he doesn't shift his gaze in my direction or change his position at all, I somehow know without a doubt that Blackheart has clocked the small movement. I freeze again, instincts flaring and telling me that running isn't an option now. No, this man is not one to run from. He is a predator made for the chase, one who would enjoy it. I wouldn't stand a chance.

Ennis looks to the tall man, who gives him a meaningful nod. Ennis takes a deep breath, as if steadying himself, and says, "Well, she's *ours*."

"I'm afraid not," Blackheart replies with an arrogant, amused smile. "She belongs to *him* now." The way Blackheart says *him*, and the way Ennis and the tall man both pale, I know in my heart that he's talking about King Dorian. Ice that has absolutely nothing to do with my Gift fills my veins. Of course, I knew deep down that there was a possibility that he would be one of the people after Tesni once word spread to the Hunters, but I guess I'd just hoped that he wouldn't be the one to find me.

Ennis swallows hard but then steels himself and pushes his shoulders back, trying desperately to come even close to reaching Blackheart's height. He fails miserably and in any other situation, I'd probably even laugh at the sight.

"I don't care who you work for, Blackheart. *We* made the plan to attack the carriage. *We* found her out here. She's *ours*."

Blackheart smiles again, but there's a cold, sharp edge to it. This man is dangerous, of that much I'm absolutely certain.

"I'll tell you what, Ennis." He cuts his eyes to me, and though I can't tell from here what color they are—black, or dark blue maybe—I can see the calculation in them as he takes me in. "If you can capture her, then she's yours. I'll let you walk away with the prize."

Ennis and I wear matching narrow-eyed, suspicious expressions. The tall man just looks confused. Well, he certainly isn't the brains of this little outfit, that's for sure.

"You swear on the Great Makers? No tricks?" Ennis asks, clearly suspicious.

"You have my word."

"And what about *him*? He'll just let a catch this big go?"

Blackheart shrugs. "I'll take whatever punishment he deems appropriate for the loss."

Ennis debates for a moment longer before nodding.

"Alright then." Ennis jerks his chin at the tall man. "Well, get her, you idiot. Should be easy enough with her Gift blocked."

The tall man nods and turns back to me again. I tighten my grip on the rock and raise it up, ready for the attack to come.

"Aw, kitten thinks she has claws," he drawls as he steps forward and reaches for me. I freeze the ground beneath him, making him lose his footing and stumble forward. He curses as I slash out with the rock, cutting him across the face. His hand flies to his cheek, his eyes wide in shock, but I don't hesitate to swing again. I backhand him with the broad end of the stone against his temple, and he falls to his knees with a groan. I swear I hear a deep chuckle from Blackheart.

"Kitten doesn't think she has claws—she *knows*," I hiss before kicking him square in the crotch. He cries out and rolls up defensively, ragged breaths sawing in and out as he moans and cups his bruised ballocks. I rear back and kick him in the jaw, sending him sprawling across the snow. He doesn't try to get up again. *One down.*

I shift my gaze to the other two men and see Ennis striding forward. I don't understand this game that Blackheart has started, but I don't have a choice but to play. His dark eyes flicker with interest as I raise my chin, telling Ennis without words that this won't be easy. Blackheart leans casually against a nearby tree, settling in to watch the show.

"Thought you were a spoiled little princess," Ennis sneers, pulling a wickedly curved dagger from his belt, the kind some of the sailors favor down at the port. "Didn't expect a fight from you, not without your Gift, I'll admit. But you're the biggest payday of my life, pet—I won't give you up to the likes of Blackheart or anyone else." He moves to the left, so I shift to my right, matching him step for step, keeping the distance between us. "Trust me, you'd rather go with me anyway. Dorian will demand a hefty ransom, and Makers know that Barony and his allies will pay it, but during the negotiations?" He makes a show of shivering violently. "Well, he'll make what I have planned sound like a walk in the park. So, just come on with me, nice and slow, and no one gets hurt."

A part of me believes that he's right, that he's the lesser of two evils here, but no way in hells I'll take either option without a fight.

"I think your friend there disagrees about no one getting hurt."

He sneers at the reminder and I eye the blade, watching as he brandishes it out in front of him like a small sword. My lips curl upward. There are two ways to hold a knife during a fight: the way he's doing it, and the right way. Another of Tobias' lessons echoes through my mind: *most men think holding a blade and waving it about is enough. Most men are idiots.*

Sure enough, Ennis is indeed an idiot. He slashes out without any skill to speak of, and I easily duck to the side. He swipes again from the other direction and I dart away once more, my eyes never leaving his hand.

"Careful, Ennis. You need her intact," Blackheart chides, his voice a mix of amusement, arrogance, and boredom.

"I won't cause any damage that can't be mended."

We circle each other slowly and I toss the rock aside. I pull at the already-torn sleeve of my dress, ripping it completely off. I hold the strip of fabric between my hands, wrapping the ends around my fists to get a good grip. Ennis quirks a brow.

"So eager to strip for me, are you, kitten? There'll be plenty of time for that on the road, don't you worry," Ennis muses in a low voice, smiling and showing off several silver teeth.

He lurches forward, swinging the knife downward in a wide arch, and I shift to the side, using the sleeve to capture his wrist. I twist my body and the fabric at the same time and use my momentum and leverage to send him stumbling forward while yanking back on his arm. He cries out when it bends at an unnatural angle, and I smile savagely when I pull harder, snapping his wrist. His scream of agony echoes through the woods around us.

"You bitch! You broke my arm!" he roars, but I spin behind him and kick out at the back of the knee. He cries out as he falls to the ground and I quickly wrap one arm around his thick neck, tucking it into the crook of my elbow and pulling tight, cutting off his air supply. He claws at my forearm with his uninjured hand, but I don't budge, only squeeze tighter. In a last-ditch effort to get me off of him before he's out of oxygen, he reaches back for my face. I pull away, but he manages to get his grubby fingers into my hair. I scream through clenched teeth as he yanks, ruby-encrusted pins scattering along the snow-covered ground and looking entirely too much like drops of blood. My braid comes free and my hair tumbles down my back. I scream again, in frustration this time, and squeeze harder. He finally, *finally* stops struggling, his hand going limp and falling away from my hair. I let his body slump to the ground and stumble backwards, panting.

And then Blackheart is there as if he'd appeared out of thin air, the tip of his sword resting against my throat and forcing my chin up to face him.

Fuck.

I glare at him, still breathing hard, and try to calculate my options. I could use my Gift and end him right here, but I hear others approaching now. If they see and I can't get away, I'm worse than dead...

"I'll admit, your attempts to fight back were admirable and unexpected—hells, they were even entertaining—but they end now. This pretty little head is worth a half a kingdom in coin, but I'll gladly relieve you of it, princess. Do you understand?" He presses the tip of the blade forward just enough to prick my skin, and I feel a hot trickle of blood making its way down my throat. "You're far too valuable to kill, but make no mistake, if you cause me trouble, I will make you wish that I had." His voice is so cold, so matter of fact, that I shiver with true fear. I give him a tiny nod, mindful of the blade, and he lowers it as another handful of men join us. They look at the others, both still lying on the ground. Ennis might be dead, actually, now that I look at him. I'm not entirely sure and I don't entirely care.

"Not just a spoiled princess after all then?" one of the newcomers asks.

"Not quite," Blackheart says, his dark eyes cold and intense, and I look away, feeling like he'll somehow be able to see right through me if I don't, see every secret I'm trying to hide. "Bring her."

He strides away and I look up again, watching him as he goes. He slides his sword into the scabbard on his hip in a smooth, practiced motion, and doesn't look back.

Two men step on either side of me, each taking an arm, and I have to fight every instinct to turn my skin to ice, to burn them and fight back. *You're far too valuable to kill*. If I want to survive, I have to pretend to be my sister, at least for now. Dorian may like to collect Gifteds, but even he would be enticed to trade me for the unholy amount of coin I'm sure Barony and the Alliance will be willing to pay. So, I need to keep up the ruse. It will buy me time to figure out a plan, some way to escape this nightmare.

We finally make it to a small clearing where horses and more men are waiting. I'm happy to see that they've brought the horses that were pulling the carriage as well, their harnesses sporting the winged lion of Lyanna, and didn't leave them to fend for themselves out here. A large trunk sits on the ground and I eye it curiously. It's beautifully made, deep, gleaming wood inlaid with rows of glittering gemstones and a golden latch. Blackheart throws it open, and he and another man begin rifling through the contents, tossing garment after garment out onto the snow-covered ground. Blackheart cuts a glance my way and it takes me a moment to realize that he's expecting a reaction. *These are meant to be my belongings*, I remind myself, *the belongings of one of the most famed and powerful Gifteds in all of Hypathia*. What would Tesni do? Throw a fit like a spoiled princess, I imagine, just like they keep calling me. I take a settling breath, hoping I can play the part well enough.

"Stop that!" I snap, pulling against the man who still holds one of my arms. "Do you have any idea how expensive those are?"

Blackheart smirks.

"Not nearly as expensive as the cost to get you back, I'll tell you that much, Red."

I frown. Red? What in the hells is he talking about?

He rises and stalks towards me and I force myself not to take a step backwards when he approaches. I have to crane my head upwards to meet his gaze, but I do. I refuse to cower, and though she is a spoiled, high maintenance princess, Tesni also believes herself to be untouchable. She wouldn't be afraid of this man, and I will not allow myself to be either. He reaches out and I do flinch back instinctively ever so slightly. This seems to amuse and delight him, his blue-gray eyes sparking. He reaches again, and this time I don't move when he grasps a lock of my hair and holds it out between us.

"Red," he says pointedly, as if I'm an imbecile and the men around us laugh. I blink, shocked to see that he's right: my hair is a bright, fiery red once more. *Great Makers, I haven't seen it this color in so long.* But of course, Tesni would have changed my hair and eyes back to match her own. I look like *me* for the first time in almost fifteen years. Would I even recognize myself if I looked in a mirror now? Blackheart arches a dark brow and I again remember the part I'm to be playing. I slap his hand away and scowl, and he chuckles low, a cold, mocking edge to it, before walking away.

"A lot of coats for a Fire Witch who I suspect is always nice and toasty," Blackheart observes, toeing the large pile of clothes they've pulled from the trunk.

"It's called fashion," I sneer, doing my best to look down my nose at him. "Something you disgusting mongrels obviously know nothing about."

One of the men laughs.

"Sharper tongue than I was expecting," he observes. Shit. Did I mess this up already? Is this not how Tesni acts?

"Not even half as sharp as I've heard it can be," Blackheart counters. Oh good. So, I was right: Tesni is just a raging cunt and everyone in Hypathia knows it. "Someone get her bandaged up," he adds, gesturing to my bleeding arm and forehead. A woman with white-blonde hair cut nearly to her scalp on one side, the other side flowing down to her waist, and sharp, angular facial features rummages in a saddlebag, looking for healing supplies, I imagine, but I only watch her from the corner of my eye. No, my gaze remains on the barrel-chested man who leers at my exposed thighs, the low cut of my dress, a dark look in his eyes that makes the hair on the back of my neck stand on end.

"Turner," Blackheart barks, and the man pulls his gaze from me. "Help Gilroy put all this shit back in the trunk."

He nods and walks away as the woman comes towards me with a bundle of cloth. She wraps my arm quickly and inspects my forehead, but decides it doesn't need anything more than wiping the dried blood away. I wince and hiss.

"Ow! You'd do well to be careful," I snap. "Didn't you hear? I'm *expensive*."

The woman glares at me and I glare right back until she eventually rolls her eyes and walks away. I turn to find Blackheart staring, his eyes are dark and cold.

"You're just as bad as they say," he spits, shaking his head. He mounts a giant Northland, black as midnight and taller than any horse I've ever seen. He juts his chin towards another Northland, this one a shade lighter and a few hands shorter, but still massive. "Up you go."

"No collar?" I ask, frowning. I'm surprised that a group of obvious Hunters wouldn't be more prepared. Shouldn't their first order of business be to subdue my Gifts with something more long-lasting than the poison from the carriage?

"I'm not worried about you, little fire witch." I narrow my eyes and he gives me a look that's half amused, half challenging. "You want to try? Go ahead." He spreads his arms in invitation. I clench my jaw, knowing damn well that I can't do a thing, and even if I could, *Tesni* would know better than to try. Whatever game he's playing, it's a stacked deck. Anyone who couldn't see that would be a fool. He chuckles darkly when I do nothing but cross my arms and press my lips into a thin line.

"So, as I said: up you go." I eye the horse warily and Blackheart huffs out a mocking laugh. "Surely King Barony's great Gifted knows how to ride? I've heard he has prize winning Elysians in his stables." It's true. King Barony has some of the most beautiful horses in all of Hypathia, and Tesni and I both learned to ride at an early age. Of course Tesni would have continued that throughout her life and would have no problems with this beast, but *I* haven't ridden in years. I take a deep breath and hope that I remember enough to look competent.

"Of course I do," I snap irritably. "I'm just used to superiorly bred animals," I add, bitingly. I hate how easy it is to sound like my sister, to play the spoiled, entitled, ungrateful fire bitch that she's known to be.

"Oh, my apologies, My Lady," Blackheart says mockingly, the sarcasm so thick that I'm surprised the bastard doesn't choke on every word. "*Up*," he says, all humor gone and that cold, commanding tone ringing loud and clear.

I grip the horse's saddle and begin to hoist myself up when I feel uninvited hands on my ass, pushing me upward and squeezing greedily in the process. I clench my jaw and throw my leg over the horse, and when I'm settled, I turn to find Turner grinning, clearly proud of himself and daring me to say something. There is a darkness in this man, one I've seen too many times to count in my life. He's the kind of man who thinks he has a right to take what he wants from a woman, whether she agrees or not. The kind of man who doesn't take no for an answer. The type of man I'll kill without a wisp of guilt in my heart if he tries anything more than what he's just done.

"Get on with it, Turner. I want to make camp by nightfall," Blackheart barks. Turner raises a length of rope and I grit my teeth, but don't fight as he binds my wrists and then ties the length of rope between my horse and Blackheart's. Turner holds my gaze for another long heartbeat before walking away. Blackheart turns his horse to face me, eyeing me in a way that makes me shift in the saddle. Not in any way like how Turner had, but a way that makes my heart settle firmly in my throat. It's like he's stripping away every last layer of my defenses, seeing every secret I'm trying to hide.

"You try anything, you'll regret it," he finally says.

I swallow hard but nod once. He turns his back to me and after a few more minutes, we ride out into the unknown.

CHAPTER
FIVE

I don't know what I expected a group of Hunters to be, but it certainly isn't an entire camp of hundreds upon hundreds of people, all looking...formidable. We'd ridden for an hour or so through the forest in what I assume was to the northeast, towards Duskthorne, and I'd come up with and discarded plan after plan of escape. I'd finally given up, frustrated and exhausted, and decided that an opportunity will present itself at some point and I'll be ready to grab it when it does.

The camp is made up of rows upon rows of tents, fires burning in the open spaces between them. We approach a make-shift stable where a young boy, probably no more than fifteen, takes the reins of my horse and waits for me to dismount. I nearly stumble when my boots hit the ground, my thighs screaming, but manage to right myself before Turner can "assist" me again as he did before. The boy looks to Blackheart, and when he nods, the boy quickly unties the rope from my wrists. I rub them as I wait, the skin irritated but not injured.

I have no idea what will happen next. Will I be chained in the middle of the camp for everyone's amusement? Worse? I know that I

—Tesni—am important to them insofar as I'll line their pockets handsomely from the ransom—or so they think. What the hells will happen to me when the ransom never arrives? When Hastings disappears with the coin and jewels to meet Tesni and I'm left in the hands of a monster? Surely they'll send another ransom, won't they? But what if they find out the truth about me before then? Or if Barony does? Would he want me in his clutches or would he leave me to suffer at the hands of Dorian?

I clench my hands into fists, knowing that all of the questions are useless. I have no intention of actually arriving in Duskthorne, so there's no reason to worry about any of this yet. Now, I need to focus on the more immediate threats—like what feels like hundreds of pairs of eyes staring at me. I shrink back instinctively, the need to stay hidden in this part of Hypathia so intense it feels like something clawing at the inside of my chest, but then I remember that I'm supposed to be my sister. I'm supposed to be King Barony's prized and coveted Gifted with a reputation for being a haughty bitch. So, I shove my shoulders back and do my best to look down my nose at everyone who dares to look my direction.

"This way," Blackheart commands, not looking to see if I follow as he strides off down a muddy path between the rows of tents. I don't immediately move and get a shove from behind from Turner. I stumble forward a few steps before turning to glare at the man. He smiles, crooked teeth gleaming in the light from the setting sun.

"Touch me again, and it will be the last decision you ever make," I spit, putting as much icy venom into the words as I can, my Gift coiling in the center of my chest. For a moment, I forget about my need to hide, my need to keep up this charade that will possibly save my life. For a moment, I'm all too happy to throw all of that right out the fucking window and teach Turner a lesson, teach every man like him one.

"I wouldn't," Blackheart calls and I whip my head around to find him watching us, that cold amusement in his eyes again. "You can try, but I advise against it."

Part of me wonders how many people I could kill before they could subdue me, but something in Blackheart's gaze tells me I really don't want to try. There's a calm, lethal power in this man, a coiled viper waiting to strike. So, with one last withering look, I turn my back on Turner and stride forward to follow Blackheart through the camp. I hear the rumblings as we walk, some whispered, some not bothering with that at all:

"Is it really her? Barony's fire whore?"

"Doesn't look so formidable to me."

"She burned my entire village to the ground."

"Thought she'd be prettier in person."

"I'd still fuck her."

"I heard that she can set entire leagues ablaze with the flick of a finger."

"Makers damn her and her Gift to the pits of the seventh hell."

I try not to cringe away at their words, each hitting like a slap though I know they aren't truly about me.

"You've quite the reputation," Blackheart says casually over his shoulder when we approach a larger tent set apart from the rest, a smaller one beside it. I remain silent as he steps inside, clearly expecting me to follow. I don't particularly want to, but don't suppose I have much of a choice, so I step beneath the flap and am immediately enveloped in warmth, almost to the point of stifling. A large fire burns in a brazier on one side of the space, a bed covered in furs sits on the other, a chest thrown open beside it overflowing with weapons. What looks like *armor* stands on a life-size dummy on the other side of the room near a large desk, the surface covered in maps and parchment. I frown. I'd always heard that Hunters were typically small, rag-tag groups of outlaws and criminals who found a way to make a living doing terrible deeds that were technically legal. This is a group of at least three hundred from what I could tell, and this man looks like he's ready for battle, not the capture of a single Gifted.

What in the hells kind of Hunters are these people?

Blackheart removes his sword belt and hangs it on the stand next to the desk. A dragon adorns the grip, wings spread out along the crossguard, ruby eyes staring and fangs on full display. I remember now that the sigil of Duskthorne is an ice dragon, though they've been extinct for centuries. He pulls a bottle of something dark from a drawer and pours himself a drink, not offering me anything, before leaning back against the front of the desk. He runs a hand through his hair, the dark strands a tangled mess, and watches me over the rim of his glass as he drinks.

I stand in the center of the space with my arms crossed and try to keep my nerves in check, try to keep from shaking so violently that my knees buckle.

"What do you plan to do with me?" I ask, trying to sound strong and unconcerned.

"I plan to take you to King Dorian, who will negotiate with Lyanna for an obscene ransom for your safe return." Just as Tesni planned, but something nags at the edges of my mind. King Dorian is known throughout the world as a cruel and avid *collector* of Gifteds. So why would he negotiate at all?

"Why?"

"Why what?" Blackheart asks, quirking a dark brow.

"Why return me instead of keeping me for his collection?"

Blackheart sets his glass on the desk and shrugs out of his coat, tossing it into one of the chairs. He eyes me as he rolls the sleeves of his black tunic up to his elbows, revealing swirling lines of dark ink.

"I wouldn't think you'd want to be part of the collection."

"Of course I don't," I snap, "but...why wouldn't he want me for it?" For all that I hate my sister, there is no doubt that her power is vast and terrifying. Surely she would be a prized addition to someone like Dorian, especially knowing he took her from another kingdom.

Blackheart shrugs, rubbing his hand across the thick stubble at his jaw.

"Think he's already got a fire wielder in a cage somewhere—he doesn't need another." My skin prickles at the thought of people trapped in cages in Duskthorne, cold radiating out from my chest in fear and revulsion and fury. "And what Barony and his little Alliance will be willing to pay to get you back far outweighs the need for Dorian to keep you as another pet." He says *little Alliance* like the joined kingdoms are a mere annoyance, a gnat buzzing near your ear that you shoo away. Perhaps Hunters don't pledge allegiance to any particular kingdom since they travel the entire continent for bounties, so he doesn't really care who decides to ally with whom.

"And until negotiations are concluded?"

He lets his gaze travel over me, not in a leering way, the way Turner had, but like he's taking my measure, assessing Makers know what.

"Until then, you remain my prisoner. You'll travel with us to Duskthorne, you'll do as I say, when I say it, and you'll not cause trouble. Simple."

"Simple," I repeat, incredulous. I have to get out of this place. The sooner, the fucking better.

"Glad we're in agreement," Blackheart says, a cruel smirk on his lips.

"Is Blackheart your name, or simply a monomer given based on your personality?" I spit. His smirk turns into a true grin, revealing straight white teeth.

"I'll let you be the judge of that. Now—" he shifts his gaze over my shoulder and beckons to someone. I turn to find a beautiful woman with warm brown skin and ice blue eyes walking towards me. She's dressed in black leather pants, a long-sleeved black tunic with a black leather vest over top. Myriad daggers are attached to it —what in the hells would someone possibly need with so many knives??--and the firelight sparks off of the blades like stars. Apparently the uniform of these Hunters is black to the core. "—Odessa will escort you to your tent."

"No chains? No collar?" I ask before I can stop myself.

"Do you need them?"

"You can't possibly think I won't—"

"I don't think, I *know*," Blackheart interrupts. My eyes fly wide, real anger rising, not merely the feigned outrage that I'd forced to act like Tesni before.

"You have no idea—"

He pushes off of the table and closes the distance between us in three long strides, cutting my words off quite efficiently. I force myself not to flinch back, but my entire body tenses and goes cold, my Gift rearing up inside my chest. I swallow hard and crane my head up to meet his gaze and he narrows his eyes.

"Go ahead and *try*," he growls. "I fucking dare you, Red."

I want to. I want so fucking badly to freeze the bastard's heart inside his chest and shatter the damn thing into dust. But I can't, especially not with Odessa here to witness it. I could kill her as well before she could strike, I'm sure, but there are *hundreds* of others outside. I can't possibly attack everyone at once. I've never used my Gift for something of that scale. I can make the glasses at the tavern nice and cool in the heat of summer. I can coax a snowstorm from the clouds. I can slice men to ribbons with daggers of ice—but only two or three at once, at most. Taking on hundreds? It's out of the realm of possibilities for me. Maybe Tesni could, but she's had far more practice than I. If I tried something so large, I'd push my Gifts past their limits. I'd be ripped apart at the seams by the power of it.

"Come on, I know you'd love to burn me to ash, right here, right now, wouldn't you?" he taunts. "I've heard that you absolutely delight in the smell of burned flesh." His lip curls in disgust and my stomach roils at the thought, at the knowledge that deep down, he's probably right about Tesni. She has a blacker heart than even this man before me. "Not even a single flame?"

He smirks when I merely stare, jaw clenching so tightly that my teeth ache, as if he's won some kind of battle. I want to scream in frustration but only stand there, mute and frozen.

"Well then," he says, crossing his arms over his chest, that simmering darkness settling back into the shadows, the mocking levity back in his voice and eyes now. "If you ever decide to give it a go, know that you're more than welcome."

I narrow my eyes again, not sure what he's getting at. Why does he *want* me to try? Why does he think it will be so easy to stop me? Unless...I nearly gasp, eyes going wide. Could it be possible? I've never heard of such a thing, but it would make sense for an elite Hunter to be a Gifted himself, one who can *block* the Gifts of others. No need for collars. No way for the Gifteds to fight back. It would make his job infinitely easier. It's genius, really.

So, he wants me to try just to show me that I can't do a damn thing, to show me fully just how fucked I am in this place, that I am fully at his mercy and under his control. I decide to test my theory another time when those stormy eyes aren't studying me so intensely it's as if I can feel it like a physical touch, a skating of claws over my skin. I swallow hard and his gloating smile widens.

"We leave at dawn. Be ready to go, or I'll drag you out of that tent myself, ready or not. You may go now."

Effectively dismissed, Odessa gestures for me to walk in front of her out of the tent. Though I'm surprised she doesn't just grab my arm and steer me where she wants me to go like Turner did, I do appreciate her lack of intrusion. I step out of the tent and breathe in deeply, letting the cool air fill my lungs and settle me.

"This way," Odessa says, not entirely unkindly, but not warmly by any means either, as she turns to the left. I follow a step behind her, letting her lead the way. Her dark hair is in three thick plaits starting from her crown that hang down to the middle of her back, and it reminds me of something that I can't quite place. She's taller than me by a head, and though she's lean, she's muscular. Strong. Formidable. I have no doubts she can wield all of those blades strapped to her body with ease. I wonder how she came to be a Hunter, what turns someone to a life of tracking down innocents.

She stops a few seconds later and I nearly run into her back.

"Here you are."

I blink and turn my head to look back at Blackheart's tent, merely feet away, then turn back to Odessa and arch a brow.

"I needed an escort for *that*?"

She gives me a look that says I need whatever the hells Blackheart says that I do, and reaches to pull up the flap, looping the circle of fabric around the hook attached to the outside of the tent to keep the doorway open. She gestures for me to enter first so I sigh and walk inside. It's smaller than Blackheart's, but clean at least. A cot sits on one side of the space, a small brazier on the other with a fire burning low within, and beside it a small table and water basin. To my surprise the trunk of "my" belongings is beside the cot as well.

"Food will be brought to you shortly," Odessa tells me. "There is water in the basin should you wish to wash up."

"Thank you," I say absently, exhaustion and despair trying to pull me under. Odessa furrows her brows and I want to kick myself. Tesni would never thank this woman. She would never thank anyone for anything. I force more bite into my words when I add, "I'm fully aware of what a wash basin is for." I make a show of looking her up and down. "Though I can't be sure you could say the same." The words taste like ash on my tongue. I've never been the type to be unnecessarily cruel. She, in fact, looks like she could be Brienne herself made flesh, a gloriously beautiful and fearsome goddess, and she's certainly far more put together than I must look right now with my ruined dress, tangled hair, and covered in dirt and blood.

Odessa clenches her jaw and her blue eyes flare brightly, like shards of ice with fire burning behind them. She looks as if she loathes me, which I guess is what I intended, but it doesn't mean that I enjoy it. I tell myself that this cruelty is necessary. This is about survival.

"Don't try anything stupid, princess," she snaps, the word *princess* thrown like an insult, and leaves the tent, closing the flap behind her. Once she's gone, I start to pace, rubbing my temples as I try to sort through everything that has happened, but it's too much. Everything attacks my mind at once, all of the possibilities and consequences and emotions slamming into me over and over like lashes of a whip. It's hard to breathe and I hit my knees, wrapping my arms around myself as I break apart.

My sister betrayed me—*again.* She sent me off to be kidnapped and taken to a place known to be hells on earth for Gifteds, to a place where the king is cruel and sadistic and forces women to do unspeakable things. I have no idea what will happen when we arrive —or even how long that might take—or what will become of me once the ransom goes "missing." I wonder if I'll ever see Math and Cece again, if they're safe.

It feels as if my ribs are shrinking, pulling inward, squeezing, squeezing, squeezing.

Breathe, Thea, I tell myself. *You have to breathe. You have to think. You have to fight.*

Fight. Yes. I've fought my whole life and I won't give up now. I will get out of this. I will return to Math and Cece. I will live the life I deserve, the one I made for myself against all odds. I dig my fingers into the fabric of my dress, focusing on the feel of the thick wool. *Focus on what you can see and feel and smell.* I focus on the orange glow from the brazier, the soft, cold earth beneath my knees, the smell of snow in the air. Slowly, so fucking slowly that I think I might suffocate, my ribs expand once more and I can finally suck in a deep, ragged breath. I take four or five deep, controlled breaths after that, letting my body and mind settle. After what could be minutes or hours, I can push myself up from the ground. I move to the bed and sit on the edge, putting my head in my hands.

"Ok," I whisper. "Ok. You can do this. One thing at a time."

I try to think through everything again, this time forcing all of my thoughts into an orderly line the way Cece does with the sailors on particularly rowdy nights and they all rush the bar like a pack of wild dogs. First things first: I need to see if my Gift is truly useless here. I take a deep breath and let my power flow through me, cold filling every vein and making my heart flutter with excitement. I can feel the cold beneath my skin in my palms, traveling up my fingers, and I try to force it outward and create a small icicle.

Nothing happens.

I try again, putting more strength into the command, willing my skin to turn to ice. Nothing. I try for a light frost. No luck. I try for dropping the temperature in the tent around me, but it remains warm and pleasant, the wood popping loudly in the fire as if to mock me.

"Fuck!" I spit through gritted teeth. So, he *can* block my Gift. I wonder how far his power extends...and then my heart plummets. If his Gift depends on proximity, I fear that I won't be allowed to stray too far from him. Desperate I try one more time, letting the power pool deep in my chest, pulling up from the depths of my soul. I hold my palms out, willing ice to form, begging...

I scream through clamped teeth in frustration when once again, not a damn thing happens. I flop back onto the bed and bury my face in the pillow, not even bothering to move when someone slides a tray of food inside the flap of my tent a few minutes later.

CHAPTER SIX

Hours later, I finally force myself up from the bed. The fire has burned down to embers, and while I'm not bothered by the cold, I need the light. I manage to coax it back to life, thank the Makers, and get the two lanterns burning as well, filling my tent with a nice warm glow. I peek outside, expecting to find armed guards at my door—*er, flap?*—but find nothing. I'm not naïve enough to believe that I'm not being watched, even if I can't see them, and know that a camp this size would have patrols roaming at all hours just to be safe, especially if word has spread that this particular group of Hunters has the Flame of Lyanna. So, no, escape is out of the question, at least for tonight. I glance towards Blackheart's tent and see that his lanterns are still burning bright. The rest of the camp is mostly dark, though the fires still burn along the paths. I have no idea what time it might be, but it must be late, most everyone asleep in preparation for our dawn departure.

I sigh and retreat back inside. I pull off the ruined dress and do my best to wash the grime and blood away in the basin. I wince when I wash the scrape on my temple and bite my lip as I peel the bandage away from my arm, the dried blood making the process far from pleasant. The cut beneath isn't too bad, but it's sore and tender. I'll have to find another bandage, but first I unplait what's left of the braids atop my crown, wincing when I encounter tangle after tangle. Ennis had managed to yank most of it down already, but a few stubborn strands had found themselves into more of a knot than a braid at this point. Finally, I work them all out and let the tresses hang loose down my back, rubbing my sore scalp as I rummage through the trunk.

"Fucking hells, Tesni," I whisper. Not a pair of trousers in sight, just more heavy, flowing dresses, thick fur coats, and hats that I would rather die than be seen wearing by a soul on this earth. I slap the edge of the trunk in frustration and squeeze my eyes shut, taking deep, deliberate breaths in through my nose and out through my mouth. I find a soft handkerchief, her name stitched in gold thread along the edge—*Tesni de Moreau*—and tie it around my arm as a makeshift bandage, getting the tiniest bit of satisfaction knowing that she'd be pissed to see my blood ruining her fine accessories.

I pull on a thin shift for now and climb beneath the furs. I wouldn't have thought sleep would find me in this place, but it embraces me like an old friend and pulls me beneath the waves of darkness the moment my head hits the pillow.

"—up!"

I bolt upright, gasping. I'd been dreaming of fire, great serpents made of flames chasing me through a black forest, gnarled trees reaching out their wickedly sharp branches to slash deep gouges into my skin. I'd run and run and run, but Tesni's laughter had never faded, seeming to hover above me as her beasts pursued. I wipe sweat-soaked hair from my brow and blink into the dim light. It takes a heartbeat for me to realize where I am, to remember everything that had happened yesterday.

"Get up," Odessa snaps, apparently not for the first time. "He wasn't joking, you know. He *will* drag you out of here in your shift and not give two shits if you freeze your ass off or chafe the skin right off your thighs as we ride. So, unless you want that, I suggest you get up and get dressed *now*. You have five minutes."

I blink to try to clear the sleep from my eyes and nod. She strides out of the tent, letting the flap close behind her. I untangle myself from the blankets and stagger to the basin. I splash the cool water over my face and neck, and run my fingers through my hair, quickly plaiting it in one long braid over my right shoulder. I choose the least offensive dresses I can find, something I believe Tesni would deign was indeed for riding, though her idea of riding through pristine gardens will be vastly different from what I'm going to be doing today I imagine. It's a deep midnight with gold stitching, and thankfully allows for a bit more movement than the monstrosity I was in yesterday, with slits in the sides to allow one to mount a horse easily. I pull on the heinous boots and exit the tent to find Odessa waiting.

"One minute to spare. I'm impressed."

She tenses, snapping to her full height at some unseen signal or threat. I furrow my brow but turn to find Blackheart emerging from his tent. He's back in the Hunter uniform again—black leathers, black coat, sword at his hip—and he strides forward with an easy grace.

"And I was so hoping I'd get to drag you out," he says, smiling coldly. He keeps walking, not seeming to care about my response, and Odessa falls into step behind him, making it clear I'm to do the same. I don't bother asking about the trunk—someone put it there before. If they want me to continue having it, they'll move it again—and hold the hem of my dress up from the muddy path as we walk. I jut my chin up, pressing my shoulders back as we walk past the rows of tents, most in the process of being taken down and packed away, and ignore the comments and stares. The sun is just coming up over the mountains in the distance and bathing the camp in beautiful, soft golden light.

We walk back to where the horses are kept and I see the same horse I rode yesterday waiting, the young boy putting his saddle on him. The horse has a white spot on his neck in the shape of a star, and I secretly name him Zaro after the Maker of the sky. Blackheart walks off to talk to a group of men and women, all in the same black clothing, while Odessa stands beside me.

"Are you to be my keeper, then?" I ask, making sure to put that annoyingly haughty tone into my voice.

"If that's what he wishes, then yes," she says tersely, but then adds with a cold smile, "no matter how demeaning and beneath me such a task may be."

I press my lips into a hard line and she smirks before a young girl with dark brown hair and light green eyes approaches cautiously. She must only be nine or ten, far too young to be a Hunter, certainly? Odessa softens and smiles warmly at the girl, nodding encouragingly at her. The girl ducks her head, but takes the last few steps so that she's standing closer to us. Is she afraid of me? My chest twists at that. People shouldn't cower before a Gifted. We're supposed to use our Gifts to help people, at least that's what I've always believed. We're no better than anyone else, we were just given the opportunity to be vessels for blessings from the Makers, to help where others cannot. The fact that Tesni has allowed her Gift to be turned into something so dark and twisted, something that strikes fear into the hearts of people, something to be bought and paid for, makes me sick.

"Finally awake, are we Mia?"

The girl looks up at that and rolls her eyes. "I was only a few minutes late, Dessa. Anyway, I brought breakfast for you and..." She peeks at me from beneath her lashes and I see the smattering of light freckles across her nose. She's adorable now, but will be stunning one day. I want so badly to smile, to tell her that Mia is a beautiful name, ask her what she's doing here. But of course, I can do none of those things. "And for her," she finishes, pulling her gaze away quickly. She holds out a hand towards each of us, and I take the offered piece of bread with some kind of cheese baked on top. It smells delicious.

"Thanks, Mia. Tell Cookie it smells delicious, yeah?" Mia nods and someone calls Odessa's name. She turns slightly away from us and Mia chances another glance my way. I shouldn't, but I can't help myself. I let my cold mask slide away, smiling at her and winking. She looks a little confused, blinking and narrowing her eyes slightly, but after a moment gives me a very small smile back before turning and running away. Odessa turns back to find me nearly done with my bread already. It's the most delicious thing I've ever eaten, the bread baked to perfection, the cheese thick and flavorful and toasted just enough to be crunchy the way I like.

I don't even know when the last time I've eaten anything was. On the ship before I met with Tesni? And how long ago was that? Days? My stomach makes an obscenely loud grumbling sound, demanding more, and Odessa quirks a dark brow, the two golden rings through it glinting in the sunlight. I pretend that I didn't hear a thing and instead decide to see if I can glean any useful information from her.

"Are all Hunting parties this large? I always thought Hunters traveled in small groups. Did he really think hundreds of men—and women—were required to subdue me? I'm flattered, really, but—"

"Hunting...?" she interrupts with a frown.

"We'll be riding most of the day," Blackheart says, striding towards us. "If I hear complaints, I'll gladly gag you." He smirks like he hopes that he'll have the opportunity to do just that, popping a piece of some kind of cooked meat into his mouth that smells like heaven. He catches me staring. "Apologies that our humble fare isn't up to your standards, Highness."

I grind my teeth, choking down the first few retorts that come to mind knowing full well that the insults to his mother that I learned from the sailors in the port would never be something that Tesni would possibly know, let alone dare say. I think that Blackheart may just be the most infuriating prick in Hypathia.

Thankfully, my horse is ready to go and the boy holds the reins while I hoist myself up, without Turner's hands on my ass this time. Thinking of him apparently summons the bastard. He strolls down the path with a small group of men behind him, his eyes immediately shifting to my thigh, the slit in the dress putting it on full display again. Out of all the men that I've seen since being brought here, Turner is the only one who stares like this, who makes it clear what he wants…and I don't think he's afraid to try to take it.

I sigh but wait patiently while Odessa secures my wrists again and tosses the end of the rope to Blackheart. He smiles as he wraps it around the pommel of his saddle and pulls it tight. We end up riding out from the camp in waves, twenty or thirty in each group. The morning passes in a blur, and I honestly don't remember much of the trip. I let my mind wander, half because it's the only way I can keep my panic at bay, and half because it takes the focus off of how sore my thighs and ass are getting and how the rope is chaffing my wrists.

We eventually stop at a wide stream to let the horses rest and to refill the water stores. After being untied, I walk to the water's edge a bit away from everyone else, though of course my shadow is watching me closely. I cup the cool water in my hands and, with a glance around to make sure no one is nearby, try once more to use my Gift. The water remains just that in my hands despite how much I will it to turn into ice.

"Fuck," I whisper, letting the water fall from my hands.

"Rumor has it that you could boil this entire stream in a heartbeat if you wanted," Odessa says as she approaches, holding out a small package to me. I rise and take it, just stopping myself from thanking her again. I unwrap it to find some strips of dried meat, salted and seasoned with something that smells mouthwatering, and small hunks of cheese. I hike a shoulder as I nibble on one of the pieces of meat, my eyes nearly rolling back at the taste. *Makers I'm fucking starving.*

"If that's what the rumors say, then it must be true," I spit, letting my frustrations get the better of me.

"Well, I can tell the rumors of you being an absolute cunt sure are true." She turns and walks away before I can respond, not that I have a damn thing I can say anyway. I'm already weary of this charade, and it's only been two days. How the fucking hells am I going to keep this up for…however long it takes to get to Duskthorne? I move to sit on a large rock at the stream's edge and watch the others while I eat my rations. The group, though large, moves easily and efficiently, as if they've done this a thousand times. Water barrels and canteens are filled, the horses are tended to, food packages distributed—all with barely a word or order uttered. Something is strange about the group, but I can't quite place what.

"I expected much more complaining, if I'm being honest," Blackheart says, startling me. He seems to be holding back laughter when I gasp and nearly fall over. I narrow my eyes, not having to act like a cold-hearted bitch where he's concerned. I smooth my braid over my shoulder.

"How long will it take for us to arrive in Duskthorne? The faster I can be away from you and this band of degenerates, the better."

"Weeks, maybe months depending on several factors." My eyes go wide.

"*Months?*"

"Trust me, I don't find the idea of being saddled with you for such a long trek appealing either, but Dorian will not negotiate until you are in his possession—and neither will Barony and the Alliance, for that matter. A lot of things can go wrong on a journey like this. Why pay a ransom when the prize can't even be guaranteed yet?"

"I…but…" I sputter, not knowing what the hells to say or how to wrap my head around being out here for possibly *months* without my Gifts. But then again…the longer we're out on the road, the more opportunities I'll surely have to escape before we reach the nightmare that is Duskthorne. So, maybe the long journey is a good thing in the end?

I let out a long breath and try my best to act as if I don't care, but he doesn't walk away. Instead, he turns to watch the group with that intense gaze he has, as if he's seeing a thousand different things at once, things no one else can. Calculating and recalculating and noting every little detail.

"What other factors?" I finally say, the silence feeling heavy and uncomfortable between us. He turns back to me and gives me a bored look. "You said it could be months depending on several factors—what factors?"

"The weather, for one." He looks upward, as if he can predict what will come by staring at the sky. "Heavy snowfalls will make for slower travel, especially once we reach the outer Obsidians." The Obsidians are the mountain range surrounding and encompassing Duskthorne. "And battle, of course."

I rear back and blink in surprise. *Did he say...*

I look back to the group and realize what had seemed strange earlier: they're all carrying weapons. Not tavern-brawl daggers or the thin rapiers some of the sailors carry, but *real* weapons: long swords and great iron hammers, balls on spikes and double-bladed axes. And Odessa's braids—they're *warrior* braids. I've seen paintings of the legendary Oska—stalwart female warriors from the wilds in the north that are now part of Duskthorne—fighting epic battles, their braids and blades coated in blood and wildfire in their eyes. I can see Odessa among them in my mind's eye and wonder if perhaps she's a true descendent of them. And if, perhaps, I should watch my tongue around her a bit more.

"This is an army," I say slowly.

Blackheart quirks a brow. "Of course it is. Did you think..." He barks out a laugh. "Did you really think all of this was for *you*?" He throws his head back and laughs again and I press my lips into a thin line. He goes on and on, to the point where others start looking our way curiously. Finally, his laughter subsides and he wipes tears from his eyes—fucking *tears*, the prick—and says, "Oh, thank you for that, Red. I needed a good laugh. But no army was necessary for you. I could have captured you alone with my eyes closed and one hand tied behind my back. Your location happened to be in our path, so." He shrugs. "Two birds. One stone."

"Why the hells is an army parading about anyway then?" I snap, sounding petulant and annoyed.

He looks at me seriously now, narrowing his eyes and tilting his head.

"I can't tell if you're joking or not." When I give him a dry look, he curses and runs a hand through his hair. "Great fucking Makers, you really are a self-absorbed, spoiled little princess, hiding away in your fucking castle until someone can scrounge up enough coin to pay for your services." Anger makes his blue-gray eyes blaze and churn. "A war is brewing out here. People are *dying*, innocent fucking people. What in the hells did you think the Alliance was doing? Having tea? Throwing parties?" He curls his lip in absolute disgust and fury, and I actually flinch backwards from the fire of it. "You have no idea what's really going on, what your precious Barony and his friends are planning, what they're already fucking doing."

I can only stare. A *war*? We'd heard rumblings down in Helios, sure, but it was just gossip and rumors, wasn't it? But...Tesni's note flashes behind my eyes now: *There will be no winners in this war for our kind.* She'd mentioned Barony's Alliance moving against Duskthorne, wanting to take their Gifteds. *Fucking hells.*

Blackheart is truly fuming now, surprising me in his anger. He serves the worst royal in all of Hypathia, doing Makers knows what in Dorian's name and allowing horrific things to happen under his watch within the walls of Duskthorne. I may not know what in the hells he's talking about Barony and the Alliance's plans, but whatever it is, it can't be worse than what he himself is a part of. How the hells can he be so self-righteous? But before I can ask just that, he pulls himself up to his full height, towering over me even sitting atop the rock, and glares down at me, sending my snide retort dying on my tongue. His eyes truly look like the North Sea during a storm now, more gray than blue, and churning just as violently.

"You want to know the real reason Dorian wouldn't want you for his collection?" he seethes, "Because even someone as despicable as him wouldn't want someone like *you* anywhere near him. You are the worst kind of Gifted, the worst kind of *person*. The world would be a better place without you in it."

I flinch away again, his words hitting me like a physical blow. He's not even talking about *me*, not really, but the fire and hatred in his eyes feel all too real and tears well. I blink them away, determined not to let him see them fall, and he storms off, barking orders at a few what I understand now to be soldiers.

Odessa shoots a glare my way, blaming me for Blackheart's sour mood, I assume. She's not wrong. Her demeanor around him makes much more sense now—he's not the leader of a band of Hunters; he's her superior officer in an army of warriors.

"Great fucking Makers," I mutter, putting my face into my hands.

CHAPTER
SEVEN

By the time we stop for the night, I'm sore, exhausted, frustrated, and starting to lose hope. No one spoke to me on the second half of the journey and I didn't mind, really. I wasn't much in the mood to chat. I still can't quite make sense of everything Blackheart said. There's a war going on, at least the beginnings of one. How is that possible? And why? What are Lyanna and its allies planning? I'd forced myself to think about the conversation with Tesni over and over and over as we rode, and more details finally crystallized. She'd said that six of the nine kingdoms had allied and planned to attack Duskthorne and take their Gifteds.

She said *take* them—not *free* them. And she'd said something else before Hastings had cut her off. Something about adding the Gifteds to Barony's...His what? Does he have more than just Tesni now? Does he have the beginnings of his own collection, like Dorian? If so, why doesn't anyone know about them? Why would the other kingdoms ally with him simply to get their own Gifteds? Couldn't they just offer to buy one from Dorian? Surely he'd be willing to part with a few for the right price.

"Ughhh," I groan, my head pounding. I have a thousand questions and no answers.

"If you'd like to bathe, now is your chance," a voice says from the entrance to my tent. I raise my eyes to find Odessa standing there, looking annoyed. I don't have the energy to be rude or haughty, so I merely nod and grab the silk pouch, a nightgown, and fur-lined robe to put on afterwards from the trunk. She eyes the bundles of fabric in my arms but doesn't comment. She probably thinks they're as ridiculous as I do and I want so badly to tell her just that, to have a real conversation with someone and maybe not feel so alone in all of this. I'm suddenly so keenly aware of how badly I miss Cece and Math that my chest feels like it's collapsing in on itself. *Makers, please keep them safe.*

I follow Odessa away from the lines of tents to a bend in the river guarded by a thick line of trees. On the other side, an inlet juts out from the river and forms a small pool surrounded by rocks. Odessa holds out a thick towel. Surprised, I take it and nod.

"There's a hot spring not far that feeds into this inlet, so the water will be warmer. This is probably the last bit of non-freezing water you'll find before we reach Tithmoore. Better make the best of it."

I shudder at the thought. Just because I love the cold doesn't mean that I don't also love a good hot bath. I walk to the edge of the water and set all of my belongings on one of the flat rocks. I start unlacing my boots and then a thought occurs to me.

"Um, will...will anyone else be joining us?" I scrunch my nose. That's not exactly how I meant for it to come out. "No, not joining, like it's a bathing party. Not that bathing parties exist." I blow out a long breath and pinch the bridge of my nose. "I mean—"

"Instructions were given for you to have privacy," Odessa, blessedly interrupts me and looks for half a heartbeat like she wants to laugh. "I'll be standing watch over by the bend in the river."

"Thank you," I say, not even caring if it's not what Tesni would do. She eyes me, but doesn't comment, and turns to go back to the bend, as she said. I strip down and wade out into the water, moaning quietly in delight. The water is somewhere between warm and hot, and it feels so good to really wash away all of the grime from the last few days finally. I pull out the contents of the silk pouch and try not to be grateful for Tesni for putting it in the trunk. It was full of delicious smelling soaps, oils, shampoos, and lotions. I choose a soap that smells like honeyrose now and scrub my skin until it's nearly raw, and wash my hair twice for good measure. Though Odessa told me to make the most of this opportunity, I know that I can't stay here all night and I highly doubt the soldier would have any qualms about pulling my naked ass right out if I take too long. So, with a sigh, I leave the warm pool and dry off.

I pull the satin nightgown over my head—the only thing I've found of Tesni's so far that I do actually enjoy—and throw the robe on, wrapping it tightly around myself before I walk back through the camp. The thought of Turner seeing me in just the nightgown makes my stomach twist.

"Done," I say to Odessa as I approach the spot where she's standing sentry, cleaning her nails casually with the tip of a dagger.

"Well, you sure as hells smell better, that's for sure," she says, twirling her blade before sliding it into one of the many slits in her vest. I huff out a laugh at that and she blinks in surprise. "Come on, dinner should be ready."

I nod and fall into step beside her back towards the camp.

"Is there really a war starting?" I ask, not sure if she'll answer me or not, but deciding it's worth a try.

She snorts. "The fact that you don't know the answer shows how truly sheltered you've been up in your tower, princess." I roll my eyes. I'm already tired of the princess comments, but I know they're mostly deserved.

"Yes, I am. But I'd still like to know the answer."

She eyes me sidelong, but finally sighs.

"Yes, a war is coming. It's already here, really, but things will get much bigger before it's all said and done."

"And it's Lyanna and its allies against...Duskthorne?"

"Pretty much."

I purse my lips, trying to think through what that might mean. Why now? After all these years, why did Barony suddenly decide he wanted to unite the kingdoms against Duskthorne and take their Gifteds? Not just take them, but fight a full out war for them, *kill* for them. And why in the hells would the other kingdoms be so easily swayed to this cause? Tesni said that six of the nine had joined Barony.

"And why are all of the other kingdoms so eager to join this Alliance?"

Her jaw clenches. "Amon Luterian is very...persuasive."

My stomach roils at that. Even I've heard of Amon Luterian, the leader of Nocadian's army and the personal Guardian of the Queen. Folks around the tavern call him The Abyss because his chest is as hollow and dark as one. No heart within, no feelings to speak of, only cold death and ruin. He's the only reason that no one has challenged Queen Viola's seat on the throne—she's barely more than a child, an easy target, her throne a beacon for the greedy. Amon eliminates all potential threats, and, if rumors are to be believed, decorates the palace with the bones of all those he kills. Why he doesn't just kill the child and take the throne himself is beyond me, but there must be some tiny shred of decency in his chest to keep him loyal to her.

I'm about to ask another of the questions burning on my tongue when we pass Turner and the same small group he always seems to be around. Perhaps the soldiers are assigned to specific groups that they must stay with—*or maybe they're all just friends, you idiot*, I say to myself. That makes more sense.

"Could use someone to warm my bed. What better than a Gifted fire bitch to do the job?" he calls. The men around him all laugh, though some seem to do so uncomfortably. I pull my robe tighter around me and Odessa narrows her eyes on Turner, a hand shifting subtly to one of the knives at her hip. I don't think Turner even sees the movement.

"Fucking prick," I mutter quietly after we've moved past them.

"Agreed," Odessa says to my surprise. She stops in front of my tent, gesturing for me to go inside. I glance towards Blackheart's tent, just beside mine once more and again I wonder how far his Gift extends, at what distance would I be able to unleash my ice again? I can see him within, his large shadow pacing the length of his larger space. I suppose we have that habit in common.

"I'll have someone fetch your dinner...oh, looks like she beat me to it," Odessa says with a smile, her entire demeanor softening as Mia approaches. She clearly has a soft spot for the girl and curiosity burns in my chest. Math calls me nosey, but Cece lovingly calls it inquisitiveness instead.

"I brought dinner for..." Mia trails off, glancing up at me nervously. "For, the, um..." It seems like she can't decide what she's supposed to call me. Gifted. Prisoner. Future slave. Bitch. Dead girl walking. Any number of things apply, really.

"Th—" I stop myself and bite the inside of my cheek. No, I'm not Thea, not here. I'm...*her*. My chest constricts, like my heart is trying to pull away from what I'm about to do, declaring out loud that I'm Tesni. I know the name I need to say...but I don't fucking *want* to be Tesni. She's a terrible person, a monster, and even taking on her name feels as if it's tainting my soul somehow.

So, no. I won't do it. I'm playing the part, but I decide that I don't have be her completely.

"Tess," I say instead. "You can call me Tess." Tess was the sister I loved. Tess was the sister who loved me back and had goodness inside of her before the darkness took hold. If I can't be myself, I can settle for being Tess.

Mia seems to consider this, glancing quickly to Odessa as if for permission. The woman gives her a nod and then Mia straightens her shoulders and holds out a metal bowl with a handle on the side, and a piece of bread towards me.

"I brought dinner for Tess."

I smile at her and take the offered gifts gratefully, nodding in thanks. The girl tilts her head at me, studying me in that way that children do, like they can somehow cut through all of the layers of bullshit that a person puts on themselves for protection or to hide everything they don't want the world to see. What does she see in me?

Odessa reaches out and tugs on the end of one of her braids.

"Off with you then. I'll be there soon." Mia nods, casts me another look, and then turns and strolls away, alternating between walking and running and skipping. Whatever is in the bowl—a stew of some kind by the looks of it—smells absolutely delicious and my mouth waters. Odessa turns back to me and though I don't say a word, the curiosity must be clear in my eyes. I don't know if it was the moment of almost truce by the river or our shared disgust with Turner, but she lets her guard down for a moment and answers my unasked question.

"She's my sister," Odessa says quietly, surprising me. "Not by blood, obviously," she adds, the hint of a smile pulling on her lips. It's true that they're complete opposites physically—Odessa with her brown skin and icy eyes and Mia, ivory and freckled, with those stunning fern-green irises—but there's a certain likeness between them. Some shared mannerisms, similar quirks of their lips. Something siblings would share being raised together, blood or not. "She's a squire, technically, so that she can travel with me since our parents..." She trails off and clears her throat.

"I'm sorry," I tell her honestly, chest clenching at the clear pain in her eyes though she tries to hide it, at the thought of Mia losing her mother and father so young. She seems to shake herself, that guard going back up again, and gives me a hard nod.

"We leave at day light again. Be ready."

She turns on her heel and strides off, and I cast one last glance at Blackheart's tent—only to find him standing outside watching me intently. I inhale sharply in surprise and hold his gaze for a heartbeat before I swallow hard and quickly step through the flap into my tent. The fire is burning low already and I toss my robe onto the trunk before settling onto the bed with my meal. I devour the stew and bread, and find fresh water in a canteen beside the water basin. I braid my wet hair into two long plaits and settle beneath the furs. I try not to think about the coming war or what it might mean, not just for me, but for all of Hypathia—and especially the Gifteds. I stare at the top of the tent for a long time but can't settle my mind. I glance over to the open flap on the other side that allows the smoke from the fire to escape and pull myself out of bed. I grunt and curse as I drag the cot across the space—the damn thing is sturdier than I would have thought—until it's positioned just below the opening.

I climb back in and lie down, staring up at the stars now. I sigh in contentment as I watch them, finding familiar shapes, remembering the stories and silly names Tesni and I used to make up for each of them as children in my canopy bed, remembering the correct names for them that Tobias had taught me as we traveled the road all those years ago, recalling all the nights Math and Cece and I laid on the roof of the tavern together, drinking and laughing and thanking the Makers for the life we'd managed to make for ourselves.

I drift off with a smile on my face, and tears in my eyes.

THE NEXT WEEK IS MUCH OF THE SAME: WE RIDE; WE REST; WE CAMP. The only real changes are the landscape and the weather, and perhaps the stares and insults thrown my away are fewer, though most certainly not gone completely.

We're making our way toward Tithmoore to re-supply before we'll enter the true northlands on our way to Duskthorne. Tithmoore is one of the only kingdoms that hasn't allied with Lyanna, though they haven't allied with Duskthorne either, apparently. They're remaining neutral—I wonder how long that will last when one side or the other demands that they choose, most likely at the tip of a sword.

"How in the hells are these fruits always fresh?" I demand when I open the package that Mia handed me this morning. She now smiles at me before scampering off, a true smile, the trepidation from before gone, and it makes me happy. A bright spot in this dark, uncertain time. The bundle contains moonberries and a variety of melons, in addition to the cheese and meat. "It's impossible. The first day, sure, I assumed fresh fruit was purchased in Lyanna before my untimely capture," I roll my eyes and Odessa's lips quirk. She, too, is starting to thaw towards me ever so slightly, that guard still up but not quite as thick. "But now? A week later?"

She gives me a look that says I'm daft and I give her one back that says *ok, maybe I am, answer me anyway*.

"You really can't figure out how we have fresh fruit—and vegetables, for that matter, in case you haven't noticed those in your dinners—out here as we travel? Truly?" She looks at me, willing me to understand.

And then I do.

"A Gifted?? But...Blackheart...?"

"He can choose who is blocked." *Holy fuck*. Great Makers, he must be even more powerful than I thought to be able to distinguish each Gift somehow inside his mind and only block those he wishes. A thought sends cold fear through my veins, but I discard it quickly. Of course he can't know what *exactly* the Gift is, otherwise he would have known in an instant that I wasn't Tesni. He must just be able to sense an energy or something like that, some signal that only he can detect and know who it's coming from.

"Cookie is a Gifted with agricultural specialties."

I glance around the camp, all the people milling about preparing for today's journey. How many of them are Gifteds? It would make sense to have Gifteds with offensive powers, or healing ones perhaps, in an army. And one who can grow fresh food within the camp, apparently. Odessa follows my gaze, tracking my thoughts.

"Yes, there are Gifteds in this army—serving willingly."

I blink, storing all of this away to think about as we ride, wondering what other kinds of Gifts may be useful in an army and if

I've crossed paths with any of the wielders. The only other Gifted I've ever known was Tesni. I think it might be nice to talk to another person who understands what it's like—though none here are likely to talk to the Flaming Cunt, as someone so lovingly called me yesterday, spitting at my feet as I passed. I sigh and finish my breakfast and we prepare to leave, the routine becoming familiar to me already.

Late in the afternoon, Blackheart drops back beside us and orders Odessa to arrange a scouting party and have them disperse within the hour. I'm no longer bound to his horse, thank the Makers, but he never rides far from me.

"Yes, sir," she says, inclining her head and riding off towards the rest of our group a few yards behind us. He stays beside me, studying me. I keep my eyes forward and remain silent, trying not to let his enormous presence unnerve me. He's physically imposing, of course, any fool can see that, but it's more than that. His entire being takes up space, demands to be seen and obeyed. It's both intimidating and captivating. If he wasn't such a prick, it might even be sexy as hells.

"What can you tell me about Lyanna's military and defenses?"

I start, turning to stare at him in confusion. Of course, I know exactly ruddy fuck about Lyanna's military and defenses, but would Tesni? I honestly don't know what Barony would have shared with her—or Hastings for that matter.

"And why would I tell you a damn thing?" I reply, pushing my shoulders back and adopting Tesni's haughty tone, bluffing for all that I'm worth.

He hikes one broad shoulder. "Perhaps if you're willing to cooperate and share information your stay in Duskthorne could be more... hospitable."

I bark out a humorless laugh. "So, I spill secrets and I'm not tortured and raped? Wow, what a deal you propose." The sarcasm is so thick that I fear I might choke on it. My power roils in my chest, radiating through my body at the thought of all Dorian might plan to do to me, that he's already doing to countless others. His jaw ticks, something flashing in his eyes, but it's gone quickly and he smooths out his features, that damned mocking smirk tilting his lips.

"You want to use that fire of yours so damned badly against me right now, Red. I can *feel* it." Even though I know he can't know the truth, I swallow hard as fear skitters up my spine. His smile widens and I turn my face away to look forward again, body tense. "Oh yes, I can feel it. You're strong, I'll give you that. If I believed for a second that I could trust you, I might even offer you a place here in my army."

"Yes, a fire bitch would come in quite handy against your enemies I imagine," I say in a bored tone. I turn to look at him then before I add in a cold voice, "And I do so love the smell of charred flesh."

Knowing damn well it's a stupid decision and could have dire consequences, I still spur my horse onward and ride ahead, leaving Blackheart to stare after me in what I hope isn't complete and utter rage.

CHAPTER
EIGHT

"What is this place?" I ask Odessa a few days later as we ride into what looks to be an abandoned town of some sort. I slide off of Zaro, finally used to riding so much again and far less sore than the first week, and hand the reins to Jacob, the squire. I give the horse a loving pat on the neck before walking down the wide path that seems to cut through the middle of the village. Or town. Or whatever the hells it was.

"It was a trading post once upon a time, but it's been abandoned for decades now."

I can see how having a trading post here would be ideal—we're in what most call The Perilous now: a vast, dangerous span of land between Lyanna and Tithmoore with unpredictable and treacherous terrain of thick forests, raging rivers, and rocky mountains, and beasts of legend said to be lurking within. There are no villages or towns in either direction for at least a three days' journey—and that's only so long as the snow holds off. I look upward, knowing it will start within the hour. I can feel it heavy in the air, calling to me, reaching out in welcome like an old friend. I sigh, wanting to embrace it back. I've missed it so much that my heart aches, but at least I'll see it again soon. With a snowstorm, it could take a week to get to the nearest town, and being stranded would be a nightmare.

So, yes, having a point halfway through The Perilous could be the difference between life and death. I wonder why it was abandoned.

"A newer one was built farther south. Travelers take that route across The Perilous now—it's safer," Blackheart answers my unasked question, making me jump as he seems to materialize out of thin air behind us. *How in the ruddy fuck does he move silent as death like that?* His lips quirk for a heartbeat, apparently amused by my surprise. "The ice dragons and frost cats like this area a bit too much for most people's liking," he adds, before walking on without a backwards glance.

"Are they truly real?" I whisper to Odessa. I've managed to crack her outermost shell of irritation towards me, so though she still doesn't like me, she tolerates me without outright disdain now, which is a win in my eyes.

"Oh, most definitely," she says with a sly grin, and I can't tell if she's serious or not. We haven't come across any as of yet, and I've always assumed they were merely myths, but...I glance around now, as if one of the beasts is going to burst out from behind a building any second. Odessa notices and laughs lightly, rolling her eyes. "Frost cats, yes. Dragons, no. They used to exist, but they've been gone for a long time now." She sounds sad about that. "But make no mistake, The Perilous truly is filled with all manner of beasts that would happily make a meal of you."

I glance to the woods again, the dark mountain peaks, and can only hope that the sheer size of the army is enough to keep them at bay as we make the crossing. We walk past several long cabins, large enough to house the entire army I'd wager—and apparently that's exactly what they're for.

"Sleep houses," Odessa explains, nodding to the rows of cabins on either side of the path. Travelers must have been able to pay for a bed within when this was still an active trading post. "Everyone gets a break from the tents tonight, thank the Makers." My stomach twists at the thought of sleeping in a giant open room with hundreds of soldiers, plenty of which still give me scathing looks when I pass, but most importantly, Turner and his brood.

"That's the kitchen and dining hall," she continues, nodding to another large cabin at the end of the path. "Bath houses." She points to four smaller structures to the left of the kitchen.

We keep walking, though I'm not quite sure why—shouldn't she be showing me to my assigned cot for the night? I don't complain though as I'm not in a hurry to be cooped up inside with all of those bodies. I want to stay out and enjoy the cold as long as possible.

"This was the main commissary, where everyone brought their wares to sell and trade. There are private quarters upstairs, which is where you'll be sleeping tonight."

"But why...Oh," I finish, realizing the answer before the question is even out of my mouth: I need to be watched. I'm still a prisoner. I nearly laugh—I'd almost forgotten that was the case for a few minutes. Pity flashes in Odessa's icy blue eyes for a heartbeat. Pity fills my own heart, but then it's forgotten and I sigh in utter contentment, my lips curling into a smile. *Here it comes.*

"Why are you smiling?"

"I'm home," I whisper, so quietly I know she can't have heard me clearly.

"What? Are you alri—oh!" she gasps as the first flakes fall from the sky, thick and fluffy and so beautiful my eyes water. I'd made it snow that day I was captured, sure, but then I hadn't been in a position to truly feel it then, to appreciate it and revel in it and let its presence fill me with utter contentment. I feel like I'm whole again, like a part of me has been missing for fifteen years and I've finally found it once more. I love my life in Helios. I love the sun and the crystal blue water, the sights and the smells and the sounds, but *this* is who I am. *This* is where I belong.

"I love the snow," I say simply, tilting my head back and grinning at the sky as the flakes fall, faster now.

"That's funny," Odessa says. I turn my head slightly to quirk a brow in question, but keep my face upward. I feel like an old wound I've been ignoring all this time is slowly healing with each flake that touches my skin. "That a fire wielder would love the snow." I merely shrug. After a moment, she adds quietly, "We love the snow too. Duskthorne gets heaps of it, as you can imagine. Mia is going to be so excited."

Other soldiers start calling out orders and Odessa curses under her breath.

"I need to help get some things taken care of before the snow gets too heavy." She points to the commissary building to our left. "Up the stairs. You'll be in the room at the end of the hall. Your trunk should already be there. I'll come get you for dinner soon." I nod and take one more minute to enjoy the snow while she jogs off into the melee. I finally sigh and head inside. It's a bit dank and dusty, but overall, it's in fairly decent shape for an abandoned building in the middle of The Perilous. I find the stairs in the back of the room and though they look a little rickety, I'm assuming if two men hoisting that trunk could make it up, I'll be fine.

I start down the hallway just as Blackheart steps out of his room, pulling a tunic over his head and I stutter step, eyes wide, mouth dry. I blink. And blink again.

Great. Fucking. Makers.

His body is...immaculate. Ropes of muscle beneath taut skin, more tattoos snaking up his ribs. His leathers sit low on his waist, showing deep indentions beside his hip bones and a fine trail of dark hair leading downward from his navel...

I make a sound that's somewhere between a gasp and a cough, and he quirks a brow once his shirt is in place. I suddenly hate the fabric with the fire of Sola, the sun Maker herself. I swallow hard and tell myself to get my thoughts in line. But instead, I find my gaze following a droplet of water from his damp hair as it slowly treks down his jaw and along his throat. I have the strongest urge to wrap my arms around him and capture it with my tongue, to tangle my fingers in his hair and pull his mouth to mine, to have him lift me up and press me against the wall...

"Red?" he asks, voice low and rough. Or am I imagining that? What in all seven hells is wrong with me? He's my captor. He's the leader of an army defending a monster. He's a prick.

A man can be both a prick and incredibly sexy, I remind myself, *you can hate someone and still have them fuck you within an inch of your life...*

I scowl at that tiny little voice until it retreats into the dark corners of my mind, cowering. I shake myself and meet his gaze, taking a small step towards the other side of the hallway to put extra distance between us.

"It's snowing," I say cooly because I honestly don't know what else to say and I need some words to come out of my mouth or I might just let that little voice speak up again, let it take the reins and do something incredibly fucking stupid. Not that he'd allow it, of course, but that would be even worse, to be rebuffed and ridiculed mercilessly afterward.

"I can see that," he says, nodding towards my hair. I reach up and realize I still have snowflakes there, just beginning to melt. I pull the mess of hair over my shoulder, cursing myself for not braiding it today, and comb through it with my fingers, shaking out the remaining flakes. I glance up to find Blackheart staring, his eyes intense, but not in the way I've seen before. This feels...different. The air in the hallway suddenly feels thick and heavy. It only lasts a heartbeat, but *something* passes between us...doesn't it? But when he straightens and looks as if nothing is amiss, I think maybe I imagined the whole thing.

I quickly turn my nose up and walk away, ducking into my room and closing the door.

"What in the ruddy fuck??" I hiss to the empty room. I shake myself and take a few big gulps of water from the canteen on the table. The room is in surprisingly good shape, with only a crack in one window showing any signs of disrepair. There's a bed, a small writing desk, two highbacked chairs near the fireplace, an armoire, and even an old tub in the corner behind a screen.

I pull one of the chairs from in front of the fireplace over to the window and settle into it, watching the snow fall and feeling more at peace than I have in too long to remember.

"Tess?"

I blink my eyes open to find Odessa standing beside me, gently shaking my shoulder.

"Makers, I didn't mean to fall asleep. How long—"

"A few hours. I came earlier but didn't want to wake you, but don't want you to go all night without supper. Are you hungry?"

I stand and stretch my arms over my head. "Starving," I admit. Odessa's lips curl.

"Come on, we'll scrounge you up something."

I grab the coat from the back of the chair and pull it on before following her down the stairs, eyeing Blackheart's door warily as we pass. Maybe I'd dreamed the entire encounter. Though I don't really need the coat for warmth, I do pull the hood up to keep the snow from my hair.

"Wow, it really came down, didn't it?" I say as we step outside. The snow is piled up to my knees, though paths have been cleared between the buildings. I gasp quietly. "Zaro!"

"Zaro?"

"My horse. Er, the horse I've been riding. I named him Zaro because of the star—you know what, it doesn't matter. Are the horses ok?"

"They're fine. They're bred for this and we have tents up for them." She studies me.

"What?"

"You're just...different than I thought you'd be. At least sometimes."

I don't have a response to that and she thankfully doesn't seem to expect one. I know I should be mindful of showing my true self and keep up the wall that Tesni puts between herself and the rest of the world, alienating them, but I can't seem to care at the moment.

We make our way down the cleared path towards the kitchen. It's empty now, but the space is full of tables—some circular, others rectangular or square—and I can imagine it as a bustling meeting space once upon a time, where people gathered and laughed and fought. It reminds me of the tavern a bit and a pang goes through my chest. I wonder what Math and Cece are thinking right now—do they have any idea that I'm in danger? Do they think I'm still with Tesni? Are they worried? More importantly, are they safe? A wide center aisle runs down the middle of the room, the tables set up in random patterns on either side.

"Cookie should have some leftovers in the back. I'll be right— Mia? What are you doing up??" I turn to find Mia slipping in the door, cheeks tearstained. My stomach dips, my power flaring to life as if I can fight off whatever made the girl upset. "Mia! What's wrong?"

"Nightmare," the girl says brokenly before plowing into Odessa, wrapping her arms around her sister and burying her face in Odessa's shirt. I get the feeling she's embarrassed about it.

"Sweetheart, it's ok," Odessa tells her softly, gently stroking the girl's hair. The moment is so tender that I feel as if I'm intruding. Over Mia's head, Odessa says quietly, "She gets them sometimes, ever since our parents died."

I nod, telling her I understand.

"I have them too," I say, and Mia twists so she can look at me, still holding on to Odessa for dear life.

"Really?"

"Uh huh. All the time. They're nothing to be ashamed of." I lean forward and look around dramatically before whispering conspiratorially, "I bet even *Blackheart* has them."

Mia laughs a little at that, sniffling. She turns back to Odessa.

"Can you walk me back and sit with me until I fall asleep?"

Odessa looks to me, clearly torn between her duty and her sister.

"Go take care of her. I'll stay here until you get back." She worries at her bottom lip, cutting her gaze between me and the door, clearly torn. "I know it doesn't mean much, but I give you my word that I'll stay here and wait for you. I'm not going anywhere."

"She'll stay," Mia says confidently. "I know it." I smile at her and she returns it, thankfully seeming to feel better after her dream.

"Ok, I'll be back soon, I promise." Odessa takes Mia's hand and leads her back to the door.

"Good night, Tess," Mia says, waving.

"Good night, Mia. Sweet dreams."

Just before they step through, Odessa looks back over her shoulder.

"Thank you," she says, making sure to hold my gaze, telling me she means it. I incline my head and she disappears out into the darkness. I promised I'd stay, but I didn't promise I'd wait for her to return before I found some dinner, so I head to the back room. I find the food stores and make myself a plate of one of the leftover meat pies, some cheese, and a handful of melon. I'm just walking back into the dining area, picking through the cheese and not paying attention to much else, when a voice sounds through the room, making me jolt and nearly drop my plate. Turner and two other men step through the door, locking it behind them.

"Well, well, well. It's about ruddy time, pet."

CHAPTER NINE

"You really don't want to try this," I tell him, assessing the situation, Tobias' steady voice in my mind: *look for exits; run away if you can, but be prepared to fight if you have to; don't let them get at your back; anything can be a weapon.* I tighten my fingers on the tray in my hand and think about running back into the rear room, but discard the idea quickly. There's no exit, no place to hide, and tight quarters. There's surely another entrance somewhere, maybe down one of the hallways that branch off the main area on the left and right. I can't chance running for an exit that I don't know actually exists though, possibly getting trapped. No, it's better to be out here in the open where I have a better chance at fighting back. So, I remain at the end of the aisle, waiting.

"Oh, I think I do. I think I do, very, *very* much," Turner says, the smile pulling his lips while his gaze roves over my body making me ill. "Makers must be smiling down on me tonight—imagine my surprise when I saw you coming in here with your keeper, only to see her finally fucking leave you alone."

The other two men slowly walk towards me, each moving as far to the edge as the pathway will allow, attempting to come at me from both sides, I assume.

"Do we get to take turns?" the taller man asks. I don't recall his name, though I remember that the shorter one is Gregor.

"You can have her when I'm done with her," Turner grins.

"I don't want your scraps," Gregor says, sounding glum.

"It's never stopped either of you in the past."

He smiles at that, and he and his taller friend both chuckle low.

"Get her so we can start our fun," Turner says, crossing his arms over his chest. "I don't think we have much time."

"I don't need much," the tall man says.

"Somehow that is not shocking to hear," I tell him, curling my lip. It takes a moment for him to realize what I've implied and then his face twists with anger.

"That's not what I meant!" With that, he lunges forward and I slam the metal plate across his cheek, food and blood flying as his head whips to the side. I move to kick him, only to find that I can't because of this fucking dress.

"Ruddy fucking fuck!" I spit through gritted teeth as the man rights himself again. He pulls a knife from his belt just as Gregor comes at me from the other side. I spin away but he manages to grab my coat, yanking me backwards. I drop the plate and pull my arms free, stumbling away just as the other man slashes out with his knife. I scream out in pain as the blade slices through the sleeve of my dress and into my upper arm.

"Oy! No more of that you fucking idiot! Can't have her all sliced to ribbons," Turner snaps.

The pain burns like fire and blood pours from the wound, hot and thick. I know the cut must be deep but I grit my teeth against the pain, and it slowly fades from the forefront of my mind. I back away from both men, keeping them in front of me.

I note that Turner's staying back and letting the other two do the hard work. He's a coward, then, as well as an asshole.

My Gift roils within me, icy vipers desperate to strike, but I'm still blocked by Blackheart. *Fucking prick.* If I could use my Gift, this would have been over in seconds. No matter. I learned long ago to defend myself without the use of my power, and this isn't the first time I've had to do it. I quickly assess the two men, going through options before I settle on one. One that I hate but know that it's the best one that I have, so I take a quick breath and then let the man with the knife grab me. He turns me so that my back is to his chest and holds the blade near my throat, just as I knew he would. Men are nothing if not predictable. Gregor grins, but it falters when I wink at him. His thick brow furrows in confusion but he doesn't have time to do anything more before I drop to the floor like a sack of flour.

"What the—" the tall man barks, thrown off balance from the unexpected dead weight. He pitches forward as he tries to catch me, and I take advantage, grabbing his tunic and pulling him down as I roll. He hits the floor and groans, and I kick him in the ribs hard enough to hopefully break one or two. I push up to my knees just as Gregor lurches forward to help. I punch him square in the crotch and he cries out in pain, a keening, high pitched whine that makes my ears ring. He folds, covering his bollocks, and I spring upward with all of my strength, using my momentum to put as much force as I can behind the punch I aim at his nose. Bone crunches, blood gushes, and I smile wickedly even as pain screams up my arm. I use my elbow to land another blow to his temple and he flails backwards, landing with a grunt and a thud. He lies there, groaning quietly, so I turn back to the other man.

He rolls, panting, and pushes himself up to his knees, brandishing the knife.

"You bitch," he sneers.

"It's always *bitch*," I say, eyeing him and calculating the next blow. "Can none of you come up with something more original or creative than *bitch*?" I make a show of moving to punch him with my left hand, and his eyes track the movement. I reach out with my right hand instead and latch on to his wrist, squeezing in the exact place Tobias taught me, the place I know will send a spike of pure agony through his arm. Right on cue, he screams and drops the knife, and keeping a firm grip on his wrist, I grab his hand with my other and twist. The bone snaps and he screams again, cradling his broken wrist to his chest. I curl my fingers into his hair and yank downward, forcing his face to meet my knee as hard as I possibly can. He chokes out a pained groan, and I do it once more for good measure before I let him tumble to the ground, blood squishing beneath my boots.

I swoop down to grab the knife and see that my entire arm is coated in blood. The pain is still distant, but I know that will only last so long. I'm breathing hard when I straighten and face Turner. He curls his lip, clearly furious that his companions weren't successful.

"Come on, you fucking coward. Face me yourself," I spit.

"That won't be necessary," a low, lethal voice sounds from a darkened corner of the room. Turner pales, head whipping to the side as Blackheart strides into the light. I must have been right about the other door. My heart races as I take him in, a cold, calm fury radiating off of him so forcefully that I take a step backwards and swallow hard. I have no idea *where* this anger is directed: Turner for attacking? Me for fighting back? Most likely the latter, I think with a sinking feeling. After all, Turner is one of his men and I'm the prisoner fire bitch who he plans to deliver to his king to have Makers know what done to me. I won't delude myself into believing I have much of a chance of fighting back against someone as big and skilled as Blackheart, but I keep the knife in my hand, steady and waiting all the same. I won't give up without a fight.

"Blackheart," Tuner gasps, voice quavering ever so slightly. "I thought you were—"

"Otherwise engaged, yes, I'm quite aware," Blackheart says in a flat voice, stalking forward. Turner stumbles back.

"It-it's not what it looks like."

Blackheart cuts his gaze to me, taking in my bloody arm and missing coat, the men on the floor, the knife in my hand. He clenches his jaw and turns his stormy eyes back to Turner.

"I very much doubt that. You have ten minutes to gather your men and whatever supplies you can carry on your back." I blink at that, clearly having misheard him. *Your* men? What does that mean?

Turner's eyes bulge. "What? You can't possibly be serious. Over this Gifted cunt??"

Blackheart only stares, deceptively calm. "Nine minutes and forty-two seconds." Turner sputters at that. "You can leave with supplies, or you can leave with nothing but the clothes on your back, the choice is yours. But you'd better make it soon. Now get your fucking friends and *go*." He all but bares his teeth, reminding me of a feral wolf, or the dragon on the hilt of his sword.

I frown, not understanding what the hells is happening. Why would Blackheart care about this? Especially enough to, what? Banish his own men to face The Perilous in a snowstorm? I'm so confused that my head starts to pound, though that could be due to the gaping wound in my arm. I blink away the spots threatening at the edges of my vision, and just stop myself from swaying as a wave of dizziness rushes over me.

Turner looks like he wants to say something but knows he can't, so he stalks towards me, eyes blazing with hatred. I take a step backwards and twist the knife so that the blade is facing backwards and lying against my forearm, ready if he wants to do something stupid. Out of the corner of my eye, I see Blackheart's brow furrow ever so slightly, missing nothing. *Fuck.* Tesni shouldn't know the right way to hold a knife. But I can't make myself worry with that right now. Turner manages to rouse his companions and they limp warily to the door.

"Please, sir, I didn't...I mean, I wasn't going to do anything, I was just following Turner's orders, I didn't mean anything by it," the man who'd cut me begs when they get close to Blackheart. Quicker than I can track, Blackheart sinks a blade into the man's side. His eyes go wide and Blackheart's remain cold and steady, not a flicker of apprehension or remorse. Turner gasps and steps back from the man, while Gregor curses, trying to hold the other man upright on his own and struggling. The man sucks in a wet, rattling breath and I know that he will be meeting Noxum, the Maker of death, very soon.

"You knew the rules within my camp. You chose to ignore them." He pulls his blade free and the man falls to the floor, Gregor unable to support his now very dead weight any longer. Blackheart shifts his gaze back to Gregor and Tuner. "You can share his fate, or you can go. Eight minutes," he adds, casually wiping the blood from his knife on his pants.

"Fucking hells," Gregor rasps, clearly terrified, and fumbles with the lock, desperate to escape. When he throws the door open, there are ten soldiers waiting, all armed.

"Escorts," Blackheart explains with a cold smile. He shifts his gaze to one of the men at the front of the group. "Seven minutes, northwestern edge of the post." The soldier nods and though he looks like he wants to protest, or possibly tear Blackheart limb from limb, Turner steps out into the night with Gregor on his heels. The snow is still falling and I inhale deeply, letting the smell and feel of it settle me. Odessa bursts through the group of soldiers as they lead the other two men away, eyes wide in horror and fear.

"What happened here?" Blackheart asks her calmly. "You had an assignment, Dessa." I blink at that, surprised to hear him call her by a nickname. It's what Mia calls her as well. I try to figure out what that might mean—are they...together, perhaps?—but then the room sways and I grip the edge of a table to steady myself, gasping. *I will not faint. I will not faint. I will not fucking faint.*

"I..." Odessa swallows hard, but shifts her shoulders back, brave and ready to accept her punishment, whatever it might be, but before she can say a word, I cut in, stepping forward and willing my knees not to buckle.

"I snuck out here on my own," I say firmly. Odessa snaps her head to me and Blackheart's gaze follows more slowly. His eyes bore into me, as if daring me to continue what he knows to be a lie. I somehow shift my shoulders back and hold his stare despite the cold fury still wafting from him. "Odessa had no idea I was out of my room. Turner and the others must have seen me walking here alone and took the opportunity to try to take what they wanted."

The silence that follows is deafening, but I hold strong. Odessa's eyes dart between me and Blackheart, unsure, though not fearful despite how truly fucking terrifying Blackheart looks right now. I honestly don't know what's keeping me unflinching at his intense gaze, at the quiet, restrained power within him. But Odessa doesn't deserve to be punished for taking care of Mia. None of this is her fault.

"Try," Blackheart finally says softly and my brow furrows.

"What?"

"*Try* to take what they wanted." He studies me in that way he has, the one that makes it hard to believe he doesn't see right through every last one of my lies. "This is the second time you've been outnumbered and bested trained men." My blood chills. He's pulling at a thread that could unravel everything.

"Not well-trained," I say, jutting my chin stubbornly. He gives me a look that says he's expecting an explanation and will get one, so I give him a semi-plausible answer. "King Barony made sure that I was trained in self-defense in the event I was ever taken prisoner and collared—or blocked by another Gifted," I add pointedly. Surely that's believable, isn't it? I know damn well that Tesni would never lift a finger to train physically, not believing for a moment she would ever be without her Gift, but a rational person certainly would. He seems to mull that over but before he comes to a decision, another wave of dizziness crashes into me so forcefully that I fall to my knees with a gasp, the pain coming quickly on its heels. Blinding. Burning.

"Tess!" Odessa cries, at my side in a heartbeat. "This is bad," she says to Blackheart as I pant through gritted teeth and try to make the world stop spinning.

"Get her to Copeland immediately. Then bring her." With that Blackheart strides out into the snow. Once he's gone, Odessa turns back to me.

"Can you stand?"

"Yes, I'm fine." I'm not completely sure it's the truth, but I will it to be. She nods and helps me rise, quickly scanning the room and running to a nearby table. She comes back with a rag and wraps it tightly around my arm. I bite my lip to keep from crying out, but tears burn my eyes, sliding down my cheeks.

"Sorry, sorry, sorry." She secures the rag and grips my elbow to steady me as we walk from the room. "Why would you do that?" she asks quietly, ducking her head against the falling snow. "Lie for me like that?"

"I don't know what you mean. I haven't seen you all evening. I did sneak out by myself."

I see her staring at me from the corner of my eye as we walk, the cold giving me strength, her dark brow furrowed. I turn to meet her gaze and give her the best smile I can muster, which admittedly isn't great and comes out more as a half grin, half grimace. She huffs out a small laugh, her lips curling up as she shakes her head.

"My mistake, then." After a few moments she adds softly, "Thank you."

We make it to one of the long cabins and Odessa settles me onto a chair while she fetches Copeland. He turns out to be an old man with long, white hair that's pulled back into a knot at the top of his head, and a long white beard to match, reaching the middle of his chest.

"Makers, what happened here, then?" he asks, voice raspy but gentle.

"I met the...pointy end of...a blade," I say through gasping breaths, and he laughs lightly, giving me a warm smile.

"Nothing this old man can't fix, my dear. May I?" he asks, reaching his hand towards my arm but stopping before he touches me. I blink, shocked and confused by the question, but nod. He unties the rag and gently grips my arm just beneath the wound. I don't want to look, but I do anyway and immediately regret the decision. I wouldn't call myself squeamish, exactly, but seeing a gaping hole in my own arm, flayed skin and muscle and catching a flash of what I think is bone, is enough to make me gag. I put the back of my other hand to my mouth and take deep breaths through my nose to steady myself, not wanting to vomit on this very nice man. "You'll feel heat, but hopefully no real pain. Are you ready?"

Odessa puts a reassuring hand on my shoulder and I nod. Copeland hovers his palms above the wound and an intense heat flares up and down my arm. It doesn't hurt, but it's not exactly comfortable. I close my eyes, determined to keep my composure no matter how long this ordeal takes.

"There we are. All finished."

My eyes flash open and I stare at my arm, mouth gaping.

"Great fucking Makers," I whisper, and he and Odessa both laugh.

"Copeland is one of the most powerful healing Gifteds in all of Hypathia," Odessa says and the old man inclines his head in modest thanks.

"Thank you," I tell him. "That was...that was amazing." I move my arm, bending and flexing, and find that it's as if the wound was never there at all.

"I hope you won't need my services again any time soon, but I am always happy to help if the need does arise."

"We need to go," Odessa says urgently. "Thank you, Copeland."

Confused, I follow Odessa outside, still shocked at how fully and easily I've been healed. Duskthorne truly does have quite the collection of Gifteds. We hurry towards...I have no idea what.

"Where are we going?" I ask quietly as we near a crowd of soldiers.

"To witness," Odessa says, voice laced with anger, and lead settles into my stomach. We make our way to the edge of the group and find Blackheart standing a few yards out in the thick snow, the tip of his sword resting on the ground, his hands resting casually on the pommel. Before him is a group of seven men, Turner and Gregor among them, all looking uneasy. Blackheart turns his head towards us, sensing my Gift, I assume. He meets my gaze for a heartbeat before turning back to the men.

"You can't really send us out into this!" Turner complains, throwing an arm out towards the woods in the distance, dark and menacing and dotted with thick hills of white.

"I can and I am."

"I won't go. You can't force us to—" I gasp when Blackheart moves faster than any man his size should be able to move, the tip of his sword now resting at Tuner's throat, just as it had rested against mine that day by the stream. The dragon on the hilt seems to be snarling, begging for a taste of the bastard's blood.

"You're right, I can't. But I can give you two very clear options: leave, and take your chances, or stay, and die."

The other men in the group mumble to each other, exchanging glances. They come to the only real decision and slowly trudge out into the darkness with nothing but small bundles on their backs. Blackheart is truly sending them out there alone? *Great Makers.*

Turner's jaw ticks but he finally turns and follows the group. The rest of us watch in tense silence as he goes, but a strangled cry of warning escapes my lips when he stops a few yards away, whirling and throwing a knife. The bright moonlight glints off of the blade as it flies towards Blackheart, end over end. In a movement that shouldn't be possible, Blackheart shifts his body to the right and catches the hilt as it sails past his cheek.

"Holy ruddy fucking fuck," I whisper. I see Odessa turn to gape at me from the corner of my eye, as if me cursing is the astonishing thing here and not Blackheart catching a fucking flying knife like it was nothing. If he hadn't moved, that blade would have gone right through his skull. Turner's eyes bulge and a dark smile spreads across Blackheart's face. He flips the knife, pinching the tip of the blade between his thumb and forefinger, and throws it with far more force than Turner had managed. He can't move the way Blackheart does, and the knife finds its target: right through his left eye. He's barely able to grunt before his body goes limp and he hits the ground. In the moonlight, the blood spreading across the snow looks black as pitch.

The rest of the men being turned out from the camp stare in utter shock before taking off, running as best as they can through the snow drifts until their torches look like fireflies dancing within the trees. Blackheart says something about a scout team following them, but I can't imagine they'd dare come back after what they just witnessed.

"What the hells just happened?" I whisper to Odessa.

"We have rules. They broke them," she says simply, as if that even begins to answer my question. "Come, I think it's time for bed."

As soon as she says the words, exhaustion settles over me like a heavy blanket and all I want to do is crawl into bed and perhaps never come out again. So, I nod and we follow the rest of the soldiers as everyone files back to the cabins.

"Thank you," Odessa says again at my door.

"There's nothing to thank me for," I tell her honestly.

"Can I ask you something?"

I tense.

"I can't promise I'll answer..."

"That's fair. But...where did a spoiled princess locked away in her ivory tower learn to curse like that??"

I huff out a laugh, completely surprised by her question and she smiles back. I can feel that something shifted between us tonight. Perhaps we aren't friends, exactly, but I believe we could be. Or we would be, if our lives were different, if we were on different paths and I wasn't pretending to be someone I'm not to have a chance of escaping the master she serves. I sigh just as Blackheart mounts the stairs. Odessa straightens but doesn't snap to attention like she does when we're out among the rest of the soldiers. Perhaps they really are together, and I wonder if it's against some rule and that's the reason they keep it hidden. I make a note to watch next time we camp, to see if she comes to his tent during the night. *Inquisitive, not nosey.*

She flashes me another smile before heading down the hallway.

"Nice move with the dagger, showoff," she tells him as she passes, and I don't think I'm meant to hear it. Blackheart's lips twitch.

"Goodnight, Dessa."

I wait outside my door and once Odessa has disappeared down the stairs, Blackheart turns back and meets my gaze, brow arched, clearly waiting for the question he seems to know I'm going to ask. He shifts and leans his shoulder against the doorframe, crossing his arms over his chest.

"Spit it out, Red."

Part of me wants to leave without a word just to defy him, the thought sending a strange, ridiculous thrill through me, but I have to know. So, I cross my arms over my own chest, mirroring his stance, and turn to face him fully.

"Why would you do that?" I ask.

"You'll have to narrow that down."

"Cast them out like that."

"Are you upset that I sent them away?" he drawls, that sharp edge beneath the velvety smoothness. "Would the princess rather I had them drawn and quartered? Line them up and let the archers use them as target practice?"

I clench my jaw. Makers, he really is a prick.

"No," I say slowly, trying desperately to keep my annoyance in check. "I just meant, why would you send your own men out into The Perilous to die because of...well, as Turner put it, a Gifted cunt like me?"

"Those were *not* my men." My brows draw down. "They are Hunters who had hopes of grabbing you, but arrived on the heels of your capture. I allowed them to travel with the army as a courtesy—and in exchange for information about the Alliance. Traveling with an army across The Perilous is far safer than going at it with a group of only a few. But there are rules within my camp, rules that are very clear and that I expect to be obeyed, even by guests."

"Rules?"

His gaze shifts to my torn, blood-stained sleeve, the spot where a gaping wound had been not even an hour ago, before he meets my eyes again. He stares for an endless moment before he says, "Things are not *taken* here. Not by me. Not by my men. And certainly not by fucking pricks like that who are treading upon my hospitality." I know exactly what he's saying and while I appreciate this rule for myriad reasons, I don't understand.

"But...but you serve a monster. You're delivering me *to a monster*. How can you care if people are raped or abused or Makers know what else in your camp?"

His jaw ticks and I search his stormy eyes, suddenly desperate to figure out this man.

"Dorian may run his kingdom however the fuck he chooses. *I* decide what happens in *my* camp with *my* army." There appears to be no love lost between Blackheart and his king and I wonder if perhaps he doesn't serve him willingly after all. But he speaks again before I can say a word, ending the conversation.

"Get some sleep. We'll be heading out early and tomorrow will be a long, rough day on the road after this storm."

With that, he pushes off the wall and goes into his room, closing the door firmly behind him. I sigh and go into my own room, pulling off my dress and trying not to look at all of the blood, trying to ignore the sharp, tangy smell of it. I ball the fabric up and toss it in the corner where it can stay forever for all I care. I pull on the satin nightgown that has become my favorite, and settle into the bed. It feels so good to sleep in an actual fucking bed that I nearly whimper.

I don't want to think about what happened. I will, at some point, but not tonight. It's too fresh and real right now. So, instead, as sleep gently pulls me into its embrace, I try to solve the puzzle that is Blackheart.

CHAPTER
TEN

Things shift after Turner and his group are gone. Odessa is no longer required to escort me everywhere—though she does still walk with me often when she's not doing other army-related things—and I'm free to wander as I please when we camp. So, Blackheart was...protecting me? No, more like protecting his investment. Of course he couldn't risk Turner or his men getting carried away and killing me before Dorian could negotiate his ransom. But no matter the reason, I'm grateful for it, and though it takes me a few days, I start to explore my newfound freedom. Blackheart seems to be entirely certain that no one under his command would dare try to touch me or harm me in any way. So, I guess I trust in his trust of his men—and women. I'm pleased to find that Odessa isn't the only woman in Blackheart's army. I know that Lyanna doesn't allow women to fight in their ranks, only cook or clean or tend to the animals, which I think is horseshit.

I've learned that Odessa isn't just a soldier, she's a Captain, which apparently is extremely high-ranking, and while I would assume watching me would have been far beneath her duties, I realize again that perhaps it was because Blackheart was taking no chances on his investment. He put one of his best warriors in charge of protecting me. *Makers, just how much coin is Tesni worth?*

I've started walking to Cookie's tent to fetch my own dinner instead of having Mia deliver it to me, but she's taken to walking with me all the same and the girl has lost all traces of shyness around me since that night she had the nightmare. I don't know if Odessa shared with her the lie I told to save her sister punishment, or if the girl just decided on her own that perhaps there's more to me than meets the eye, but either way, I'm happy that she's taken a liking to me.

"What was it like living in a *castle*?" she asks, awe in her voice. "I've been in the palace in Duskthorne, but living there is completely different. I bet you had servants and a closet full of ball gowns and I heard that Lyanna has a…" She scrunches her freckled nose and I fight a smile. "Maginery? Full of animals?"

"Menagerie," I tell her with a smile and she snaps her fingers.

"That's it! I knew it was something like that. Well, is it true? Did you have a menagerie?"

"Lyanna has a large menagerie, yes," I tell her honestly, though of course I haven't seen it myself in nearly fifteen years. I used to love spending time there though, would visit almost every single day. Her eyes light up.

"Did you have dragons?? I've always wanted to see one. Dessa claims that she's seen an ice dragon before, but I don't believe her." She rolls her eyes, exasperated at the lies her sister apparently told her. "She says it was once when she was about my age when they were playing up in the mountains and that she saw a pair of golden eyes staring at them from the next peak over. No one else did, so I think she's just full of sh--" She stops herself, eyes going wide and cheeks turning pink as I quirk a brow. "I think she's making it up," she amends quickly and I pull my lips in to hide my smile. "Anyway, dragons have been gone from Duskthorne since way before I was born, but we used to have them. Yara says they'll come back one day. I hope she's right," she sighs. I don't ask who Yara is, assuming one of her friends or a teacher perhaps. "Can you imagine soaring through the skies like that?" she adds wistfully. I don't want to imagine it even for a second, the thought making me sick.

"No dragons I'm afraid, but we had lots of other amazing things." I tell her all about my favorites as we walk until a yell draws our attention.

"Oye! Flame of Lyanna, how about a little help here?" a soldier with white-blonde hair calls from a fire pit not far away. To my surprise, he doesn't sound mocking or cruel. He and a few others look to be trying to get the flames to catch but are having a hard time.

"I'm afraid your Commander won't allow that," I call back, relieved beyond measure that my supposed Gift is blocked.

"Oh, I think I could let your power off its leash for this," that damned cool, velvety voice responds as Blackheart steps out from behind a nearby tent. Does he just follow me around and wait for opportune moments to step out of the shadows??

"Remember what I said about cooperation? Helping my men would go a long way with earning favor with Dorian." There's snow stuck in his beard and Mia giggles. To my surprise, the big man looks at her and grins before shaking his face like a dog, making Mia laugh even harder.

The blonde man whoops loudly, grinning. "Yes! Light it up, Red!" he calls. He turns to one of the others and hits him on the shoulder. "Watch this. I've heard it's amazing to see in person. Flames out of nothing just like that." He tries to snap his fingers but frowns when he can't because of his thick gloves. I fight a smile and try to ignore the way Blackheart is watching me so intently, as if this is a test and...he wants me to pass? I'm not sure why, really. Maybe he hopes that if I cooperate, as he says, Dorian will decide having a fire wielder in his army will outweigh the hefty ransom he could get. A tiny part of me wonders if he would be just as happy with an ice wielder, if maybe I could tell Blackheart the truth of it now and stop this whole ruse. Of course, I wouldn't actually stay and fight with him...so, no, I need to keep being Tess for now.

"I..." I glance between the group and Blackheart, and he quirks a dark brow in challenge, and damn if part of me wants to accept it, to create frozen flames ten feet high just to shock them all and prove my worth, to show that I'm just as powerful and competent as my sister that I...matter. *Makers, I'm pathetic.* I lift my chin. "Didn't you hear? I don't work for free."

I stride off to groans from the blonde man and his friends. I couldn't truly help them anyway, but I still feel awful for having to act like...well, Tesni. I hate all of this so much. I just want to find a way to escape and go the fuck home. My chances of doing that are better now that I'm not under constant supervision by Odessa, but leaving while we're still in The Perilous is a horrible idea. I'd be no better off than Turner and his men—who did not make it far, from what the scouts sent after them reported back according to Odessa. So, no. My best chance to flee will be once we reach Tithmoore. Perhaps I can convince someone to hide me, or possibly make it to the coast and find a ship to take me back to Helios. I have Tesni's jewels I can trade. Shockingly, Blackheart didn't take them though they're worth a fortune.

Mia catches up to me quickly.

"Why didn't you want to help them?" she asks, sounding disappointed.

"I don't know," I tell her honestly, suddenly exhausted by of all of this. "I'm not a very nice person I'm afraid."

"I don't believe that."

I turn to look at her. "Really?"

She eyes me seriously, that studying look on her face.

"I think you're nice but pretend not to be for some reason." I can't say much to that, so I just give her a sad smile and keep walking towards the tent she shares with her sister. Odessa is out beside one of the communal fire pits with several other soldiers, laughing and drinking what looks to be some kind of ale, and playing quills.

She smiles widely when we approach and reaches for her sister immediately. She wraps Mia in a hug and kisses the top of her head in a very motherly way that makes my heart clench and my throat feel tight. It's the kind of thing Cece would do. Makers I hope she and Math are ok, that Tesni wouldn't think to go after them as insurance for my cooperation or anything of the sort. I wonder if I could send a letter...No, probably not. And it might put them in even more danger if I involve them at all. I have to assume that they're safe and happy in Helios and that the war doesn't find its way there before I can get back to them and figure out a way to keep us all safe. Giving up the tavern feels like giving up a part of my heart, but we could all leave, we could go to Sol or one of the other islands until all of this war business blows over. I suppose that part of Tesni's plan wasn't so terrible actually.

I'm about to turn away and go back to my own tent when an idea occurs to me. I turn back and jerk my chin towards Odessa.

"What do I have to do to get a few pairs of trousers?" I can use the tunics from Tesni's trunk that were meant to be paired with various skirts, but I would do just about anything for some fucking pants.

Odessa quirks a brow. "You've never struck me as the pants type, princess." I don't mind when she calls me that so much anymore. It's shifted subtly from an insult to an almost affectionate nickname.

"All of this mucking about in the wilderness is ruining all of my dresses," I say, gesturing angrily towards the hem of my skirt, which is in fact caked with mud and snow. That's a plausible enough reason. Odessa nods to herself, seeming to agree.

"You can trade for some once we reach Tithmoore, I suppose..."

"How about we play for a pair?" I suggest, nodding toward the board painted with different color rings hanging on a post a few yards away.

"You know how to play quills?" one of the men asks skeptically. Tristan, I believe his name is. I shrug and Odessa's lips curl up at the corners.

"Alright then. You win; you can have two of my old pairs of leathers. I was saving them for when Mia got tall enough for them, but that's going to be quite a while." Mia sticks her tongue out at her sister, and I huff out a laugh.

"And if you win?" I ask, stepping forward and taking the set of feathered darts from Tristan.

"My pick of anything from your trunk," she says quickly, an eager sparkle in her eye. I blink in surprise, not having pictured Odessa as the type to want jewels and finery. *But why not?* I chide myself. Why shouldn't she be able to like stabbing things *and* wearing gorgeous gowns?

"Done. You can go first." I hide my smile as I gesture for her to go ahead. She hikes a shoulder and steps up to the throwing line drawn in the muddy ground. The drifts of snow were cleared for us to make camp by a Gifted with the ability to move things with his mind. Now *that* is a Gift worth having in an army.

Odessa throws her darts, the red feathers flapping gently in the breeze when the points land just outside the smallest circle in the middle of the board.

"Impressive," I tell her, giving her shots an appraising look. She gives me a cocky one back.

"Why is it even called quills?" Mia asks, playing with the feathers on another set of darts, these sky blue. "You throw darts, not quills."

"When the game was first invented, the darts were made of basilisk quills," I say as I step up to the line. The legendary beasts had fans of quills around their throats that would stand on end when angry. They fell off often, the way birds lose feathers or dragons lost scales, and people started using them in all manner of things because of their strength and durability, and, in the case of this game, their razor-sharp points. Everyone goes silent and I glance around before throwing.

"I had tutors," I remind them, which is technically true, but I learned this from Math. He has an unquenchable thirst for knowledge and knows the most random facts about pretty much everything. I shift my body slightly and eye the target like I've done too many times to count at the tavern. I take a deep breath and release my first dart. Dead center of the smallest circle, the dart's black feathers quivering. I smile when I hear Tristan whistle behind me—and Odessa curse. The second dart hits directly beside the first, and the third just below them both. Whoops and cheers and cries of incredulity ring out from the small group, and I turn to find Odessa looking shocked and impressed and a touch disgruntled.

"How in the fucking hells does a spoiled princess like you know how to throw darts like *that*??"

"A castle can get very boring. I had to find ways to entertain myself. Now, about those trousers..."

"A deal is a deal!" Tristan calls, laughing as he jogs to the target to retrieve the darts.

"Yeah!" Mia echoes, clearly having fun. "A deal is a deal! Fetch the pantaloons!" she cries and then laughs herself silly. I snort, unable to help myself and wondering where in the hells she learned the word *pantaloons*. I don't think anyone under the age of a hundred uses it anymore.

"Alright, alright, all of you shut it." Odessa holds up a finger and walks the short distance to her tent, emerging a few moments later with two pairs of leather trousers. I nearly whimper when she hands them to me, the leather buttery soft and supple.

"You can still pick whatever you want from the trunk," I tell her, hugging the trousers to my chest like they're a newborn babe and precious to me. She huffs out a laugh, shaking her head in an *I don't think I'll ever understand you* gesture.

"Oh, I couldn't...who am I kidding, yes I can and I most certainly will." I laugh out loud at that and she smiles.

"A and C companies!" a man in full battle dress calls as he strides between the rows of tents. Odessa straightens. "Armed and ready in ten minutes!"

A few people from the group by the fire set down their cups and quickly disperse.

"What's happening?" I ask quietly, watching people starting to move with organized urgency as the man continues to call out his message as he walks past us, spreading the word.

"Battle," Odessa says matter-of-factly. No fear. No apprehension. I wonder what that must be like? To be trained to expect war and battle, to long for it even, based on the excitement in the eyes of some of the soldiers I see running past. Odessa tugs me out of the way and closer to the fire so I don't get trampled.

"Battle??" I repeat, unbelieving. I know she and Blackheart both confirmed a war truly was happening, but I've still managed to keep it as an intangible, fictional thing inside my mind. But now, hearing the commands being called, seeing men and women marching in dark armor with weapons strapped to their hips and backs, it is all very, very real.

"Nothing too bad," Odessa adds, apparently seeing the worry on my face. Though I know that I'm not going anywhere near this battle, my heart starts to race at the very idea of it, the thought that any of these people might not come back. How far away is this threat? Who is it? Lyanna's soldiers or one of the other kingdoms in the Alliance? "If only A and C companies are going, it's barely even a battle. A skirmish, really. It might not even amount to anything at all. Scouts most likely just saw some troops moving towards us and Blackheart likes to strike early. Not to worry." I nod absently.

"You aren't in A or C, are you?"

She gives me one of her sly smiles. "Would you be worried about me if I were?"

"Yes, you idiot," I say plainly, not even caring to keep my Tesni pretense up. I like Odessa. I don't want to think about her in battle. I know she's strong and skilled and formidable, but I can't picture her out there fighting. She blinks, her features softening a bit.

"Let's get you back to your tent, alright? Mia, go see if Colton needs help with packing up provisions." She nods and scurries off, ducking between the soldiers with ease. Just as we start to walk, Tristan calls out for Odessa, asking her to help him find something or another. She shakes her head in exasperation, but smiles. "He would lose his own cock if it wasn't attached to his body, I swear." I snort at that.

"I'm fine, I can make it back to my tent alone. You aren't my prison guard anymore, remember?" She gives me a dry look but smiles and nods.

"I'll see you tomorrow."

I walk back to my tent, trying to avoid the melee as much as possible and not get in the way. Blackheart is leaving his tent just as I arrive and my brow furrows.

"What?" he asks, striding towards me as he adjusts leather gauntlets that cover his wrists and forearms. He looks equal parts menacing, handsome, and almost regal in his full battle dress. All black of course, but his armor shimmers faintly, like oil, and a silver dragon is engraved across his chest plate. His hair is pulled back from his face, his sword strapped across his back, the hilt peeking over his right shoulder. He looks even taller somehow, more muscled, and I think if I saw him riding towards me across a battle field I might just shit my newly won trousers. *No wonder he's such a feared warrior.*

"I didn't think you'd actually go into battle. Don't Commanders usually stay back where it's safe?"

His lips curl, excitement sparking his blue-gray eyes. He stops just beside me and leans down. I suck in a sharp breath. Having him so close is...disconcerting. And intense. And horrible. And that last one might be a lie.

"I'm no ordinary Commander," he whispers conspiratorially, as if he's letting me in on a big secret. He straightens, an actual smile spreading across his face. Makers, the man is practically giddy. "We'll remain here for another few days. You're smart enough not to try to escape, aren't you?"

"I don't care to starve to death in The Perilous or get eaten by a beast of some sort, so, yes, I will remain here within the safety of the camp." *For now.*

"Good answer, Red. But there is the matter of your Gift..." And now it hits me: he'll be gone from the camp. My Gift won't be blocked anymore...so of course he won't allow that to happen. "One of the lieutenants will be along shortly to collar you. Do not do anything you'll regret." I take his warning and nod easily enough. I have no plans to try to run yet so there would be no reason for me to harm whoever comes to put the damned collar on me.

He strides off and the words bubble up from my throat before I can stop them or even think about what in the hells I'm doing.

"Be safe."

He stops and glances at me over his shoulder, eyeing me suspiciously. I could say something scathing like I seem to be getting the opposite of what I wish for lately, so by wishing him safety, I'm ensuring his demise, but I find that I don't want to. I do actually want him to be safe, to return to the camp breathing and whole and —*Makers, I'm a fucking idiot.*

I just quirk a brow in challenge and walk inside my tent, but I swear I catch him grinning before I do.

ON THE FOURTH DAY, THEY RETURN FROM BATTLE. THERE'S A FRENZY OF activity when they ride back, and my stomach twists when I see some of the soldiers being carried on canvas stretchers, blood-soaked cloths wrapped around wounds. They rush them to what I've learned is the medical tent, run by Copeland and a few other healers —the regular kind, not the Gifted kind.

"Why doesn't Copeland go with them? Heal everyone as they're injured on the field?" I ask Odessa and Tristan, and a few others who have decided to tolerate me being included in their group: Kendall, Jonathan, and Lucinda.

"He's too important to risk being hurt or killed out there. So, we have to do our best to hold everyone together until we can get them back to him," Lucinda says, wincing as Odessa braids her white-blonde hair. "Ow! You're pulling on purpose," she spits with a scowl. "I swear I'll gut you, Graveryn..."

Odessa snorts. "I'd like to see you try, Luce."

Jonathan clears his throat, bringing the conversation back to the original point. "Any that don't make it back to the camp belonged to Noxum already anyway—His will be done." He and Kendall both touch their foreheads with two fingers, the sign of respect for the Maker of death. I've found that most soldiers have a very healthy respect for Noxum, which I suppose is understandable. When you might meet him at any given moment, it's probably best to be on good terms with him.

"So...since they've returned mostly intact, does that mean you won?" How is a winner even decided in a battle? Do they just tally up who lost the most soldiers at the end of the day and the side with the fewer casualties is crowned victor?

"We *always* win," Kendall says, grinning.

"I can't tell if you're serious."

"Well, in your defense, he rarely is," Jonathan says, and Kendall shoves him in the shoulder. "But in this case, yes. Blackheart does not lose. He does not retreat. He would die on the battlefield before running away."

I mull that over, watching the procession of the soldiers back through the camp. When I see Blackheart, I exhale in...relief? Oh fucking Makers. *No. No, no, no.* I grit my teeth. I don't care if he dies, not really. Except...he's been kind to me when he didn't have to be. He protected me, no matter the motives behind it. He's a good leader who fights with his men, men who seem to genuinely respect and admire him.

No, damn it! He took me prisoner. He plans to deliver me into the hands of a monster known throughout Hypathia for his horrific treatment of Gifteds, a monster who will do Makers know what with me once the ransom goes missing or he learns the truth. So, no, I am not feeling any kind of way towards Blackheart. End of story.

Even still, my eyes track him as he dismounts his horse and

strides toward the medical tent. Is he hurt? There are no obvious signs of it, no bloody bandages or missing limbs, but that doesn't necessarily mean no injuries.

"He likes to be near for the ones who are too far gone for Copeland and the others to save," Odessa says quietly, watching me watch Blackheart and reading the question in my mind. I shake my head. I don't understand a damn thing about this man. Could he really be a decent person? It did seem like he hated the king when we spoke after the incident with Turner, so again I wonder if perhaps he doesn't serve the monster king freely. Maybe he's being forced, a loved one being held hostage to ensure compliance?

"So was it all just rumors then? About the level of your cuntness—" Kendall frowns. "Cuntitude?" I choke on a laugh and Jonathan looks as if he's praying to the Makers for patience. Odessa and Lucinda both laugh, shaking their heads and mumbling insults under their breath. "You seem pretty normal to me." He shrugs magnanimously.

I freeze for a moment, knowing that I shouldn't be here laughing and joking with them, that I should keep the damn walls up, but then decide I just don't fucking care anymore. I'm so tired of being awful to everyone. They have no reason not to believe I'm Tesni, even if I'm not as much of a raging bitch as they'd initially thought, so I let it go. I remind myself that I'm the only one who knows she has a twin. Of course they'll believe I'm her regardless of how I act. So, I let myself keep the wall down, at least here with this small group.

"Nah, I think she'd just never been properly socialized," Odessa says, grinning at me. "What can you expect of a spoiled princess who's only ever been surrounded by butlers and maids and the royal ass-wiper? 'Course she was a cunt before."

I give her a dry look. "Royal ass wiper? Really?" She only smiles widely in return, finishing with Lucinda's braids. I'm tempted to ask her to do something with my own hair, but decide that's entirely stupid.

"What's it feel like, then? Your Gift?" Kendall asks and this time

Jonathan smacks him in the back of the head. "Oy! What was that for?"

"You can't ask people that," Jonathan insists through clenched teeth, and I laugh as Kendall rubs the spot mournfully, ruffling his sandy blonde hair and making it stand on end.

"Idiot," Tristan mutters, but he casts his friend a warm smile.

"It's alright," I tell them, perfectly fine steering the conversation away from why I'm not being a heartless bitch. "It's kind of like this... energy within me, I guess. I can feel it like a part of me deep inside my chest. It starts there and radiates outward through the rest of my body. My palms are where it gets the strongest and where I can... push it out I guess it is the right term. Wield it." I want to explain how I can radiate the cold over my skin, turn it to solid ice, make it snow—but of course I can't say any of that. I assume Tesni can do something similar with her fire, but I'm not sure.

"Does it hurt?" Lucinda asks.

"Not at all."

"And you aren't afraid that you'll ever, you know...blow yourself up or something?" Odessa asks, surprising me. Her cheeks heat when I quirk a brow at her but then she rolls her eyes.

"A Gifted *can* push too hard. We call it the Brink. There's a point where your power can become too much for your body to handle and it gives out—or goes up in flames," I add.

"That's terrifying," Lucinda says, shuddering.

"But you can feel that coming? So you know when to stop?" Tristan asks.

I nod. "I've never really gotten close before, but I've heard that you know when you're at your limit, so you *choose* to keep pushing. No one hits the Brink by surprise."

One of our regulars at the tavern was married to a Gifted who hit the Brink in an attempt to save him and their children from a cyclone. He was the only one who made it, and he drowned his memories in ale on good days, in hard liquor on bad ones. But he said he could see it in her eyes the moment she made the choice, the moment she knew what she was doing but decided it was worth it to try to save those she loved. I can't imagine having to make that choice, knowing you were going to die but pushing on anyway.

"And does *that* hurt?" Lucinda asks, nodding toward the collar at my throat. I run my fingertips along the cool metal chain at my throat.

I shake my head. "It isn't painful it just feels...strange. It's the same when Blackheart is here blocking. I can still feel my Gift inside me, it's just that I can't call it all the way out or wield it. Think of it as being locked inside a glass box. I can see it. I know it's there. I simply can't touch it."

"Huh," Jonathan says, sounding thoughtful. "I never really thought much about it."

"Your father helped create the collars, how do you know nothing about them or how they work?" Odessa asks. Jonathan's father must be an alchemist then. I don't understand how they work either, honestly—something about the specific mix of metals blocking the energy somehow—but I know that there must be alchemy involved.

"And when he starts to talk about them, my brain begins to hurt. It's all far too complicated for me. I barely know the difference between iron and steel. Da is a genius. I just poke things with pointy sticks." He winks at me and though I'm surprised, I smile back.

Kendall looks wistful. "I wish I was a Gifted."

"I, too, wish you were blessed with the Gift of silence," Jonathan says solemnly.

"Alright, that's it," Kendall says, lunging for the other man. The next thing I know, the two are play fighting in the middle of the path, pushing and shoving and landing mostly harmless blows until Jonathan lifts Kendall over his shoulder as if he weighs nothing and walks behind the row of tents.

"Hey! Knock it off!" we hear him call and Odessa, Lucinda, Tristan and I exchange confused glances before all running to follow. We get past the line of tents in time to see Kendall tossed unceremoniously into a giant snowbank. Odessa laughs so hard she snorts, and I can't help but feel lighter than I have in weeks. Here, in this moment, I'm able to forget the danger I'm in, the razor's edge that I'm walking with this ruse. I can forget that I'm supposed to be Tesni and just be me, just a girl having a laugh with her friends. Or as close to friends as I can have here, anyway.

"Come on, let's get some food," Tristan suggests, wrapping an arm around Odessa's neck and kissing her temple. She leans into him with a smile, resting her hand on his forearm. I quirk a brow. So... maybe Odessa is sleeping with Blackheart *and* Tristan? I take in Tristan with his golden tan skin, deep brown hair hanging to his shoulders, and cheekbones that could cut glass, combined with that leanly muscled frame and just the right amount of swagger. I give an inward approving nod. *Good for her.*

After bowls of stew, Kendall grumbling all the while that he'd never be warm again and Jonathan threatening to toss him in all over again if he didn't stop complaining, I have my collar removed by another of Blackheart's men and take a walk through the camp. The others wanted to visit with some of their injured comrades and pay respects to those lost, and that didn't feel like something I should be trespassing upon, so I said my goodbyes for the evening.

"And where in the hells did you get *those*?" the voice I'm now all too familiar with asks from behind me as I near my tent, low and... gruff? No, surely not. Then I remember that his voice may very well be hoarse—I can only imagine how much yelling is done during a battle, though to be quite honest, I'm having trouble envisioning what a true battle even looks like. I don't think I really want to see it, even in my head.

I turn and find Blackheart not far behind me, looking tired but no worse for the wear. I tilt my head, realizing that though exhaustion is clearly weighing on him, his body is tense and alert, his eyes blazing. Is he angry about the trousers? I narrow my eyes. Does he think that I stole them? I shift my shoulders back and barely stop myself from planting my hands on my hips before I start my tirade.

"I won these fair and square playing quills, I'll have you know, and if you don't believe me, I have several witnesses from your own soldiers who can attest and—"

"They...suit you," he interrupts, eyes drifting downward over my body in a way that makes my pulse race. He clears his throat and pulls his gaze up to meet mine again. "Are you truly not cold?" he asks, dark brows arching.

"I'm fine."

"So, it's true that you run hot then," he muses, studying me and slowly closing the distance between us. It's true that while the cold doesn't bother me, Tesni *is* always warm, so it doesn't really bother her either. Both of us can survive equally well in the freezing north or the blazing south. I wonder then, if Tesni would be more at peace in Helios, the way I am here. I can't believe I've never thought of that before now.

"The cold doesn't touch me," I answer truthfully without actually confirming his assumption. He nods and we stand in silence for a few moments. It isn't uncomfortable, exactly, but it starts to feel heavy as his eyes bore into mine and I find my gaze drifting from those stormy depths to his lips, wondering what would happen if I just...

I shake myself and take a step backwards before my body stops taking instructions from my mind. It's been known to happen a time or two.

"Was it awful?" I ask, willing my voice not to come out breathless. I halfway succeed.

"Hmm?" he asks, sounding as if his thoughts are a thousand miles away.

"The battle," I clarify. "Was it awful?"

"Oh," he frowns. "I never really think about it in terms of awful or not. It was a small contingent from Nocadia, nothing we couldn't handle easily."

"Do you always fight with them? Even in battles that can be handled easily?"

"I try to, yes. It seems wrong for me to send my men to fight, possibly fall, while I stay safe and warm in my tent."

I study him. "That's only part of the reason," I finally say.

His lips curl at the corners. "Oh really?"

"You get a rush from it. A thrill that you can't seem to find anywhere else." I can't even explain how I know it, but I do, sure as I know my own name. He hikes a big shoulder and winces the tiniest bit, covering it quickly enough but I catch it all the same. "Are you hurt?"

"I'm fine," he says, brushing the question away, but I'm already in front of him, reaching up to pull the edge of his coat and tunic away without thinking. There's a bloody gash across his shoulder, leading down over the top of his chest. I glance up to scold him, only to find that he seems to have stopped breathing completely, his eyes wide and staring. Now I realize what I've done, touching him so casually, our bodies so close that I can feel his heat warming me, smell the snow and dirt and blood, and his own wild, wintery scent beneath that.

I clear my throat quietly. "Why didn't you have this healed? It would have been easy work for Copeland."

"He should focus on the worst of the injuries. This is a scratch and will heal fine in a week or so." He puts his men first, their healing above his own. I feel something inside my chest start to shift and I force it to stop in its tracks. No. I fucking refuse. I cannot and will not do what I fear I might be doing. *No, no, fucking NO.*

"Idiot," I mutter, and I honestly don't know if I'm talking about him or me, but he laughs lightly.

"I have never claimed to be otherwise."

"Let me help you bandage it at least. I can fetch some supplies—"

"I have some in my tent, but you don't need to—"

"Come on then."

We both fight smiles at our interrupting conversation, and I charge towards his tent before I can fully realize how stupid this is.

He follows behind and when I step through I find that it is set up much the same as it was at the very first camp. I don't know why I was expecting anything different, really. I eye the bed, but quickly discard that idea. It isn't that I don't trust myself not to ravage him if we were near a bed, but...well, maybe it is a bit that I don't trust myself not to ravage him if we were near a bed. I'll examine my traitorous body's thoughts on this matter later when I am alone and away from the walking temptation that is Blackheart.

I point to the chair in front of his desk.

"Sit. Supplies?"

To my surprise, he obeys, tossing his coat onto the desk and sliding into the chair with a heavy sigh. He points to the weapons trunk.

"There's a pouch of bandages and salves in there somewhere." I rummage through it, mindful of the many, many sharp points within.

"Aren't you afraid I'll swipe a dagger, slit your throat in your sleep?"

"I never pictured the Flame of Lyanna as having such a wonderful sense of humor," he says, and I glance back to find his head tilted back, eyes closed. He really must be exhausted. I find the pouch and hurry back over to him.

"Erm...this will be easier if...well..."

"I'm naked?" he says, lowering his head and seeming to force his eyes open, but smirking in a way that should be a crime. I somehow manage to give him a dry look despite the wave of heat that crashes through me at that look, and he chuckles, low and rumbling. I like the sound. Oh, fuck me, I sound like those girls in the tavern, fawning over the sailors who stole their hearts away—without realizing that those same soldiers had a ship full of hearts they'd taken from nearly every young girl in the damn port.

"Do you want help or not?" I snap.

"No, I don't. It was you who insisted—ow!" His mouth pops open and he stares at me in shock tinged with amusement when I yank his shirt aside and slap a bit of cloth soaked with the cleansing tonic onto his wound. I happen to know it burns like fire. Serves him right.

"Apologies," I say without sounding apologetic in the least. He laughs again and tugs his tunic over his head, making me shift away, taking the cloth with me. My mouth goes dry. My blood turns to fire. My eyes take no orders from my mind and rove as they please, drinking in every inch of his bare torso. I got a glimpse at the outpost, but great Makers I somehow forgot how magnificent his body is. More tattoos spread across his chest and down the right side of his ribs, disappearing into the waistband of his pants. I realize now that they aren't just swirls of ink, they're symbols of some kind. Ones I don't recognize or understand, but I know that they have some sort of meaning. I don't dwell on them too long, my eyes still drinking him in. His stomach is taut and rigid, line after line of muscle, clenching tightly as I watch. I swallow hard, staring for one more eternal heartbeat before I finally manage to get my hands to cooperate once more, reaching out to wipe the wound with the cleansing tonic again, taking dried blood with it and causing fresh blood to well.

"What happened?"

"Walked into the pointy end of a blade." I meet his eyes, wondering if he somehow overheard me say something similar to Copeland that night or if we're simply very alike in our senses of humor. "I wouldn't recommend it."

"I'll keep that in mind," I say, forcing myself not to smile. I continue to clean the wound and try not to think about the fact that I can feel him watching me. I peek up at him from beneath my lashes and find those blue-gray eyes staring between wayward strands of midnight hair that have fallen over his forehead.

"Will you show me?" he asks quietly and I frown. "Your Gift," he clarifies. My entire body shoots through with tension. I keep working on his wound, adding a salve that will ward off any infection and help the skin heal.

"I'm not a dog performing tricks," I say through gritted teeth, hoping it comes off as anger and not fear. What if he demands that I show him? What will I do then?

"Has your power grown weaker over the years? Is that why Barony was giving you away? I've heard Gifts like yours can wane."

"My power is just fine," I say, and while I mean for it to come out biting, it's only a soft whisper.

"We could use you, you know. In the army, in this fight. Hells, even just on this journey your Gift would make things far easier." It was true that they have the telekinetic Gifted and another who has heat, but not fire—she can only do so much to melt the snow before she grows too tired. Fire, on the other hand, would make quick work of it all. "You could fight back against the very person who tossed you aside."

I finish securing the bandage over his wound, telling my fingertips not to linger, though they don't quite obey, and finally sigh, meeting his eyes.

"I'm not to be trusted," I tell him. "I'm not a good person, Blackheart. The second you stopped blocking my Gift, I would use it against you, against this camp." His eyes narrow a fraction. "I might be playing nice with the others, but the only thing I care about is myself. I would betray anyone, hurt *anyone*, even my own blood, to get what I want. You could never rely on me in this fight." My heart aches that it's the truth—not about me, but of Tesni. How could such awful things be true about my own sister, my twin, the other half of myself? How did we turn out so, so differently? He seems to see the sadness welling up in me, and out of the corner of my eye I see his hand lift from his lap, as if he's going to reach for me, but he quickly drops it again and clenches his fingers into a fist.

"How do you do that?"

"Do what?"

"Lie and tell the truth at the same time? I can see it in your eyes. All of that is both deceit and truth. How can that be?"

I inhale sharply, wondering how this man can possibly read me better than anyone else in this world after only knowing me for such a short while. That old familiar pang echoes through my chest, seeming to reverberate down to my bones, threatening to shatter them. No one can ever truly care about me because they can never truly *know* me. And as ridiculously stupid as it is, in this moment, I want Blackheart to care about me. I want him to know me. I want to tell him things I've never told anyone, even Math and Cece. I want to tell him the truth of who I am and why I'm here.

But no.

No matter what wild strangeness is passing between us tonight, he is still the leader of Duskthorne's army. He still serves King Dorian. He will still deliver me to that monster. I clear my throat.

"All done," I say softly, stepping away and only now realizing how close we'd been, how I'd been standing in the cradle of his thighs, my hands on his body. My cheeks heat.

"Thank you."

I nod and ball up the bloody rags. I look around for a bin to place them in but shrug and just toss them over my shoulder. He huffs out a laugh and despite myself, my lips curl upwards, just the smallest smile, but he notices.

"Alright, I'm going to go now." *Before I do something very fucking stupid.*

"Goodnight, Tess," he calls softly.

I freeze mid-step, my entire body tightening. I inhale softly but quickly exit his tent and flee to mine.

That was the first time he's ever used my (false) name. Not Red. Not Princess. Not Highness.

And fuck all the Makers—I liked it.

CHAPTER
ELEVEN

A sense of eerie foreboding has settled over The Perilous. Everyone seems to feel it as we make our way slowly through the treacherous woods, jagged rock formations and caves here and there hiding Makers know what. Everyone seems more tense, more alert, heads whipping at every beat of wings and snapping branch.

"Something is out there," I say when we stop to rest midday. I scan the thick forest around us, their branches looking all too much like bony, reaching fingers.

"Did you see something?" Odessa asks, hand reaching for her bow leaning against the boulder beside us.

"No, I can just...feel it. Can't you?"

She nods. "I feel like we're being watched."

"But..." I lick my dry lips. "But the scouts would have seen if there were...enemies out here, right?"

Odessa laughs. "Yes, there are no armies lying in wait, don't worry. No, whatever's out there isn't human."

"Oh, because *that's* so much better," I hiss, making her laugh even harder. The stories around the campfires these last few nights have spoken of all manner of beasts found out here. Ice dragons who can breathe fire, frost cats that can stalk their prey as silent as Noxum himself with fangs as long as my hand, arctic bears with blood red eyes and paws the size of dinner plates, wolves larger than horses, basilisks forty feet long, bats that feed on blood—none of them sound like anything I'd like to encounter. They're all regarded as silly tales, just legends and myths, but that feeling pressing against me, that unease swirling in my belly, makes me wonder if the legends might just be true.

"It just feels like something is coming." I rub the heel of my hand against my chest, the strange feeling welling there making me want to claw through my skin and bone.

"Have you seen Mia?" Odessa asks, scanning back through the long line of soldiers and wagons as best as she can. I frown. She normally comes to find us as soon as we stop.

"No," I say slowly, an icy pit forming in the center of my stomach, but I try not to let any worry show in my voice when I continue, "She's probably helping Ansel with the provisions still, that's all."

"Uh huh," Odessa says absently and I can tell she has a pit of her own to mirror mine. There's just something about this day, about these woods...

"I'll help you look. Come on."

We set off through the throng, making our way through the line, asking along the way if any has seen her.

"She was here," Ansel says with a frown. "She went off that way, but I thought she was going to relieve herself, so I didn't go with because...you know. She's a *girl*." Ansel is fifteen and an imbecile, though good-hearted. "But that was...hells that was ten minutes ago, at least. I got busy with the rations..." He looks worried, his doe eyes nearly drowning with it.

Odessa immediately strides off in the direction he pointed, away from the bit of forest that passes as a path we've been traveling, and into the deeper, more unruly woods. I follow, and unsurprisingly, Blackheart is at my side in a few moments. I saw him watching our exchange with Ansel.

"And where are we off to?" he asks.

"Mia," I say, not bothering to be biting or mocking, the worry making it impossible to focus on anything but putting one foot in front of the other and finding that little girl.

"Fuck." He shifts subtly then, his entire body focused and tense, eyes scanning the trees. I stumble through the underbrush, roots and bushes hidden beneath the snow, though I manage to stay upright. Thank the Makers for the trousers. I can't imagine trying to do this in a fucking dress.

"Mia!" Odessa calls.

"Mia!" Blackheart and I both yell in unison.

Over and over we yell, making our way through the brush, getting farther from the rest of the group, deeper into these Makers' forsaken woods, that feeling of unease doubling, tripling, making it hard to breathe.

"Mia! Where are you?!" Dessa shouts again and I can see her starting to fray. "Mi--"

"Dessa!" we hear from off to the right. Odessa turns to the sound and bursts forward, faster than I've ever seen her move. I follow as best as I can, but can't move nearly as nimbly. I remember that she was raised in a place like this, Duskthorne with its constant snows and imposing mountains and forests. Blackheart seems torn between staying behind with me and getting to Mia.

"Go, you idiot," I snap. "She might be in trouble!"

He nods and takes off, quickly leaving me behind. I'm out of breath by the time I reach them, bursting through the last row of trees, afraid of what I might see—only to have a shaky laugh burst from my lips.

Mia is sitting in the snow in the middle of the small clearing, a pure white rabbit in her arms. She glances up at me and grins.

"Look, Tess! White rabbits are good luck, you know!" She strokes the rabbit, his floppy ears admittedly adorable. I shift my gaze to Odessa who gives me a look that's somewhere between exasperated, relieved, and amused.

"Make good stew, as well," Blackheart says casually and all three of us stare at him incredulously. "Not that I would cook this one, of course," he adds hastily, eyes darting between the three of us. My lips curl upwards but then that uneasy feeling skitters up my spine. Though I don't hear a sound, I know deep, deep to the very core of my being, that there is something behind me. Something big. Something not human. My heart seems to stop but also race all at once and I can't seem to breathe at all. My power flares, ice coursing through my entire body. Useless, of course, with Blackheart blocking me, but it still rises up, ready.

"Tess," Blackheart says quietly, tension thick in his voice. "Don't. Move." He pulls his sword free in the blink of an eye.

"Great Makers," Odessa whispers, grabbing for Mia and pulling her up, putting the girl behind her protectively. Mia's eyes are wide and she clutches the rabbit to her chest, whether to shield him or for comfort, I can't be sure. Probably both.

I can feel the beast moving closer at my back now and every instinct is telling me to run, screaming at me to get away, to do something—but then all at once, they stop.

Something shifts—the entire world, part of my soul. Everything —and I'm suddenly unafraid. I feel a strange connection snap into place, like a fiery vine wrapping around my heart, the other side wrapping around his, a warmth filling my entire soul.

Because I know the beast behind me now, as if I've known him my entire life. He is a friend. He is a part of me. He is—

-*Mine*,- a voice whispers through my mind. I gasp quietly and Blackheart tightens his grip on his sword, raising it.

"No," I tell him. "No, it's alright." Despite knowing that everything is alright, I still swallow hard and take a deep breath before I start to turn.

"Tess," Odessa hisses.

"It's alright," I tell her again and Blackheart's eyes fly wide.

"Great Makers," Blackheart whispers, lowering his sword, mouth going slack. "It's...bonded her. Fucking hells, it's a *familiar*."

"What?!" Odessa whisper-yells back. "That's rubbish from campfire tales! Bedtime stories we tell children! Familiars aren't...real?" she finishes, though it sounds far more like a question than a fact. "At least not anymore."

I've heard stories as well, about Gifteds who bond with exceptional beasts. They protect their bonded one, love them, and bolster their power, making them far stronger than a Gifted could ever be on their own. Legend says that a familiar is only called to bond when the Makers themselves demand it, when something important is on the horizon. I never believed a single tale.

Until now.

I fully turn and come face to face with ice-blue eyes, almost the same shade as Odessa's, though these are ringed with deep gold that seems to glow like the sun. He's huge, easily the size of a small horse when he's standing upright, but sleek, and I know without a doubt he's agile as the wind. His fur is white as the snow surrounding us, with black and gray patches that I would guess help him blend into the rocks and trees, and I can only imagine the dagger-like teeth he's hiding.

"He-hello," I whisper, feeling a little silly.

-*Hello,*- the frost cat replies inside my head.

"Holy ruddy fucking fuck," I whisper and I would swear the cat arches a brow. Do cats even have brows? I clear my throat lightly. "My name is...Tess," I say, not sure that lying to your familiar is a good idea. The cat tilts his massive head.

-*No, it is not.*- I glance nervously over my shoulder, having no idea how to explain. -*You may speak to me this way as well. Without words*- My brows fly up at that.

"Really?"

"Is she...having a conversation with it??" Odessa whispers incredulously before Blackheart shushes her.

-*Try. Imagine a pathway between your mind and mine, and direct your words there.*-

I take a deep breath and do as he says, looking inside my mind and finding a silvery doorway of sorts. I push it open.

-*Umm...like this?*-

-*Very good. It would be a shame if the Makers bonded me with an imbecile.*- I huff out a nervous laugh. Is this frost cat...making jokes?

-*My name is Thea.*-

-*Why do you lie when the humans can hear?*-

-*That is a very long, complicated story and I promise I will tell it to you later.*-

The cat inclines his head. -*Alright. You may call me Soren.*-

I nod and start to turn to the others, but quickly whip back to Soren.

-*You won't hurt them, right?*-

-*Not unless they give me reason to.*-

I'm not sure what would qualify as a reason, but decide that we're safe for now. I turn back to find Odessa staring in absolute shock, Blackheart with that intense calculation, and Mia grinning like she just gained a new pet.

"Um. This is Soren. He says he won't eat you."

-*I said I wouldn't unless they give me a reason. That is an important distinction.*- he says and makes a chuffing sound from behind me, his breath tickling the back of my neck and ruffling my hair. I pull my lips in to hide a smile.

"Unless you give him a reason to," I add.

"This is...great fucking Makers, Tess, this is insane." Odessa shakes her head and runs a hand over her braids.

"Can I pet him?" Mia asks, peeking around her sister's back, still holding the rabbit.

"He's not a housecat," Odessa scolds from the corner of her mouth, as if Soren won't be able to see or hear.

-*I like the young one. She may pet me.*-

"He says yes, Mia."

Her eyes light up and she sets the rabbit down, patting him once more on the head before running forward without a care, as if she truly is running towards a housecat instead of a lion-like beast that could rip her to shreds with ease.

"Careful," Odessa warns, stepping forward hesitantly, clearly torn between protecting her sister and not wanting to anger Soren.

Mia stops beside me and reaches out a hand, palm facing outward, and waits, letting Soren make the decision. I give her an appreciative glance. She truly has an affinity for animals and I wish so badly for a moment that I could show her the menagerie back at Lyanna. Soren lowers his head and presses his nose into her waiting palm. She giggles and moves her hand down the side of his face and neck.

"He's so soft," she whispers in wonder. "And handsome," she adds, smiling at the cat. He chuffs again, clearly pleased. I can scarcely believe this is truly happening, but the utter *rightness* running through my veins like a rushing river makes me know that this isn't some sort of strange dream. I turn to Blackheart, suddenly worried that he'll try to turn the cat away.

"He has to stay with me. I can't...he can't..." I close my eyes, trying to sort through everything flowing through my body and mind right now. We are connected. We are bonded. His strength is my strength, my pain his pain. We simply cannot be apart now.

"He stays," Blackheart says firmly. I blink and surprise and he goes on, "The legends of Gifted familiars are revered in Duskthorne, from the ancient days of Hypathia when Gifteds were thought to be touched by the Makers themselves. There hasn't been a familiar in a century, at least, not that I've heard record of any way." He looks at the enormous cat with something close to wonder. "He stays," he says again.

I incline my head in thanks.

-That was an excellent choice. I would have hated to have to tear him to ribbons. He is...important to us.-

I narrow my eyes, not having any idea what that might mean. *Us* as in Soren and myself? *Us* as in Gifteds? *Us* as in the world? I choose to ignore his comment because I'm honestly a little afraid to go down that road. I don't need Blackheart to be important to me in any way. Once we reach Duskthorne, I'm no longer his charge. I'm Dorian's property until the ransom negotiations, and then when Hastings disappears with the coin...well, I don't know what happens to me, but I know that Blackheart won't be around to save me from it. Caring about him at all, letting him be important to me, will only lead to more hurt in the end.

"I'm going to go make an announcement and try to prepare the men," Blackheart says, striding back in the direction of the rest of the group but giving Soren a wide berth, keeping an eye on the cat. I can only imagine how everyone is going to react to a frost cat in their midst. They're almost as legendary as ice dragons, and rare to be sure.

"I can't believe this," Odessa says, sidling up beside me. I let out a long, shaky breath.

"You aren't alone there."

"Well one thing is for sure," she says, watching Mia pet the great beast like it's a puppy before turning her gaze to mine and smiling, "things are never dull with you around, princess."

CHAPTER
TWELVE

I stay up nearly the whole night talking with Soren, explaining my situation, my history with my sister, asking if he knows the reason he was called to me. He'd explained that he hadn't heard a voice, exactly, but something inside of him awoke with knowledge of me and how to find me, a piece of himself that was connected to me and would be forever rising up and helping to guide him. I had sort of been hoping that the Makers had given him a full explanation in great detail of what in the fucking hells was happening, and I do get the feeling that he knows more than he's letting on, but for now, he's only sharing that he was called to find me, so he did. Simple as that.

I still don't quite know how to handle having a familiar or the intense power simmering deep in my chest, stronger than I've ever felt. Blackheart had been watching me curiously throughout the rest of the day until we made camp, but I'm not sure if it was because he could feel the increase in strength or just because he was still reeling from Soren's appearance, from the knowledge that familiars aren't just the legends we all thought.

Walking back to the rest of the group with a frost cat in tow was...well, if I thought I'd gained attention as Tesni when I first arrived, it was nothing compared to this. Half of the soldiers looked like they might piss themselves, while others watched in reverent awe at Soren as we walked up the line towards our horses, some even bowing their heads and putting fists to their hearts. Some of the horses were skittish at first, but settled after a time, and Zaro didn't seem to care at all.

By the time we made camp, the entire army had gotten word about Soren and our bond, and the whispers were so loud I'd hidden in my tent as soon as it was up and ready. I was starting to become commonplace here, no one really paying me much attention anymore which is how I liked it, but now? *Everyone* is looking, and the harder people look, the more the cracks in this house of lies will spread.

Mia had spent most of the evening with us, already completely smitten with her new companion, and Soren seems equally enamored. He'd been perfectly content to let Mia stroke his ears and lean against his massive body until she'd fallen asleep. Odessa had hoisted the girl up without waking her, as if she'd done it a thousand times.

"You don't know any other familiars by chance, do you?" I ask him now, the morning coming all too quickly. He stares at me with those icy eyes, clearly saying that that is a horrifically stupid question. "Ok, ok, don't answer that." I rub my eyes and flop back onto my pillow. "I just wish I knew why you were sent to me, why the Makers chose to bring us together now. Why *me*?"

-The reason will make itself known when it is time. Until then, we travel north.-

"And what happens when we get there?" I whisper, not really looking to him for an answer.

-What is meant to happen.-

He seems to believe that everything has happened for a reason, that we are all part of a great plan that the Makers have put into place, including Tesni betraying me again and putting me on this path. I can't deny that part of me might even believe it too. After all, if I'd never gone to see Tesni, if I was never put in her place in that carriage, I would never have been in a place to find Soren, and though it's so new, barely hours, really, it feels as if this bond has been in place since the day I was born, maybe even longer than that. It's hard to explain, but I can't help but be a little thankful to the treacherous bitch that is my twin for bringing me here.

I turn to look at Soren where he's lounging on a pile of furs on the other side of the small tent. He said he didn't need them, but didn't complain too much once I put them down and he settled upon them. If it bothers him to lay on another animal's hide, he doesn't show it. Maybe he hates bears and is perfectly happy to sleep on top of his fallen foes.

Maybe I need sleep. As if on cue, I yawn widely.

-*Sleep.*-

My eyes are already sliding closed, so I whisper goodnight inside his head and drift off feeling more at ease than I have in my entire life.

"Can you feel it?" I ask Blackheart a few days later as we finally near Tithmoore.

"Feel what?"

"My Gift. Or everyone's Gifts, rather. I mean, how does your Gift work, exactly?" I honestly don't really expect him to answer, but I've been burning to know and now seems like as good of a time as any to ask. His brow furrows, as if he's never been asked the question before and isn't quite sure how to answer, which gives me hope that perhaps he will. It takes him a minute, but he finally speaks.

"Every Gifted has a sort of energy that regular people don't. I can sense it. Feel it, like you said."

"So, you could stare into a sea of people and know if there were Gifteds hidden within? Because you could sense this energy?"

"Mostly, yes."

"And you can just choose which energies you let past your wall, so to speak?"

"It's quite a talent, don't you think?" he asks with a cocky smirk and I roll my eyes. "Yes, I can choose which Gifts to let pass."

I think about that, trying to imagine wielding such a Gift, and quickly thank the Makers that it isn't mine. I suppose here on the road or within the camp it might not be so difficult, with only a handful of Gifteds, but what about when he's home in Duskthorne? He'd be surrounded by hundreds upon hundreds of Gifteds if the rumors of Dorian's collection are to be believed. I would think that would be...overwhelming to say the least. The more I think about his Gift, the more questions I have, so I keep pushing, wondering if there's a limit to how much information he'll share. Things have shifted subtly between us, but not so much to call us friends who have casual chats.

"And how do you do that? Know which Gift you're letting through?"

"It's a bit hard to explain, but each person, each Gift, has a different...feel to it."

I blink at that. "So...everyone's energies *feel* different to you? I feel different than Cookie?" He nods. Overwhelming was perhaps an understatement for how he must feel back at Duskthorne.

"Is my energy different now since I've bonded?" He opens his mouth to answer but someone calls for him and he sighs, seeming frustrated to end our conversation. I'd be lying if I said I didn't share the sentiment, not just because I'm intensely interested in his Gift, but because I am a fucking idiot and just like talking to him.

"I have to go, but we can continue this later." I nod, the fact that he doesn't seem to have hit any limits on sharing with me about his Gift making me happier than it should. He inclines his head and rides off.

-interesting...-

-I'm learning valuable information about our enemy, that's all.-

-More lies from my fated soul-bound,- he says with mock disappointment and hurt.

I glare at the cat and he laughs inside my mind while he growls softly at me out loud, flashing his fangs. Having him with me is still a little strange, yet so much a part of me already that I can't imagine being separated from him. I never could have imagined having conversations with an animal, sharing secrets and learning about each others' lives, but it feels as easy as doing so with a friend. He slinks off into the woods as he's prone to do during our travels. He likes to take to the trees sometimes to check for any dangers our, er I mean, *Duskthorne's* scouts may have missed. Plus, just because he's my familiar now doesn't mean he isn't still a frost cat. He still hunts and lurks and speaks to the other animals, as he did long before I came into his life. He's at home in these woods and I suddenly worry how he'll cope when—*if?*—we ever return to Helios.

-I think I'd rather enjoy seeing these white beaches you spoke of, not to worry.-

It seems that short distances make no impact on our ability to communicate, which eases my mind whenever he does go on his little adventures away from me. I smile and Odessa pulls her horse up beside my own.

"What are you smiling about?"

"Just imagining Soren lounging on the beaches in Helios."

She frowns. "Have you ever been there?"

"Oh, of course not," I say quickly, waving that away. "They never seemed to be in need of my services, so Barony and I never traveled there." I shrug. "But I've heard stories and seen paintings and for some reason I was just picturing Soren there on a beach beside the palms."

She seems to be trying to imagine it herself and then huffs out a laugh. "It is a funny thing to imagine. I would love to go there one day. Maybe after the war is done."

"You've never been either?"

She shakes her head. "No, coming to Karthania with this contingent is the farthest I've ever traveled from Duskthorne." I've learned that they came at the request of Queen Nicolette, to discuss the possibility of her kingdom leaving the Alliance and joining Duskthorne, but it was apparently a waste of time. "My mother's people came from Sol generations back though. Many settled in Helios as well. It was my father's family that came from the north and despite her love of the sun, mum loved him more and never went back." She smiles sadly and then shakes herself. "I feel like going there will help me feel closer to her again," she admits quietly. She glances at me sidelong. "Is that stupid?"

"Not at all. I hope you make it there one day." I want to tell her that I'll take her myself, that I'll show her all of the most beautiful hidden coves that no one knows about, that I'll introduce her to Cece and Math and that I'll help her find all the pieces of her family left there. But I can't. So, I just hope that one day our paths cross there and I can make good on these silent promises she'll never hear.

"Me too." After a few moments, she asks, "What about your parents?"

"I know nothing about them, really," I tell her with a shrug. "I know nothing of my father, and not much of my mother save that her name was Aura. One of them must have had Gifteds in their line somewhere—how Barony knew, I'm still not sure—but he thought there was a chance that we would be as well."

She frowns. "We?" My heart freezes for a minute at my stupid, stupid mistake, but I try to keep my expression blank.

"I had a twin at birth, but she died." It's a bit of the truth. The person I was died the day I fled all those years ago. "Anyway, Barony adopted me and got lucky that I did have a Gift, I suppose."

"Lucky would be an understatement, I think. Not only did he get a Gifted against the odds, but he got one with a formidable Gift—and one of the most powerful Gifts I've ever heard of to boot." She shakes her head. "It's almost as if the Makers orchestrated the whole thing."

My brow furrows, suddenly feeling like my entire life truly has been planned by the Makers. But *why*? Why me? Why now? What the hells does any of it mean?

"Well, I would have preferred for them not to have orchestrated me being kidnapped, personally," I say dryly. She smiles at that.

"Oh, come now, we aren't so bad as that, are we?"

"I do like Mia. And Cookie's cheese bread."

She snorts and I grin at her.

"Well, it will be nice to be in a proper town again for a few days," she says, looking wistful. We're to arrive in Tithmoore tonight and remain for a few days to rest and gather supplies before setting off for Duskthorne. "Real beds. Real baths. Real shopping." I quirk a brow and she hikes a shoulder. "What? I like to shop."

"You are a woman of many facets, Odessa Grayvern."

She winks. "That I am, princess. That I am."

TITHMOORE IS MUCH LARGER THAN I EVER REALIZED, THE KINGDOM MADE UP of twelve different sectors with King Ryker's palace at the very center. The army has been given lodging across three of the sectors, and Odessa was right: being back in a proper town is truly amazing. I stayed soaking in the tub in my room until the water had turned cold the first night, just luxuriating in the honeyrose oils. The citizens had been a mix of awed, terrified, and respectful of Soren, who had waltzed right into the middle of the kingdom by my side as if frost cats strolled into town every day. Though Tithmoore hasn't pledged an allegiance to either side in this war, they welcomed the army and offered any assistance they may require. I'm told they would have offered the same to any other kingdom, but from the quiet mutterings I heard while walking through the markets with Odessa our second day here, I think many of the members of this kingdom would gladly choose Duskthorne. Which is crazy...isn't it?

"Captain," Julius, one of the higher-ranking officers—though not as high as Odessa—calls as he approaches us from across the tavern we'd found. I'm slowly learning some of the ranking distinctions and pecking order, so to speak, within the army, but still don't know much. "You're needed." We both immediately stand, though I throw back the rest of my drink before we leave. Julius eyes me with a bit of amusement.

"No need to be wasteful," I say, grabbing Odessa's cup and draining it as well before wiping my mouth with the back of my hand. Odessa laughs lightly and we make our way to the inn where Blackheart and some of the other officers are staying—and me, of course, since the prisoner can never be too far from the jailer, apparently. To be fair, this prisoner is still plotting ways to escape, so Blackheart keeping me close is wise.

A group of soldiers is standing outside when we arrive and Blackheart looks up, beckoning us over with two fingers. Well, he's probably actually only beckoning Odessa, but I come anyway.

"I need you on this scouting team," Blackheart tells her. "I've been doing my best to keep you here with Mia but—"

"I understand," she says quickly, inclining her head. "She'll be alright here."

I hover on the edges, not really a part of the conversation but not wanting to walk away either as they start talking about logistics and other things I don't understand, and apparently I'm making that obvious. Tristan steps to my side.

"King Ryker told us of rumors of a large contingent of Lyannian and Karthanian soldiers moving in from the northeast. Not so large that we can't handle them, don't worry," he adds, "but we want our best scouts to go out and confirm the information."

"And Odessa is one of the best?" I ask.

Tristan nods, pride shining in his hazel eyes as he looks to the woman. "She is one of the best archers in all of Duskthorne."

"And what happens if the rumors are true?" I ask, trying not to sound worried.

"We'll meet them in battle before we reach Duskthorne," he says simply. My stomach drops at that, the idea of them going into a large battle. I know there have been fights along this journey, but this seems different to me. "Not to worry," he says again, smiling, as Blackheart dismisses the group and they all disperse to gather their things I assume. I thank Tristan for explaining things and make my way over to Odessa, falling into step beside her easily as if we've been doing it for years instead of weeks.

"We leave within the hour," she says.

"Are you…are you afraid?"

She purses her lips. "No one's ever asked me that before." She mulls it over before answering. "Yes and no. I've trained for this for half my life. I am not scared to fight, but I think if you aren't afraid of death, you have nothing to live for." She glances up the path towards the small cottage she and Mia are staying in. "And I have something very important to live for," she adds softly. Fiercely. As if daring Noxum himself to take her from this world.

I lay a hand on her forearm and she meets my eyes.

"I'll look after her. You have my word."

She smiles at me and places her hand over mine, squeezing gently.

"Thank you. I know she's safe here and that everyone will take care of her, but it's comforting to know there is one more set of eyes watching over her."

-Make that two,- Soren says inside my mind. I glance over my shoulder just as the cat jumps down from the top of the building lithely, landing as silent as death. He stalks towards us, nudging my back with his forehead affectionately as he passes and sits beside us, tail curling around his paws.

"He says to make that two sets of eyes."

Odessa smiles and the cat inclines his big head to her.

"I appreciate you both."

❄

Mia says that she doesn't mind staying by herself, but doesn't fight too hard when I insist that she stay with me and Soren instead. Blackheart has the men bring a second bed into my room and though it groans a bit under his weight, Mia beams when Soren leaps atop it and curls up beside her. She falls asleep almost immediately, her head resting against his chest and fingers tangled in his fur, and my own chest warms as I watch the two of them.

The next day, I accompany a group of soldiers out to the mountains on the southern edge of the kingdom. Blackheart offered additional hands to assist with the harvest of the chryil crop, the root vegetable that grows within the caves deep inside the mountain. Chryil is only grown here in Tithmoore and one of their most lucrative trading items throughout Hypathia, but this final harvest of the season before deep winter arrives is what will help to feed the entire kingdom until spring. King Ryker was more than happy to accept the assistance of Blackheart's men to expedite the process as much as possible.

Mia, of course, wanted to be included and is doing her fair share from what I can tell. Though I wouldn't mind helping, I still have a part to play. I may not be acting as awful as Tesni, but she wouldn't be caught dead doing manual labor, especially for free, so I merely stand in the shade of a blood pine, its red leaves and sap giving the tree a sinister but beautiful look. Soren is off hunting, so I'm standing alone when Blackheart steps up beside me.

"You're not nearly as sneaky as I originally thought, you know," I say without turning to look at him.

"Oh really?"

"I used to think you were silent as Noxum himself stealing in to take souls, seeming to appear out of thin air."

"And now?" I can see out of the corner of my eye that he's suppressing a smile, his arms crossed over his broad chest as he watches his men and the Tithmoore farmers bringing out carts full of chryil from the fields deep within the mountain and disappearing back into the mouth of the cave entrance.

"Now, I can sense when you're coming. You can't surprise me anymore." I turn to look up at him finally. He meets my eyes and his lips pull up on one side into a crooked grin that's somehow adorable and sexy all at once.

"Oh, I imagine I still have plenty of tricks up my sleeve that could surprise you, Red." The words are innocent enough, his tone playful, but a slow shiver works its way up my spine all the same. The implications. The possibilities. The desires. I swallow hard, but don't pull my gaze away as the heat between us seems to grow hotter and hotter. I feel like I'm going to combust and I wonder for a second if playing Tesni all this time has somehow truly given me her Gift, if I'm making this heat between us.

"Tess!" Mia shouts, breaking the bubble that had surrounded us. I shake myself and turn to find her running towards me. She's grinning widely, dirt smeared on her cheek and across her nose, and she holds up a beautiful flower with deep crimson petals. "For you."

I smile and take the flower, gaping when I examine it more closely. There are patterns of small golden stars running up the middle of each petal, as if the stars are shooting across them from the center of the flower, and that they've been dusted with glitter, a faint shimmer in the gold as I turn it in the sunlight.

"It's beautiful," I whisper, holding the flower to my nose and inhaling deeply. It smells of the crisp, clean bite of snow and a hint of sweetness, like honey but not quite as heavy.

"It's a daska," says Blackheart and Mia nods emphatically. "We have them in Duskthorne as well—they manage to grow deep inside the mountains, despite not having the sun that most colorful flowers need. No one quite knows how or why."

"Mum used to say that it's because they're the most stubborn of all flowers, that someone told them long ago that they couldn't possibly grow inside the mountain, and so the daska did just that to prove them wrong." I laugh at that and she smiles. "She used to call Dessa *daska* instead sometimes because she's so stubborn." Her smile turns a little sad, but she recovers quickly, waves, and darts off towards the mouth of the cave again.

"My mother used to tell a similar version, but she said that it meant that the most beautiful of things can be found in the darkest of places." I meet his gaze again, the blue-gray dark and burning. "It is a symbol of hope, of never giving up no matter how dark things seem." I can't seem to look away, his words sounding like a message he's desperate for me to hear, but I don't quite understand. Does he mean the darkness of Dorian? That I need to hold onto hope throughout whatever ordeal I'm still heading towards?

I force myself to break eye contact first, frowning when I realize that we're practically alone in the field. Nearly everyone has gone back down inside the mountain to load up more carts. Mia waves from within the cave, standing just before the long, man-made path that leads deep into the mountain's center with a farmer waiting beside her and smiling warmly. I smile and wave back, but my smile falls when the ground beneath my feet begins to shake. Blackheart grabs my arm to steady me and yells sound out from within and from the few folks still outside, people shouting out warnings, words like "rockslide" and "cave in" slamming into my mind too quickly to process.

Before anyone can so much as move, the mouth of the cave begins to crumble before my eyes.

"No!" I try to scream, but it only comes out as a soft gasp as giant stones cover the entrance to the mountain, Mia's wide, terrified eyes the last thing I see before the opening is just...gone.

CHAPTER THIRTEEN

I'm running before I even make the decision to move. The people still outside are shouting, but I can't make out what they're saying. All I can think about is Mia. I'm almost to what used to be the entrance to the cave, now just a solid wall of rocks, when strong hands yank me backwards.

"Let go!" I yell, thrashing.

"Wait," Blackheart's low, commanding voice hisses in my ear. "Just wait, Tess."

"I can't! I have to—"

Another deluge of stone rumbles down the mountainside and slams into the ground just in front of us. Blackheart pulls me back with him just in time, his arms like iron bars around me, pinning me to him. We stand there for a few moments, waiting for the last few pebbles to skitter downward.

"There is almost always a second slide," he says softly, releasing me.

I don't have time to thank him or even acknowledge what he's said. As soon as I'm free, I fling myself at the rocks, desperately searching for a hole, a gap, a sliver of space, but find nothing.

"Mia? Mia!?" I scream so loudly my throat feels like it's being ripped apart. My heart's in my throat, my entire body cold as ice as I wait, but no response comes. "Makers, no..."

"Go for help!" Blackheart yells at someone, the command in his voice unyielding and absolute. "What about the auxiliary tunnels?" He asks someone else. "Go check—*now*!"

I keep searching for a hole, my hands flying uselessly over the packed, finding nothing. *Fucking nothing!*

"Mia!" I call again. "Mia, answer me!" *No, no, no. Come on. Come on.* "MIA!"

"Tess!" Her small voice makes its way through the wall of stone and a broken half-gasp, half-sob tears from my throat in relief.

"Mia!! Are you alright!?"

"I...I think so," she calls back. "My arm is bleeding...my forehead too, but it doesn't hurt much. One of the farmers shielded me. He...I don't think he's ok, Tess." I can hear the tremble in her voice, the tears threatening, but she's holding them back. She's so strong, so brave.

"It's going to be ok, Mia. We're going to get you out. Just hold on!" I feel Blackheart at my back, his presence somehow calming. One of the soldiers runs up then.

"Sir, the auxiliary tunnels are both blocked as well."

"Fuck," Blackheart rasps. I know that can't be a good thing, but I keep my focus on Mia.

"How many people are there with you?"

"We were the only two up here. Everyone else was down in the farming caves, but I can hear them running up now that it's stopped."

"Ok, that's good."

"They should stay down in the caves, by the fields. It will be safer there in case of another quake. They'll have places built within the farms for shelter just for these events."

I brace my hand on the stone, rough beneath my palm and Blackheart steps up beside me.

"Mia, go down into the farm with the others, alright?"

"No!" she cries. "No, I want to stay up here where I can hear you." Her voice breaks and I can feel how terrified she is. It claws at my chest, but I swallow hard and steady myself before I reply. I can see Blackheart watching me from my peripheral. I don't know what he's thinking and frankly don't fucking care.

I keep my voice calm and even when I say, "I know, but it's safer for you to be down there. We're going to get you out soon, but I need you safe until then, ok? The others will help you. We have to move all of these rocks out of the way, so it will take just a little bit of time, ok?" They should have some provisions and medical supplies down in the caves too. "Have someone bandage your arm and forehead, and drink some water."

"But..."

"Please, Mia." I close my eyes, willing my heart to stop trying to beat through my chest.

"Ok," she finally says, resigned. "Tess? You won't...you won't leave me in here, will you?" I can hear the wobble in her voice and can see her lip trembling in my mind's eye, see those pale green eyes filling with fear.

"Never," I say fiercely. "I *promise* I will get you out of there." I lean my forehead against the stones and grit my teeth. "Don't worry. Just go down into the caves and see if anyone else needs help. You're always helping, so do that now, ok? They need you."

"Ok," she says quietly.

After a few seconds of silence, I assume she did as I asked and I let out a long, shuddering exhale. I snap my eyes open then, fire filling my belly, scorching through my every thought. All I can think of is getting to her. All I can see is the path to rescuing her. It's my only goal, my only purpose.

I grab one of the small rocks and throw it aside, then another, and another. I will dig her out stone by stone, piece by fucking piece if I have to. Blackheart and the others step up and start doing the same. They speak but I don't know what they say, it's all just muffled buzzing, my head too full of worry and this frantic need to get through this wall to Mia.

Soren is at my side then, a low, worried growl rumbling in his throat. I honestly don't even remember sending anything to him through the pathway, but I must have in my panic.

-*You were screaming,*- he says solemnly, clawing at the stones with his massive paws and dislodging the loose ones in a small avalanche of rocks and dirt. My heart soars, thinking it might be easier than I thought it would be, but then it plummets, right to the pits of the seventh hell. The outer layer is loose, small stone that gives way easily, but beneath that? It's like trying to tear a building down with my bare hands, but I don't care. I keep digging, keeping wedging my fingertips into the minute cervices between the stones, pulling and clawing and heaving. I don't know how long it will take help to arrive, but the few of us here keep going, determined to find a way through.

What feels like hours later, I stop for a brief moment to wipe sweat from my brow. Every muscle in my body is screaming, but I can't give up. So, I let out a long, slow exhale, pull up strength from deep within myself, and keep going. I curse my Gift as I dig, wishing it was something that could be useful right now. Telekinesis would be perfect, like Charles has, but he's out in the scouting party with Odessa. My heart clenches as the thought rocks through me: Odessa is out there, possibly in danger, and has no idea what's happening here with Mia. What if we can't get to her? What if Odessa comes back and I have to tell her that Mia is gone? That I broke my promise? That now she's not only lost her parents, but her little sister?

NO, I snarl silently at the Makers, letting them know loud and clear that they will not touch either of these girls, these two people who have shown me kindness when it wasn't warranted, these two people who have become my friends. Not today. Not ever. No, neither of them will be taken from me. My Gift surges and I gasp quietly when the rock beneath my palm is suddenly coated in frost. I feel Blackheart start beside me, whipping his head towards me. Did he feel my Gift break through his wall? The rock is in a pile with the others before he can possibly see the ice, and I force my power to settle.

I keep going, not even acknowledging that he's staring at me, acting as if nothing happened. I dig, and scrape, and claw, moving along the wall when I can't find a way through, my mind racing in a manic, frenzied storm of panic that won't ebb no matter how much I try, no matter how much time passes.

"—ss!" Blackheart's voice crashes through the haze of exhaustion that's settled over my thoughts. His hand is on my shoulder, pulling me gently. I blink and look at him, forcing my vision to focus. "Tess, I've called your name three times. You need to rest."

"No, I can't." I try to pull away but he holds fast. A low, warning growl rumbles in Soren's throat. Blackheart eyes the cat but doesn't let go.

"Tess, you must, look at your hands—"

"I WON'T!" I scream, my Gift rising up again and filling my entire being so quickly, that despite some part of my mind still aware enough to know I can't let it break through his wall again, not with him touching me or watching me this closely, I would swear the temperature around us drops a few degrees. "There are good people trapped in there!" I fling my hand towards the cave, towards the wall of stones still standing strong. *How is it still fucking standing??* "People who are just trying to feed their families, the families of everyone in this kingdom! Our people are in there too, damn you. I won't leave any of them, and by all the fucking Makers I will NOT leave that little girl! She is scared and her sister is gone and I will not stop until I get to her and make sure that she's safe. Do you understand me? I. WILL. NOT. STOP," I seethe, baring my teeth, my power roiling inside of me like an icy tempest. Soren growls in earnest now, pulling himself up to his full height behind me and peeling his lips back from his massive fangs.

Blackheart looks between my familiar and me again, and seems to decide that I will not be moved.

"Alright then."

He lets go and I continue clawing at the rock. It's then that I notice my hands: covered in blood, nails cracked and jagged and even altogether *gone* in two cases. The pain is behind some kind of wall, thank the Makers, so I keep digging, screaming in frustration and fear and exhaustion until finally, finally, someone shouts that they've made a hole. I sprint over, Soren at my heels to clear a path of anyone who would dare try to stop me. The man who'd made the hole—W something. Warren? Wadson? I make a quick promise to the Makers to find out later and thank him—steps aside quickly after a low growl from the frost cat beside me, and I peer into the darkness within.

"Mia! Mia!!" I wait, exhaustion trying desperately to pull me down, but I hold steady, ignoring its claws in my back. I grip the rocks on either side of the hole so tightly they cut into my palms, more blood mingling with what's already there. "MIA!!" I scream, my heart falling. What if she'd been hurt more than she realized? What if we're too late? How long have they been down there? Hours? Days? I have no idea. Surely they have enough air and provisions to last for a while if these rockslides are common, right? But there were so many more people than usual, maybe too many. My thoughts simply won't stop spinning and my vision starts to blur, my head pounding and my chest aching.

Please let them be ok. Please...

"Tess!!" Her voice is far away, but tears burn my eyes and I thank every fucking Maker I can think of. She's ok. She's alive. "Tess!" she calls again, closer now, and then I can see her pale face in the dim lantern light within the cave. I reach my arm through the hole, and she latches onto my hand, squeezing for all that she's worth.

"I told you," I say, relief filling every inch of my soul. "I told you I wouldn't stop. Are you ok? Is everyone alright?"

"Yes, we're ok. A few people got hurt a little, but everyone is alright, I think. I'm not bleeding anymore."

"Mia, we can get you all out of there in just a few more minutes, alright?" Blackheart says from just behind me. "We just need to move a few more stones. Can you step back for just a little while longer?"

"Yes, sir," she says bravely, nodding. She meets my eyes again, hers red and puffy from tears, a streak of dried blood coating her temple and cheek. "Thank you," she whispers.

I don't think I can say anything without breaking down completely, so I simply nod, squeeze her hand, and force myself to let go and step away. A few other men immediately swoop into my place and start maneuvering more stones out of the way. Someone even makes some kind of harness to put around Soren, and the great cat starts pulling the large chunks of stone out of the way with his massive strength as the men put thick branches in to keep the remaining stones in place.

She's safe. Mia is safe.

I smile even as my knees buckle and darkness speeds in from all directions. The last thing I feel are arms catching me before I hit the ground. The last thing I see are Blackheart's worried, beautiful eyes. The last thing I hear is his deep, rumbling voice saying my name over and over. *No, not my name*, I think as the darkness pulls me under. *Not my name.*

THE LOW RUMBLING OF SOREN'S WHAT I CALL PURRING BUT HE INSISTS IS nothing of the sort is the first thing to break through the darkness. It's such a comforting sound that I savor it, letting myself lie there for a few more moments before prying my eyes open.

-*Finally,*- the cat mutters in my mind, though I can feel the relief in his thought. I wonder how long I've been asleep.

"Good to see you too," I croak, my throat feeling as if I swallowed a bucket of sand. I push myself up on the bed. I frown. The bed? How did I get here? I don't remember...

"You're awake!" Mia cries from the doorway, running across the room and dropping the bowl of stew to the floor just before she throws herself at me. I *oof* quietly but hug her back tightly when she wraps her arms around my neck and squeezes. Everything comes crashing back into me now: the quake, the rockslide, digging and clawing and refusing to give up. I close my eyes as tears burn and bury my face in her hair, thanking all the Makers again that she's here and safe and whole. Soren bumps the back of her head softly with his nose and chuffs, his breath ruffling her hair and making her giggle before he leaps lithely off of the bed.

-I'm going to hunt now that you've found your way back from the dead.-

-Thank you. For helping. For staying with me afterward.-

-I will always stay.-

Soren slips from the room as Mia pulls back and I brush wayward strands of hair from her temples, smoothing them back against her plaits and scanning her face, looking for the injuries that I know were there.

"You're alright?"

She nods and smiles. "Copeland healed me. It was just a small cut here," she touches just above her temple, "but he said head wounds like that bleed a lot, even when they aren't bad, and my arm was barely a scratch, really." I exhale in relief. "He healed your hands too," she adds quietly. I blink and look down to find my hands looking perfectly ordinary, but I remember how bad they'd been, bloody and mangled. But it didn't matter. All I cared about was getting to Mia. To everyone trapped, of course, but mostly her. I didn't break my promise to Odessa.

Blackheart clears his throat from the doorway.

Mia glances at him and then turns back to me, whispering, "He's been worried and waiting for you to wake up. He's been pretending he hasn't, but I know he has." I try to suppress my smile and she grins before hugging me again and hopping off of the bed. Blackheart smiles at her as she walks back, patting her braids affectionately as she passes.

Once she's gone, he watches me from the doorway, arms crossed. I worry for a moment what I must look like after everything that happened and then apparently sleeping for Makers knows how long like the dead, but he isn't looking at me as if I look like a horrific mess. He's looking at me like...he's never seen me before. I swallow hard.

"You refused to stop digging," he finally says quietly. I hike a shoulder, not sure what to say to that. "You kept digging, despite your fingers bleeding, your nails splintered or gone, one bone actually broken for fuck's sake." I wince at that, not having realized it had been that bad. He continues on, "Despite being so exhausted you could barely stand. You kept digging to save those people, to save that girl."

"Of course I did," I say, my voice coming out smaller than I intend.

"And yet, you claim that you aren't to be trusted, that if I stopped blocking your Gift, that you would use it to hurt anyone in your path."

My heart starts to beat loudly in my ears. *No, no, no. Don't start pulling at this thread, please...*I stare back, trying to make my eyes cold and hard, but I don't think I succeed, because...fuck me, when I look at him, I don't want to be anything like Tesni. I want to be *me*. I want him to see *me*.

"I believe that I can trust you, Tess." I can feel it the moment he stops blocking my Gift. It's like a soft pressure against my chest disappears, my power surging forward now that it senses its freedom. My palms go cold, the icy feeling flowing down to my fingertips, ready to be used. "Show me."

"I..." I don't know what to say. I don't know what to do. What would happen if he found out the truth now? Something between us has shifted, I know that much, but is it enough for him to overlook the fact that I'm not Tesni? That I'm not useful to him and his King? At least not in the way they initially intended.

"What did they do to you?" he says when I can't respond, a

strange anger in his voice that I don't quite understand. I know the anger isn't directed at me, it's directed at whatever *they* he means. But what the hells is he talking about?

"What do you mean? Who?" I ask honestly, more confused than I've been in weeks. He studies me, seeming to search to the depths of my soul for...something, though I don't know what. He finally shakes his head and exhales.

"Copeland healed you?" he asks, though I know he already knows perfectly well the old man fixed all of my injuries. *Changing the subject.* I want to push, needing to know what he was talking about, but I don't, not now. Instead, I glance down at my hands once more, moving and flexing my fingers.

"Yes, I'm fine."

"Good. King Ryker has requested that you accompany me to his palace for dinner this evening." I blink at that.

"Me? Why?" I ask, incredulous. Blackheart's lips curl into that crooked smile that I'm finding myself becoming addicted to.

Instead of answering he says, "At least you have cause to wear one of your fancy dresses again, Red."

TITHMOORE'S PALACE IS STUNNING, THOUGH COMPLETELY DIFFERENT THAN the only other castle I've ever been in. Where Castle Lyanna is all white and gold, Tithmoore is decorated with deep, rich woods, gemstones, and understated finery. It feels more regal to me, more refined somehow, like King Barony needed to *prove* his wealth and position, whereas King Ryker knows he doesn't need to go to such lengths.

The man himself exudes royalty, but again, in a calm, understated way that makes me feel at home despite being in the presence of a king. He's waiting for us in the royal banquet hall, but I barely notice him at first as I take in the room. Lanterns burn at intervals along the brocaded walls and in the huge chandeliers hanging above our heads, making the gemstones shine and glitter. I crane my head up, up, up and find the soaring ceiling painted with beautiful swirling stars, looking so much like the night sky that for a moment, I wonder if there's truly a ceiling there at all. I smile, memories of Tobias pointing them out to me all those years ago coming back again. *The Hunter. The Lost Queen. The Bull and the Lamb.*

I notice Blackheart watching me and I pull my gaze away from the ceiling. I clear my throat lightly and hike a bare shoulder.

"I like the stars," I whisper tersely. "What of it?"

"Nothing at all," he says, a smile pulling at his lips. His gaze drifts slowly down my throat, across my bare shoulders, lower...A shiver runs up my spin, heat pooling in my belly and my pulse racing, just as it had when I first saw him waiting for me at the bottom of the stairs at the inn. He's in some sort of dress uniform that I've never seen before and holy fucking Makers does he wear it well. It's tailored to hug his massive frame, black, the same as his usual attire, but this uniform has delicate silver stitching along the cuffs and neck. A thick black cloak hangs down his back, pinned over one shoulder with a silver broach in the shape of an ice dragon's snarling mead. His hair is slicked back and more tamed than I've ever seen it, and he's trimmed his beard and mustache close to his face. He looks...devastating.

So devastating, in fact, that I'd completely missed the final step because of my gawking and nearly broken my ankle. Copeland had to be called in for an emergency—and very embarrassing—quick healing job. I'm fairly certain Blackheart was completely aware of the reason for my misstep, but neither of us acknowledged it. At least not yet. I get the feeling he's holding on to it to toss in my face at an opportune time in the future.

But I wasn't the only one caught staring. More than once in the carriage that King Ryker sent for us, Blackheart couldn't seem to keep his eyes from roving over every inch of me. The dress I'd chosen is a deep forest green, sleeveless, with the bodice cut to resemble the top of a heart, and from the way Blackheart's eyes kept darting downward, he was a fan of the workmanship. We rode in silence, but I was aware of every small movement he made, every inhale, every hitch of my own breath when I let my imagination run wild with all of the possibilities...

It was the longest ride of my life, though it only lasted less than twenty minutes, and by the time we arrived, my fingers were sore from clenching them so tightly in my lap in an effort to stop myself from reaching for him in the dimness, from climbing into his lap and wrapping my arms around his neck, from pressing my lips to his in the way I've been dreaming of far too often. I've been dreaming of far more than that, and my cheeks heat as our eyes meet and hold once again, remembering all of the wicked things we've done inside my mind. His throat bobs as he swallows and my heart starts to race.

"Welcome," King Ryker says with a warm smile, breaking the tension building between Blackheart and me. I quickly shake myself and shift into a deep curtsey, bowing my head, and silently tell Soren to behave himself.

-I will not eat this king, don't worry. He is known throughout the animal clans across the north for being exceedingly kindhearted, especially to my kind.-

I straighten and glance sidelong at the cat. He's sitting just behind me on my right, making it perfectly clear that he's there to protect me.

-What does that mean? Especially your kind?-

-There was an epidemic of poachers hunting the frost cats in this area. Many, many of my kind were taken or killed. King Ryker put a violent end to them. He saved many of us and even gave us lands protected within his kingdom to live and recover.-

I look at Ryker with a new respect. He beams at the cat and Soren dips his head in respect. The two stare at each other and I would swear they were having a conversation.

"Magnificent," Ryker says in soft exaltation. "Absolutely magnificent. He is your familiar, yes?"

"Yes, your majesty."

"It's been so long…" He shakes his head, smiling, as if a familiar returning is the best news he's ever heard. "May I?" he asks, gesturing towards me and I don't know if he's asking me or Soren, but we both incline our heads in acquiescence. I swear I can feel Blackheart laughing lightly beside me but I don't dare take my eyes from the king as he steps forward. I watch in shock as he dips into a low bow and kisses the back of my hand. I blink, wondering if Ryker is a bit mad, like Dorian. That's a sign of the utmost respect across all of Hypathia. *But why…*

"Thank you," Ryker says, straightening again and clasping both of my hands in his. My brow furrows. "I was told what you did at the mountain—all of you," he adds, looking to Soren and Blackheart in turn, "but especially you, my dear. I heard that you dug into those rocks with your bare hands until your fingers bled, and even then, you *kept* digging. You even screamed at this one when he tried to stop you," he adds with a smile and a twinkling in his golden eyes as he glances to Blackheart.

Heat creeps up my neck and into my cheeks.

"Oh. Well, I…" Have no fucking idea what to say to that.

He smiles wider, skin crinkling beside his eyes. He's what I imagine a loving grandfather to be like, though of course I have no personal frame of reference for such a thing and he's too young for that. An uncle then, perhaps. Regardless, I feel instantly comfortable and safe with him, his warmth seeming to wrap around me like a soothing hug.

"I know you were mostly fighting to save the young girl, but I know what you said, about helping *everyone* trapped within, good people trying to feed their families. I know that you said you wouldn't leave any of them trapped, my people included." I don't know what to say to that, so I remain silent while he studies me. "You are much different than your reputation would have me believe," he finally says and my heart thuds against my chest. Of course Tesni never would have helped those people, not unless it served her own purposes somehow or unless they could pay some outrageous sum. Even then, if she couldn't use her Gift to help, she most certainly wouldn't have lifted a finger.

I sigh. I wouldn't change what I did, but I'm not helping myself by continually slipping in this ruse. It was one thing to stop trying so hard to be a raging cunt around Odessa and the others, but I should probably do better about keeping up appearances for the rest of the world.

Blackheart is still as a statue beside me, watching the exchange and thinking Makers know what.

"I am in your debt, Tesni de Moreau. Should you ever need my assistance, you must only ask." My eyes fly wide at that. A debt owed from a king is quite a thing. He winks at me, reading my stunned reaction easily, and I huff out a laugh. He turns to Blackheart. "I have thought long and hard on where Tithmoore will fit in this war. I am afraid that remaining neutral isn't an option any longer after reports I'm hearing from my eyes and ears throughout the continent."

My stomach twists at that, wondering what types of reports he's hearing. Is Helios still keeping out of things? Are Math and Cece alright? Makers I need to get to them, to make sure they're safe, to tell them to run, even without me.

"I've been around for a while. I know how bad things used to be and though I have great respect for the changes that have been made, I remained unsure." What in the hells is he talking about? "This woman has swayed me." Ryker glances back to me but continues speaking to Blackheart. "She has shown bravery and self-lessness and unyielding loyalty, despite the circumstances in which she finds herself." He turns back to Blackheart. "If she can trust in you, then so can I."

Blackheart swallows but otherwise remains completely still. I glance between the two men. Is Ryker saying what I think he's saying? He extends his hand to Blackheart.

"Tithmoore stands with Duskthorne." I inhale sharply, and Blackheart extends his own hand. The two men clasp each other's wrists. "I'll come to Duskthorne soon to work out the details with...

Dorian," he says, smiling at Blackheart in a way that makes the Commander grin back. A real smile unlike I've seen in all these weeks. A smile that transforms him into a different person, one that makes it hard to breathe he's so handsome. A smile that shreds through any last line of defense I've deluded myself into thinking I still had.

Blackheart cuts his eyes to me and I reach up to twirl my hair, suddenly nervous that he could read my thoughts too easily, only to remember that I've pinned it up loosely at my nape. I curl my fingers into a fist and clear my throat lightly, giving him a bland smile back. He narrows his eyes but looks back to Ryker, the two of them sharing another look that's most definitely familiar. These two obviously have a history of some sort, sharing in small jokes that only the two of them understand. Soren chuckles inside my mind and I narrow my eyes at him.

-*What do you know that I don't?*-

-*A great many things. I could make a list, but I fear you will grow very old before I am finished.*-

-*Have I ever told you that you're an ass?*-

-*I love you too.*-

I can't help but smile and Soren huffs out a quiet breath.

"Now," Ryker says, smiling widely and gesturing towards the enormous dining table, "let us eat and celebrate the joining of our kingdoms in this Makers' forsaken war."

We spend the next several hours eating course after course of some of the most delicious food I've ever had. Elk and pheasant and several types of fish caught off Tithmoore's coast that aren't found in the southern seas, stews and spiced spreads for the various types of bread, roasted vegetables that put even Cookie's to shame. Something I don't want to look too closely at is brought in on an enormous silver platter for Soren and he practically dives on it as soon as they set it down. Apparently it's some sort of boar that is only found within Tithmoore's borders and it's delicious, according to the cat.

Ryker asks me many questions, but thankfully many of them I

don't even have to really lie about to answer. He asks about my favorite foods and hobbies, what kinds of things I've seen and experienced since coming to be with Blackheart's army, about Soren, and though I have to choose my words carefully, I find I can give pieces of the truth about myself to this kind man, that I *want* to give him pieces.

Blackheart watches all the while, seeming to be dying for each new kernel of information, begging silently for Ryker to keep asking me questions. When we finally depart, I'm full to bursting and feel as if I've made a great friend in King Ryker. Who would have ever guessed that the outcast Gifted who's been hiding for most of her life would be friends with a king? I smile to myself at the thought as the carriage pulls to a stop in front of the inn, surprising me. I'd been so lost in thought, I'd barely noticed the ride at all.

"What are you smiling about?" Blackheart asks softly. It's the first he's spoken since leaving the palace.

"I'm just...happy," I tell him, honestly. "I had a wonderful time tonight. It was nice."

"It was," he agrees, shifting forward and resting his elbows on his knees. "This alliance is crucial for our cause. And it wouldn't have happened without you."

"I didn't do anything," I say, though I wonder suddenly about why Ryker would possibly ally with a monster like Dorian when he seems like such a good person. There has to be some explanation, something I'm missing, I'm sure of it. But the worry fades away when I find myself staring at Blackheart, thoughts veering very, very far from alliances and wars and kings.

"You did," he insists, voice low and sending a warm shiver down my spine. "What I don't understand is why." He studies me in that intense way of his, his eyes looking nearly black in the low lantern light within the carriage. My heart speeds, my pulse thrumming like the wings of a hummingbird at my throat in what should be fear of him finding out the truth. But it's nothing to do with that at all. It's only this man, the way he's looking at me, the strength of the things I'm feeling...

But a moment later, we lurch to a stop. He blinks and shakes himself before exiting the carriage without another word. I let out a long, quiet exhale before moving to exit. I step up to the edge of the doorway, ready to maneuver myself down in this ballgown, but I gasp in surprise when Blackheart's big hands settle on my waist. My hands fly to his shoulders to steady myself as he lifts me down, setting me to the ground, but not immediately letting go or stepping away. My heart thunders and my breath hitches as his thumbs move in lazy circles over my hips, somehow scorching me through the thick fabric of the dress. Neither of us moves away. *Stupid, stupid, stupid...*

My hands slide slowly from his shoulders down his chest, my right index finger tracing over the dragon broach.

"Who are you, Tess?" he asks quietly, reaching one hand up to brush a strand of hair from my temple, his knuckles skimming my cheek ever so gently. My lips part on a soft inhale and I curl my fingers into the front of his shirt, desperate to pull him closer, to never let go again. The forcefulness of the thought startles me, but I don't care. It feels right. It feels fated. Just as Soren has always been in my path, so has Blackheart, I know it somehow, deep in my bones.

"What's your name?" I ask quietly, eyes darting to his lips. "Your real name, I mean. Surely your mother didn't name you Blackheart, that seems very rude..."

He chuckles low. "Killian," he says, voice rough, leaning down towards me. "Call me Killian." The words have a strange edge to them, like he's been desperate to say them for so long.

"Killian," I whisper as his face nears mine. He sucks in a sharp breath, his fingers clenching on my waist as he tugs me forward so that our bodies are even closer. He seems to shudder at the sound of his name on my lips, and right now, I need far more than only that on them. I need his mouth on mine, his lips and tongue and teeth...

"Tess!" a voice cries out from a few yards down the lane. Blackheart—Killian—and I leap apart, and he curses low, taking another step away and straightening. "Tess!" Odessa cries again, sprinting forward.

"Oh, I didn't know you were back! How—*oof!*" I grunt as she throws herself at me, nearly knocking me over. She wraps her arms around me and squeezes so hard that it's a little hard to breathe.

"They told me," she says, nearly sobbing, "they told me what you did for Mia, that you wouldn't stop, that you wouldn't leave her. That you dug at the rocks until you were *bloody*." She pulls away and cradles my face so that I have to meet her intense gaze. The lanterns above us glint off the tears in her eyes. "*Thank you*," she says so seriously that I have to swallow several times to get around the sudden lump in my throat. "Thank you, Tess. Thank you for being there for her when I couldn't be. Thank you for not giving up on her. I'll never be able to repay you for this."

"It's nothing," I tell her, gripping her wrists. "Truly. The little brat is annoyingly likable. I couldn't leave her stranded in a cave." I smile at her and she huffs out a choked laugh, sniffling a bit.

"She really is, isn't she?"

"*So* frustrating."

I look her over. She's still in her fighting leathers, her hair in her warrior braids. I can't tell in the dim lantern light if the dark smudges on her face and neck are dirt or blood. "Are you alright? Did everything go ok?"

"I'm fine," she says, waving my worry away. "We got in a tiny tussle with a group of their own scouts, but we came out on top in the end. We lost Charles," she says solemnly and though I didn't know him well, barely exchanged a few words over these past few weeks, the loss of a Gifted hits me in a strange way. We are so rare, that it feels like another light extinguished in the darkness, only a few candles still burning.

"But I don't want to talk about that right now," she says, wiping at her eyes, and I can tell that she needs time to process the loss and whatever she went through. But I know that she knows that I'll be there to talk about it if she wishes when she's ready. Whatever last bit of a wall that had been between us has crumbled to dust now, and no matter how stupid it may be given the uncertainty of my future, I've gained a true friend in Odessa. "I want to talk about this fantastic dress." She steps back to admire the garment. "Why are you in this? Bored of trousers already?"

"Oh, we were invited to dine with the King," I say with mock haughtiness, straightening and looking down my nose at her—which is quite a feat since she stands a head taller than I do.

"We?" she asks, pierced brow quirking. I turn to look at Killian only to realize that he's gone.

"Oh. Um, Blackheart was with me, but he seems to have disappeared. Soren went too. I tried to put a jaunty little hat on him, but he refused." Odessa laughs, pulling me into another hug.

"I need to hear all about this."

"Well come on, then. Mia is in my room anyway."

I glance over my shoulder again as we head inside, as if Killian might appear, but he's nowhere to be found. What would have happened had Odessa not interrupted? Was it a good thing that she did? Is exploring this connection with him the right choice given our strange circumstances? After all, soon enough he'll hand me over to a monster. How can I want to be with the man who plans to do that??

I can't. I shouldn't.

But great fucking Makers, I do.

CHAPTER
FOURTEEN

I wait nervously in a parlor in the palace, alternating between standing and sitting on one of the oversized armchairs and standing again to pace. I don't know if this is a good idea, but I know this is the only chance I have, so I must take it. If the roles were reversed, I would be going out of my mind with worry.

"Another visit so soon," King Ryker says as he enters the room, smiling warmly. The early morning sun filtering through the oversized windows brings out light streaks of red in his dark hair. "The Makers must be smiling upon me." I curtsy low and return his smile when I rise. "To what do I owe this pleasant surprise?"

I take a deep breath and shift my shoulders back. "You said that you owed me a debt. I've come to collect." His brows rise.

"So soon?" he asks, clearly amused.

"Yes." I nod, but add quickly, "If that's alright, of course."

"What can I do for you, my dear?"

I take a deep breath and hold out the envelope. I found a stationary set in the bottom of Tesni's trunk and though I refused to use the Lyannian seal, throwing that out into the snow behind my tent, I was grateful for not having to ask anyone for writing supplies.

King Ryker eyes the envelope, clearly confused, but waits patiently for me to explain.

"I need this letter to find its way to Helios, but..." I lick my dry lips and try to swallow past the desert that's taken up residence in my throat. "But I can't explain why. I can promise that it's nothing having to do with Lyanna or the war or anything about my location or ransom. It's...I just need someone to know that I'm alright, that's all. I wish I could explain more, but I can't, not now. Maybe one day. I'd like that, actually, to explain everything to you. If you'd like of course. You're a king and have far more important matters to worry about than me and my confusing, somewhat pathetic story, annnnd I'm rambling, I'm sorry." I squeeze my eyes shut for a moment and breathe. When I open them again, I find Ryker studying me, but he doesn't look suspicious or angry, merely interested and amused.

"Please, it's important. Not to Hypathia or the war or the Alliance, but to me."

King Ryker reaches out and takes the letter, patting my hand gently as he does.

"Then it is important to me as well." I exhale in relief, the knot of tension in my stomach unfurling like the petals of a flower opening for the sun. "I will make sure that it finds its home and will do so with the utmost discretion."

"Thank you, Your Majesty."

He eyes me for another moment. "Is this truly what you would ask for my debt? To send a letter?"

"Yes," I say, brow furrowing. "Why?"

"You could ask for nearly anything. I am one of the most powerful royals in all of Hypathia, after all. You could have asked for riches beyond imagining or your freedom from Dorian." I start at that, the thought never having crossed my mind. "But you asked for a letter to be sent, not for any personal gain, but merely to put someone else's mind at ease."

"I...I suppose that's right," I say, my cheeks heating. I don't want to examine too closely why I didn't think to ask him to save me from Dorian...by taking me away from Killian.

"Hmm," is all the old man says, amusement and calculation sparking in his golden eyes. "You know," he says very quietly, very carefully, "I heard a secret many years ago."

"A secret?" I ask, brow furrowing.

"That Barony didn't just have *one* Gifted, but a set. Twins."

I snap my eyes to his, my entire body going cold in a way that has nothing to do with my Gift. *He knows. Oh, great fucking Makers, he knows.* I try to tell myself to calm. He only knows that there were twins, not that I'm not Tesni. *Breathe, Thea. Breathe.*

-*Thea...*-

-*I'm alright*- I assure Soren. I don't need the frost cat ripping through Ryker's guards or scaling the palace to reach me for no reason. -*I'm fine*-

My Gift rises, readying to fight my way out if needed, but I find it blocked. Killian must be near the palace.

"It was a secret that King Morthan knew—but after his untimely death nearly fifteen years ago, I believe I may be the only other holder of such knowledge." Fifteen years ago. When I escaped. My mind races: did Barony have Morthan *killed* after I fled? It would make sense, I realize, pieces falling into place. Barony wouldn't risk the knowledge of a second Gifted escaping his grasp leaking throughout Hypathia. He would look weak and that is something Barony would not tolerate. So that's how Ruby took the throne. I'd been too worried about staying alive in those days to concern myself much with empire business, but I did hear about a new Queen of Enola along the way, a vicious woman—with ties to Barony. Makers, they'd probably plotted it together. After all, Enola was considered a weaker kingdom years ago. Now, it's powerful and feared. My head throbs as I try to think through everything, but all of that must wait. The most important thing right now is that Ryker might know the truth...

It takes me a moment to find my voice. "And how did you hear the secret of my sister, Your Highness?" He leans towards me and speaks quietly.

"I have a Gift of my own, one that allows me to speak with animal kind. They bring me secrets from all across the empire." My eyes fly wide. Ryker is a Gifted? He presses a finger to his lips, letting me know that we're sharing many secrets between us this day. Then I remember dinner the previous night, when it had seemed as if he and Soren were speaking. They fucking *had* been.

-*You couldn't have told me??*- I hiss at the damned feline.

-*His was not my secret to tell.*-

I grit my teeth but can't really blame Soren for keeping Ryker's secret.

"And...and do you know what happened to my sister?"

"She died, of course." He gives me a knowing look, and though I should be terrified in the knowledge that he knows this forbidden, dangerous truth, I only feel...safety. Relief. Suddenly not so alone in the world.

"Yes, it was very tragic," I reply, watching him closely for any signs that I'm about to be betrayed yet again, though I can't imagine it. Then again, I never would have thought Tesni capable of it all those years ago either...

"Exceedingly so. I daresay that my intuition tells me that if the sister had had the chance to live, she would have become a remarkable woman." My nose burns as tears well, making my vision blurry. He smiles again, saying so much with that gesture, with these layered words. I clear my throat.

"Do you think King Dorian could possibly know this secret?"

"I don't believe so," he assures me. "Though...well, he is a mysterious man." I tilt my head at that, wondering what he could mean. He gives me a smile that says he'll say no more, but will await the day I figure it out on my own. "Well now, I'm sure you are anxious to get back and prepare for the journey."

The army has been resupplied to bursting, Tithmoore's citizens hefting as many gifts as they could spare at us in thanks for our assistance with the harvest as well as after the cave-in. We start the final leg of this journey to Duskthorne in the morning and while I'm still afraid of what might happen, I can't deny that I'm not ready to part from Odessa and Mia…and Killian. I'm nowhere near ready for that, and I might be more terrified of what that might mean than I am of Dorian. I am well aware of how ridiculous and stupid it is, but it's the truth.

"I will take care of your letter, you have my word. Speaking of letters, I have a gift for you. Wait right here." He strides out of the room and I wait, wondering what this gift might be. He comes back in and I nearly gasp: a stunning silver raven sits on his arm.

"This is Alexi. He'll deliver messages to me—discretely and directly—should you wish to write." The bird seems to preen, puffing out his chest and waiting for Ryker to stroke his feathers. I reach forward tentatively, stopping before I reach the bird in question. Alexi spreads his wings for a moment, as if to show them off, and then folds them against his body as he lowers his head in invitation. I stoke my fingers gently along his head and beak and he makes a soft cooing sound, making Ryker smile.

"He's beautiful."

"He likes you," Ryker says, rubbing his knuckles down the bird's back. Alexi turns to give the king a playful peck before flying off with a soft caw. "Alexi will always be near, though you may not always see him. Soren will be able to reach him any time you wish for his assistance."

I furrow my brow. "May I ask you something?" He nods. "Why are you being so kind to me?"

"Because you deserve it," he says simply. Ryker has always been rumored to be a great king, a beloved ruler who cares deeply for his people, but to see the proof before my eyes, his care extending to a stranger, is truly something. So…why would he ally with Duskthorne, with a monster like Dorian? I frown inwardly, trying to make sense of it all, but knowing I can't possibly. There are far too many things at work that I don't understand, that I have no knowledge of, things that must make sense to Ryker. One thing I can tell about him above all else is that he will do whatever he must to protect his people and ensure their safety. I shake myself, deciding to think on it on the many days of travel we have ahead of us.

"Safe travels, my dear...Tess. All will be well, I promise." It seems as if he's trying to tell me something, though I have no idea what.

"Thank you. For everything." He kisses the back of my hand again and I huff out a laugh, shaking my head before I walk towards the door. I stop just before stepping through and turn back to him. This is a terribly stupid idea, but the need is so demanding inside my mind that I know I can't fight it. I don't really *want* to fight it, if I'm being honest with myself. I take a quick, settling breath.

"Thea," I say, so softly I worry that he can't hear me, but he blinks in surprise and I know he's heard it. The word that I haven't been able to say in almost six weeks now. The word that could be my downfall. The word I need someone else in this world to hear, in case things go badly, despite Ryker's promise that everything will turn out ok. I wait, wondering if I've made a terrible mistake, but then the king's lips curl upward in a soft, genial smile.

"It is lovely to meet you, Thea," he says quietly, inclining his head. I nod in return and leave, my heart thundering in my chest and my soul filled with joy—and hope.

-THERE IS A BIRD FOLLOWING US,- SOREN GRUMBLES, ICY BLUE EYES narrowed at the sky as we begin the slow, painstaking trip away from Tithmoore.

-*His name is Alexi. He's a gift from Ryker.*-

-*I'm aware of his name. He is very pompous. I'm going to eat him.*-

"You will do no such thing," I tell the cat, narrowing my eyes at him from atop Zaro.

-*I make no promises.*- He does a half-chuff, half-growl of annoyance and streaks off ahead of us, fading from view completely in the snow almost immediately.

"He really is terrifyingly good at disappearing," Killian notes, riding up beside me in Soren's wake. I huff out a laugh.

"That he is."

I glance at him. We haven't had much interaction over the last week since leaving Tithmoore, always seeming to be pulled in opposite directions, but every time our eyes meet, that connection snaps between us the same as it did that night after our dinner with Ryker. My pulse starts racing now, my fingers itching to make their way over his body, to learn every inch of him, trace every tattoo, memorize each dip and hollow. His gaze drifts to my lips and he wets his own, the sight sending a jolt through my core and making my toes curl. He clears his throat and pulls his gaze away.

I know it's madness to want him. I'm his king's prisoner. I'm a bargaining chip at best, and a new member of his collection to be tortured and used at worst. There's no future in which Killian and I can be together, but that doesn't stop me from wanting it. For the first time in my life, I want it so badly I could scream.

"How long do we have?" I ask. I mean to ask how long the journey will be, but he seems to understand my true meaning: how long do we have before all of this is gone, before our time together comes to an end.

"A few weeks." His jaw clenches and I nod.

"Alright then."

He leans in towards me and adds quietly, "It would go faster if you wished to use your Gift to rid us of this snow...but it's quite a shame that the bastard leader of this army continues to block you." He flashes that crooked smirk and I try and fail to hide my answering smile.

"Such a shame. He truly is a bastard. Weeks it is then," I say, mockingly resigned. He huffs out a laugh and then I ask the question that's been burning in the back of my mind. "What did you mean when you asked me what they did to me? Who is *they*? And what would they have done?"

His amusement vanishes then and he studies me for what feels like hours. What he's trying to find, I have no idea, but whatever this is about, I know it's very important to him.

"You truly have no idea?" he finally asks, still that edge of incredulity to his voice. I shake my head and shrug, and he exhales. "Come to my tent tonight after dinner and we can discuss it."

I blink but nod. "Alright."

His gaze roves over my body and he looks like he wants to say more, perhaps something about clothing being optional at this meeting, but he only gives me a sharp nod and rides off. I let out a long, slow breath, the air coming out in a puffy white cloud in front of me. How much colder will it be as we move farther into the true northlands?

I wonder what Duskthorne will be like as I follow the line of our group onward. Not Dorian and the horrors to be found, but the kingdom itself. I've heard that it's surrounded completely by a ring of mountains, the only passage is carved directly through the stone, miles and miles of it. Dorian's palace is built directly into the side of the highest peak overlooking the entire kingdom, the famed Duskthorne forge and their great temple on the peaks on either side. It's hard to imagine, but I'll admit it sounds like it could be magnificent to behold. I try not to think about what the dungeons within might be like, the cages where the Gifteds are kept. Now that I've been bonded with Soren, I don't believe I'll be used or abused like the others—Killian spoke of familiars as things to be revered and honored and respected. I can only hope that his king believes the same.

If he doesn't...well, I'd like to see them try to cage me or Soren. Though I'm still uneasy about what's to come, I no longer fear Dorian the way I once did. My power is far stronger with Soren by my side, and he is stronger than any normal frost cat now. The two of us could cut quite a path of blood and carnage through Duskthorne should we need to.

-With pleasure, should they try to touch you,- the cat purrs menacingly in my mind.

-Same, should anyone try to touch you.-

The thought of Soren being hurt or threatened makes my Gift roil inside me, ice spearing through my veins. I see Killian up ahead tilt his head and turn back to look at me over his shoulder. He must have felt the surge. He purses his lips but turns away again quickly to speak to one of the men on his right.

-But you needn't fear anything in Duskthorne.-

I snort. *-Just because I don't think we'll be caged or tortured doesn't mean there's nothing to fear.-*

This plan could still go terribly wrong.

-One day you will learn that I am always right, Thea.-

-And so humble too.-

He laughs lightly in my mind and then fades away from the pathway between us. We ride a few hours more before making camp for the night. Murmurs ripple through the camp about why I still refuse to help, or why Blackheart refuses to *let* me help, depending on who you're talking to, but I don't have a good answer, so I don't respond to any of them.

"Come on," Kendall begs as we huddle around a fire. "Can't you just show us a tiny little flame? Just one spark?"

I shake my head as Jonathan slaps Kendall in the back of his head —his favorite pastime, it seems. I'd be surprised if Kendall doesn't have a permanent bruise there.

"She's blocked, you idiot. She can't do anything with the likes of Blackheart holding her power back. He's one of the most powerful Gifteds in all of history."

"But she's bonded now, I bet she's even stronger than he is. Have you tried to push past him?"

"I can't," I say, though it's not complete truth. I think I *could* push past him, if I really tried. Or perhaps it's more that he'd let me. I can't be sure, really, without outright asking him, which of course I won't do. He still seems to believe that my power—Tesni's power—has waned over the years from so much use. It's possible, I suppose. Gifts like ours are rare, so it's not out of the realm of possibilities that they could fade over time more than typical Gifts that aren't as strong. I shake the thoughts away. There's entirely too much that I don't know about myself, my people. Perhaps I'd know more if I hadn't been in hiding all this time, but I think the more likely answer is that Gifteds aren't able to speak freely out of fear of being enslaved. *Of course* we don't have much knowledge of each other, of how our power truly works, our lifespans or how our Gifts might age with us.

"Well, it would come in bloody handy right about now," Lucinda grumbles. "I haven't missed the winter, and my mam says that the ancient texts claim this is going to be one of the worst ones in history. This war may be put on hold if no one can make it out of Duskthorne after the first snow."

"Can that truly happen?" I ask. "I mean, do you really get stranded there?" I hadn't really thought about it, but it makes sense if there really is only one passageway in and out of the kingdom.

"It's happened once or twice in the past, though we have everything we need there," Odessa tells me, leaning into Tristan's side as he puts an arm around her. I haven't outright asked, but the two of them are most definitely together. They share these tender moments and I've seen her sneaking in or out of his tent a time or two when Mia is asleep or otherwise occupied.

"But...if I'm to be ransomed and returned..."

Odessa's face falls slightly, as if she'd forgotten that I'm not meant to stay with them forever. She clears her throat lightly.

"We have months before true winter arrives. I'm sure they will negotiate your price and you'll be returned safely to Barony and his friends before then, not to worry."

I want to tell her that I don't want that to happen. It's partly true. I don't want to leave her or Mia. I don't want to leave Killian. I've somehow managed to find another small family, like I did in Math and Cece, and the thought of never seeing them again makes my chest ache. But I can't remain. I can't pretend to be my sister forever, and I still don't know what will happen once the ransom goes missing along with Hastings. Will Barony simply send another? Will Dorian demand an even higher price when he learns that the first payment was lost? Will he decide that a fire bitch from his enemies is too valuable to part with, no matter how much Barony is willing to pay?

I don't know what I'll do if that's the case, but I'll deal with it when it comes. Cece always says that we don't need to worry about the curve in the path until we reach it. So, I'll leave the curve be for now and find a way to navigate it when I arrive.

I tell everyone goodnight, trying to sound casual but Odessa gives me a suspicious look.

"A little early for bed, isn't it?" she asks pointedly. She has no idea that I'm to meet Killian, but I think she suspects a good many things where he and I are concerned. She's far too perceptive for my liking.

"I trekked through miles and miles on the back of a smelly oaf of a horse today. I want to bathe and rest, thank you very much." I suppress a smile and one of her own curls her lips.

"My mistake, princess. Goodnight." The others take no real notice of our exchange, arguing over who cheated during the last round of cards, and call out distracted goodbyes as I leave. Odessa mouths *details later* and I roll my eyes but smile. I've decided that she must not be fucking Killian if she's so keen on he and I doing...whatever it is we might be moving towards. No, the more I've watched them, the more I've found the relationship to be that of best friends or siblings—normal ones, not like my bitch of a twin and me.

I grab a fresh tunic and trousers from my tent and take my turn in one of the bathing tents. The water is frigid, but I take my time, scrubbing away all of the grime from the road and lathering every inch of my skin with the soap Odessa got for me from one of the markets in Tithmoore. She claimed it was because she couldn't stand the honeyrose scent I'd been using, but I know that really it was a small token of thanks for Mia despite me telling her over and over that no thanks was necessary. It's made from the daska flower with a petal suspended within the clear bar, the shimmering golden stars on full display, and smells absolutely divine.

I finally decide I'm as clean as I can possibly be and dry off, putting on my trousers and tunic. It's a deep midnight blue and cut into a low v between my breasts, thin laces crisscrossing the delicate skin there. I chose it for…no reason at all, of course. I make my way back to my tent, glancing towards Killian's but not seeing him. I tell myself to calm down, I'll see him soon enough, and head inside. I brush out my hair and dig through the trunk until I find the ruby-lined hair clip. A loud caw rings out from the other side of the tent. I yelp and spin to find Alexi standing on my cot, tilting his head at me as the clip sails past him and hits the side of the tent with a muted thud.

"You scared the shit out of me, you little…" He caws again, eyes narrowing, and I stop the admittedly unflattering words wanting to pour from my mouth. "Hello, Alexi," I say instead and the bird ruffles his feathers, cawing in a more affectionate way now. I walk over and rub my fingers gently down his head. "What are you…oh!" I realize then that there's a letter attached to his leg. I quickly untie the string and rip open the envelope.

Tears immediately spring to my eyes and I cover my mouth with my hand to stop the sob from escaping. Cece's handwriting is as familiar to me as my own and I run my fingertip along the neat, looping letters as if I can somehow touch my friend's hand through the ink.

"Cece," I whisper.

I swallow hard and wipe away the tears so I can read what she's written.

T–
I'm so glad you're alright. We were so worried, but

knew that you would find a way to keep fighting, no matter the situation. You always do. You are stronger than you'll ever know.

I have always wanted to travel to the north. If now would be a good time to do so, please do write back soon.

We love you and we miss you.

-C & M

I wipe away more tears, reading her words over and over. She's kept things vague just in case someone else was to read this letter, but I know what she's truly saying: they'll journey to Duskthorne to rescue me if I ask them to. I huff out a laugh, imagining Cece riding in like an avenging angel to fight all of Dorian's army herself if it means saving me, Math at her side as he always is.

I quickly scrawl out a response, knowing that Alexi will get it back to Ryker who will take care of getting it to Helios once more. I tell her not to worry, that I'm alright and that true winter is not a good time for a holiday in the north. I promise to write soon, remind them how much I love them, and tell her to be careful and vigilant. I still worry that Tesni might target them in this insane ploy of hers, but there's also the threat of war now. I can't tell her as much as I'd like right now, but hopefully soon. I debate on telling her to run to the islands, but hold off for now, hoping that somehow, the war will stop before it reaches them. Plus, if I tell her to run, she'll know there's danger and will immediately come for me instead. I hadn't revealed everything in my first letter, but they know that I'm hiding in plain sight in the middle of a scheme of Tesni's. I told them we were headed for Tithmoore, though I was already there when I wrote the letter, because I knew if I mentioned Duskthorne they'd both already be on their way.

So, as far as they know, I'm as safe as I can be for now and that's what matters. Besides, it isn't a lie. I *am* safe for now.

I write a second note to Ryker, thanking him a thousand times and promising to write him more soon as well. I seal both letters and tie them to Alexi's leg. He's much larger than a usual raven, even larger than Barony's messenger birds, and can handle the weight of the letters with ease. I give him a few pieces of bread left over from my dinner before he takes off.

Feeling almost giddy, I race to Killian's tent—only to find him walking out, in his full armor. My heart plummets.

"What's going on? What's wrong?"

"Nothing to worry about," he tells me, flashing a smile. "I'm sorry for missing our...appointment." He frowns at the word and I huff out a laugh, despite the worry winding its way through my veins like an angry serpent. I glance back to the rest of the camp and most of the soldiers are milling around, eating or laughing near the fires, not preparing for battle. So it must be a small group going. If it's that small, surely they'll be fine...right?

"I'll be back soon."

"Be safe," I tell him and he nods. He looks like he wants to say more, to *do* more, his hand rising as he takes a step towards me, but he quickly drops it and straightens.

"Sleep well, Tess."

With that, he strides away and I head back into my tent, admittedly pouting. I pull my tunic off, glaring at the top and the fact that it didn't serve the purpose I'd hoped it would this evening, and unlace my boots. I'd gotten some proper riding boots when we were in Tithmoore and they're far superior to the blasted things Tesni had in her trunk or had dressed me in that first day. I shimmy out of my trousers, pull on a short silk nightgown with thin straps, and flop onto my cot, staring through the hole in the roof until the light fades and the stars appear. Soren slinks inside and settles on his furs.

-*They will be fine. It is a small group from the enemy army. A scouting party of some sort.*-

I turn to look at him. "Why do they keep sending these small groups, do you think? It seems silly to me."

-Perhaps they are hoping to find weaknesses in Blackheart's army, in their responses and tactics, before sending in their full contingent.-

I mull that over. It makes a kind of sense I suppose. I let out a long, measured sigh, my head pounding trying to keep track of all of the things I don't know or understand, all of the worries and *what-ifs*. I wait for someone to come and collar me, but no one does. I start at that, bolting upright. Now would be the time. We could run, I could use my Gift and we can escape. Despite their new alliance, I feel certain that Ryker would shelter me if we made our way back to Tithmoore.

But I don't move.

I lie back and tell myself that I don't leave because it's probably a test of some sort and there are armed guards waiting just outside to watch me, but the truth of the matter is that I don't *want* to leave. Not like this. Not without saying goodbye.

Not without him.

I turn and bury my face in the pillow, groaning. Soren chuckles low and I curse him silently. I sigh and roll back over to stare up at the stars once more, trying not to worry about the group going out to meet this threat, trying not to worry about the fact that I've lost my heart to a man who may or may not still be my enemy, trying not to worry about this war and my friends and the fate of the entire fucking empire.

-Sleep, Thea,- Soren commands quietly, sensing my tumultuous thoughts, and before I can protest or tell him that I don't need mothering from a cat, my eyes are sliding closed and sleep is claiming me for its own. Perhaps I do need a bit of mothering from a cat. I hear him laugh lightly within my mind and then I know nothing more.

I WAKE TO KILLIAN STANDING AT THE ENTRANCE OF MY TENT. I BLINK IN THE low light from the brazier in the corner and sit up, turning the knob on the lantern beside my bed to burn brighter.

"Killian?" I ask, rubbing my eyes. It's still night, the sky above dark as pitch, clouds gently sweeping past the stars.

"I'm sorry to wake you, I just..."

"Are you alright?" My heart races. Did something happen? Is he hurt? Is the full force of the Alliance headed our way?

"Yes. I'm fine...Actually, no, I'm not," he adds after a heartbeat, changing his mind. Before I know what's happening, he crosses to the bed in three long strides and drops to his knees, taking my face between his hands and pressing his lips to mine. I'm so shocked that I forget to breathe, but the feeling of utter relief that rushes through my entire body is staggering. He's here and he's whole and he's kissing me. *Great fucking Makers, Killian is kissing me.* His lips are cool from being out in the frigid air, but soft as he presses them so softly against my own. Starlight bursts behind my eyes, my entire world seeming to explode.

Just as I finally find that I can command my body once again and raise my hands to grab his shirt and tug him closer, to deepen the kiss and demand that he never stop, he pulls away. I sway, my head swimming, and I blink several times to try to clear my thoughts. Everything happened so damned quickly, I can barely even process it. Is this even real? A dream?

"I know this is madness. I know it cannot be. But I couldn't go another second without knowing what your lips felt like, Tess. I *needed* to fucking know." I blink, barely able to breathe, certainly not able to respond. He has blood and dirt streaked across his cheek and forehead, splashed down his throat. What the fuck had happened tonight? Is this blood his, or someone else's? But he says nothing more, only rises and walks away, leaving me gaping in the silence.

-Well, that was...interesting,- Soren says in my mind a few moments later, and I whip my head to the side to find him staring, his eyes shining like mirrors in the dim light.

"You just sat there and watched?" I hiss.

-Well, I thought it would have been far more awkward if I got up and left in the middle of it.-

"Why didn't you wake me when he first arrived?"

I swear the cat shrugs. *-I wanted to see what would happen. He stood there for quite a while, just watching you. He seemed...very serious.-*

"Fucking hells," I groan, running a hand through my hair, trying to figure out what just happened—and what to do next. I can still feel the whisper of his lips against mine and my fingers drift upward, lightly tracing my skin. Such a brief touch, so gentle...

"You know what? No. Absolutely fucking not." I throw my legs over the side of the bed and shove my feet into my boots, not bothering to put on pants. I do throw a coat on over my nightgown though because it seems like a better idea than charging through a war camp with my ass nearly visible through this thin silk.

-No?- Soren drawls, stretching his long legs, claws digging into his pile of furs and his tail flicking from side to side.

"That wasn't good enough, not for me."

He chuckles inside my mind. *-There's my daska-* I straighten at that and arch a brow. *-Stubborn flower. It fits you oh so well, don't you think?-*

I narrow my eyes, but don't argue. He isn't wrong, after all.

"Stay here."

I stomp outside, crossing the small distance between our tents when Soren's voice whispers through my mind again.

-He isn't there.-

I pause with my hand on the flap of Killian's tent. I don't hear any movement inside and I'm on a mission, so I sigh in annoyance.

-Where is he then, you absolute ass?-

-How you wound me, my beloved bonded.-

-Soren,- I growl back, warning clear in my voice and my Gift pulsing through my body, my palms growing cold.

I can hear the amusement in his voice when he responds. *-The cave three hundred yards to the northeast, just past the stream.-*

I look up, finding the stars Tobias taught me to navigate by all those years ago, and set off to find Killian.

The cave is set into the face of a small rise of stone—a small mountain, I suppose?—and I see his boot prints along the small, worn path leading upward. Once inside, I see nothing. Pitch black darkness greets me and I wonder if Soren is playing a joke. I grit my teeth and vow to freeze the damn cat completely when I see a tiny flicker of light in the distance. I charge forward and find that the light is coming from a tunnel. I follow it, shouting.

"Killian Blackheart! That's *it*? Really? After all these weeks, all that build-up between us, and *that's* all I get?! Well, I've got news for you if you think you can just kiss me like that and walk out, mysterious and yearning and..."

I stop dead and gawk when I emerge into an even larger cavern, an underground spring flowing through the space and creating a giant pool in the center surrounded by a low stone wall. Stalactites hang from the towering ceiling, covered in glowing flowers that fill the space with a soft, purple light. It reflects off of fragments of diamonds embedded in the rock walls.

It's absolutely breathtaking, but all of it pales in comparison to the sight of Killian shirtless, knee-deep in the pool. He's still got his leathers on and I don't know if that's a good thing or a bad one. He holds himself perfectly still, staring at me and looking uncertain. I let my eyes drift slowly down from those intense blue-gray eyes, down his throat and over his broad chest, droplets of water cascading downward, his tattoos dark and mesmerizing. They drift lower still, down the hard planes of his stomach and over the...jagged, angry red line that was most assuredly a gaping wound not long ago.

"What happened??" I gasp, running forward, worry cutting through everything else swirling inside my mind. He strides out of the pool, water sloshing down his body.

"I'm alright," he says, voice low and gruff. He inhales sharply as I settle one hand on his stomach, the other gently touching the spot on his right side, just below his ribs.

"What happened?" I ask again after I determine that the wound is, in fact, closed, looking up to meet his eyes. He sighs.

"I was overconfident and careless. It was a mistake." When I give him a look that clearly says he's nowhere near done explaining this to me, he runs a hand through his hair and I realize that my hands are still on his body. I don't move them and he doesn't ask me to. "I was...apprehending a scout to interrogate, assuming he was unarmed, but he had a hidden blade. He was able to get it between the plates of my armor."

"Copeland healed you?" He nods and I frown. "But why is there still a mark then?" When he'd healed me, there hadn't been anything to show that I'd been injured at all save the faintest pink line, and even that faded quickly. This would surely leave a scar behind.

Killian clenches his jaw. "I asked him to leave it. As a reminder."

"A reminder?" I whisper, pulling my gaze from his and letting it trace across his chest and arms and stomach again, noting every scar. Some hidden beneath the ink, some more obvious, but all there by design, I realize. He *chose* to have these scars remain on his body if Copeland is at his disposal at all times.

"A reminder that I'm human, that I'm not infallible. A reminder of what mistakes can cost." After a moment he adds, "A reminder that life is far too short."

I meet his gaze again, and amusement sparks in his eyes. They look more blue than gray in the purplish light sparkling down on us, and I'm reminded all over again how beautiful they are.

"What was it you were yelling when you stormed in here, Red? Something about *'that's all I get'*?"

"Oh." I clear my throat lightly and my cheeks heat. "Well, yes, I..." He gives me a challenging look and I narrow my eyes. I love that he pushes me. I love that he doesn't back down. I love that he's playful. *I love...*

I shift my shoulders back and hold his gaze.

"I was just curious if that pathetic excuse for a kiss was really all you had to offer."

He tilts his head at me slowly. "Pathetic. Excuse. For a kiss," he repeats.

"Oh, good, your hearing was unaffected by this little skirmish you were involved in."

He moves so quickly I barely even see it. I squeal when he lifts me up and gasp when he grips my thighs and coaxes my legs around his waist. He moves his hands to my ass, holding me tightly against him as he walks us away from the pool. I shrug out of my coat as we go, letting it fall to the ground and sling my arms around his neck, tangling my fingers in the hair at his nape. He doesn't kiss me though our mouths are so close, *so fucking achingly close*, and with each thundering beat of my heart, the more desperate I become.

Suddenly my back is against the stone wall and his body is flush against mine. I gasp again, the feel of him hard against me turning every inch of me into pure fire. He pins me to the stone with his hips and moves his hands to my thighs, sliding his palms beneath the hem of my nightgown and making me moan low in my throat. His hands are rough and calloused, and a shiver runs down my spine at the contact. He's exactly the kind of man I want, the kind I need.

He was made for me. He's mine, maybe always has been. I believe in this moment that the Makers really have been steering my entire life, leading me here, to this moment and this man...this army? Maybe I can turn this entire situation on its head. With Killian by my side, maybe we can convince Dorian that I'm an asset to his victory. I don't have to be a hostage while I pretend to be my sister. I don't have to be a prisoner or a bargaining trip or an imposter. I can be *me*.

Killian leans in close, still not kissing me, but hovering with his lips a hairsbreadth from mine and all other thoughts vanish from my mind.

"Pathetic, you say?" His voice is a low, sinful promise. I try to close the distance, to press my lips to his, but he pulls just out of reach. I groan in annoyance and he chuckles.

"Ah, ah, ah. Not yet, Tess."

I clench my teeth. I want him to say *my* name. I want him to know *me*, the true me. But then...he *does* know the true me. The surety of it sears my bones to ash, makes my soul burn brighter than the sun. No matter what name he might say, he knows me. Somehow, against all odds and reason, he knows me better than anyone ever has. So, I let the worry over names fall away and give him a slow, sultry smile.

"I believe my exact words were *pathetic excuse for a kiss*, if you want to be perfectly accurate."

He smirks at me, leaning in and nipping quickly at my lower lip, the contact enough to make me gasp in surprise and groan with impatient need when he pulls away again before I can get what I truly want.

"Damn you, Killian. *Kiss me.*"

"Are you begging me, Red?" he asks, a mix of playful and sexy that should be criminal. Not to be outdone, I smile wickedly and hold his gaze as I answer.

"I think I'd need to be *on my knees* for that, so if you'd kindly let me down, I'm more than happy to show you just how well I *beg*..."

He groans, his eyes sliding closed as he takes my true meaning. They flash open again, the stormy blue blazing just before he finally slams his lips to mine. Every nerve in my body explodes, heat and ice both flooding my veins at the feel of his lips on mine, warm now, and demanding as he shows me exactly what he wants and how he wants it.

And great fucking Makers is it exactly what *I* want and how *I* want it too. He seems to know exactly what my body desires, exactly what it needs. He sucks on my lower lip and I moan loudly, clenching my thighs hard around his hips. I pull at his hair, desperate, as his tongue slips against mine, rolling, thrusting, dominating.

"Killian," I rasp as he kisses along my jaw. "More."

"Always," he promises low in my ear, making me shudder. He takes my ear lobe between his teeth and the sound I make is obscene to be quite honest, but I don't care. This man knows how to coax the most intense sensations from the smallest touches, the most illicit pleasure I've ever felt. And this is just a fucking *kiss*. I can only imagine other things he has in store for me and my power surges at the thought. *Holy Makers.* That's never happened before. It must be because of the bonding with Soren?

"You can let it out, Tess," Killian whispers as he kisses along my throat, and I know he felt my Gift flare. "You don't have to hide with me, not anymore." I wish that was true, but I can't possibly tell him the truth, not now, not yet. I force my Gift back into the well deep inside my chest, slamming an iron cover over it to keep it locked away.

"Don't want to hurt you," I pant, which isn't a lie. My Gift could easily hurt him, kill him even. He's strong but there's no guarantee that he could block me in time if I really did unleash my power. I force his face back to mine with a tight grip on his hair and kiss him again, hard. He groans and moves his hands up my thighs, gripping tightly but I only want him to grip me tighter, kiss me harder, hold me forever.

He turns suddenly, holding me up easily as he walks us Makers know where, but then I'm sitting on the rock wall by the water's edge. The stone is completely smooth, like a polished opal, and feels almost soft beneath my bare skin. He pulls back just enough to speak, his lips still brushing mine.

"Tell me yes," he says, pleading, surprising me. "Tell me I can do whatever I want to you, Tess. Because great fucking Makers do I *want.*" I gasp quietly. *Whatever I want to you.* I shiver with all of the possibilities that simple phrase holds. "I've been wanting since the moment I saw you beside that creek, ready to fight your way out and nearly doing just that. I didn't want to want you then. You were the spoiled, cruel Gifted of my enemy, and yet, I did. I've tried to stop myself from wanting all these weeks—and I've failed time and time again."

I swallow hard, his words sending a thrill through my blood, an ache through my heart. He leans in once more, kissing me deeply before taking my bottom lip between his teeth, tugging gently.

"So," he whispers, trailing his hand downward, fingers brushing gently over my breasts, my pebbled nipples jutting through the thin silk, moving farther down over my stomach and over the top of my thighs, only to skim back upwards between them, stopping just short of where I need him so fucking desperately, driving me absolutely mad. "*Tell. Me. Yes.* Please, Tess."

"Yes," I breathe, arching my hips forward, begging. "Yes, Killian."

He lets out a long, shuddering breath and kisses me again before sliding to his knees. I inhale sharply, eyes following him down. He unlaces one booth, then the other, and tugs them both off. I watch, breathless, wondering if he's going to do what I think he's going to do...

He rucks my short nightgown even farther up my thighs then and rips my panties clean in two as if they're nothing but parchment, tossing the ruined pieces of silk aside. Slowly, gently, he presses my knees apart. I don't fight him, actually spreading them farther in clear invitation. I've never been shy in this regard and he isn't the only one that's been wanting all this time.

"Great. Fucking. Makers," he rasps. "There's no...you're...*bare.*" He sounds somewhere between incredulous and awed.

"Is that...alright?" I ask, breathless. Though other men seem to have loved this little side effect from the tonic to alter my hair and eye color, I worry suddenly that Killian will be dismayed by it.

He glances up at me. "Alright? *Alright??* Fucking hells, Tess, I don't think I've ever seen anything so arousing, so...erotic in my life." His gazes shifts back between my thighs and he scrubs a hand across his jaw. I can hardly breathe as I watch him, looking at me like I'm a marvel. "Lie back, Red. We're going to be here for a while..."

I nearly whimper at that but do as he asks, lying back on the smooth, cool stone. A heartbeat later, my back bows upward at the first feel of his tongue. I cry out at the ecstasy and he groans, a deep rumble in his chest. He settles my thighs over his shoulders and I lose all track of time and place and reason as he licks and nips and works his tongue like the expert he clearly is.

"Fuck, fuck, fuckkkk," I rasp, writhing, clawing, trying to hold off for as long as possible, wanting to enjoy every sensation this man wrings from me for as long as possible.

"You taste like the heavens, Tess. Could lick you for hours and hours, until you can't fucking take another second..."

I whimper but it turns into a cry of absolute pleasure when he pushes a finger inside, pumping and curling it in perfect rhythm with the flicks of his tongue over my clit.

"Killian, oh great Makers, *don't stop.*"

"Never," he all but snarls.

I don't know how much longer I can last, no matter how much I want this to go on forever, the pleasure within me climbing and climbing, so high that the fall my very well kill me, but oh what a way to fucking go.

"It feels so good, Killian. *So fucking good.*"

"Then come for me, Tess."

I gasp quietly and push up to watch him down the length of my body. *Dear. Fucking. Makers.* It's too much. Seeing this man, this great warrior, the Commander of Duskthorne's entire army for fuck's sake, on his knees before me, his head buried between my thighs, sweat beading his forehead and his hair the unruly mess I love, it's *too fucking much.* His eyes flash open and I explode the second they meet mine. I scream and arch my back off of the stone once more, my body spasming and my Gift trying to break free from its imprisonment of my own making. I don't know if it's the increase in power because of being bonded or just the fact that I've never felt anything near to what I'm feeling now with Killian, but my Gift has never reacted like this.

Killian makes some low, animalistic growling sound that sends shudders of pleasure through me, but he doesn't stop, prolonging the pleasure and making my entire body feel like it's melting from sheer bliss. I pant and writhe and flail, barely able to comprehend the heights Killian has brought me to. Stars flash behind my eyes, burning so brightly I think they'll forever be branded there, an eternal memory of this perfect moment. Finally, *finally,* I somehow push myself upward and tug him towards me. He grunts in surprise and protest but doesn't fight me too much when I press my mouth to his and rip at the laces of his leathers. I tunnel my hand inside, wasting no time wrapping my fingers around his shaft. *Holy. Fucking. Hells.* Killian is...blessed.

Blessed may be an understatement.

Blessed may rip me in two.

"*Great fucking Makers*," he chokes out against my lips, tangling his fingers into my hair. I tighten my grip around him, gliding my fist up and down his cock, spreading the moisture beading on the thick crown with my palm. "Don't stop. For the love of all the Makers *don't fucking stop*."

"Never," I whisper, echoing his own words before sucking his bottom lip between my own as I glide my fist up and down. Faster. Harder. He rocks his hips in time with my movements, clutching at my waist with one hand, the other still tight in my hair holding me to him. His beard tickles my skin and I smile against his lips.

"Fuck, you're going to make me come, Tess."

"Like this?" I pant, the idea making desire boil inside my veins.

"Just like this," he growls. So I don't stop. I keep pumping my fist, kissing him hard and thrusting my tongue against his. "Ah Makers... going to...FUCK!" His hips jerk forward again as he comes hard, his entire body going rigid, every muscle clenched as I keep pumping, gentler now. Something about it is so arousing and heady. Making this hardened, lethal warrior come with just my hand, trousers still on? It sends power sizzling through my blood. I grin as he finishes and he rests his forehead against mine, breathing hard.

"Well that didn't take much," I tease.

"Woman, you could look at me the right way and I'd come," he says, completely unabashed. Warmth fills my chest, my cheeks flushing. Having power over this man is...intoxicating. Addicting.

"Think I'll try that sometime," I tease. He laughs lightly, forehead still resting against mine. I turn serious as my fingers drift over the new scar on his side. "I'm glad you're ok," I whisper.

"I saw your face."

"What?" I pull back and look up at him.

"When the blade sank home and I felt that it could be a mortal wound if I couldn't get to Copeland in time, your face flashed behind my eyes. *Yours*, Tess. I knew that I had to get back to you, I had to kiss you, at least once. I had to tell you..." He trails off and swallows hard. "I vowed I would get back to you, and somehow, I did." He cradles my face with both hands, thumbs tracing soft lines along my cheekbones in a gesture that seems far too tender for a warrior like him, one that breaks my heart into a million pieces in the best possible way. I close my eyes and lean in, kissing him softly and conveying the words I can't quite make myself say out loud yet through this touch. I can't tell him how I feel until I can tell him the truth about me, who I really am and how I came to be here, and I can't do that until we reach Duskthorne.

"We should get back," I whisper. He sighs but nods, stepping away and striding back into the water to clean himself up. I hop off of the rock and nearly stumble, my legs still shaky from the things Killian did...the things I'm dying to have him do again. My mind runs wild with the other things I want to do, but it's probably for the best that we didn't take things much further tonight. When we're finally together, completely together, I want it to be *my* name that he's yelling to the rafters and whispering into the night, *my* name that he says over and over like it's a prayer. *My name*, forever, no one else's.

I rinse my hands at the water's edge and pull on my boots before grabbing my coat and tugging it back on. Killian trudges out of the water, shaking his hair out like a dog and making me laugh. He gathers his armor and cloak, leaving his ruined tunic on the ground near the pool. He wraps his cloak around himself and leans down to kiss me once more before gathering up the lantern and leading the way back to camp. It's quiet as death when we approach, almost everyone deep in sleep at this late hour—everyone except my nosey familiar, apparently.

-*Well, well, well...*-

-I hear in Enola, they use feline entrails to make musical instruments.-

I can practically hear his answering smirk inside my head but roll my eyes and slam the pathway between us shut for the night. I shake my head and take a step towards my own tent, turning to tell Killian goodnight, only to find him right in front of me, one hand snaking around my waist.

"And where, exactly, do you think you're going?" he whispers.

Heat floods through me and my pulse races with the promises hiding beneath his words.

"Killian, we should…" I clear my throat lightly. Every cell in my body screeches in protest when I say the next words, but my heart and mind know it's the right decision. I need him to be with *me* when we're together like that. Not Tesni, the Flame of Lyanna. Not Tess, the prisoner of Blackheart. Me. Thea. The girl who is tired of hiding.

"We should take things slowly. I want to wait before we…"

He gets that playful spark in his eyes, and I know he's going to make me say the words.

"Before we…?"

I narrow my eyes, but if he wants to play, I'll play.

"Before I ride you hard like a wild Northland stallion until your eyes roll back in that pretty little head of yours and you cry out my name so loudly that the very mountains shake around us."

He curses and barks out a choking cough, and I grin, biting my lip.

"Makers, you're going to be the death of me, Red," he mutters, shaking his head before leaning down and kissing me softly.

"I just want to sleep beside you, Tess, that's all. I'll wait as long as you need me to for anything else, but I still want you to stay with me until then. Please."

I study him for a few heartbeats, wondering what the rest of the camp might think if anyone finds out, what rumors might fly…but then I decide that I don't fucking care. Let them talk. Let them think what they want.

"As long as you don't snore, I suppose I could be persuaded..." I smother a yelp and subsequent giggle as he lifts me over his shoulder with one arm as if it's nothing and stomps into his tent. "Killian!" I hiss, laughing and beating my fists uselessly on his back.

"Quiet, fire wench," he rumbles, tossing me onto his bed. I laugh as I right myself, wondering not for the first time how we got here. Laughing and playing, well on our way to loving deeper than any two people have ever loved.

He puts his armor on the desk and tugs his cloak off, throwing it over the pile. He stokes the fire, eyeing me for a heartbeat as if to say *you could do this, you know. I won't stop you*, before striding back to the bed. He sits on the edge and unlaces his boots, and I can't help but go to my knees behind him, pressing my chest against his back and wrapping my arms around him. I kiss his neck and he groans quietly, tilting his head to give me better access. I make mental notations of the spots that he seems to particularly like, like just below his ear and the spot where his shoulder meets his neck.

"Mmm, you keep that up and we won't be getting any sleep, Red..."

I laugh, place one more kiss at his nape, and settle back as he tucks his boots beneath the edge of the wide cot.

"I have a very serious question to ask you," he says, turning those stormy eyes on me. I gulp, suddenly worried about what this might be. "Do you think you can control yourself while I change my pants?"

I press my lips into a thin line and grab one of the pillows from behind me, smacking him in the shoulder with it. He chuckles lightly and rises from the bed, crossing to his trunk. I watch as he starts to unlace his pants, but suddenly his question doesn't seem so ridiculous. I'm honestly not sure if I *can* control myself if I see him completely unclothed right now. He eyes me for a moment, but just as he starts to tug them off, I groan, flopping back and covering my face with the pillow I'd hit him with. He laughs loudly and I flash him a single finger—a gesture that means something entirely unrefined throughout Hypathia.

"And where in the seven hells did a spoiled princess like you learn a gesture like that??"

"From your mother," I snap, another retort I picked up being around all of the sailors down at the port that Tesni most certainly would never say. He laughs again, louder, the sound so easy and carefree that I truly wonder if I'm dreaming.

"Move, you feral, wanton little thing," he says from just beside the bed. I remove the pillow and my eyes immediately drift downward to confirm that he is actually wearing pants once more. These are silk and loose, and hang indecently low on his waist, showing off those deep indentions beside his hips, the trail of dark hair leading down from his navel...

I clear my throat and meet his gaze again, and he gives me that crooked smirk that tells me he knows exactly what I was thinking. I shift over in the bed and he settles in beside me, tucking his arm beneath me and pulling me to his chest. I lay my head just above his heart, my right arm thrown over his stomach, and I don't think anyone has ever fit so perfectly beside another. He holds me close, arm wrapped around me tightly, as if he's afraid I'll run away or disappear. He pulls the fur blankets up around us and I exhale in utter contentment.

"Sleep well, Tess," he whispers softly, kissing the top of my head. Sleep comes for me swiftly, far more swiftly than I would have thought possible, but before I'm dragged away, I need to tell him something.

"Killian?" I murmur.

"Mmmm?"

"Thank you for coming back to me." He pulls me tighter against him, as if he needs to be sure that he truly did make it back, that this is real.

"Thank you for being my reason to."

I snuggle deeper into his side, throwing my thigh over his, and smile as I drift off into the darkness.

CHAPTER
FIFTEEN

I wake the next morning and find myself alone. I frown, wondering for a moment if I'd dreamed the entire evening, but when I inhale deeply and smell Killian all around me, his woodsy, wintery scent lingering on the pillow and furs, I know that it was all real. I stretch across the large bed and take a few minutes to just revel in everything that happened, in the knowledge that I'm not alone in these feelings, in the warmth of his bed cocooning me. I snap my eyes open when I hear him enter the tent, stomping snow from his boots.

I push myself upwards and brush wayward curls from my face, wishing for a moment that I'd taken the opportunity to get up and make myself a bit more presentable before he came back, but when he looks at me, he stares as if I'm dressed in all the finery of a royal, and I don't worry about my tangled hair or rumpled nightgown.

He strides over and hands me a steaming mug of something that smells sweet and delicious.

"Is this…Abrashian chocolate??" I gasp, taking another greedy inhale over the cup. I haven't had chocolate in years, not since I left Lyanna. Something about the way the Abrashians create the mixture makes it melt before it could ever reach Helios. It can only be found in the north.

"It is," he nods with a grin. "I have a slight addiction to the stuff, truth be told, and I'd heard rumor that Barony kept cases full of it in Lyanna. I assumed that might have been for you."

I make a noncommittal sound and blow across the top of the mug, the dark brown liquid rippling gently. Tesni actually hates it. It's Barony himself who has the weakness for chocolate of all kinds. Deciding I can't wait another moment, I take a heaping mouthful and moan loudly, despite the scalding of my tongue and throat. *Worth it.*

Killian chuckles. "I don't know if I should be offended that your moaning over hot chocolate sounds extremely similar to you moaning over my tongue on your pu—"

I choke, coughing and spluttering, and he throws back his head, laughing. I wipe my mouth and glower at him, but can't fight my smile. I glance over his shoulder and bite my lip.

"Do people...I mean, does anyone know that I'm in here?"

"It's not for my men to know or comment on my activities, but no, I don't believe anyone is aware."

"Is this something that should be kept secret?" I gasp quietly as a thought occurs. "What will Dorian do if he finds out that you've been bedding his captive?"

He strides over, that cocky swagger firmly in place and so damned attractive that my blood heats and my heart races. He leans down so that our faces are only inches apart and holds my gaze.

"First off, I haven't bedded you yet, Tess. You wouldn't be able to walk this day if I had." I gulp at that, clenching my thighs at that challenge and promise all wrapped up in one. "And secondly, let me worry about Dorian." He closes the small distance between us and kisses me, slow and deep, and soon my head is swimming. He pulls away.

"Mmm, you taste good," he rasps, voice low and gruff and making my toes curl. Memories of him saying something very similar last night when he knelt before me flash and I shiver. He seems to know exactly what I'm thinking and nips playfully at my lower lip. "I can't wait for another taste."

Before I can pull him down into the bed and forget every promise I made to myself last night about waiting to have sex until he knows the truth, he pulls away and taps the tip of my nose with a forefinger.

"Get dressed. We'll be leaving in a few hours."

He leaves to take care of army things I assume and I peek outside, making sure no one is nearby before I dart to my own tent. I find it empty, though Soren's spot still holds a bit of warmth, so he must have left only recently to hunt. He likes to do it before first light most mornings, taking down enough for himself and to bring back for Cookie to help feed the army. Any who weren't completely comfortable with the frost cat being in the camp at first quickly changed their minds once they started having fresh meat almost every day in their meals.

-A good evening I take it?- the cat purrs inside my mind.

-Go away.- I splash my face and neck with cold water from the basin and close my eyes, trying to sort through everything that happened and wrap my mind around the intensity of these feelings, of the sureness deep in my soul.

-Aren't humans typically in a better mood after they've been satisfied? Perhaps the rumors about the Commander's prowess in the bedchamber—or cave I suppose, in this case—are entirely fabricated...-

-I'm in a fine mood,- I grumble but then purse my lips. *-...and what rumors have you heard?-* I pinch the bridge of my nose. *-You know what, I am not having this conversation with you-* He laughs. *-Finish hunting. We're leaving in a few hours.-*

He slides out of my mind, the pathway dimming. I get dressed and braid my hair into a crown across my head, one long plait resting over one shoulder.

"Can you do mine like that?" Mia asks, peeking into the flap of my tent. She glances around, clearly hoping to find Soren here, and her face falls ever so slightly when she doesn't spy the snowy white bastard. I smile. The two of them have become thick as thieves, even more so since her almost entombment.

"Sure, come sit." I gesture to the bed. She runs and leaps atop it, and I turn her to face the side of the tent so I can stand behind her and work. "Where's Dessa? She normally does your hair, doesn't she?"

"She's in some meeting about the war. I think there's a big battle coming." My fingers still in her strands, just a few shades lighter than my chocolate this morning.

"Why do you think that?"

She shrugs. "I heard them say something about a big group moving in, much bigger than the others so far. I think Commander Blackheart wants to attack, but Odessa shooed me along before I could hear more and told me it wasn't my place to eavesdrop on army business." I can hear her rolling her eyes and smile despite the worry starting to course through my belly. A bigger group. A larger battle.

I wonder if Killian will tell me about all this himself now that we're...together? I suppose we are, aren't we? We didn't make any declarations outright last night, but it was clear how we felt... wasn't it?

I shake myself. Regardless, is army business, as Mia calls it, something he'll include me in now? Do I *want* to be included? I chew my lip as I braid Mia's hair. I honestly don't know if it would be worse to know what's happening, going out of my mind with worry about it when he's gone, or to be in the dark of exactly what's going on out there.

I finish with her hair and an hour or so later, the army is on the move again, the groups slowly making their way ever north. The temperatures are dropping by the second, the clouds overhead thick with coming snow. We've had a reprieve from it for the last day, though it's still thick on the road beneath the horses and wagon wheels. It's nice to be on a proper road on this leg of the journey instead of bumping along beaten paths in The Perilous.

I raise my face to the sky as we ride, the feel of true winter calling to me, comforting and familiar. Everyone is covered nearly head to toe now, thick woolen scarves pulled up over mouths and noses, hats pulled low, thick fur-lined gloves keeping fingers from getting frostbitten. Kendall grumbles about wishing *he* had a constantly toasty ass like a certain red-headed fire wielder he knows, though it's all muffled behind his scarf.

I give him a half-hearted apologetic smile and Jonathan draws his sword, smacking Kendall on the back with the broad side of it.

"Must you always abuse me??"

"Yes, I must. I believe it the very reason the Makers put me on this earth."

I snort as Kendall mutters artful curses behind his woolen mask, putting even Math to shame. I've learned the two are cousins, raised more like brothers, and can't go more than ten minutes without bickering like this.

The next few days are uneventful, though Killian becomes increasingly on edge.

"There's something coming, I can feel it," he says while I lay on his chest, his fingers sifting through my hair, his voice contemplative.

"Did something happen?" I ask, pressing up so I can look at him. His hair is a tangled mess, dark strands tumbling across his forehead. His stormy eyes are narrowed in concentration, staring deep into the distance, seeing far more than what's inside these four canvas walls.

"Not exactly," he says. "Just more reports of a larger contingent moving in from the west. Still not large enough to be of much worry, which is the worrying part."

"What do you mean?"

"Well, *why?* Why isn't Amon coming with a larger force? What we're hearing is that he only has a fraction of his might with him. If he's coming this far into the northlands to attack us, why would he not bring his full strength?"

"I...have no idea." I frown, remembering that I had similar questions about all of these strange small attacks. "It really doesn't seem to make any sense."

"And Amon is no fool. He has led the Nocadian army for decades and won nearly every battle he's engaged in. It's why almost every kingdom was so quick to join Lyanna's alliance once Nocadia was on board. No one was stupid enough to want to fight Amon."

"Except for you," I point out, smiling, and he shifts his gaze to me, answering with a smirk of his own.

"Yes, except for me."

"And Tithmoore and Helios, too," I add.

"Ryker has long been an ally of Duskthorne, but was hesitant to formally declare alliance because of the fear of Amon's might. He cares only for his people's safety and I can't fault him for that. A good king will do whatever it takes to protect his kingdom." He gives me a look then, something in his eyes that I can't quite read, but continues on. "He came around in the end—because of a certain red-headed fire bitch, I hear."

I narrow my eyes but he only grins.

Choosing to ignore him, I ask, "Why does Helios stay out of... well, most everything it seems?"

"They always have. Decosta would break Helios off of the continent completely and join Sol if he could, I suspect." He smiles a little at that. "He's a good man, but very...idealistic. He only wants peace and happiness and good ale. So, he keeps away from Hypathian politics and war and everything else. And the other royals let him—all of the exports that come through the port are too important to jeopardize, so." He shrugs.

"If it isn't broken, don't try to fix it?" I supply and he smiles, nodding.

"Yes, exactly. The unofficial arrangement—we leave you alone and you keep trade lines open—has been working for decades, before I was even born. Of course, the Vines make it easier for them to stay separate in most things, the rivers forming a natural barrier that's fairly easy to defend, and I know that the port itself can be closed as well. So, they can hold out against siege for a time."

I swallow hard at what his words mean, what they might mean for Math and Cece, for Randolph and all of the other sailors and traders and even the handful of loveable pirates I've come to know.

"You think the war will get so bad as to make its way to Helios, to make him close the kingdom off completely?"

He looks at me, eyes soft, and brushes hair back from my face.

"It's already there, love," he says breezily, not knowing what the words will do to me, what Helios means to me. I bolt upright, my heart in my throat and my Gift roaring within me, my skin turning frigid. Thankfully Killian had already dropped his hand from my face and didn't feel the sudden change. I force the chill away and my Gift to calm.

"What?? What do you mean?"

He frowns, clearly confused by my distress.

"Forces from the Alliance are on their way there now."

"What?" The word barely has sound, mostly just a whispered exhalation. I can't breathe. I can't think past the roaring in my ears.

"Tess, are you alright?" He cradles my face and I force myself to focus on his eyes, to keep in mind who I'm supposed to be. It's more important than ever now that I make it through these next few weeks. I will find a way to get back to Helios. I will make sure that Math and Cece are safe.

"I...I just..." I take a deep breath. "I just still find it hard to believe there's truly a war going on, that's all."

"It's yet to truly begin. These small battles are nothing compared to what's to come."

"But I don't understand why. Why did everyone decide suddenly to fight against Duskthorne?"

"Because we want to stop Barony and the only way he could stop us from stopping him, was to get the rest of Hypathia on his side." He all but snarls the words, true hatred and rage simmering in his eyes. Stop Barony? Stop him from what? Before I can ask, he exhales roughly and leans in to kiss me. "Enough talk about war." He kisses me again, this time on the corner of my mouth, slowly moving across my jaw and my pulse races. I force the worry for Helios and my friends away, needing to lose myself in this man for a while before the anxiety and fear can eat me alive.

"Killian?" I whisper, nearly breathless when he kisses the spot at the base of my throat where my pulse beats frantically beneath his tongue.

"Mmm?" he rumbles, sliding the strap of my nightgown aside and kissing my bare shoulder.

"You said that I tasted good…"

"Better than anything else on this earth," he breathes, one hand trailing down my side, his touch burning me through the silk.

"Well, I think it's my turn to taste *you*." He freezes and pulls back to stare at me in question. We haven't done anything more than kiss and sleep since that night in the cave, both of us having been exhausted the last few nights from the journey and Killian being called away to meetings with his highest-ranking officers.

"Tess…" The word is half warning, half pleading.

My lips turn up into a wicked grin and I shift, pressing his back to the bed. His hands settle on my waist as I straddle his hips, leaning down to kiss him slow and deep, teasing and biting before I make my way lower, down his throat and chest, tracing my tongue along swirling ink and kissing old scars. I slide down as I kiss, lower and lower, over muscles that are so hard and smooth I would swear they were carved from marble. He hisses in soft breaths as I go, muscles tensing and flexing beneath my fingers and lips and tongue. I tug his sleep pants down and my eyes go wide when his cock springs free. I'd been right that first night: blessed was an understatement. He's thick and hard, straining. Fucking *mouthwatering*.

I don't waste a second, immediately wrapping my lips around him.

"Fuckkkk," he rasps, hips arching off the bed and tangling one hand in my hair. I moan around his length, taking him deep and twirling my tongue. There's no way that I can take him all, so I add a hand, curling my fingers around his shaft, pumping in time with the bopping of my head. "Ah Makers, *don't stop.*"

I don't, couldn't even if the Maker's themselves demanded that I stop. The sounds he makes, the way he moves under my touch, it's a whole different kind of power, one that I might well become addicted to. I lick and suck and pump my fist and all the while, he moans and shifts his hips beneath me, fingers clenching in my hair, breaths coming in ragged pants. I settle my other hand on his stomach, nails dragging along his rigid muscles. He shifts his grip on my hair, sweeping the long strands from my face and curling them around his fist—for a better view, I imagine. Sure enough when I look up, I find blue-gray eyes staring at me, burning with such fierce desire that my stomach clenches.

"Ahh that's right, keep those beautiful eyes right here, Tess." *One day*, I think. One day, he'll say those words with my name attached. Even so, they send a shudder of pleasure through me. I do as he commands, holding his gaze as I slide my mouth down his cock, taking him deeper than before. "Oh, fuck me...Makers, your mouth on my cock is the sexiest thing I've ever seen. Keep going. Just like that."

I do, licking and sucking and dragging my teeth ever so gently along his shaft. He bucks and moans and curses and prays.

"Going to...ah, fuck, you must stop unless you want..."

I quirk a brow and suck him harder, moving my hand faster, demanding my due. He curses low, watching, biting his lower lip until he throws his head back and calls out my name, thankfully remembering to keep his voice low enough that the whole of the fucking camp can't hear, coming hard as he bucks his hips. I close my eyes and swallow everything he gives me, moaning quietly as I do. When he's finally spent, I release him and collapse back onto the bed, grinning.

His chest glistens with sweat and he's breathing hard as he runs his hands through his hair.

"Great fucking Makers," he mutters.

"It is a common mistake, but alas, I am a mere mortal woman. Surprising, I know, I—" I break off in a squeal as he shifts so quickly I barely see him move, settling his big body over mine, pinning my hands to the bed on either side of my head.

"Has anyone ever told you that you're the cockiest little wench in all of Hypathia?"

"It isn't cocky if you can prove your claims—which I believe I just did."

He laughs lightly and leans down to run his nose along mine.

"I never imagined you'd be like this," he whispers. "I'd heard terrible things, really fucking awful things. I didn't feel bad at all for the whole kidnapping business. I sure as hells never thought that we'd..." He pulls back to stare at me. "You don't want to go back to Lyanna, do you?"

"No." I can tell him that much with absolute honesty. "But...does what I want even matter? Dorian will want his payment, and Lyanna will demand me back to keep up their alliance with Marrowood."

"Perhaps not. If you agreed to help us fight, that could change things. After all, we'd rather have your power on our side than any riches that bastard Barony could ever promise." He looks away as he speaks, not quite meeting my eyes and a whisper of unease snakes around my heart. There's something he's not telling me.

"I..." I don't know what to say. I can't say all the things I want to: that I want to stay with him forever, but that I also have a life and family in Helios that I can't just walk away from. Tesni wouldn't have any real reason to not want to stay and fight Duskthorne. So, what the hells can I say? He saves me from having to come up with anything.

"I don't want to lose you, Tess," he finishes softly, holding my gaze again. Before I can say anything else, he kisses me and rolls off to his back, tucking me into his side and pulling the blankets over us. "Sleep."

I want to demand answers, but decide not to push it. He has a right to his secrets. Makers know I've got mine. One day, there can be complete openness between us, but for now, I'll take the safety and comfort of being here with him, surrounded by his warmth and surety.

I don't know how this story will end, how we will find a way to our happiness, but I will do whatever it takes to make it happen.

Because I don't want to lose him, either.

CHAPTER
SIXTEEN

"You don't think anyone has noticed that you've instructed my tent be set up closer and closer to yours each night?" I ask Killian in a low voice as we ride a few days later. I still have my own tent, of course, as things with us are still a quietly kept secret—except for Odessa. She knows all and keeps assuring me that everything will turn out alright, that I need to just keep hope, like the stubborn flower we've both been called. But my tent has gotten suspiciously close in proximity to the Commander's each night when we stop. It does make sneaking back to my own each morning easier, it's true, but we practically share a wall now they're so near.

"I don't give a flying fuck if they've noticed," he says easily as he sits astride his giant Northland as if the two were made for each other. Both proud and strong, with a quiet ferocity that no one can deny. I shake my head and laugh, and he winks, flashing me that crooked smile. There are flakes of snow caught in his dark beard from the short fall we had this morning, but it thankfully didn't last long enough to hinder our journey. I can feel a bigger storm on the horizon though, and I honestly don't know what it will mean for the army to be caught out in it. So, I ask.

"What happens when this storm hits us true? Your army is strong, but they're only human. They can't survive being buried in ten feet of snow."

He eyes the sky. "It may hold until we reach Duskthorne's gates. We only have another two weeks, possibly less."

My stomach dips a bit at that. Two weeks. Two weeks until I meet the monster and my fate is decided. Killian seems to think he can sway his king, that I won't be ransomed if I don't wish to be and that I could join their cause. But what about Helios? What about Cece and Math? I need to get back to them somehow. But maybe joining Duskthorne is the way to do that. As horrible as that kingdom is, it has the might of Killian's army and Tithmoore's as well. That may be my way to get to Helios—maybe I can make it a condition of my cooperation. I'll fight with them if they get my friends to safety first.

Of course, that's assuming that my revelation that I'm not actually my sister is met with...open-mindedness. Though I'm bonded now and know my power is far stronger than ever before, I've never really *used* it for much. I've sure as hells never wielded it in battle. So who's to say I could even be helpful in this war at all? Regardless, I need to be sure of Dorian's intentions first. If he is determined to ransom Tesni, I can't reveal the truth. Which means I must continue to lie to Killian.

I groan inwardly, all of the questions and possibilities and secrets making my head ache.

"It won't," I tell him. "The storm will only hold a few more days."

"A weather expert now, are we?"

"It is one of my many stunning attributes." He chuckles at that.

"We are an army bred in the depths of the frozen Northlands, Tess. We will be alright, I assure you."

"But—"

-*Something is wrong,*- Soren rumbles in my head.

I tense and Killian, ever vigilant, marks the change immediately.

"What's wrong?" He scans the trees around us, waiting for a

threat. His hand flies to the sword at his back, ready to pull it free in a heartbeat if needed.

-*To the west. I can smell it on the air.*-

-*What? What's going on? What can you smell??*-

-*...death.*- His voice is tight and I can feel the strain within him as he speeds back towards us through the trees. I blink and whip my head to the west, having no idea what to expect...and then I see the smoke.

"Look," I tell Killian, nodding in the distance. It's difficult to see with the heavy clouds, but I was sure...yes, there. Smoke curling upward in the distance. "What's there?"

"A small village," he answers, frowning. "There are a handful of them out here. A few hundred people at most. They're part of Duskthorne, technically, but we call them Outskirtters. They prefer life outside the walls of the kingdom proper, the wilds running deep in their veins from years long past, before Duskthorne even existed."

"Soren says that he smells...death."

Killian stiffens. "Hold," he says shortly and rides off down the line of soldiers, calling for his lieutenants and captains. I pull Zaro to a halt and wait. A few moments later Soren joins us, leaping to my side, hackles raised and claws and teeth bared. Zaro snorts at the cat but remains mostly aloof, as usual. I swear nothing could truly worry the horse.

"Do you know what happened?"

-*No, only that...*- He hesitates and cold dread pools in my belly. I meet his gaze, icy blue and gold grounding me despite the knowledge that what he's about to say is something terrible. He sighs. -*Only that the bodies were burned*-

I rear back.

"What??"

Before Soren can answer, Killian rides back to me.

"Stay here. I'm taking a group to see what's happened."

"I'm coming with you."

"No, you're not. We don't know what we're going to find, Tess, you need to stay—"

"I'm coming," I tell him again, voice hard and unyielding, and Soren peels his lips back from his fangs, growling low and making it perfectly clear that he will fight any that try to keep me from what I want. I don't even know why I want to go so badly, but something is telling me that I need to, that I need to see. Killian glances from me to Soren and rolls his eyes.

"You can put those away," he tells Soren. Turning back to me, he continues. "You stay behind me at all times and you do as I say, when I say it, do you understand?" He pins me with that stormy stare and I feel the command in his voice, but below that, the worry. He wants me safe. I nod and he looks back to Soren. "You will get her out if there is danger." It isn't a question, and though Soren is not one to appreciate being given orders, he doesn't object. He inclines his head to Killian. The two are in agreement about my safety, it seems.

He barks out a few more orders and the group going to investigate the village set out. Odessa rides ahead of me, her silver bow at the ready. My heart remains in my throat, a completely different energy around me now than ever before. This isn't a trek through the country. This isn't a leisurely journey from one camping spot to the next. This is a group of trained warriors on the way to possible battle, going to meet danger head on.

And while I know I should be afraid, a part of me I never knew existed rises up inside my chest. It stands at attention, a sense of duty and honor and the need to help shining like a beacon and warming me to the core as my Gift cools my blood and fills my veins. It wants to help too. I blink at that and glance to the white and gray streak beside me that is Soren.

-You couldn't have thought I would be given any but a true warrior as my bonded- he scoffs.

A warrior? No, I'm not that. I ran away. I hid. All these years, I've hidden away in Helios, forgetting everything and everyone else in Hypathia. I kept my Gifts locked away...but now, I feel how badly I want to use them to fight. Against whom or what, exactly, I don't know, but I know deep in my bones that I'm meant to do it. I'm meant to come out of the shadows and use this Gift the Makers gave me to do something more than keep the tavern cool in the sweltering southern heat.

I'm meant for more.

-More than you could ever know, daska...-

I wish he'd be less cryptic, but he's firmly refused to answer my questions about what he knows, the knowledge given to him by the Makers when he was called to be my bonded.

We finally make it to the village and the first of our group stop dead, horses rearing back and stomping their giant hooves. A cold finger of dread whispers down my spine. Why are they stopping? Why aren't they riding in, swords drawn ready and ready to fight? Or rushing to help at least?

-Because there's nothing left to fight. There's no one left to help,- Soren says solemnly, bowing his head.

"What?" I whisper. "I don't understand..."

But then I do.

The smell hits me when the wind shifts, blowing the scent of charred flesh and ash into my face. I cough and gag and tears burn my eyes.

"No," I whisper. I slide from Zaro's back and rush forward, despite Killian's orders to stay behind him. There's no danger now though, apparently. Soren is at my side, his strength keeping me afloat in what I know will be an ocean of despair in a matter of heartbeats.

"Tess," Killian says urgently, a warning in his voice as I break past the front line and see the absolute horror before me. I slow, barely able to remain upright, and Soren presses against my side to help. I settle my hand on his back, fingers knotting in his fur as the air rushes from my lungs and my heart shatters.

The village was indeed small, just as Killian said it would be. It's built in a wide circle, spokes of small buildings fanning outward into the woods and a packed earth path running through the center. Every single building had been burned. Charred stone and smoldering piles of wood and ash are all that remain, smoke still rising like gray fingers reaching for the heavens and orange embers glimmering through the haze.

And there, in the center, is a pile of bodies, white bone shining through the dark ash and burned flesh, tongues of fire still licking at the edges. I open my mouth, to scream or to cry, I'm not sure, but no sound comes out.

-Breath, Thea.-

I can't. I don't understand what happened here. I *can't* understand it. Who would do this? And why? For a moment, I wonder if this was Tesni's doing somehow, but no, she would never come out of hiding and risk her safe, cushioned future with Hastings and the ransom for this.

I can't seem to pry my eyes from the pile, despite the bile rising in my throat and Soren's whispered pleading for me to look away. My eyes scan every inch of mountain of death before me. I see long, tumbling locks of charred hair, and small hands reaching...

Women and children.

Women and fucking *children* were burned alive in this place.

"Makers." It's a choked whisper, and then Killian is there, reaching for me.

"Tess, look away. You don't need to see—"

"Why??" I cry, tears blurring the morbid visage before me, cold and scalding and I swear they're leaving deep scars in my cheeks, a brand that will never, ever leave me. "Why would someone do this?"

"It's a message," he says, voice low and laced with such white-hot anger that fear skitters down my spine. I've never heard him sound so...terrifying. Soren growls low, echoing Killian's fury.

"A message?" I rasp, throat aching, fingers still digging into Soren's fur. I still can't seem to breathe, my chest aching as a deep, resounding sorrow fills my heart. All these people. The fear they must have felt, the agony...

"From Amon," he growls and my stomach drops. Amon. The Abyss. That heartless monster did this. I finally tear my gaze away and look at Killian.

"Why?" I whisper, eyes stinging from the smoke and tears.

"He knows we've been watching him, tracking his forces. This is his open invitation to battle."

"I don't understand," I say, clawing at my chest with one hand, desperate to ease the pain, desperate to breathe. "What is so important about this fucking war that *this*," I throw a hand out towards the pile, "is a part of it?!" I scream and my Gift nearly breaks free, the raw power and rage making it course through my veins like never before, like it's a living, breathing beast desperate to lash out and punish. Killian quirks a brow, obviously feeling the spike in my Gift's energy with his own. I knew that Amon was fierce. I knew that there was war brewing. But I couldn't have imagined it was like this. So...brutal. So intense. So horrible. And for what? To try to take some Gifteds from Dorian?? It makes no fucking sense!

"Tess, I'll explain it all to you soon, I swear it. Right now, we need to get back."

"We can't...we can't just leave them like this," I whisper.

"There's nothing to be done, love," he says quietly, so quietly only I can hear. Odessa strides up and puts a hand on my shoulder.

"Come, Tess," she says, gently.

I turn back to look at the horror before me, something inside of me shifting and hardening at the sight. *This* is why I needed to come here. I needed to see this, to allow the seeds of understanding to begin to take root within me. This is all much bigger than I knew, and I'm to be a part of it. I know it now, somewhere deep in my soul.

So, I look. I memorize every single detail of this horror before me. I say a silent prayer to every Maker I can think of. I tell the souls in the blasphemous funeral pyre that I'm sorry and that I will make sure this never happens to anyone else again. I don't know how in the hells I can make such a promise. I'm one Gifted. A scared one at that, one who has hidden her whole life and never truly used her power.

But I make the promise all the same.

Finally, I turn away, walking with Odessa as the snow begins to fall.

THE INVITATION TO BATTLE IS ONE THAT KILLIAN ACCEPTS IMMEDIATELY. WE travel a few more hours before making camp and they begin preparing. Scouting reports say that Amon's army waits not far from where we've stopped, which makes me nervous, but Killian assures me that we're perfectly safe.

"He won't attack here. He'll meet us on the battlefield."

"War is strange," I mutter, surprised at the odd...civility of it, the sharp contrast to the brutality of what's to come, of what I saw at that village. "You schedule a time to meet and kill each other like you're meeting for tea or a standing appointment to fuck."

He quirks a brow at that, his hand freezing mid-slide as he sharpens his great sword.

"Have many standing appointments to fuck, do you?"

I roll my eyes and ignore that. "And you just *trust* each other? After what we saw him do?"

"There is an honor in war, a code..." He shakes his head. "It's hard to explain. But yes, in this, I trust that he will not attack this camp as we will not attack his. It's cowardly."

"What he did to that village was cowardly," I say in a deadly voice, fists clenching against the cold pooling in my palms. I can't stop seeing it. The bones. The ashes. The bodies. The faces set in eternal agony. I squeeze my eyes shut and try to breathe around the memories, swearing I can still smell the burning flesh. It had taken me hours before I could speak to anyone, even Soren, though his presence inside my head was a quiet, necessary talisman that I held on to for dear life.

Big, rough hands are suddenly cradling my face ever so gently. I open my eyes to find Killian staring, fire in his own stormy ones.

"We *will* avenge those people, Tess. I promise you. The ones in the village, the ones that Lyanna has taken, all of them."

I frown, not quite understanding what he means. What people has Lyanna taken? Now isn't the time to ask. I need him focused on the battle to come—and on coming back from it. He presses his lips to mine and crosses back to his desk, looking at the map once more. He runs his fingers along the worn parchment, all of Hypathia before him.

"We'll meet them here, on this tundra." I get up and come to stand beside him, staring at the map. My eyes drift immediately to Helios and I send a quick prayer to the Makers to keep the forces at bay, to keep Cece and Math safe. I shift my gaze to where Killian's finger rests.

"And we're here?" I ask, pointing to the area just on the other side of the small forest beside what will soon become a battlefield. He nods.

"And Amon's forces are here." He points to an area to the northwest of the tundra.

"How many are there?" I ask, twirling my hair around my finger. Killian watches, a slow smile curling his lips. "What?" I ask.

"You do that when you're nervous or worried or thinking," he says. I drop my hand.

"A very old habit," I tell him, another truth I can share. "Can't quite seem to break it." Warmth fills my chest realizing that he's noticed enough to know when I do it.

"Our scouts say three hundred or so," he says, answering my initial question. "Nothing we can't handle." Odessa told me that they are nearly six hundred strong. I should feel better knowing that Killian's men outnumber Amon's but something still feels wrong.

"I still don't understand why he's coming at you without more troops..." And then it hits me. "Oh! He has Gifteds."

"I'm fairly certain, yes."

My lips curl upward. "But they don't know that you can block them?"

"That knowledge is a closely guarded secret," he says with a wink.

"So, he thinks he's going to have the upper hand with offensive Gifteds on his side..."

"And will be unpleasantly surprised to find that his Gifteds are utterly fucking useless."

I let out a long, relieved sigh, feeling much better. I know that it's still battle and there are still lives to be lost on both sides, but at least these people that I've come to think of as my own are safer than I initially thought.

"I wonder what kind of Gifts they wield for Amon to think he'll be able to thwart the great Killian Blackheart."

Killian grins, and shifts, pinning my body between his and the desk, quickly lifting me atop it. I gasp quietly but immediately spread my knees to let him wedge his hips between my thighs. He puts his palms flat on the table on either side of me and leans in close.

"None so brilliant as my great Flame of Lyanna," he says softly, face so close that his breath tickles my lips. "Although, I do believe we should change that moniker. You don't belong to that bastard anymore." He leans in and kisses just below my ear, making me shiver. My hands slide beneath his shirt, settling on the hard planes of his stomach.

"And who do I belong to?" I whisper, gasping when he sucks gently on my pulse point, an appreciative rumble vibrating through his chest when he feels how hard it's racing. He pulls back and meets my gaze, and I wait for the words I know are coming. *You belong to me.*

"You belong to yourself, Tess," he says seriously, his dark eyes intense and unyielding, and I inhale quietly in surprise. "No one owns you. You are your own, your *Gift* is your own." Tears spring to my eyes. How can someone from a kingdom where the regent collects people like artwork feel this way? But I know in my heart that he does. Again I wonder why he serves Dorian, what hold the king has on him.

"Killian," I whisper, voice nearly breaking.

"You belong to yourself," he repeats, "but you also belong *with* me. You are your own, but you are also mine—as I am yours." My heart stutters and I want to cry from bittersweet joy. I know he's saying these things to me, but I still feel as if they're somehow a lie because he's not saying them to *me*. I want to tell him the truth so badly but I have to wait until we reach Duskthorne. I have to find out what Dorian's plans are for me, but I also know that if I reveal the truth now, I'll be putting Killian in a horrible position, having to choose between me and his king. It's clear that he doesn't have any love for King Dorian, but he is sworn to him for reasons I don't know yet. So, no, I'll keep my secret until I can face the king himself, and then I'll…I don't know what yet. Tempt him with the power of a bonded Gifted and reveal my true identity, I think. I can bargain for Cece and Math's rescue and then give myself over to Dorian to serve at his will in this war. I don't let myself think of the fact that he might choose to try to keep me for other reasons, to serve other purposes…

"I…" I don't know what to say, swallowing hard and trying to force words to come, but none do. He smiles and kisses me, a soft touch of lips so tender my heart splinters.

"You don't need to say anything, not yet. I know things are… complicated and uncertain. I don't expect you to make any declarations until we reach Duskthorne…until you have all of the information." He searches my eyes for something, though I'm not sure what, but I hope that he can read what I feel for him there, even if I can't say the words yet. I want to ask what kind of information he means, I want to ask about the war, what he meant about the people Lyanna has taken, but I don't, not now. He's riding into battle in the morning. Now is not the time. When he comes back safely, then I'll demand answers.

Until then, I'm perfectly content to spend the evening wrapped up in the man that I love. I may not be able to say the words yet, not until he knows the truth, but I can feel it and acknowledge it in my heart. In my bones. In my soul.

Well, perfectly content isn't exactly accurate. It takes all of my self-control not to rip his trousers off and beg him to fuck me until I can't remember my own name, but that's another thing that must wait. So, I move my palm up his body, settling it over his heart and letting its reassuring beat calm the worry trying to drown me.

He kisses me then, long and deep, and we lose ourselves in every other pleasure we can conjure save actually having sex. Hours later, sated and exhausted, I lie on his chest as my lids get heavier and heavier, but just before I fall asleep, I murmur the most important words I've ever said:

"Come back to me, Killian."

"Always, Tess. Always."

I WAKE THE NEXT MORNING STILL EXHAUSTED. TERRIBLE DREAMS PLAGUED ME most of the night, the scene from the village visiting me over and over, but in the dreams every body on the pyre belonged to someone I love. Their faces contorted in pain, screams and pleas echoing in my ears so loudly it felt as if my head might explode.

I'm not surprised to find that Killian is already gone when I pry my eyes open. I squeeze them shut again and stretch my hand across the bed, imagining I can still feel him beside me. I give up after a moment, knowing it will do no good to lie here and wallow and worry all day. So, I hoist myself up, dress in my leathers and an emerald tunic, and plait a braid along the top of my head, leaving the rest of the curls free to cascade down my back. I walk outside to find Soren prowling back and forth in front of the tent.

"How long have they been gone?" I ask, looking out over the camp. Seeing it so empty makes my chest clench but I grit my teeth and try to force the unease away. I remained, of course, along with a small cadre in case Amon didn't honor the rules of battle, and other non-combative members of the army: the squires, Cookie, Mia—those types.

-*Not long.*-

I nod and cross my arms over my chest, warding off a cold that has nothing to do with the weather or my own Gift. No, this is the cold of the unknown. The cold of those left behind to wait and wonder. The worst cold I've ever known.

I decide to spend the time waiting with Mia, knowing she must be just as worried about Odessa, but just before I make it to her tent, a commotion stops me short. Shouts are coming from some of the soldiers left to guard the camp.

-*Something is wrong...again.*-

My heart turns to ice and I rush towards them. A soldier I don't know is yelling, frantic and out of breath.

"We have to get to them. We have to warn them!" he pants, trying to push the others away as they hold on to him.

"Hawk, calm down! Tell us again, slowly," Tristan demands, sharing a quick glance with me. Killian claimed that Tristan was being left behind for a purpose *other* than keeping me safe, but he couldn't actually come up with a reason when I'd pressed him on it. I'd only kissed him in answer, and let it slide. I do feel better having not only someone formidable—Tristan is second only to Killian himself when it comes to swordsmanship—but someone I actually know and care about here to guard me.

Hawk sucks in ragged breaths, and I wonder where the hells he's run from. The battle? No, that doesn't seem right, he isn't in full armor and he said something about...warning them. My heart jumps into my throat and I try to keep it from strangling me.

"The prick that the Commander brought for interrogation, the one who stabbed him—" I flinch, remembering that wound, remembering the scar Killian chose to leave behind as a reminder...and blush ever so slightly as other memories from the night flash.

They're not enough to chase away the worry though, and all too soon they're gone and the gravity of the here and now settles over me once more. "—he was acting like a madman, laughing and cheering as if they'd won the whole bloody war. He said...he said that we were all as good as dead."

"Oh come off it, Hawk, he's just talking shite," another soldier tells him, waving it off. I think his name is Edmund. Tristan tenses, clearly worried about his brothers in arms, but mostly about Odessa.

"No, you don't understand! They don't have three hundred men like we thought. They have *a thousand*."

I blink and the other soldiers exchange glances. Some skeptical, some worried.

"No, that's not possible. We've been scouting. We would have seen..."

"They have a Gifted who can somehow conceal the others!" Hawk cries, eyes wide and frantic.

"But Blackheart can block—"

"He wasn't there," I whisper. They all turn to me. I clear my throat and force the words from numb lips. "Commander Blackheart wasn't with the scouts. He couldn't have blocked the Gifted. The scouts would only see what Amon wanted them to." I swallow hard. "But he'll be able to block them now..." And right now, he'll be seeing the truth of the situation. He'll be seeing a thousand enemies across the frozen plain. He'll be seeing the end of his army—the end of his *life.*

I share a brief, horrified look with Tristan before whipping my head to Soren, unable to say the words but my familiar doesn't need me to. He knows my heart.

-*Get on,*- the cat demands.

I leap onto his back and dig my fingers into his thick fur. He streaks away from the soldiers as they yell protests. After all, I'm still a prisoner and now I'm escaping. But I don't give a fuck. Let them try to stop me.

-*Stop* us,- Soren corrects. -*Hold on tight, daska.*-

He runs ever faster, bounding through the drifts of snow with ease, and I settle down low on his back as the wind whips at us like a tempest. *Please, please, please. Please let us get there in time. I can't lose him. I can't lose Odessa.*

I don't understand it all yet, but something tells me that we can't lose this army. We can't lose this war. Dorian may be a monster and Duskthorne hells on earth for Gifteds, but Amon is worse, and if Barony is allied with him, then it means I know where the true evil must lie.

But I don't care about any of that right now. I don't give a fuck about the Alliance or Barony or anything else in this entire world. All I care about is getting to Killian and the others.

I don't know how long we run but it feels like no time at all when Soren reaches the crest of the hill overlooking the tundra. My breath catches when I see the sea of scarlet across the expanse of the tundra, flags with the crossed scythes of Nocadia flying high.

Holy. Fucking. Makers.

The captured soldier said a thousand, but it looks like *tens* of thousands to me, the line stretching all the way across the width of the plain and extending so far backwards that it disappears into the distance.

-*Fuck,*- Soren growls.

-*Go!*-

Soren leaps from the hillside and I brace myself as we hit the frozen ground, sliding towards the army waiting patiently to die. Mutters and cries of alarm ring out as we streak through the ranks, a few swords even whipping out towards us in their shock and surprise. Soren snarls when a blade grazes his side.

"Soren!" I scream, feeling as if I was the one who was cut.

-*I'm fine,*- he assures me. -*Barely a scratch.*-

I can feel the truth in his words and know that he'll be ok, so I put it to the back of my mind and focus on the utter terror in front of me as we weave in and out of the soldiers, desperate to get to the front lines.

"Fuck, fuck, fuck," I grit out, and urge Soren on, desperate to do... I don't know what, exactly, but my Gift rises in my chest, ready and waiting...but Killian is blocking me. I can feel it, thicker than ever before. *Fuck!* Of course he'd be blocking anything and everything here, using the full power of his Gift in case anyone on the enemy side has powers to use against them. I grit my teeth, knowing I'll have to push past him somehow, hoping that I can. I don't know what aid I can truly render, but surely I can at least knock out the first line or two of their men with my ice? I don't know if it will be enough to truly help with numbers this large, but I have to try, I have to do *something*. Everything inside of me is screaming to, telling me that this is where I'm meant to be, that I will somehow make a difference here.

We speed forward, somehow moving so fast that the world around us is just a blur of black armor and white snow, but so slowly that I think we're running in place, not moving an inch.

We're almost to the front line when I hear the sound, a strange shift in the air that I can't immediately place...until I look up and see the sky above Amon's forces filled with arrows. Thousands of them, maybe more, some on fire, all deadly.

"No!" I scream just as I hear Killian yell for his men to hold. His voice cuts to the heart of me and nothing else in the world matters. I slide from Soren's back and roll, the way Tobias taught me should I ever be thrown from a horse or the wagon, wincing as I tumble over the ice. The big cat roars his denial and protest inside my head, a snarl breaking free from his mouth for all to hear. Confusion ripples through the men closest to us, but most of them are distracted, staring at the incoming assault. I push myself up and run through the last line of men, breaking into the open space in front of them. I see Killian then out of the corner of my eye whipping his head from the sea of arrows flying towards him and his men to me. His eyes go wide and a roar tears from his throat.

"TESS!!"

The arrows reach their tipping point and begin their descent downward, the wind whistling as they fall, closer...closer...

I hit my knees and slide forward across the icy ground, unleashing my Gift like never before with a scream that feels as if it's ripping my throat apart. I feel Killian's wall blocking me for a fraction of a heartbeat before I crash right through it, crumbling it to dust. I hear him shout my name again, but I grit my teeth and push with all my might, sending ice out across the tundra, a great, roiling wave of it. I can see the edge of the Brink on the horizon.

-*Thea!*- Soren roars inside my mind and I feel him dig his claws into my soul, a wave of his strength crashing through me, refusing to let me go. I cling to him and the Brink fades away like the setting sun disappearing beneath the waves in Helios. Even so, my heart feels as if it's going to explode, my every vein on fire and feeling as if it's trying to rip free from my body. Is this what it feels like? To be torn apart by your Gift?

But in this moment, I understand that woman from the story the man told us at the tavern. I understand seeing my own end and choosing to meet it in order to save those that I love.

It all happens in a matter of seconds, but it feels like ages to me, time crawling like a snail along a window ledge. I can barely breathe, but I realize that I've done it.

The arrows don't fall. The army doesn't advance. Killian is safe.

My vision tunnels, darkness closing in from all sides. I feel something wet and hot above my upper lip and when I wipe my hand across it, my fingers come away red. I turn to see Killian rushing towards me as the darkness takes over completely, and then I'm gone.

CHAPTER SEVENTEEN
KILLIAN

It's a strange feeling to accept death, to know that Noxum is waiting in the wings to take you by the hand into the hereafter, whether it be to the heavens or one of the hells. There's a freedom to it that's surprising. The ever-present question of *is this my last day? Is this when it ends?* that all men have in the back of their minds finally quiets now that I know the answer. This. This is my last day. This is where it ends. I knew it the moment we entered the field and saw *thousands* of warriors in crimson across the plain, waiting and eager for our blood. I don't know how it's happened, how they hid so much of their might, but there's no use dwelling on that now.

Stranger than the freedom that quieted my mind, knowing this was the end, is the pain. Any other time in my life, I wouldn't have felt it. I'm a warrior, born to fight and defend. I have people that I care about and want to protect, a whole continent that I had grand delusions of trying to save from Barony and the treacheries he's been hefting upon Gifteds for years, a whole army under my command that look to me for answers and guidance. And yet, before now, I would have met Noxum without fear or doubt, no pain or regret settling in my veins colder than the frozen lands around me.

Because before now, I didn't have *her*.

Tess' beautiful face stays ever present behind my eyes as I stare out at my downfall. Piercing green eyes like emeralds set aflame that somehow look to the heart of me; deep, fiery hair that feels like silk beneath my fingers; the perfect bow of her lips, soft and giving beneath my own; the small scar in the shape of a bird just beneath her collarbone and the quiet gasps that escape when I run my tongue along it.

I cursed the Makers the day I laid eyes on her beside that stream, running for her life but also prepared to stand and fight for it, because I knew, I fucking *knew* in that instant, that I was gone. I hated them for making me so drawn to her the moment she shifted her shoulders back, fire in her eyes, ready to do battle with the men trying to take her. *Warrior,* my mind had whispered, a true warrior to her core. It was the opposite of what I'd envisioned the Flame of Lyanna to be. Stories and songs had painted her as a cruel, cold-hearted bitch who looked down on anyone and everyone, who was selfish and spoiled, someone who didn't deserve the Gift she was given.

I'd been all too happy when word of her journey to Marrowood reached my ears, the rumbling among Hunters about the outrageous bounty that would come from her capture. And to find that I could collect her myself? A boon from the Makers themselves, I'd thought. I was fucking *eager* to put her in her place, to teach her a little bit about the real world outside of her palace walls, to watch her struggle to be powerless and cold and dirty, to hear her complain and curse me and mine to the depths of the seven hells, and I'd grin all the fucking while as she did.

Imagine my surprise when she did none of that. She was cold and callous, sure, but it never seemed like it was truly her. She didn't try to hurt anyone within my camp, though she clearly could have, skilled as she was at fighting—another surprise. She didn't attempt to unleash her power and burn us all to ash when I'd taunted her to try time and time again. Slowly, her coldness began to thaw. Only with Mia at first, then with Dessa and some of the others.

And when she clawed at those stones, desperate to get to Mia and the others until her fingers were bloody, broken messes, I knew that everything I'd been told about this woman had been a lie. I didn't understand why, why she felt she had to pretend to be so awful, but there must be a reason. We all have our secrets and play our parts, after all.

Against all the odds, and admittedly, my better judgment, I let myself give in to that immediate connection I'd felt from the first moment, that draw that lured me to her like a moth to the flame. I grew closer to her, finding myself noticing every fucking detail, missing her every second I wasn't nearby. I used to mock those fools that spoke of intervention from the Makers when it came to matters of love, that they made plans for us all and that things happened for reasons they demanded. It was utter bullshit. Children's tales. Ridiculous.

Now, I understand it all. Now, I realize that I was the fool. She was meant for me. I was meant to find her that day, meant to bring her into my life. She is the piece of me that has been missing all these years. When I'd finally given up all pretense and kissed her that night —and more. Great fucking Makers the *more* of that night is a constant memory at the forefront of my mind. The way she moaned. The way she tasted. The feel of her losing herself completely on my tongue. Even now, a slow shudder rolls through me at the thought. When I'd finally crossed that line and she hadn't hesitated to leap headlong across it with me, I knew that we were truly fated by the Makers.

And we barely fucking had time. I curse the Makers now, for that. How cruel to show me a glimpse of the heavens I was supposedly promised only to snatch it all away before we'd even had a chance to truly begin, before I had the chance to tell her the truth of it all, not just my feelings, but all of it. She deserves to know. I guess she will, eventually, but I wanted to be the one to explain it all, to make her see...

I take a deep breath and share a look with Dessa. She's my oldest and dearest friend and though I know she's beside me because she has the heart of a warrior and wouldn't be anywhere else, I still feel responsible for what's about to happen. My chest clenches thinking of Mia.

She knows what I'm thinking, as she always seems to, as she always has. I wouldn't have survived the horrors of childhood if not for her. She presses her lips into a thin line, sorrow filling those icy blue eyes, but then she inclines her head, telling me without words that it's alright and that she'll find me again when we cross over.

"The mountains do not move."

I give her a sad smile, and finish the battle cry we made up as children, fighting imaginary foes with wooden swords in her father's armory, raging imaginary battles across the mountainsides. We've brought it with us into every fray since. It's only fitting that it's with us at the last.

"And the dragons do not yield."

I hold her gaze for a moment longer and turn to look out across the plain to my enemies once more. Accepting death and giving up are two entirely different things, so the cold calm of battle settles over me, and I grip the pommel of my great sword, sending up a quick prayer to Brienne, the Maker of war, despite me cursing her brethren only moments ago. I will cleave through all the seven hells to try to get back to Tess. I tense as their archers let their arrows fly, a whole sea of them sailing towards us.

"Hold!" I roar, knowing there's nothing else we can do. Those that fight with shields raise them, hoping to ward off the worst of the blows, but I know this first strike will take many of my men. I commend their souls to Noxum and ask that he watch over them.

Startled gasps and curses ripple through my army, unlike them even in the face of death, and a moment later, I see a figure burst forth from the front line a few yards to my right, and my heart freezes in my chest. Long, red hair billows behind her like a banner of war as she races forward.

No.

"What the fuck!?" Dessa breathes, fear etched on her fierce, beautiful face.

No, no, no. She can't fucking be here. What in the seven hells is she doing?? Even if she can burn some of their line, she can't destroy the whole of the army. There are at least a thousand, maybe more. Even if she destroys some of them, then she's here, in the middle of a fucking battlefield and I can't protect her and why would that fucking cat let her do this and *I can't fucking breathe.*

"TESS!" I roar just before she slides to her knees across the frozen ground and...

I rear back as if I've been struck. Her Gift rips through my walls with unreal ease—I hadn't even thought to let it down, too much whirling through my mind to focus—and...*ice* bursts forth from her extended palms.

Ice. Not fire. Fucking *ice*. A great wave of it, turning into a solid wall as it sails across the tundra and through Amon's forces. The few that managed to scream only get the luxury for mere heartbeats before the sounds cut off as if they've been severed with a blade—quick and clean.

It only takes a few moments for the *entirety* of the army to be entombed in a block of ice miles wide and just as thick.

All. Of. Them.

A thousand men, at least. The power is unlike anything I've ever seen, but...

"What the fuck?" Dessa whispers from beside me, eyes wide and incredulous, but I barely spare her a glance. I'm already sprinting for Tess. Blood pours from her nose and she sways. Soren leaps towards her, sliding beneath her before she can hit the ground and cushioning her fall with his big body. I'm there a moment later, gathering her into my arms.

"Tess? Tess!?" I push her hair from her face, her brow covered in cold sweat. Ah Makers, did she push herself too far? I've never seen any Gifted wield like this. Even bonded, what I've just witnessed is fucking impossible. There's no way she could do this without reaching the Brink, could she? Frantically, I check the pulse racing at her throat, her heart beating wildly, but strong, in her chest. She's ok, I think. I still want to get her to Copeland as soon as possible to make sure, but she's alive, at least.

"Sir, what...what just happened?" Lucian, my first lieutenant whispers at my back.

"Tell the men to hold until I say otherwise," I tell him, still trying to figure out the answer to his question myself. I feel him walk away and hear him roaring my command to the others, telling them to remain. I know my army—not a single soul will move until I tell them to. Soren prowls back and forth before me. "Is she alright?" I ask the cat. He inclines his head to me and huffs, and I nod in thanks, accepting that she must be ok. He wouldn't be this calm otherwise. The stories say that once a pair is bonded, they can feel each other's pain, and the loss of one is worse than death for the other. If he's ok, then she must be as well.

I shift my focus to the other end of the tundra, to the frozen army there as I try and fail to understand. I gently lower Tess to the ground just as Dessa drops to her knees beside me. She looks at Tess worriedly, taking in the blood still smeared beneath her nose and across her cheek.

"Is she...?"

"She lives," I say gruffly, throat tight. How close had she come to the Brink? How close had I come to losing her? And how in the absolute fuck did she just wield *ice*??

"Did you know?" I demand in a low voice, sharp as a whip.

"What?? No, of course not! She's the Flame of Lyanna. The Burning Beauty. The Fire Bitch. I don't fucking understand, Kill."

"Neither do I."

"Well, either way, I'm glad you let her past your wall," she says, looking toward the wall of ice across the field.

"I didn't," I whisper, and Dessa whips her head back to me.

"What??"

"I didn't let her through. She broke it like it was nothing. I didn't even feel her here until I saw her." I shake my head, anger at myself rising. I'd put my full power into my Gift to ensure any Gifteds fighting for Amon were rendered useless. When I do that, all the energies just blend together, a steady hum forced beneath the might of my wall. If I'd known she was there, I could have picked her Gift out and allowed it through like I do with our own Gifteds, but without that prior knowledge, it was just another stream of energy that I pushed down with the rest.

"She...*broke through?*" She glances back to Tess, unconscious on the ground. Dessa knows damn well that no one has ever been able to do such a thing, not even close. "Who is this woman?" she whispers in wonder. *Who, indeed.*

"Stay with her," I say before I rise and bark for a few of the lieutenants to join me. We march cautiously across the tundra to get a closer look at what's happened. It's truly unreal. I glance up as we near the wall, staring at the sea of arrows suspended above our heads in what resembles the crest of a wave, curling back to meet the top of the wall. I place a hand on the thick, smooth sheet of ice before me. We can see through it, clear with a faint bluish tint, and within it are bodies. Thousands of bodies, frozen in an instant where they stood, mouths open in silent, eternal screams.

"Great fucking Makers," Malik mutters.

"You two, go around the edges and see how far back it goes, see if any of their troops remain on the back side."

Phillipe and Callum incline their heads and take off.

"You know, I thought the Flame of Lyanna would yield, well, flames," Nigel says, running his hand down the wall. He is rarely upset by much, and it's for that reason that he's one of my best officers. He's taking even this in stride whereas I am trying extraordinarily hard to act as if I'm doing the same. Inside, everything is complete chaos, every thought in my mind churning too quickly to grasp any single thought. None of this makes sense. I have seen first-hand the ruin left behind after Tess' work. Scorched fields and ashen forests and great floods after an entire hillside of snow was melted too quickly. So...she has two Gifts? I've never heard of such a thing but perhaps it has to do with being bonded with Soren. But even the legends of familiars never told of them bestowing a second Gift.

"Do we just...leave them?"

"Not much else we can do," I say, turning to walk back toward my own army, leaving the forever frozen one behind. "Send missives to Barony and the rest of the Alliance, tell them that Amon's forces here were defeated without a single drop of blood shed. Tell them that is the power of our might and they should plan accordingly. Have Ryker send messages with his ravens to all of Hypathia. I want rumors of this victory spreading like wildfire." I glance up and see a silver raven circling overhead and know that Alexi will get word back to Ryker before my men will have a chance. I wonder what he'll think of all of this, if there are any records of two Gifts in their archives.

"Yes, sir," Malik nods, running off.

"Nigel, get the troops back to camp. I'll meet with you all later after I've...figured out some things."

I gather Tess into my arms and though I'm confused beyond measure, I send a prayer of thanks up to any Maker that might be listening for the woman in my arms.

CHAPTER EIGHTEEN
THEA

I wake with a jolt, a scream trapped in my throat as I tear free from dreams of battle and blood. What had happened? Had I stopped the arrows? Had I stopped enough of Amon's forces to give Killian and his men a chance? My heart races and panic thunders through my veins.

"Easy," the low, rumbling voice that's quickly become the center of my world says from across the room. I blink, brushing hair from my face, and realize that I'm in Killian's bed, safely back inside his tent. He's sitting at his desk, watching me from the shadows. Relief rushes through me. He's ok. He's here and he's ok and he's—

Oh fuck.

I'd used my Gift. He knows the truth. Or, he knows I have the power to wield ice, at least. I swallow hard and lick my dry lips. As always, he seems to read my mind.

"Water on the table."

He sounds...neither angry nor happy. Even-toned. Closed off. I don't know if that's a bad sign or not, and decide I need the extra minute to collect my thoughts, so I pour a glass and drink the entire thing in a few long gulps, gasping, but quickly refilling it again. I feel alright, physically, though I'm still tired. I remember the blood on my hand before I passed out and instinctively reach upward. My fingers of course come away empty.

"Copeland checked. You are alright. The...exertion strained your body and caused the blood. I'm assuming it was because you were close to the Brink." His voice tightens at that.

"Oh," I say, not having any idea what else to offer. I remember the feeling, of seeing the limits of my power, feeling the weight of them trying to tear me apart—and choosing to keep going. For those soldiers. For Dessa and Mia.

But mostly for him. Everything I have and everything I am, is for him.

"Is everyone alright? The battle..."

"There was no battle," he says, tone still flat. "You froze the whole of Amon's army in their tracks." He says it matter of factly, but my eyes bulge and I cough on the water, nearly choking. My heart races. There's no way that's fucking possible. He has to be mistaken.

"That's...impossible," I whisper.

"The thousand men permanently entombed in ice would beg to differ, I'd wager."

I run my hand through my hair, not able to wrap my mind around what he's saying. How could I possibly do such a thing?

-*I told you that you have no idea what you're capable of, daska,*- Soren purrs in my mind. -*I'm glad you're awake. I'll leave you to your... conversation.*-

He says *conversation* as if he truly means confession and possible battle following thereafter, and my heart thuds against my chest again for completely different reasons.

-*Good luck...*-

"I'm waiting, Tess," Killian finally says after I remain silent for a few moments, trying to gather my thoughts, trying to figure out how to fix this. My finger snakes into my hair, twirling, twirling, twirling, heart hammering.

Killian rises and stalks towards me, dragging the chair with him and placing it just beside the bed. He sits again, leaning forward to rest his elbows on his knees, and meets my gaze. His eyes are more gray than blue in the low light, but they're churning with too many things to name. Thankfully none of them seem to be rage.

"Tess," he says again, softer. A plea.

I think about lying. I could make up a story about a second Gift that I'd hidden away all these years, or maybe he would believe I gained a second when I bonded—little is really known about familiars anymore. It could be a possibility for all we know...But I discard the ideas as quickly as they surface. I don't want to lie to him anymore. I want to tell him everything, every last detail about who I am and the life I've lived. I need him to know. I'll figure out the rest after we get to Duskthorne. If I can freeze an entire army, surely I can convince Dorian that not having Tesni to ransom isn't such a bad thing, in the end. Though, I'm not sure I could do something that extreme again...

So, feeling as though it may be a terrible idea, I take a deep breath, and I tell him the truth.

"My name," I say softly, "is Thea."

"What?" His brow furrows, every line of his handsome face etched with confusion. Whatever he'd been expecting me to say, it sure as hells wasn't that.

"I will tell you the truth, all of it, every single detail if you wish it, though I'll warn you that many are unpleasant, but...but I need you to let me get everything out before you ask questions." I know I need to rip the bandage off, as Cece would say. Open the gates and let everything out all at once. This will be the first time I've ever told my entire truth out loud to anyone. There are parts that even Cece and Math don't know.

He stares at me, jaw clenching and unclenching, his fists doing the same. He finally seems to force his body to heel, his jaw relaxing and his fingers unfurling. He runs a hand across his bearded chin before finally saying, "Alright."

"Tesni is my twin sister. We—"

"Twin?? No, that's not possible. Barony's Gifted doesn't have a —" I give him a look and though it seems like it physically pains him, he presses his lips into a hard line and nods.

"Tesni is my twin," I say again. "Barony adopted us when we were four years old with the hopes that we would have Gifts. I lived in the castle with my sister until we were twelve." I swallow hard around the lump in my throat as the memories of that awful day come flooding back, but I tell him all of it. I tell him about Barony's twisted game of forcing the two of us to choose who would stay and who would be sold; of how I never would have thought either of us could play, but Tesni leapt at the chance; of how the sister I thought I'd known died that day, the cruel, heartless bitch that he'd heard tale of taking her place. I told him how I escaped, the fear and the pain and the utter despair I felt as I fled. I tell him about the long, awful days afterward hiding in ditches and alleyways, digging through rubbish bins for food, dodging Barony's soldiers prowling through the kingdom to find me. I tell him of the months on the road as I made my way south, of the men who were...unkind to a young girl on her own. His knuckles turn white from how tightly he clenches his fists at that, and he rises to pace. I spare him all of the details, of the things tried and the harm I caused in response, skipping ahead to Tobias instead.

"He saved my life in more ways than I could possibly count," I say, bittersweet memories making my heart swell and shatter at once. "He took me in and protected me, fed me, taught me to defend myself and how to find my way by the stars, how to be smart and strong and kind, no matter how bad things got. My surname is from him: Sparrowhill. He called me Sparrow in those first few months, when I was too afraid to speak the truth, because of the cut—now scar—just here," I say, tapping on my collarbone. The spot that Killian likes to kiss, the memories of his tongue and lips there making my pulse jump.

"His surname was Hill, so I combined the two when I was brave enough to reclaim my own first name, the only thing I was able to keep of myself for a very long time." I clear my throat around the lump lodged there before I can continue. "He got sick a few years after we met. It happened quickly, thank the Makers, so he didn't suffer long. After that, I took all that he taught me and found my way to Helios. I'd planned to find passage on a boat to Sol and leave the continent behind completely, but I met Cecelia and Matthais and they saved me all over again. Tobias taught me how to survive. Math and Cece taught me how to live again."

I tell him of the crazy dream Math had to open a tavern right at the port, drawing in all of the sailors and living with paradise right outside our front door, and how we all worked ourselves to the bone for three long years before we saved up enough to buy the building and get the tavern up and running.

Killian stops pacing at that and exhales, deciding the worst of the story has passed and coming to sit once more.

"Not long after we opened the tavern, I got a letter from Tesni telling me that she knew where I was, and so long as I stayed hidden away, she would keep my location and the fact that I was still alive, a secret. She left me alone for years after that, as promised. I lived my life, changed my appearance, and became someone else entirely. Until one day…"

I tell him the rest of the story and he keeps his promise to remain silent until I finish.

"And…and that's all, I guess." I let out a long, slow exhale and twist my fingers into the fur blanket, more anxious than I've ever been. What will he think? What will he do? "I wanted to tell you the truth, but I couldn't, not until we reached Duskthorne and I found out what Dorian wanted to do with me." He clenches his jaw but nods, seeming to understand. "Are you…angry?"

He blinks at that. "Angry?"

"That I'm not who I said I was. That I've been lying to you all this time."

"You were lying to save your own life. You were lying to protect yourself and people you care about." His eyes burn with a sudden intensity then, as if the words are some of the most important he's ever said. "How could I be angry with you for that?"

The vice around my heart that had been tightening and tightening while I waited for his response finally releases its grip and relief floods through my veins like a raging river.

"And you haven't been lying to me," he says softly, "not really." I blink and he sighs, running a hand through his hair. "You may have been hiding your true Gift and you may have been using a different name, but I know you down to your soul...*Thea*." The sound of my name on his lips, finally *my* name, makes heat wash through me, a shiver of pleasure rippling up my spine. His lips quirk at the corners and I know that he noticed.

"I know that you're kind and thoughtful and that you care about others so much that their joy is your joy, their pain your pain, even complete strangers." I know he's thinking of the village and I quickly push those thoughts away. "I know that you love Abrasian chocolate. I know that you are excellent at quills but cheat at cards and cups." My mouth pops open to protest, but he only smirks and continues on. "I know that you love to look at the stars, especially when you can't sleep. I know that you scrunch your nose when you're trying to hold back tears and that you hum when you braid your hair, and that you twirl this lock around your finger whenever you're deep in thought or worried about something." He shifts forward, voice going low and rough when he says, "I know the sounds you make just before you're going to come, that hitch of breath and the quiet, gasping moan..." My entire body shudders and my cheeks heat, and his lips curl on one side.

He reaches out and takes my hand, running his fingertips over my knuckles before meeting my gaze again.

"And I know that you've said that you love me in your sleep almost every single night since the cave." I suck in a sharp breath, having no idea that I'd said something so important in my fucking sleep. I'm somewhat mortified, truth be told, thankful that I haven't said anything else before now that could have revealed my secret.

"But I would do fucking anything to hear you say it true, Thea."

My eyes burn and he's right: I scrunch my nose to try to keep the tears at bay. I don't think I've ever felt so loved or understood or seen in my life, and my belief that the Makers brought us together solidifies. Killian was made for me, to be mine, and I was made for him. I don't know what the future holds. I don't know how this works between us, or if Dorian will allow it to continue once we reach Duskthorne, but I will do anything to be with this man, to take this love and burn down the entire world for it if needed.

I crawl out of the bed and he shifts back in his chair as I approach, watching me with burning blue-gray eyes. I slide into his lap, straddling him, and wrap one arm around his neck, tangling my fingers into his hair. I slide my other hand across his cheek, his beard tickling my palm, and his big hands grip my waist, the heat of him seeming to burn through the thin silk of my nightgown. Thank the fucking Makers that he put me in this after the battle, that only this tiny bit of fabric stands between us now.

I hold his gaze for a long, long moment, finally giving myself permission to leap, to fly with this man beside me forever.

"I love you, Killian Blackheart."

His eyes slide closed and he leans his forehead against my own. He exhales, long and slow, and pulls back to look at me once more. He reaches up and brushes hair from my face, grazing his knuckles along my cheek, and I wait for him to say the words back, the three words I've been waiting my entire life to hear.

"I tolerate your presence more than most, I suppose—ow!" He laughs when I pull his hair, and I try to fight a smile.

"You are a horse's ass."

"And you love that about me."

"Makers fucking help me, I do," I sigh, shaking my head. "I really do."

He grips my chin gently between his thumb and forefinger, and guides my face to his. Just before our lips touch, he says quietly, "I love you, Thea Sparrowhill. No matter what's to come, no matter what obstacles try to block our path, I will never stop loving you and fighting for you, for *us*."

Perfect contentment settles over me and I finally feel as if I'm right where I'm meant to be, like I've been running my entire life towards this moment, here, with this man.

I press my lips to his then, not able to hold myself back for another second. I tangle both hands into his hair now, holding his face to mine and he growls in approval low in his chest. A frenzied desperation rises up in me, all of these weeks together, all of the years waiting to find him, how differently the battle against Amon could have gone—everything coming together in a storm that I can't escape. I rock my hips, feeling him hard and ready beneath me. The kiss quickly spirals, far from gentle or soft. It's hard and deep and greedy. Teeth and tongues and lips clash, my hands dig into his hair and neck and shoulders, ripping at his shirt as he tears my nightgown down the middle, the silk parting easily beneath his fingers.

I gasp when rough palms cover my breasts, kneading and pinching and driving me wild. He kisses down my throat, dipping his head to flick his tongue over one aching nipple and making me cry out in sheer bliss. He closes his lips around the peak, sucking hard and making me writhe. I grind atop him with abandon, the feel of his cock through his leathers gliding against me feeling so fucking good that I'm already close, that coiling deepening. Just a few more thrusts with him in that spot *right there* and—

As if reading the thought and being entirely offended by it, Killian stills my hips and growls low in his chest, the animalistic sound sending shivers of sweet anticipation through my body.

"Oh no you don't. You'll be coming on my tongue first, love."

I make a sound that's somewhere between a gasp and a whimper as he stands, setting me to my feet. I sway slightly but ask in a breathy whisper, "How did you know...?"

His crooked, cocky smirk pulls his lips. "I told you—I *know* you, Thea. Every sound, every breath, every scent. *Every fucking one.*"

I swallow hard, that knowledge somehow incredibly sexy.

"Now," he whispers, pressing me back against the tall chest beside the bed, "you'll want to hold on to the top of that. Your legs will be giving out soon."

"Fucking Makers," I moan, breathless, and he slides to his knees before me. He leans in and kisses my stomach, just below my navel, then lower, and lower still..."Fuck!" I cry when he licks me, one long, slow lap of his tongue that sends a wave of pleasure through my entire body. He groans and grips my thigh, placing it over his shoulder and shifting so I'm spread before him, his to devour.

"Makers, I will never tire of seeing you like this, Thea. Smooth and dripping and needy for me."

I swallow hard but look down and meet his eyes. "And I'll never tire of seeing you on your knees before me."

"I'll kneel for you forever, Thea, like the queen you are. Only you. Always you." I reach down and run my hand through his hair, and use my grip on the strands to guide his mouth back to me. He grins and sets to feasting like a starving man. I scream. I writhe. I come so hard that my legs do give out, just as he promised, but my iron grip on the trunk keeps me upright long enough for Killian to rise and lift me, tossing me to the bed. I'm breathless, sweating and panting as I push up onto my elbows to watch him. He unlaces his leathers and I watch, rapt, as his cock springs free. He grips his shaft as he steps free from his boots and pants, and I lick my lips as he stands there, stroking while he watches me.

"You'll tell me," he says gruffly, eyes burning as he continues to stroke, as his gaze shifts to where I've let my knees fall wide in clear invitation. Not so much an invitation, really, but a demand. I need him more than I've ever needed anyone or anything. "You'll tell me if it's too much."

"It won't be," I promise him. I can tell he's warning me not just about his size, but of other things. I've caught glimpses already of how he likes to be. Rough kisses and nips of teeth, tight grips and groans of pleasure when I dig my nails deep into his skin, demands and commands and words that would make the most devout priestess blush and forgo all of her vows. We are alike in so many ways, and our preferences in the bedchamber are among the many. *Thank fucking Makers for that.*

I hold his gaze and make sure he can see the absolute truth in my words before I speak.

"I want everything you have to give, Killian. All of it."

His eyes slide closed for a moment, a small ripple of pleasure cascading down his lean, powerful body. He opens them once more and they're absolutely blazing, a flame beneath a tempest. He smiles a sultry, sinful smile as he climbs on to the bed.

"As my queen commands it."

CHAPTER NINETEEN

KILLIAN

It will take me some time to truly wrap my mind around all that...Thea has told me this night. Thea. Not Tess, but *Thea*. A fucking twin. I can scarcely believe it all, but I'd be lying if I said that the fact that she isn't Barony's Gifted after all doesn't ease something inside my chest. It turns out Tesni's reputation is even more accurate than I could have guessed, the fire bitch that betrayed her own twin and left her to fend for herself at only twelve. I burn with fury at all that Thea has endured, all that she has overcome, but a fierce pride wells beside that fury. She is strong and resilient. She is kind, despite the world showing her the worst it has to offer. She is smart and giving and powerful beyond measure.

And she is mine.

I settle above her, bracing myself on one straightened arm as I grip my shaft and position the head at her entrance. Wet heat kisses the crown and I hiss between clenched teeth. Finally, after these weeks of holding ourselves back, I'm going to bury myself in this woman that was made for me, this woman who, despite having to have hidden herself from everyone, I know better than anyone else in this world.

I lean down and kiss her, deep and long, sweeping my tongue against hers and running the head of my cock along her pussy until she's writhing beneath me.

"Killian," she whisper-groans and I can't tell if she's cursing me for teasing her or begging me to give her more. Both, I'd wager.

"Ready?" I ask, voice low and husky with need.

"Yes," she breathes, arching her hips, desperate. I chuckle low but don't deny her any longer. I slowly press forward, feeding my cock inside her. She sucks in a sharp breath and I curse low. *Great fucking Makers* the feel of her, hot and wet and tight as a fist. I press forward, forcing myself to go slowly despite the clawing need to slam my hips forward, to bury my cock so deep inside her that she'll feel me for days. She digs her fingers into my lower back, and I pause.

"Alright?"

"Y-yes. Just...Great fucking Makers, Killian, I don't know if I can..." she pants and I can see the touch of panic in her eyes. I grip her chin between my thumb and forefinger and force her to meet my eyes.

"Breathe, Thea. You can take me, love, I know it. Just breathe and keep your eyes on me."

Her green eyes blaze at that, burning emeralds that I know just how to coax to life. She obeys, taking a deep breath, holding my gaze, and I shift my hips forward once more, sliding deeper. It's tight. *Fuck* it's tight, her walls squeezing me like a damned fist. I gnash my teeth against the pleasure, against the desires running through my mind, but I'd never fucking hurt her, so I'll do none of it until she's alright. She has to be alright. She has to be ready.

I reach down and massage her clit, rubbing slow, gentle circles, and she moans quietly, shifting her hips and a fresh wave of wet heat sends me slipping farther inside.

"That's my girl, you're doing so well, Thea. Makers, look at you..." She moans again, louder, and I glance down between our bodies, the sight of my cock, half buried inside her making me want to come here and now. She digs her fingers into my skin, pulling me forward.

"More." She writhes as she begs, sending me deeper. "More, Killian."

"So greedy," I tsk with a grin, but press forward, sliding in to the hilt. She cries out and arches off of the bed. "*Fuckkkkk.*" The wave of pleasure that crashes through me as she takes me so fucking deep is nearly too much, the feel of her so intense I can barely breathe. "Are you alright?"

"Yes," she rasps, meeting my gaze. Her pupils are expanded, only the faintest line of green around the black, and sweat beads her brow. I shift my hips backward before thrusting forward again, still slowly, still gently. Again. Once more, to be sure she's ready. She groans and pants, eyes sliding closed, her teeth digging into her bottom lip. She looks like an angel of the Makers' own creation, fiery hair spread out across the pillow beneath her head, lips red and swollen, skin flushed with wanting. I lean in and kiss her, sucking her bottom lip between my own before biting down. She cries out, fingers digging into my back harder now, nails biting into my skin, and hips arching upward, demanding.

"Hold on, love," I say, half playful, half warning. Her eyes flash open at that and there's no trepidation there, only a sultry challenge that sets my blood aflame.

"Let's see what the great Commander can do," she whispers, and I don't think I've ever been more aroused than I am in this fucking moment. The way she teases me. The way she pushes me. The way she challenges me in the best ways at every turn. *This woman...*

I start to move in earnest then, no more gentle thrusts, but powerful ones that have her clawing at my back and crying out in pleasure over and over, her breasts bouncing from the force of it, her hair looking like rippling flames as her head thrashes.

"Ah Makers, harder Killian," she begs and it's like a song to my heart. I shift back to my knees and pull her hips off of the bed, hooking her knees over my elbows and spreading her wide. The angle sends me deeper, hitting spots that have her screaming and sweat running down my chest and back with the strain of keeping myself from coming. I won't, not until I wring another orgasm from her first. She reaches up and grips her breasts, massaging and kneading. The sight nearly undoes me, but I clench my teeth as I pound into her, forcing my body under my command.

"Fucking hells, Thea. Pinch your nipples for me, love. Ah fuck, just like that. You look so fucking beautiful, taking my cock so well..."

She whimpers and makes a sound I'm all too familiar with now, that tiny hitch in her breath, the small change in the tenor of her soft moan. I smile.

"That's it, Thea. Come for me, love. Come hard around my cock."

I thrust two more times and she rakes her nails down my stomach, leaving bloody tracks that I'll wear like badges of great honor.

"Right...there...Killian...FUCK!"

She comes in a rush, her walls pulsing and squeezing me so fucking tightly, over and over as she rides the wave of release.

"Can feel you...fucking hells, Thea." Before she even stops spasming around me, I grip her waist and flip her to her stomach. Great fucking Makers, she doesn't hesitate, immediately pressing up to her hands and knees and raising her perfect ass into the air. I make some unholy animalistic sound at the sight and run my hand over the pert curve before gripping my cock and positioning it once more. I press inside her again, hoping that one day she'll allow me to do other things from this position. At the thought, I can't stop myself from trailing my fingers downward from the base of her spine, brushing over that forbidden spot for just a moment and making her gasp and writhe. I quirk a brow, thinking that my woman may very well enjoy that.

Later, I scold myself. *Later*. We have time. We have forever. I hope...No, I press the thought away. We will. We'll deal with whatever is to come and will be stronger for it. I grip her hips and slam forward as I tug her back, fucking her hard from behind. She cries out in pleasure, digging her fingers into the bed before turning to look over her shoulder at me. *Fucking hells*, if ever there were a sexier sight in all of the empire...

She reaches back and grips my thigh, nails biting, begging for more with hoarse, throaty screams. I give her what she wants, slamming my hips over and over, pulling her backwards on every thrust to hit deeper, harder.

"Fuck, fuck, fuck, Killian...I'm close..."

"I know," I tell her, panting, slick with sweat. "Come again. Want to feel your pussy squeezing me so fucking tight..."

I grab her arms and tug them behind her, crossing one over the other across the small of her back, forcing her shoulders to lower. She gasps and I grip both wrists in one hand as I slam my hips forward.

"Oh Makers," she cries. "Yes, yes, yes..." She screams as she comes again, but in this position, she can't move away, can't writhe or escape the full power of her climax. Her entire body trembles from the force of it and I yell her name as I follow her, coming so hard that stars explode in my vision, burning everything else in the world away.

We collapse together, both of us out of breath and covered with sweat. We lie there, tangled together, neither of us speaking for an eternity, the only sounds the crackling of the fire, our ragged breathing, and the beating of my heart loud in my ears.

Eventually she shifts and turns to face me. Her cheeks are flushed a beautiful pink, her hair a tangled mess of fire. I run my thumb over her bottom lip and she kisses the pad softly.

"Are you alright?" I ask.

"Alright is not an adequate word to describe how I am," she sighs.

"Good," I lean down and kiss her, the taste of salt on her lips. I push myself up and pour a glass of water from the pitcher on the table and hand it to her. She sits and takes it, sipping it gratefully, rubbing sweat from her brow and fanning herself. It's stifling in this fucking tent. As if reading my thoughts she gives me a look that says *here we go* and I feel her Gift rising. I have no block on her now, though I can still feel her energy like always. A moment later the temperature around us drops, cooling the sweat on my chest and back.

I blink and take a deep breath, letting it out slowly, still a bit shocked about her true Gift—and the strength of it.

"I imagine that came in handy in Helios." I arch a brow and she smiles.

"We told everyone that Math invented a contraption that cooled the air in the tavern with thick blades made from palm fronds tethered together, rotating by means of a series of pulleys and gears." She snorts at some memory of them creating the fraudulent machine I'm sure. "But it kept the seats and our coffers full, everyone dying to get inside Okania and escape the stifling heat." She shrugs.

"Okania--*freedom*," I muse at the use of the old Nydic word. The language has mostly gone extinct in the empire, but a few phrases have remained and are mixed in with the common tongue.

"It seemed like a fitting name, all of us needing it in some form or another there. Math from a bastard of a father; Cece from a loving but overbearing and exhausting family of fourteen; the sailors and pirates and patrons that found a safe haven in Helios for a million other reasons." She sighs. "And me from my old life."

"But you've never really used your Gift?" She knows what I mean and shakes her head.

"That first day when I escaped the guards, and a few times since then to defend myself, but I kept it hidden as much as possible. It was the only way I knew how to survive."

"So, you've never trained with it then?"

"No." She blinks, frowning. "I...well, I didn't really know you could do that?"

I roll my eyes. "Of course you can train it. It's how you get stronger, gain more control, like any other part of your body. Thea, with the power you unleashed on that tundra..." I shake my head, still in awe of it. If she can truly learn to wield it, she would be an asset to our army. Hells, she could end this war before it even really starts. A conversation with Yara from years ago surfaces in my mind and inhale quietly. The old loon, who I love dearly, was in one of her moods, spouting nonsense about how the world had been long, long ago, how the dragons and winds and Makers and anything else you could think of speak to her of all manner of things...and how it was foretold long ago that there would be a Gifted one day that would make all other Gifteds dim in the brightness of their power. This Gifted would end a darkness encroaching upon our world and put things back to rights. This Gifted would be important to all of us—but particularly to *me*...

My heart races. Could she truly have been speaking of...Thea? I shake myself, pushing the memories away and deciding that I'm as insane as Yara.

"Let's talk about it later," I tell Thea, kissing her forehead. "You must be exhausted."

She gets a wicked gleam in her eye and those perfectly bowed lips curl upward in a sensual, teasing smile.

"Have you forgotten?" she whispers, shifting to her knees and pressing against my chest, pushing me to lie back on the bed. "I do believe I promised to ride you like a wild Northland until your eyes rolled back in your head..." She straddles my waist and wraps her palm around my already hardening cock, stroking as she meets my gaze, all manner of wicked promises held in those emerald depths.

"Now that you mention it," I rasp, tucking one arm behind my head and reaching out to grip her waist with the other, "I do recall something of the sort..."

She runs her tongue along her bottom lip and my cock pulses in her grasp.

"I believe you have mountains to shake, Commander..."

With that, she makes good on her promise.

CHAPTER
TWENTY
THEA

"Do it again!" Mia cries with glee and I laugh but oblige. I send the snow around her churning into a slow cyclone, eventually building up enough speed to lift her into the air. She whoops and screams, telling me not to stop, but after a few minutes I let the cycle toss her into a soft bank of snow. She pops out, covered in white powder and grinning from ear to ear.

It's taken me a little while to get used to the new strength of my Gift since my bonding with Soren. It's...heady, to say the least. A little terrifying too, if I'm being honest. It takes far less thought and power to do simple things now, and I can do far greater things than I ever imagined—though I of course haven't tried anything even close to what happened on the tundra that day. A part of me feels guilt for all of those lives I took, all those souls given over to Noxum in a heartbeat and forever encased in that ice. It will never get warm enough to thaw them completely.

Kendall says it will be a monument to my greatness, that people will travel from all over the empire just to see it one day. He has it in his head that I'll be the savior of the continent now somehow. I've told him more than once how absurd that is, but he only smiles and says that he is eager to spread the word that he's a friend to the great Ice Queen of Hypathia—though he insists that the Ice Queen of *Duskthorne* sounds better, hoping that I'll truly be a part of them soon enough.

I have no idea if that could ever be true. Killian seems sure that King Dorian will be all too willing to have me as part of his army and won't give two flying fucks about the ransom now, but unease still coils in my belly as we draw nearer. He's a madman. Who's to say how he'll react or what he'll think or do.

Now that I'm free to use my Gift, the journey is much easier and we're making quick work of these last few days. I can clear the snow from our path quickly and divert the worst of the storms from overhead, sending the drifts out of our way.

"I still can't believe you aren't her. Or, well, I can because you were never quite as awful as you were supposed to be, but...it's all so crazy," Dessa says, shaking her head.

"I know," I sigh. "Trust me, I never wanted any of this to happen..." I shift my gaze to Killian as he strides down the main path between the tents, talking to Nigel and a few other officers. Odessa follows my gaze and tosses the stick she'd been drawing patterns in the snow with at me.

"I'd say it didn't turn out so bad, in the end."

Word has most definitely spread about the two of us after the tundra, but now that my true identity is also known by all, there doesn't seem to be any hostility about us being together. In fact, I've had several people apologize to me for how they acted when they thought I was Tesni.

"I would have said and done far worse in your position, trust me. I hate my sister more than anyone else on this earth," I assure Michael, an older gentleman who had spat at the ground every time I walked by, cursing me to the depths of the seventh hell every day for the last two months. I still don't know all of the details, but Tesni was somehow responsible for the deaths of his family, and I add it to the very long list of things my sister will one day atone for at my hand. Somehow, I know deep in my bones that this will all end with the two of us. Fire and ice, fighting to the last.

I'll be ready when the day comes.

Ryker had sent a missive with Alexi a day after the incident on the tundra. A simple message that had made me smile for days.

Thea,
Welcome to life out of the shadows. I cannot wait to see how brightly you shine.
Yours truly,
King Ryker Ashdown, IV

"Do you think he's lonely?" I'd asked Soren as Alexi waited patiently for me to finish my reply to Ryker.

-*Why do we care?*- Soren had drawled, shooting a disdainful look at the bird. The raven had cawed irritably at that and Soren had grumbled, rolling his icy blue eyes. -*Ok, fine, he says thank you for worrying, but he is fine. He has many brethren throughout the lands and keeps time with them, learning of all the happenings from all of Hypathia.*-

I started at that, turning to the bird.

"Do you know what's happening in Helios? Are the people there safe?"

Alexi cawed again, jumping to the desk and nudging his head beneath my fingers

-*He says that ships have tried to enter the bay, but they have been thwarted. Helios remains safe for now.*-

I sighed in relief. "Thank you."

I sent the raven off with another letter for Cece and Math as well, telling them that I was ok, that we were nearly to the end of our journey—still not revealing where we were truly headed—and that I would find a way to them soon. If the chains had been dropped to protect the bay, finding a way to Sol would be far more difficult. Not impossible, but difficult. I told them in a coded way to be ready to flee just in case and sent the bird on his way.

"So…is it as…um…*prolific* as they say?" Dessa whispers, drawing me back to the present. Now that I've stopped having to lie, our friendship has grown even stronger and I was all too happy to join the other ranks who are allowed to call her by the shortened version of her name. I saw her pin a young lad with a glare that sent him scurrying away and probably pissing himself when he'd tried it without permission.

I look at her blankly and she rolls her eyes. "You know…Killian's… *sword*."

I bark out a laugh and clap a hand over my mouth.

"Who is *they*?"

"Everyone," she says, as if that's obvious. "There are literal songs sung about it in taverns throughout Duskthorne." I snort at that, needing to hear these tunes immediately.

"You're joking. Are you joking?" I tilt my head and narrow my eyes. "I can't tell if you're joking."

"I'm not. He is legendary for more than the strength of his Gift and his fierceness in battle." She arches a brow, the golden rings glinting in the sunlight. "He's like a brother to me, but that doesn't mean I can't be…curious about certain things when I hear about them nonstop from gossiping hens throughout the kingdom." I glance to Killian again and I can't say I'm surprised that he has a reputation. He seems to feel me staring and turns, meeting my gaze and smiling.

"Ah hells, I'm sorry, does that make you upset?"

"Upset? No. Why would it?"

"I mean, you're not jealous?"

I snort at that, laughing. "I don't think a man can look and act like *that* and not have women—and men, for that matter—begging to be in his bed. He had a life before me…and I was no nun before I met him either," I add with a waggle of my brows. She laughs.

"I'll need to hear of these exploits once we're home." Home. For her, it is. For me? I have no idea. Odessa presses on. "So…the songs are true then? You're the only one I know personally who has firsthand knowledge of the…situation. The barmaid at the Wolf's Head *claims* she does but I don't believe a word out of that wench's mouth. I mean, he's the—" She seems to choke on the words, biting them back and searching for different ones to use. I frown. "He's the Commander of the army and has chambers in the palace at his disposal. Most of the women he beds are courtiers and such." She plasters a smile on her face but something is off about it, a bit too forced. I eye her but decide I'm imagining things that aren't there as the nerves draw tighter and tighter within me, the unknown gnawing at me like a dog with a bone.

I learn forward and say in a lower voice, "Calling it *prolific* would be like calling that great sword a dagger," I say, nodding towards Jonathan's sword resting at his hip. The big man wields a massive long sword that looks as if it would take at least three men to lift.

Her eyes widen and she gives me an appreciative look.

"Good for you, princess, good for you."

I roll my eyes. "You're never going to drop the princess thing, are you? Even now that you know the truth?"

"Nope," she tells me, smiling and popping the *p* loudly. We laugh but it fades quickly as I look into the distance, the looming mountains far too close now. Odessa follows my gaze and her face pinches. "You needn't worry, I promise." I must look skeptical. "Do you trust me? And more importantly, do you trust *him*?" She tilts her head back towards Killian.

"Yes," I say quickly. "To both." I trust them both with my life… though Killian is still being evasive about the war and whatever he claims Barony has been doing. He says he needs to explain it all once we reach Duskthorne, and while it doesn't help the worry slithering through my stomach, I agree to wait.

"Then, as I said, you needn't worry."

I sigh and eye the mountains again. "I guess we'll see tonight."

WE MAKE IT TO THE SEEVA LATER THAT AFTERNOON. A thin layer of ice crusts along the edges of the enormous river already as true winter draws ever closer, though the heart of it still flows strong enough to give me pause. The river is so wide here that I can't even see the opposite bank, and though a large wooden bridge stretches over the water, disappearing into the distance, it looks as if it's been here since the early days of Hypathia itself.

"Are you sure this will hold?" I ask, glancing over the side of the bridge warily into the rushing water below, swallowing hard as the wind whips at my hair. The boards creak beneath the horses' hooves and I clench my jaw. Soren leaps atop the low wall lining the edge of the bridge and I inhale sharply.

-*Get off of there! What if you fall!?*-

My heart leaps into my throat and the big cat turns to look at me, somehow managing to look annoyed and smug at once. He starts to walk casually along the narrow strip of weathered wood and I glare at him.

-*You're an ass.*-

-*You're an overprotective mother hen,*- he counters. -*I'm a fucking frost cat, daska. A bonded frost cat at that. I could scale the side of that mountain as easy as climbing a sapling now.*-

I blink at that, looking to the monolith looming in the near distance.

-*Really?*-

-*Really. You aren't the only one who was radically strengthened by our bond.*-

I knew he benefited as well, of course, but I hadn't realized just how strong he'd gotten, how agile and swift. Memories of the forest blurring around us as we ran for the tundra flash through my mind. I hadn't realized at the time just how fast the cat had been running.

-*Yes, yes, I am extraordinarily impressive, I know. Now let me have my fun, damn you,*- he adds, swishing his tail behind him in annoyance as he sprints across the wall.

"It has held for hundreds of years," Killian answers, laughing at the silent conversation Soren and I clearly just had and looking almost lovingly at the bridge.

"Telling me that this bridge is decrepit does *not* bolster my confidence, Commander," I say dryly and he chuckles low.

"Come now, the great Ice Queen certainly can't be afraid of a little river," he tsks. I roll my eyes, not loving that this new nickname seems to be gaining traction.

"You and I have very different definitions of the word *little*." I glance out over the river again, wondering how quickly someone would be swept away should they fall, and suppress a shudder.

He gets that wicked glint in his eye. "I think we agree on certain things we consider *big*, though..."

Odessa chokes, having heard the end of the conversation as she rides up beside me. Killian clears his throat, but grins.

"Nigel asked to see you up ahead."

He nods, winks at me, and urges his horse forward, riding across the bridge. I watch him go, all manner of wicked thoughts bouncing around in my mind, but I decide to change the subject before Dessa can say a word about the Commander's *giant sword*.

"Have you ever met the King?"

She stiffens ever so slightly and my stomach knots.

"Yes," she says simply.

"Is he truly as awful as they say? As mad?"

She shifts in her saddle, tossing her braids over her shoulder.

"King Dorian is...complicated," she finally says evasively. I shake my head, frustrated by the refusal of anyone to actually answer any damn questions about the man, but let it go. I decided some time ago that I don't believe he can be as cruel and terrible as rumors have made him out to be. I can't believe that people like Killian and Odessa and the other friends I've met here that all seem like good and noble people could serve someone so vicious and cold. That doesn't mean he's kind by any means, but I'm holding on to the hope that perhaps I'm not walking into the den of a true monster.

"But the people of Duskthorne—they're happy? Taken care of?"

"Yes," she answers immediately, seeming relieved by this line of questioning. "There is very little strife within the kingdom. Those that have help the ones that don't, resources shared throughout the sectors." Something again tickles the back of my mind, memories of Lyanna in those early days of my escape, something about the city outside the palace walls...but I can't quite grab onto the thought before it fades away again. "I know that I would be considered biased, but I believe Duskthorne is the happiest and kindest of all the kingdoms in the empire. It's not perfect, of course, but I think it's as close as we can get here on earth."

I ponder that as we make our way across the bridge. If the people are taken care of within the kingdom, Dorian can't possibly be that bad, right? Maybe his madness has taken him more fully than the rumors say and he doesn't truly rule anymore, advisors taking care of most of the day-to-day things like seeing to his peoples' needs. That might explain it...but also makes the thought of what he's doing to Gifteds in his maddened state even more terrifying.

The bridge doesn't collapse and send us all tumbling into the raging waters below, but the relief I feel doesn't last long. While I'm happy to finally get answers and take whatever the next steps are on this unexpected journey, I'm still so anxious my skin feels as if it's vibrating with it, tiny insects crawling just beneath the surface all over.

The mountains tower in front of us now like stone giants, disappearing into the thick clouds above and going on for miles and miles in either direction. We ride along the gentle curve of the mountain range for a few hours, the rocks dark and jagged and menacing, until

I finally see it: the passage into Duskthorne. I gape, pulling Zaro up short to stare in utter astonishment.

There's a wide opening cut into the mountain side, at least a hundred feet high, and carved to look like the gaping maw of a great ice dragon, its flaring nostrils and menacing eyes looking so real for a moment that my heart leaps into my throat. A portcullis with thick, spiked iron bars blocks the entrance into the beast's mouth and I understand now why this is the most protected kingdom in all of Hypathia. I crane my head up and see that though the peaks of the mountain are hidden within the clouds, multiple levels of battlements and ramparts have been built into the stone fanning out in either direction from the dragon's gleaming obsidian eyes. Guards in black stand at intervals, bows at the ready. Even if you could scale the mountainside—which would be nearly impossible due to the steep angle and the thick layer of ice glinting in the low light filtering down from the heavy clouds—there would be no way you could get past all of these guards as well.

"Impressed?" Killian asks from beside me.

"Yes," I tell him honestly. "It's..." I search for the right word.

"Imposing? Terrifying?"

"Beautiful," I breathe. Though it's of course both imposing and terrifying as well, it beckons to me rather than warns me away. *Home*, my mind whispers as a feeling of belonging settles over me so sure and sudden that tears prick at my eyes. *This*, I think, *this is what I've been searching for my entire life*. Cece and Math are my family and I love the tavern and Helios, but it's never felt like home, not like this. I shake myself and swallow hard, turning to find Killian studying me with a mixture of confusion and...hope in his eyes.

He glances up at the dragon, a soft smile pulling at his lips.

"I think so too," he says. "They used to live all through these mountains, you know." He's still staring up at that snarling beast reverently. "No one has seen one in too long to remember, but I hope one day perhaps they'll return. When we're worthy once more."

His gaze shifts to mine and something intense passes between us, some sort of unspoken promise that I don't quite understand, as if we're vowing to somehow make that happen ourselves. I shake myself, wondering what games the Makers are playing with our lives. I feel their hands on us, moving us all around like pieces on a Knights and Dragons board. I've never cared for the game myself, too complicated and one that caters to someone with an analytical mind, one who can see moves and countermoves rather than what's right in front of them. I'm admittedly more reactionary than calculating. *Tesni is probably brilliant at the game*, I think bitterly. But that's what I believe we are now, simple game pieces on a giant board that the Makers are controlling.

I try to hold faith and believe that whatever they're doing, we'll come out victors in the end.

The portcullis begins to rise, the sound of giant creaking gears echoing off of the stone, ice shattering and crunching as the great wheels turn. It takes a few moments for the bottom to pull free from the stone beneath and I realize that the bars must sink at least ten feet down into the ground. It truly is impenetrable. I glance up at the dragon keeping watch above. *Impenetrable unless you have wings, I suppose*, I think with a quiet laugh. I wonder what it must have been like to have these beasts flying overhead. Terrifying, to be sure, but mesmerizing I'd imagine. I'm burning with questions about them and wonder if there might be books on the subject I could read. Surely Duskthorne has a library or at the very least, written histories of its kingdom.

I wonder why Killian is worried about fighting at all. Why not just seal themselves up within the kingdom? No one could possibly attack or gain entry. Odessa said that they're fully prepared to be secluded here for long periods of time, so…why not just wait Barony and his Alliance out?

The answer comes to me as soon as I think the question, though, and I smile inwardly. This war isn't just about Duskthorne and the Gifteds within. It's about all of Hypathia, innocent people who will be hurt by the Alliance in their quest that I still don't fully understand. Killian could never just hide, protected, while others suffered. I love that about him, even as it makes my chest ache with worry about what's to come.

The portcullis finally disappears up into the stone overhead, the dragon's mouth gaping and daring us to enter.

Killian leans towards me from his saddle.

"Welcome to Duskthorne."

CHAPTER
TWENTY-ONE
THEA

Killian gestures for me to follow him inside, and I take a deep breath, steeling myself before I urge Zaro forward. Once we cross beneath the raised gate, we're surrounded by dark stone, burning torches set into the walls every few feet illuminating our way. A tunnel, I realize. The entrance is carved out *through* the mountain. Soren's hackles rise, the cat uneasy being surrounded by earth and stone.

-*Are you alright?*-

-*Fine,*- he grumbles.

I can feel the tension rolling off of him. For a creature born in the wilds, free to roam beneath the endless sky, I can't blame him for being uneasy trapped inside of a mountain, even for a short while. We ride for at least a mile but I finally see daylight streaming in ahead and a few minutes later, we emerge within the walls of the kingdom. I find myself gaping all over again, truly awestruck. Soren bounds out into the light beside me, raising his face to the sky and shuddering from head to tail. I smile at the cat and he shifts his gaze to mine, pulling his lips back from his fangs with a playful hiss.

I turn back to the view before me. We're on a slight rise so the majority of the kingdom sprawls out below us as far as I can see in all directions. Gently rolling stone streets and bridges connect the entirety of it, serpentining between the different sections—Sectors, Odessa had called them. In the distance, watching over it all, are the three peaks. The great forge burning atop one, heated from lava pits deep within the mountain, Killian had told me, a beautiful stone temple standing serenely on another.

And in between the two, the famed Duskthorne Palace. The rumors were true: it's built directly into the side of the mountain, so high up that the tallest towers and spires disappear into the clouds.

"Fucking hells," I whisper. Killian smiles and nods for me to follow him, and we make our way down a wide path to the right that winds around the outside of the inner edge of the mountain until we level out into the city below. Killian barks out orders to Nigel and the burly man leads the rest of the army to the right, continuing along the wide path to the stables or barracks or armory, I imagine. Killian, Odessa, Soren, and I turn to the left and make our way down what seems to be the main throughfare of the city.

"The King's Road," Dessa supplies from beside me. "It runs through the heart of the kingdom, straight to the palace." I nod, trying to take everything in. It's so different than Helios with its thatched roofs and open windows, the salty tang in the air from the sea, the light stone and brightly colored accents everywhere. Everything here is made of sleek, dark stone and rich red wood, the adornments all deep jewel tones and polished brass. The smell of snow and ice and pine lingers in the air, and I sigh in utter pleasure.

Images suddenly rise, as if a door is swinging open within my mind and letting out memories that had been locked away. I never saw outside the palace walls in Lyanna until the day I fled and those horrifying weeks afterwards, but I remember now that most of the kingdom was living in near squalor. I remember buildings looking as if they might fall with a strong gust of wind, broken windows and muddy streets, starving people with dirty faces and dirtier clothes. A dirty, bloody orphan wandering the streets wasn't anything out of the ordinary and probably the only reason I was able to disappear so easily and actually escape.

What the hells was Barony doing if not seeing to his people? Providing for them? Helping them? Where was all his wealth going?

"Are you alright?" Dessa asks, frowning.

I shake myself, deciding to think on it later. "Yes, fine."

"So, what do you think of our fair kingdom?"

"It's...perfect."

"I told you," she sighs, smiling. "I'm so happy to be home. I love being part of the army, don't get me wrong, but...well, Mia deserves to spend some time safe at home."

"Where is home?" I ask, wondering which part of the kingdom they live in.

"In the Inner Village." She points towards the towering castle in the distance. "The Sector closest to the palace. Many of the higher-ranking officers live there, but we've lived there my entire life because my father was the King's weapons master."

"Well that explains your affinity for the bow and all manner of pointy objects."

She laughs low. "I was toddling around with swords in my hands when I was a wee babe of two—much to my mum's chagrin of course." Her smile turns bittersweet. "She knew I was destined for the army though, no matter how much she might wish otherwise. It's in my blood. Battle calls to me, same as it did da."

"How...how did they die?"

"Mum got sick with a fever that wouldn't break. Da died of a broken heart not a week later."

"I'm so sorry," I tell her and she gives me a tight smile.

"I have Mia, so I'm still blessed by the Makers, to be sure. I remember when they brought her home, a slip of a thing, pale as a ghost—orphaned when her own parents died in a house fire out on one of the farms. Mum expected it to take me a while to warm up to the idea of a sister after being an only child for so long, that I'd be jealous, I guess. But the second I saw those pale green eyes look to *me* for reassurance in the new house full of new sights and sounds and smells, not mum or da, but me, I was done for. She was my sister regardless of no blood being shared between us." I smile at that and she grins. "I still want to skin the heathen sometimes, don't get me wrong, but I love her more than anything."

The street around us becomes more and more populated as we go. People wave from windows and cheer, children run alongside the horses, smiling and laughing. A heroes' welcome. These people don't live in fear or poverty. They aren't used or abused from what I can tell, and they seem to love the soldiers. Perhaps this place isn't so bad. I try to be like the flower Soren is so keen to call me and have hope.

The cat in question is drawing quite a bit of attention as we make our way through the city. Gasps of shock; cries of terror; exclamations of joy and reverence. He stands taller, preening and I try to hide my smile.

-*Enjoying this, are we?*-

-*Immensely,*- he says shamelessly. I can hear the smile in his voice and he flicks his tail purposefully behind him. I laugh lightly, but my humor vanishes as I hear murmurs start to rise about *me*. Not me, but Tesni. The wind blows a flaming red curl into my face and I curse myself—I should have pulled my hood up to hide my hair. In Helios, even with the red hair and my proper green eyes, I could probably pass mostly undetected, but here in the north, Lyanna's Gifted is all too well known.

"Is that…the Flame of Lyanna?"

"She's the Commander's prisoner!"

"Fucking cunt."

"Is that frost cat her *familiar?*?"

"Fire Bitch will fetch a pretty coin, that's for sure."

"Don't listen to them," Dessa whispers. "The truth will spread soon enough, the tales of how you saved this entire army. Then they'll want to throw bloody parades in your honor, believe me."

"Parades, huh?" I say, trying to sound nonchalant.

"If there's one thing Duskthornians love, it's an excuse to throw a party."

I look at her and quirk a brow. "You're joking. Are you joking? I can never tell if you're fucking joking."

She laughs, flashing her snowy white smile.

"Truly. We're a lively bunch. Parades. Soirees. Masquerades. Anything with music and dancing and debauchery, really." I shake my head, laughing. "Hard to believe?" I hike a shoulder. "Rumors are often just that—rumors. Gossip. Lies spread, sometimes for a purpose..."

I eye her at that, but she turns to smile and wave at a little boy who climbed up a tree to get a better look at the procession.

We ride on, past shops and houses, taverns and inns, and farther out from the city's center, small farms and pastures filled with animals and crops. The road veers to the right and inclines gently as we draw closer to that towering mountain, the castle high above within it. Just as we turn onto what looks to be the final stretch before reaching a towering gate at the bottom of a series of zigzagging stone paths leading up to the palace's front steps, Killian drops back to ride beside me, sharing a look with Odessa that I can't decipher but that sends cold coiling through my stomach.

"Thea, just..."

I inhale sharply and my blood goes icy when I see it: lining the street on either side are cages—large enough to fit a person. My stomach drops. So, the stories are true. Gifteds are put into cages and forced to perform like animals in the circus.

"What the fuck?" I spit.

Soren tenses, prowling to sniff at the metal bars. The cages are empty right now and I wonder where the Gifteds are. Dungeons perhaps? Chained to Dorian's bed? I clench my jaw and turn to glare at Killian. He told me things would be fine. He told me I would understand soon. He told me that he would explain everything. How can this be fine? How can I possibly understand this? What kind of explanation could he possibly give??

Part of my mind is telling me to calm, to think things through and trust in this man, the one that I love with my entire soul and trust with my life, but that part of my mind isn't nearly loud enough in this moment.

"Thea, you must understand—"

"I don't have to understand anything," I snap, my Gift roiling. I lash out with it, sending twin walls of ice shooting down either side of the street, slamming into the cages. Metal bends and screeches and snaps, iron bars crumpling into frozen heaps.

Killian arches a brow but doesn't comment, his body taut and his jaw clenched tightly. He rides ahead, wisely leaving me to seethe alone. Odessa doesn't speak either, though I can tell she wants to. My Gift is still writhing, my skin covered in a sheen of frost.

-*You need to calm.*-

-*What!? How can you say that?*-

-*There has been no human in those cages for a long, long time*- Soren points out. -*And there are many things you do not yet understand.*-

I grit my teeth so hard I fear I might crack my jaw.

-*Then. Someone. Fucking. Explain. It. To. Me.*-

-*It is not my story to tell.*-

I glare at the cat and he gazes steadily back, icy blue eyes rimmed with gold warring with emerald green. He stares, unblinking, defiant. I finally huff in annoyance and look away.

-*I win.*-

-*I will skin you and wear you as a frock coat.*-

He chuckles low and stalks forward, and I force my Gift to recede, my skin warming once more. We reach the path that leads up to the palace and a towering gate stands at the entrance, two stone dragons perched on each pillar. Two guards stand at attention on either side, nodding deeply to Killian as he passes, putting fists over chests. The path is narrower than the King's Road, but our three horses can ride beside each other if we so choose.

We don't.

I'm still fuming, though I have calmed, as Soren instructed, and

I'm trying my best to cling to hope. Hadn't King Ryker told me that things aren't necessarily what they seem? If three of the people I have come to hold in such special places in my heart can somehow serve and trust Dorian, I should at least try to let them explain, shouldn't I? And I recall now that Dorian stopped inviting guests from the empire to gawk at his Gifteds in cages long ago as his madness worsened, before he closed the kingdom off completely. So, I suppose it stands to reason that perhaps the Gifteds *aren't* forced into those cages any longer at all, guests or not. I let out a long, slow breath, telling myself over and over to keep my mind open.

Killian leads the way, Dessa behind me, and Soren walking along the ledge with an easy grace that's bordering on preternatural. We wind our way up the side of the mountain, back and forth, rising higher and higher above the city. I try not to look out over the kingdom because every time I do, the buildings below look a little smaller and my stomach inches farther up into my throat.

More dragon statues stand guard atop pillars along the way, some with wings outstretched as if in flight, some looking as if they're ready to leap from their perches, stone claws curling and digging.

We finally reach the front of the palace, the huge doors carved of the deepest obsidian, a giant silver dragon's head in their center. Several squires rush forward to take our horses as we dismount, but give Soren uneasy glances and a wide berth. The damned cat flashes his fangs and one of the boys pales, the other making a sound that's somewhere between a squeal and a yelp. He stumbles backwards, tripping, and landing right on his ass in a freshly deposited pile of dung. My hand flies to my mouth and Dessa chortles.

"Soren!" I scold in a low hiss, but I can't stop the laughter that bubbles up my throat. I meet Killian's gaze and though he's trying his damndest not to laugh, his lips curl and his shoulders shake.

-*You know it was funny.*-

-*Ok, yes, it was fucking hysterical, but still rude. You could have killed the poor boy.*-

I give Zaro a loving pat on the neck and he noses my hair.

"Thank you for being my companion through all of this," I tell the horse quietly. "I hope I'll see you again soon."

The only squire to keep his wits about him with Soren steps up to take Zaro's reins, inclining his head. He leads the horse away, the others following now that the other boys have regained some composure, and I stare up at the doors, at the dragon that seems to be watching my every step.

"Are you ready?" Dessa asks softly.

I sigh. "As I'll ever be."

We ascend the wide stone stairs and two more guards in black, silver dragon pins in the center of their chests, open the doors. The inside of the palace is breathtaking, all soaring ceilings and polished deep gray stone and silver adornments. It's dark, but not in a brooding, dismal way as I expected it to be, to reflect the dismal king himself. The corridors are wide, the staircases numerous and sprawling, the curtains and rugs and everything else refined and elegant, but not gaudy or garish.

"What do you think?" Killian asks quietly. Two young maids rush forward, assumingly to take our coats, but Killian holds up a hand to stay them. They incline their heads and slip back into one of the alcoves.

"It's...big," I say, craning my head back to stare up, up, up to the soaring ceiling, so high that it's swallowed up in shadows. He laughs low and opens his mouth to speak again, but an old man joins us then, smiling fondly at Killian and bowing low.

"Commander," he says, eyes flicking to me for a moment before shifting back to Killian. "Welcome home."

"It's good to be home, Frederick." Killian smiles back at the old man, a soft, comfortable smile. The two are obviously familiar. "Frederick this is...our guest," Killian hedges. "Frederick is the King's Second," he says to me. The older man inclines his head, his long gray hair tumbling over his shoulder as he does.

"Welcome to Duskthorne."

I find that I can't quite make myself speak, my throat suddenly dry and closed. I'm here, in the Duskthorne palace, about to meet the most despicable monarch in all of Hypathia. I know logically that I have nothing to fear—Soren will rip the king's throat out and I'll finish the job with a blade of ice if I have to, but fear isn't always logical. So, I merely nod to the man before he turns back to Killian.

"You may meet in the throne room in an hour. We have a few matters to discuss before then and in the meantime, I'm sure our guest would like to freshen up after so long on the road. A hot bath has already been drawn for you."

"Oh. Thank you." The thought of a steaming hot bath puts all of my anxiety aside for the time being. As much as I want this meeting done, the short reprieve is welcome, and I'll admittedly feel better about meeting Dorian bathed and in fresh clothes. He may be a horrible king, but he's still a king.

"Food will be brought to your room as well—for you and your, um, companion," Frederick says, sounding unsure as he glances to Soren. The cat stares back, unblinking, and Federick quickly looks away.

"I'll show her the way," Dessa offers, taking my arm and ferrying me away up the curving staircase to our left before either of the men can say a word. Soren stalks behind us as we walk down corridors and cross landings and up more stairs until I'm dizzy with all of the twists and turns. There's no way I'll ever be able to find my way back again. We finally stop in front of a polished wooden door with dark metal hinges and a dragon's head carved into the knob.

She pushes it open and I step inside, eyes widening. It's huge, the walls rounded, and I realize it must be in one of the towers. A fire burns in the large hearth and sconces along the walls shine brightly. There's a large bed set between two windows covered in midnight velvet, thick, fur blankets atop it with black silk draped between the four posts. Thick rugs cover much of the floor and I long to kick off my boots and dig my toes into the fur. A large painted screen divides part of the room, and I can see steam rising from just beyond it from the tub. I have to fight not to strip off my clothes this instant.

Soren prowls around the space, doing his own investigations. I see that a pallet of furs has been made up for him as well beside the doors to what I assume is a balcony. Truth be told, I'm a little afraid to look outside, the height must be staggering and I'm not sure I'm fond of them after the ride up to the palace. I frown, wondering why we've been given such opulent accommodations. It's true I hadn't been expecting to be tossed into a dungeon anymore, but this room seems like one that should be reserved for other royals or members of the court.

"How did you know where the room was?" I ask Odessa as she scratches Soren's head.

"I practically grew up in the palace," she tells me. "Federick and my father were old friends, and being the weapons master meant we were here often. And..." She trails off, pursing her lips. "And I know where they keep the valued guests," she finishes with a smile.

"Valued, am I?" I snort.

"You have no idea. Enjoy your bath, princess. I'm going to check on Mia, but I'll be back for the meeting—should you wish me there?"

"Yes, please, if you're allowed."

"I'll be there," she assures me, icy blue eyes sparkling. "Mia will want to see you after," she tells Soren, who gives his approximation of a meow in agreement. The archer laughs and leaves the room.

I shed my dirty clothes and practically leap into the bath.

NOT QUITE AN HOUR LATER, I'M SCRUBBED CLEAN, SMELLING OF HONEY AND some kind of flower that I've never seen before, but its fiery orange petals were inlaid within the soap and smell divine, and dressed in a fresh tunic and trousers. Someone had delivered my trunk while I'd bathed and though I debated on one of the finer dresses within it to meet the king, in the end I decided on what I felt most comfortable in. If Dorian doesn't like it, he can get fucked.

A knock on the door sounds and I open it to find Killian waiting, freshly bathed, hair still wet. He looks devastatingly handsome in a deep gray tunic and black leathers, his beard neat and trimmed. Soren joins me at the door, ready to depart.

"Are you ready? We can wait..."

"I want it done," I tell him firmly. It's time.

His jaw clenches at that, his body tense as if he'd rather eat glass and wash it down with lava than meet with the king. Is he not as sure of the king's amenability as he let on? Is he worried what Dorian will do with me? Or perhaps he's worried that he'll be punished for the two of us being together? That cold dread in my stomach spreads through my body.

-*Breathe, daska.*- The cat pushes his head beneath my hand and the feel of his soft fur, his warmth, helps chase the cold away. -*All will be well.*-

-*And if it isn't?*-

-*Then my claws and fangs will taste blood this night.*-

I look to Killian, lifting my chin defiantly and pressing my shoulders back, and despite the tension roiling off of him like waves in a thrashing sea, his lips curl into a smile.

"I'm ready."

"You truly are a daska, Red," he whispers, shaking his head. "As you wish it." I step out of the room and to my surprise, he reaches down and clasps my hand in his. He raises our joined hands to his lips and kisses my knuckles, soft enough to make a slow shiver run down my spine. I can feel Soren roll his eyes through our connection and I laugh.

Dessa is waiting at the bottom of one of the many staircases for us.

"How's Mia?" I ask.

"Happy to be home," she sighs with a smile. "She's already been running through half the city with her friends." My heart warms at that despite the cold slithering through the rest of my body. "Are you alright?" she whispers.

"No," I tell her honestly and she huffs out a laugh. "But I need to do this."

I see her bite her lip from the corner of my eye and everyone's nerves aren't helping with my own. Dorian may not be as bad as the rumors would have me believe, but they are clearly afraid of him, or of how he's going to react to this entire situation. The trip to the throne room goes by in the blink of an eye and suddenly we're standing before oversized black doors, the sigil of the kingdom inlaid in the center once more. Frederick waits for us, and two more guards stand on either side of the doorway.

"I trust your room was to your liking?"

"Oh, yes, thank you."

"Shall we?" He nods and the guards open the doors. Frederick steps inside and the rest of us follow in his wake. I inhale sharply when I behold the throne at the other end of the long room. It's big enough to seat a man twice Killian's size, carved from obsidian, the back made to look like the jagged, hulking mountains outside. Two walls are made up entirely of glass, the expanse of the city sprawling out to the right of the massive throne, the dark mountains seeming to go on endlessly behind it. We're so high up that I feel as if we must be in the heavens themselves, the city below looking like a child's toy. A tendril of fear goes through me at the sight, but it's also a bit exhilarating.

But none of that is what set my heart to racing, what makes my jaw drop in utter awe.

Curved protectively around the throne is a *dragon*.

Or the skeleton of one anyway. It's fully intact though, so it's as if the great beast truly stands just a few yards away. It's massive skull and front legs are on the left of the throne, staring out at whatever fool dares to enter this room and seek meeting with Dorian, the rest of the beast curving around behind the throne, it's back legs and massive tail standing to the right. I spy glinting silver within the bones and realize that iron has been welded to the skeleton in places to help it stand.

"Holy shit," I breathe.

"We call him Dusty," Killian whispers and a bark of nervous laughter bursts from my lips. Frederick glances over his shoulder, arching a bushy gray brow, but doesn't comment.

My heart is beating so wildly that I think it might burst right through my bones, shattering them to dust by the time we stand just before the throne. The still empty throne. There are several doors lining the walls, so I assume the king will emerge from one of them, preferring to make a grand entrance.

Frederick steps forward, walking the few remaining steps to the throne and stands beside it, turning back to face us, waiting. Soren settles at my side and I dig my fingers into his fur again, letting him ground me. Killian stands on my other side, Odessa to his left. The Commander is taut as a bow string ready to snap, and my Gift coils within my chest, ready. Waiting.

And waiting.

And waiting some more.

Just as I'm about to ask Killian if someone should perhaps go and fetch the king, Frederick sighs and gives Killian a pointed look, quirking one gray brow and clearing his throat.

Killian lets out a long, *long* exhale, and then strides forward, shoulders back, spine ramrod straight. I watch, body cold, mind somehow racing and completely blank all at once, as he turns to face me....

And sits upon the throne.

CHAPTER TWENTY-TWO

KILLIAN

Makers fucking help me.

I don't know how I'm supposed to do this. I was barely able to make my feet move to walk toward the throne. Toward *my* throne. And now my heart is beating like the stomping of a thousand Northlands in my fucking throat, so hard I can barely breathe. Thea stares, unblinking and unbelieving. *Fuck, fuck, fuck. It will be alright. I just need to explain and it will be alright.*

"His Majesty, Dorian Killian Elvania," Federick announces and I grind my teeth.

"The second," I add hastily as Thea stares, taking a step backwards. It's a small step, but it feels as if the whole of the Seeva stands between us now. I clear my throat lightly. "Technically..."

I clear my throat and Frederick chuckles low. I shoot the old man a withering look. He's known me all my life and having him beside me is the only reason we've been able to do all of the things we've done. He's the reason I'm able to lead the army—my true calling—instead of sitting my ass on this throne day in and day out pretending to be king. He truly runs this kingdom, I'm simply the one who has to hold the crown because of the bastard that sired me.

"What in the actual fucking fuck, Killian??" Thea finally snaps. In any other situation, I'd laugh at the mouth on this woman, but right now, I couldn't muster laughter if I tried. I rise from the throne and take a step towards her, but she steps backward again, shooting me a look that tells me all too clearly that if I want my favorite appendage to remain attached to my body, I'll not move again. Odessa wisely remains still. Soren's tail swishes behind him, but he doesn't look like he wants to rip my throat out, so I'm assuming he's known the truth for weeks. Animals talk to each other, after all.

"Thea, please let me explain." I hold her gaze, begging silently and though there's confusion and hurt in her eyes, there's also love. Thank the fucking Makers, there's still love. "Please," I add, so quietly it's barely even a whisper.

"Talk. Fast," she grates out, and the temperature in the room drops, my breaths clouding in the air in front of me. Federick inhales sharply and mutters a prayer. We have hundreds of Gifteds here, but none like Thea. The power she wields is…terrifying. Amazingly, beautifully terrifying.

"You asked me to let you speak without interruption once, when you told me your truth. Now I ask the same of you as I tell you mine." I hold her stare and those emerald depths seem to burn to the heart of me—or perhaps she's just wishing she could burn me true, that she really did have her sister's Gift right now. But after a moment, she nods once. I take a deep breath, share one quick glance with Dessa who gives me an encouraging nod, and begin my tale.

"My father was a monster. A despicable human to his rotten core who collected and used and abused Gifteds, just as the rumors say. I hated the man with every fiber of my being. He—" I clench my jaw, my fingers curling into fists as dark memories rise, but I push all of that away. The way he treated me as a child, the way he drove my mother to leap from the mountain to escape him and his torment, don't matter right now. I'll tell her one day, if she wishes, but right now I need her to understand the rest. "What the rest of Hypathia does not know is that my father died nearly fifteen years ago. The mantle of this kingdom has been on my shoulders ever since, but it was Frederick who knew that we could use my father's reputation to our advantage, to help us turn this hell for Gifteds into a *sanctuary*."

Her brow furrows, a small V forming between her eyes.

"The Gifteds here knew there was no love lost between me and my father, and I'd always been kind to them when I could—I'd taken many beatings for taking extra food to the dungeons and tending wounds. I'd even tried to orchestrate an escape once, but I was only ten at the time and it didn't end well."

I roll my shoulder unconsciously, remembering the pain as my father tore it from its socket, the crack that sounded loud as thunder, the vomit that rose as he punched the dislocated joint over and over...I bite the inside of my cheek but I see something flash in Thea's eyes and know that she understands there is much darkness in my past. Her eyes soften ever so slightly, concern and anger on my behalf shining there and making my chest clench. It is a very special thing to be loved by Thea Sparrowhill. What I've done to deserve to be counted among that number will forever be a mystery to me.

I clear my throat lightly and continue on. "So, against all odds, they all believed in me, in this vision. Just because my father was the most prolific and terrible slaver in Hypathia, didn't mean that he was the *only* one, and some of the others were just as awful. Barony the worst of them all," I mutter. Thea's eyes spark at that, curiosity and even more confusion burning, but I push on. We aren't there yet.

"But my father was the most feared and the wealthiest, so we used that to our advantage. We hired Hunters, more than any others in the empire, offered to purchase Gifteds from other kingdoms, let word spread farther and wider of the horrors of Duskthorne. Hunters were banging at our door to deliver Gifteds to us, and while they were always free to leave, almost all wanted to remain once they learned the truth. Because though word was spreading about Duskthorne's collection, it was also spreading about Barony."

I can see Thea stiffen at his name, tensing for what's to come. I take a deep breath and let it out slowly.

"Barony has been collecting all these years too, Thea. Your sister may be the Gifted that he parades through the continent and whores out for her power," I spit, "but she is far from his only. He has dungeons full of them…dungeons and *laboratories*."

She blinks several times, and while she remains silent, I can see her mind racing, her pulse thrumming at her throat.

"Dark alchemy. He's been having his alchemists study the Gifteds—usually by tearing them apart piece by piece—for years." My own Gift roils inside my chest at the thought. The horror stories I've heard…I shudder and press on. "He's been trying to find a way to steal their Gifts for himself. I've never seen anyone so green and sick with envy as Barony Moreau. A kingdom of suffering people, all the riches he could want, a Gifted for his own personal use to garner him even more fame and coin and reverence—but none of it is enough for him. He wants power, the kind from within us…" I take a deep breath, "…and he's found a way to take it."

She inhales sharply.

"What?" she whispers, clutching onto Soren.

"It's the reason the war started. It's the reason he's rallying the rest of Hypathia against us. He wants the power of every single Gifted within these walls. He's promised to share the power with all who join him, promising to turn them into Makers on earth, more powerful than any Gifted naturally born. The dark alchemy they've discovered, it changes the Gift, intensifies it, distorts and disfigures it. He hasn't taken power for himself yet, still letting others be the tests in these dark, twisted experiments, but he will soon."

"What…what happens to the Gifteds that he…uses?" She swallows hard and when she meets my gaze, I can see by the sorrow in her eyes that she already knows the answer. She closes her eyes and looks like she's whispering a prayer. When she opens them again, they're burning with hatred and righteousness and my chest swells at the sight. My woman. My warrior. My queen.

"Did she know?" she spits quietly, venom in her voice so thick it could poison all of Hypathia. "Did Tesni fucking know??"

"I think so, yes, but I can't be sure."

I can feel her Gift rise up, but I don't dare try to block her. I see a sheen of frost coat her skin, her eyelashes, and the temperature drops again. I feel Frederick tense and Dessa cuts me a worried look, but I hold out my hand to both of them. Thea will be ok, she just needs a moment, so I give her as long as she needs to work through everything on her own.

She takes a few deep breaths, letting them out slowly, clutching onto Soren as she calms herself.

"So...does everyone know you're both the king and the Commander?" she finally asks.

"Everyone within Duskthorne, yes."

"But how—"

"Long, long ago, we had magik in Hypathia." She frowns. "What we know as alchemy now is but a remnant of what magik truly is. Or was. It's faded from this world, but once upon a time, those with magik in their blood could do all manner of things—similar to Gifts, but so much more. Duskthorne still has a bit of the old magiks here—it's always been stronger in the north, but even more so here in the Obsidians—and it's that old magik that seals the secret of my identity within the walls of the kingdom. It's why Dessa couldn't have told you the truth out on the road, even if she wanted to."

Thea looks to Dessa then, and I can see her mind working, probably replaying conversations where Odessa seemed like she was holding something back, trying to reassure Thea about Dorian but choosing her words very, very carefully. Dessa gives her an apologetic shrug.

"I *did t*ell you all would be well," my archer quips. "So, I did tell you true. See," she gestures around the room. "All well."

"I...what...that's..." Thea makes an incoherent noise of frustration and shakes herself. "Shut up," she finally snaps, but I know all will be forgiven soon enough.

"Now the question, my dear," Frederick says gently, pulling Thea's attention back to the throne where I stand stiffly before it, the great dragon watching over us all, "is will you fight with us?" Frederick knows the truth of who Thea is. I sent a raven with word as soon as I learned it myself, not just because I share everything with the old man, but because I wanted him to start sending out scouting parties for the true fire bitch. She sent Thea to be kidnapped and tormented in her place. She betrayed my love *twice*. She would not be given a third chance or a respite from the punishment due her for all her wrongs. Tesni de Moreau *will* pay for all that she's done, mark my words.

Thea looks from the dragon over my shoulder, out the window overlooking the kingdom, and finally to me. She holds my gaze for an endless eternity, but finally turns to Frederick.

"Yes, I will fight with you."

I exhale roughly, the tension in my chest easing as if an iron fist has released its hellish grip on my heart.

"But you and I," she says, turning her burning gaze back to me, "have *much* more to discuss."

Frederick and Dessa both look between Thea and me, then share a look.

"We'll just let you chat then, shall we?" Odessa says, backing away. I shoot daggers at her and mouth *traitor,* but she only smirks, winks, and turns to run from the room, Soren trotting after her with what I swear is amusement in his eyes.

"Fucking traitor," Thea hisses at the cat, who merely swishes his long tail in response, not deigning to slow or even look over his shoulder. Frederick clears his throat lightly and I can tell he's fighting to hold back his own amusement.

"I'll see to training arrangements and send correspondence to Ryker. I'll, um, speak with you later." The old man quickly disappears through one of the doors along the side wall. It closes with a loud, echoing thud and the two of us stand facing each other. I can see her ire churning, the temperature in the room chilling further, skin shimmering with frost once more.

"I'd like to point out that you lied about your identity first," I say before she can speak. Her mouth pops open and I plow on quickly, "and I didn't *technically* even lie. My name *is* Killian Blackheart—I've never gone by Dorian and I use my mother's surname."

She sputters, words failing her. She yells through her teeth in frustration and then a ball of icy snow hits me in the chest, sending me stumbling backwards a step in surprise. I look down at the shards glittering against my leathers. I look up, incredulous, only to have two more sail at me, one hitting my shoulder, the other my stomach. She arches a brow and I read her intention just in time and block my crotch before another ball lands squarely on my cock. It stings my hand and I curse, shaking my fingers out against the sharp pain.

"Thea! Come on!"

"You bastard," she seethes, baring her teeth in a near snarl, and for a moment I'm reminded of Soren. "You let me think I was walking into a monster's den to be tortured or worse!"

"When I let you think that, I thought you were your sister! And, yes, I was all too happy to see that fear in your eyes—*her* eyes, I mean, I won't lie about that. Your sister is a fucking cunt who deserves to be dragged across all seven hells for what she's done to people all through Hypathia, but mostly what she did to you. And I vow she'll fucking pay for it, by all the Makers she *will* pay," I growl. She softens ever so slightly at that and I push my advantage. "But once I knew that you weren't like her at all, by the way you acted, the kindness you showed and the feelings I had for you, even before I knew the truth, I tried to assuage your fear. I couldn't tell you the full truth, Thea, not out there. I'm not bound to keep the secret when I'm outside these walls like the others, it's true, but I just...I needed more time with you as Killian Blackheart, the Commander you came to love before I had to be the King you'd been raised to hate. I needed more time, Thea," I say, practically begging.

"And the cages?"

"Where we keep the petting zoo on market days for the children. I swear."

She stares, studying me, another ball of ice hovering above her palm. I wait, letting her come to her decision, but I hold my fucking breath while I do. She can't possibly choose to walk away from me... can she? I had to hide things, just as she did, but everything I told her about myself, about the way I felt, it was all truth, more truth than I've ever shared with another, truth I didn't even know existed pulled from deep in my soul.

Finally, the ball of ice shrinks in on itself, disappearing with a tiny burst of powder and I blink—I've never seen her do that before. There's so much I long to discover about this woman...but first, I need her to tell me that things are ok between us. I need her to tell me that she hasn't changed her mind. I need her to tell me that she still loves me.

She closes the distance between us and brushes crystals of ice from my chest before wrapping her hands around my neck and pressing up to her toes to kiss me. I sigh against her lips, wrapping my arms around her back and pulling her hard against me.

"I understand," she whispers and I feel her lips curl upward against my own. "I still plan to make you grovel, mind you, but I understand..." She squeals when I growl and lift her up, urging her lips apart and kissing her deeply, my tongue sweeping roughly against her own. She wraps her legs around my waist and I settle my hands on her ass, squeezing appreciatively.

"I am very, very good at groveling, Red," I tell her as I walk her backwards, and she shudders. I slide her down my body just in front of the hulking throne and pull her tunic off, tossing it aside. Her corset joins moments later, and her breathing becomes quick and shallow as she waits to see what I'll do next, eyes burning and pupils expanding ever outward. I grab one leg and rest the sole of her boot on my knee, loosening the laces and tugging it off before releasing it and doing the same on the other. I unlace her trousers, and all the while, she watches, eyes wild, chest rising, pulse racing. I shove her leathers away and she steps out of them, standing gloriously naked before me, before my throne.

My cock throbs, the sight so fucking arousing that I need it burned into my memory forever. I take a few heartbeats to do just that, taking in every single detail. The way her hair falls in a waterfall of fire down her back, a few wayward curls sweeping across her temple; the way her cheeks flush and her body trembles from head to toe as my gaze drifts across every inch of her; the way the great dragon stands behind her, as if proud to have her as part of his kingdom; the way she looks like a fucking queen, head high and shoulders back, that warrior spirit nearly blinding in its ferocity.

Mine. All fucking mine.

"Turn around," I rumble. She swallows hard but that defiance I love so much rises and she cocks a brow.

"Is that a command from the king?" Her voice is breathy and sensual. I step forward and she cranes her head up, licking her lips. I grasp her hips and turn her, my chest pressed against her back now.

I lean down and whisper, "It is. Because this king is going to devour you until your screams shatter this entire fucking palace, and then he's going to fuck you on this throne, Thea, so hard and deep that you won't be able to walk come the morning." She gasps and shudders. "Now, put your hands on the armrests and—" I kiss her softly, biting her lower lip before pulling away. "—Bend. The. Fuck. Over."

She gasps but obeys immediately, gripping the armrests of the massive throne and bending at the waist before me. I use my thigh to press hers apart, shuffling her feet wider. "Lower," I command, and a soft whimper breaks free from her lips. My woman likes being instructed...and praised. I shift her hair over her shoulder and kiss her nape as I run my palm down her back, over her ass, caressing and kneading. "That's my good girl," I whisper.

"*Fuck*," she breathes and I chuckle low. I sink to my knees behind her and nearly come at the sight. *Great fucking Makers.* Her perfect ass. Her smooth pussy, already wet and wanting.

"Fuck I'm going to enjoy this," I rasp as I lean in and lick her, long and slow, hands gripping her ass.

"*Makers*," she breathes. I lick her again, tongue gliding between her lips and sending utter ecstasy through my veins. The taste of her is sweeter than the heavens. Over and over I devour this woman, fucking her with my tongue, growing harder and harder with every moan, every whimper, every curse. I dare to drag my tongue upwards, running it over that forbidden spot. She gasps quietly, but doesn't pull away, doesn't tell me to stop, so I do it again and her moans reverberate through the large room, fingers digging into the armrests of the chair and legs shaking.

"Holy fuck," she whispers. "Fucking, fuck, fuck...Don't stop!" she demands, breathless. I chuckle lightly but do as she asks, running my tongue in slow, sweeping circles.

"One day," I rumble as I pull back, kneading her ass, spreading her so I can see everything laid out before me. "One fucking day, Thea, I'll take you there if you let me—and Makers fucking help this mountain around us because I swear my roars will shake them to their fucking cores."

"Yes," she pants. "Yes, yes, yes." She clutches the throne and wiggles her ass in invitation. I smile and shake my head.

"Not yet," I say, running my hands over her curves, wanting to touch her everywhere at once, to lick and bite and kiss every inch of her. "Not quite yet, love. But one day soon..." I slide my fingers upward, spreading the moisture left behind by my tongue and pressing forward ever so slightly. She gasps again, stiffening, but relaxes a moment later, a soft moan escaping her lips. "Mmmm," I rumble, "like that, do we?"

"Again," she rasps, half plea, half command. Her entire body is trembling, sweat beading down her back, and I know she wants so badly to come. So, again, I run my fingers around that sensitive spot and then apply pressure, leaning in to run my tongue along her pussy at the same time.

"Oh fuckkkkk," she moans, legs shaking. "Don't stop, don't stop, don't stop..."

So I don't. I gently pump just the tip of my finger while I lick and suck and flick my tongue along her folds and over her clit and all too soon, she makes that sound that's become my favorite in the world. She's close. Almost there. I don't dare stop, pressing harder and flicking my tongue faster, faster...

She screams as she comes, her honey drenching my tongue. I groan and set in, taking every last drop, licking in a frenzy. Her body shudders, her legs trembling, but I keep her upright. I finally stop, needing her more than I've ever needed anything.

"Don't move," I growl as I stand and rip the laces of my leathers open, pulling out my throbbing cock. I kick her legs even further apart and clamp a hand on one hip, and with the other, guide the head to her entrance, dripping and ready for me.

"Fuck me, Killian. Ah Makers, fuck me, please."

I never wanted to rule. I took up my father's crown to help my people—whether born here or brought here—but I never would have chosen this if I'd had a true choice. But here, seconds away from fucking *my* woman, the one sent to me by the Makers themselves, on *my* throne, overlooking *my* kingdom...well, it's the first time I've ever truly felt like a king.

"As my queen commands," I rasp and glide my hips forward, sending my cock so deep inside her, her pussy wet and hot and welcoming, squeezing me like a fist. "*Fuck me,*" I bite out through gritted teeth. I wrap the length of her hair around my fist and use my grip to tug her head backwards, her back curving. "Hold. On. Tight."

She gasps but I see her tighten her grip on the armrests, ready. I shift back before slamming my hips forward again, taking her hard and fast, an animal need clawing inside my chest. Over and over, I pound into her, her screams of pleasure hitting me like whips of bliss. I need more. I'll never get enough.

"Killian," she cries. "Harder." *Makers, this woman...*

I shift my grip from her hair to her shoulder, yanking her backwards as I slam forward, again and again. Pounding. Claiming.

"Right...there...going to..."

She screams as her climax rips through her, her walls pulsing around me, greedy and demanding. I feel the base of my spine tighten, my own release climbing, climbing, climbing...

"Thea!" I bellow as I come so hard my legs shake and I would swear the walls around us shudder. I rock my hips once, twice more, before I can barely stay upright. I lean down, resting my chest over Thea's back, holding her tight and kissing her shoulder, her throat, her sweat-soaked temple. I shift, maneuvering to slide into the throne and pulling her into my lap. She rests her cheek against my chest and I cradle her body to mine, running my fingers through her hair and trying to come back down from the stars I surely touched moments ago.

"That...was...adequate...Your Majesty," she pants, still breathing hard, and I throw my head back and laugh. I feel her own echoing laugh, her lithe body shaking against my chest. I run my hand through my hair, trying to slow my heart. We sit there, tangled up together on my throne for what could be hours or an eternity, before she bolts up right, staring at me with wide, green eyes. I frown.

"What? What's wrong?"

"You...you kneel for me."

"And?"

"You're a *king*, Killian." She shakes her head, and runs her hands through her tangled hair, looking around the room as if only now realizing where we are. "You shouldn't—"

I grip her chin to cut her off, and gently but firmly guide her face back to mine, waiting until she meets my gaze to speak.

"I will always kneel for you, Thea. You are my queen, whether you ever officially want the title or not—and that will be entirely up to you. I was forced to wear this crown, but I would never ask that of you if it's not what you want—but I will always, *always* kneel for you."

She reaches out and settles her palm against my cheek, searching my eyes, her own brimming with tears.

"I love you, Killian."

My eyes slide closed and I lean into her touch, my heart cracking in the best possible way. I open them again and press my lips to hers. Soft and savoring this time.

"And I, you, Thea."

She toys with the hair at my nape, smiling softly before sighing.

"So, when do we start?" she asks and my brow furrows.

"Start...?"

She holds my gaze and seems to steel herself.

"When do we start preparing for war?"

CHAPTER TWENTY-THREE

TESNI

I pace in what passes as the grand bed chamber in this dismal chateau. It's barely larger than my sitting room at Castle Lyanna and the furnishings leave much to be desired. It belonged to some long-dead relative of Hastings, but it hasn't been in real use for years. I've hated every Makers' forsaken minute here, but I suppose when the alternative is being sold off to that wretch in Marrowood—or worse—this will suffice for a time.

"You must only endure for a short while, my moonbeam," Hastings promised the day we set this plan into motion and I stole away from the castle grounds while Thea's carriage set off in the other direction. It's getting harder and harder not to lash out and tell him what a pathetic little worm I truly think he is each time he calls me *moonbeam* or *cupcake* or one of the other equally nauseating pet names he's come up with. Kissing the man makes me nearly physically ill, doing more makes me want to burn my own skin off, but everything is a means to an end, and I will always, always find the end I desire, do whatever it takes, use whoever it takes and dust my boots with their ashes.

I should feel guilt for the things I've done, the people I've hurt along the way to get what I want, Thea most of all. And I think that I do, on some level, but it's a level that's too insignificant to matter or change my course. I have always had this fire inside of me. Not my physical fire from my Gift, but that burning desire for *more*, always more. More coin, more clothes, more jewels. My name whispered in feared reverence on more tongues. My beauty sung about in more ballads. My power praised and worshipped by more people.

Always more.

Some, however, don't call it fire. They call it darkness. Wrongness. Evil.

Perhaps it is all those things.

Perhaps I should care.

Perhaps, when I make it out of this and I'm living in luxury on one of the islands far, far away from Barony and his experiments and his thirst for his own power, I'll change and become a better person.

I snort as I drink my wine.

I will never change and it's foolish to even entertain the idea. A wolf may lie among sheep, disguised in their wool, but a wolf it remains.

"And why should I change?" I demand of the flames in the grate across the room, flicking and dancing, calling out to me as they always have. I'm the most powerful Gifted in all of Hypathia, despite what Barony is trying to do to change that. I deserve everything I've been given—or taken by cunning or deceit or the threat of fire. I deserve the praise. I deserve the recognition. I deserve the fear.

"I deserve to be a fucking queen!" I hurl my glass of wine as I scream, the glass shattering against the stone hearth. I'd practically begged Barony over the years to make it so, to make me Tesni Moreau in truth, not merely Tesni *de* Moreau, a member of his house belonging to him, but not of the royal line. I would have suffered through consummation of the damned affair easily enough if he'd demanded it. He's attractive enough, and much younger than most of the other royals. It wouldn't have been so hard to fuck him if needed. People think it's difficult to simply not care about things, but they're wrong. It's as easy as breathing if you let it be.

But he would never agree. Even when I was the one who helped him keep his crown all these years. He's ruthless, to be sure, but he isn't smart and sure as hells isn't a true king. A throne can be inherited in Hypathia—or it can be *taken*. Barony managed to take it by sheer fucking luck all those years ago, but he's only kept it because of more sheer fucking luck, and, more importantly, *me*.

And yet he refuses to give me my rightful title of queen? The one I earned over and over again, keeping the people of Lyanna in check, keeping his enemies at bay, convincing him that if he was going to continue with his experiments, he was going to need allies because even all those years ago, with his dark, twisted dreams of power in their infancy, I knew that it would all end in war with Duskthorne.

I just never thought he'd use me as a pawn within it.

I grit my teeth, flames flaring and engulfing my hands, crawling up my forearms. Thinking of that bastard selling me off as a bargaining chip to solidify his alliance, of the fact that he *collared* me, makes my power roil. The flames burn hotter, flaring higher. At least Hastings was able to get a copy of the key before I went into this loathed hiding. I run my fingers along my throat, still feeling that cold metal, that helpless feeling that threatened to drown me without the use of my power.

My power. I know that Barony covets my Gift more than any other in all of Hypathia. I suppose I should thank the Makers that the alchemists haven't been able to find a way to take a Gift without killing the original bearer. As much as Barony wants my Gift and was happy to use me in his game with the rest of the Alliance, I know he would never want me dead. I should feel bad for the Gifteds who don't have that luxury, who are being used in these experiments and paying the ultimate price for it, but again, that part of me is...buried. Cold. Broken, perhaps.

But the alchemists are working every day trying to find a way to remove a Gift without killing the Gifted. They will, eventually, and once they do, once Barony has a chance of taking my power without killing me in the process, he'll do it in a heartbeat.

And I will not allow my power to be taken.

So, this plan must work. And for this plan to work, I must bide my time in this Makers' forsaken abandoned chateau deep in the hills of Lyanna, beyond the farms and the woodlands, where no one would possibly think the great Flame of Lyanna would be hiding.

I scream through clenched teeth and the fire in the hearth soars upward.

"Oh, my flower, what's wrong?" Hastings' grating voice sounds from behind me and I curl my lip, rolling my eyes before wiping the hatred away and plastering a warm smile on my face and bringing soft tears to my eyes. It's quite a talent, if I do say so myself. I turn and run into his arms.

"Oh darling, I've been waiting for you and so worried." He wraps me in a weak embrace and I bury my face in his neck before he can kiss me with that disgusting, slobbering tongue of his. He pets the back of my head as if I'm a dog. We can't get the ransom and to the island mansion I was promised is waiting quickly enough. Then I can be rid of this pathetic little dog.

"I'm sorry it's taken me so long. Things are..." He trails off and I stiffen, pulling back to meet his eyes.

"What's wrong? What's happened?"

"Oh, my sweet, we have received reports that the whole of Amon's forces have been defeated."

My brow furrows. Amon is one of the most ruthless and feared commanders in all of Hypathia. Blackheart is formidable, to be sure, but Hastings said that Amon had a Gifted in his army that would make victory against Dorian's lapdog all but assured. Duskthorne is still nearly impenetrable, but without the great Commander and a large number of his forces, it would sure as hells make taking the kingdom easier. It would take time, but it would happen with Blackheart out of the way. *How in the hells....*

"Wait. Did you say the *whole* of his forces? How..."

He licks his lips nervously and wipes at the sweat that's beading across his forehead.

"Entombed, I'm afraid...in ice."

"No," I whisper. "No, that isn't possible." I step away from him, beginning to pace again as what this means crystalizes in my mind. *Thea, what have you done? And* how*??*

"I'm afraid so, my honeyrose. We've had scouts sent who have confirmed that it's true. The entire army is encased in miles upon miles of ice."

"But...but...no! No, this doesn't make any sense. She shouldn't be able to use her Gift at all. Why was she not collared?? Why would she risk her life like that?" Fire ripples across my knuckles as I add in a low, seething whisper to myself, "And how the hells did she accomplish something so...terrifying?" I knew Thea's power had grown in these years apart, but I never could have imagined she was capable of something like this. This is bad. This is very, very bad.

"This potentially complicates our plan. We're unaware if they know who Thea is at this point. They could believe that she's still you, and that you have a second Gift that you've kept hidden..."

I glare at him over my shoulder and he cowers. There has never been a Gifted with more than one power. Though Barony is trying to change all that, of course, as it stands, there is no possible way anyone could believe that a Gifted could control both fire and ice. So, no, they must know that she isn't me. If she's figured out how to use her Gift like that, she probably revealed all, intending to use her great power as a bargaining chip to remain out of Dorian's dungeons —or bedchamber.

Which means they won't negotiate a ransom. Which means at best, I'm stuck in this ramshackle excuse for a chateau, and at worst, I'm hunted down once more, by Hunters and the Alliance.

I continue to pace, mind whirling, creating and discarding plans. Barony has always called me his cunning little ember, so, cunning I will continue to be. Another plan forms, morphs, and solidifies. My face relaxes, that dark voice inside my mind sighing in relief, and a wicked smile pulls at my lips.

"We'll figure something out, my stardust."

"I know," I say, turning to face him.

He's still looking at me with that lovesick idolatry in his eyes as the first flames engulf him.

CHAPTER TWENTY-FOUR
THEA

Things are so much worse in Hypathia than I could have ever guessed. I still can't quite wrap my mind around the fact that Barony has been experimenting on Gifteds all this time, torturing them in his quest for power. I wonder how many have died at the hands of his alchemists. Hundreds? My eyes burn with tears for the nameless, faceless people whose blood is on his hands, all while my Gift snarls and claws and longs to make him pay.

Did my sister know? All this time, did she just sit back and let it happen? Did she...My stomach roils. Did she *help* him? Watch with that dark, twisted glee at the pain of others, or with greed at the idea of having more power?

It's something that I vow to ask her myself—before I end her.

I've learned that aside from normal Hunters, Barony had a Gifted who could detect other Gifted's energies, much like Killian, though she couldn't block them as he does. Barony used her to find Gifteds throughout Hypathia, kidnapping them himself and condemning them to his dungeons and experiments. When his alchemists finally found a way to take the power of a Gifted, he became maniacal in his quest for more fodder for his experiments, more potential power in his grasp, and he pushed her to the Brink. I'm told that she died screaming in agony.

That's when Barony set his sights on the most well-known cache of Giifteds in all of Hypathia: Duskthorne. He gained allies through promise of power or threat of annihilation, and now plans to move against us.

Us. Because I am part of them now. Always have been, really, my path always leading me here to stand beside Killian and to protect these people. *My* people. I feel as if the Makers orchestrated this to help us fight back against Barony, to punish him for perverting the blessings they gave us. Why else would they set me on this road? Why else would they send Soren to me when familiars are all but things of legend now? It all means something, it all has a purpose. I think they're making us as strong as they can in this fight.

Because we're going to need to be strong.

Our sources say that Barony's alchemists are putting the strength of *multiple* Gifts into people now, making them stronger than any unbonded Gifted should ever be. When we meet them in battle, we'll need to be ready. Killian can block a great deal, but he's never been up against anything like what we might face.

"I still don't understand how he's kept all of this a secret for so long, how he's hidden these new creatures." I refuse to call them Giifteds. They were not blessed with a Gift, they took it by force. They stole what was never meant to be theirs. Though I know these abominations most likely had no say in the matter, just more rats to be used and discarded in the laboratories by Barony and his ilk, I can't help but want them gone from this world.

"Great wealth and power can cover up all manner of sins," Killian says as we walk to a large building used for training the army. There's a sharp edge to his voice and I know he must be thinking of his father. Dorian didn't hide his hunger and cruelty when it came to Giifteds, but he hid the horrors he subjected his family to, the bruises and broken bones, the blood and fear and heartbreak. Though Killian's told me much, I know there are even more horrors that I haven't yet learned. He's stronger than I ever could have imagined.

"Why do you think he didn't just take Tesni's Gift? Even with these abominations being strong, her Gift is still fearsome. Why wouldn't he want it for himself?"

"Our ears"—which means Ryker's ravens that he sends to spy throughout the continent and report back to him—"tell us that it was a condition of Marrowood's alliance. They wanted Tesni, Gift intact, in exchange for their army and access to their mines." Marrowood's mines supply half of the empire with iron. Of course Barony would want to control that and have free access to as much of it as he might need for himself. "Plus, he has some shred of decency left, it appears: he didn't want her dead."

I snort at that. *Barony* and decency *shouldn't* be in the same sentence.

"I wonder where she is now," I mutter, twirling the end of my braid around my finger. "Will she stay in hiding or run back to Barony and beg his forgiveness? Fight with him in this war?" Part of me salivates at the idea of meeting my sister on the battlefield, of showing her just how strong I've become. To show her that I'm not the same girl she threw to the wolves not once, but twice.

"We'll find her one way or another." I remember the conversation with my sister that seems so long ago now, the day I came back to Lyanna, learning how she tracked me all those years ago by my blood. I put that thought in the back of my mind, ready to use whatever alchemy I need to in order to track my sister down when this is said and done if I need to. "And when we do...well, that will be up to you, love." I look up at him, arching a brow. "She hurt you in ways no one who shares your blood ever should. It's your right to decide her fate." I sigh and shake my head and his brow furrows. "What?"

"I just wish you would stop saying things that make me fall more in love with you," I say, mockingly wistful.

He laughs low, snaking an arm around my waist and tugging me to him. He kisses me soft and slow and my toes curl in my boots at what that soft kiss promises, all that it will lead to if I let it. But now is not the time. I kiss him once more and pull back. He lets me go, but the fire in his eyes tells me his thoughts mirror mine. *Later,* they say. My stomach clenches at the thought and I'm again tempted to run straight back to his chambers now, to show him just how much I love him...

But I know this needs to be done, so, with great effort, I step away and he gestures for me to enter the training building before him.

It's huge, three times as large as the stables and those house *hundreds* of horses. It could easily fit five thousand soldiers, I'd wager. There are multiple rings spread throughout the space, a low wooden railing encircling each one, that I assume are for sparring or weapons training. Long rows of dummies line one wall with arrows still sticking in many of their straw-sack bodies and a collection of bows, quivers, and more arrows on hooks and racks sit beside them. There are large sacks of what might be sand or possibly flour hanging from long chains suspended from the ceiling in another area. I have no idea what you do with those. Perhaps whack them with swords or...run around them?

I shift my gaze to the ropes hanging down from the rafters nearby and get the sinking feeling those are for climbing. Perhaps I won't be required to learn that particular skill. I crane my head up to where they're secured, so high up, and my stomach clenches again, but this time from terror. I've grown fond of looking out over the kingdom from the palace high up in the mountains, but still keep my gaze firmly on my feet or my horse when we ride to or from it, and stay well away from the edge of the palace balconies. The thought of climbing up a rope with nothing between me and the ground...I shudder, my stomach flipping and my throat feeling thick.

"Don't worry, I won't make you climb to the top—yet," Killian says as we walk, following my gaze and thoughts easily.

"Yet?" I repeat, mouth dry. He chuckles low.

"You'll be doing flips off of them in no time." I glare and he only laughs harder. He leads me to one of the rings near the center of the room.

"I already told you that I know how to fight."

"You know how to defend yourself against attackers, and you are damn good at it, but that's completely different than knowing how to fight an army." I start to argue, not for the first time, but he holds up a hand. "I want you in this fight right beside me, Thea. I won't be the man who tries to keep you locked away in a gilded cage to keep you safe. You're a warrior, same as I am. It's one of the many, many reasons that I love you." He cradles my face gently between his big, scarred hands. "I would never try to lock that part of you away. But," he adds, holding my gaze, "I'll not allow you to take one step onto a battlefield without proper training."

He sets his jaw and while there's unyielding determination in his eyes, there's also fear. I understand it, and as much as I don't like to admit it, his fear is justified. I may be able to hold my own against a few bastards in an alley, but an army? True battle against trained soldiers with all manner of weapons that could kill me in an instant? I haven't the first fucking clue how to handle that. So, I sigh and nod.

"Alright. Where do we start?"

WE TRAIN RELENTLESSLY OVER THE NEXT WEEKS, MY BODY AND MIND PUSHED to limits I didn't know existed. After the first few days, I could barely walk out of The Seventh, as I've learned the training building is called—the deepest and last of the seven hells, and fuck if the name isn't warranted—and if not for Copeland's ability to heal all of my aches and pains, I'm fairly sure I would have died. That might be slightly dramatic, but I don't really give a fuck. I've always felt as if my body was in good physical condition. I'm curved in the places men like to notice and flat most everywhere else, decently strong from lifting barrels of ale and cases of wine and sacks of flour and grain at the tavern, fast and agile.

But oh great Makers was I wrong.

And though he denies it, Killian damn well found it all amusing. Dessa and the others too once they all started assisting, each of them working with me on specific skills—Odessa the bow, of course; Jonathan with throwing knives; Kendall with hand-to-hand combat that differed a bit from what I'd learned from Tobias; Tristan and Lucinda with other weapons to see what I might take a liking to: small axes, throwing stars, staffs with deadly blades affixed to each end. Killian was in charge of swordplay and as much as I grumbled during the training sessions, watching him wield his blade so effortlessly, striking and blocking in a lethal dance, was amazing. And alright, arousing.

Things got a little easier every day after that initial torment, and I feel stronger than I've ever felt. I've found that while I'm fairly adept with all of the weapons I've been trained to use, I'm far more comfortable using the versions of them that I create from ice using my Gift. They feel like a part of me and I'm able to wield them with even more accuracy and ease.

I've also been training my Gift, which I can't believe I never thought to do before now. We've tested different ways to use it, limits, and strength. I can do far more with it now than I ever thought possible and I feel in my soul that I can do even more with practice.

We've learned that proximity to Soren bolsters my power even more, so he insists that he ride into battle with us. When I'd tried to object, worry for my familiar sending acid through my veins, he'd snarled and told me in very colorful language that where I go, he goes. He'd at least compromised and agreed to wear armor that's being specially made for him.

"Ryker says that Barony flew into a rage when he received word of Amon's defeat at my hands," I call to Killian from the bed in his chambers. It's twice the size of the one in the room where I bathed that first day. I never actually slept there, having been carried directly here by Killian as if I were a sack of potatoes thrown over his shoulder after our...*discussion* in the throne room. I still shiver at the mere memory, my blood turning to fire remembering clenching the armrests as if my life depended on it, Killian behind me...

I clear my throat and he strides out of his bathing chamber, shaking water from his hair like a dog. I smile.

"Why do you even bother?" I ask, shifting from my stomach to my side, resting my head on my hand and watching him stride closer, chest bare and rivulets of water slowly cascading downward over hard cords of muscle.

"Bother?"

"With pants..." I look pointedly at his crotch, biting my lip and making it clear what's on my mind. He chuckles low and swats my ass playfully as he joins me on the bed.

"Behave, you wanton little frost witch. What else is in the letter?" he asks, jutting his chin towards the parchment on the bed in front of me. I sigh but pick up the letter again.

"Let's see...more troops have been gathered to replace those lost on the tundra, some marching towards Tithmoore, some to bolster Lyanna." I worry at my bottom lip. "We'll protect Tithmoore, won't we?"

"Of course, love." He brushes hair from my face and kisses my temple. "I've already sent additional troops to his aid in preparation." I nod and go back to the letter.

"Helios is still holding out, but it doesn't appear to be a priority for Barony to take the southern kingdom." I exhale in relief, but it's short-lived. Just because he's not pushing it, doesn't mean Barony will give up on the idea altogether. I turn to Killian.

"I *have* to get to them, Killian. I can't leave them there alone, to be pulled into this fight that isn't theirs. I can't ride off into battle until I know they're safe. Maybe we can take a ship from Tithmoore and...and I don't know, I'll figure out a way to get inside the port. I just...I *have* to try. Before I can fight back against Barony, I have to know my family is safe."

He inhales softly, sharply, as if in surprise and I frown, but he only smiles, huffing out a soft laugh.

"I hate it when she's right," he says quietly, a bittersweet note in his voice, and though I have no idea what in the hells he's talking about, he doesn't give me the chance to ask. He sighs. "I'm afraid I have to say the words that I loathe more than anything on this earth: put on some clothes."

"NO, NO I CAN'T LET YOU DO THIS," I PROTEST, BACKING AWAY FROM THE old woman. "This isn't what I meant, Killian. We'll find another way, we'll—"

"This is the way, child," Yara tells me. We'd gone to the old woman's cottage atop a small rise near the mountains and Killian had explained that she is one of Duskthorne's elders. "You are too important to risk a trek around the continent right now."

"I'm not, though. I'm not anything special, I—"

"You are," she interrupts gently. "I have been around for a long, long time." She smiles warmly, weathered skin wrinkling at the corners of her eyes and mouth, her silver hair almost sparkling in the torchlight. "And I have seen the world shift more than once. Gifteds and familiars roaming the continent and helping all who lived within it." She looks at Soren reverently then, like he's a miracle brought to earth. Killian said that familiars were greatly respected in Duskthorne, so I guess I shouldn't be surprised. Soren purrs deep in his throat and dips his head back at Yara.

"And I have seen familiars becoming fewer and farther between until they were thought all but lost, Gifteds themselves becoming scarcer as well. I've seen crowns given and taken—sometimes unwillingly," she adds, giving Killian a knowing look. "I've seen kingdoms fall, only to rise again, while others never did, staying dead forevermore and new ones taking their place." I look sharper at the woman now. Just how old can she be? I've heard tales of people living well into their hundreds. There's even rumor that there's an old priest on Sol who is over a thousand years old. I'd never believed them, adding them to the long list of campfire tales that run rampant through Hypathia, but now, looking at Yara, hearing her speak and seeing the endless depths of knowledge in her eyes, I wonder...

"But I've never seen anything like what Barony is doing now, the darkness he's bringing down on us all. He is defying the Makers, taking their blessings and twisting them into unnatural abominations—and destroying innocents in the process. You are meant to stop all of it. I know it. The winds, they speak to me, child, the mountains and the rivers and the dragons."

I share a quick glance with Killian and he hikes a shoulder, as if to say *she might have a bit of crazy mixed in with her wisdom*. Yara laughs, lips curling as she looks at Killian fondly, almost indulgently as you would a child.

"I know you all think I'm mad, talking to the earth and the dragons you believe to be gone." She leans in and whispers conspiratorially, "They're wrong, you know. The dragons are still here, they're just waiting..." She tilts her head, as if listening to them even now and smiles a knowing smile. "In time," she says to herself, nodding, "in time. But all of that is to say that you are here to right these wrongs, child. You were foretold. You are awaited. You are changing *everything*."

I hear Killian inhale quietly, as if he'd been...expecting this? Had Yara mentioned this to him before? Did he...know I was coming? No, no, this is madness. I sure as hells don't feel at all like any kind of long-awaited savior, so I push it all away and focus on the reason Killian brought me here to begin with.

"Even if what you say is true, it's not worth the price. It's too much."

"If it is my time to meet Noxum, then I shall greet him as an old friend at last. He's been poking around these last few centuries, after all, checking in as it were." I choose to ignore that, again wondering if age has started to addle her mind—and if she could possibly be speaking true when she says *centuries*...

"But—"

"You four are meant to stop Barony." Four? I frown and look at Killian who looks as baffled as I do. Does she mean Math and Cece? No, that doesn't make any sense. Neither of them are Giifteds or soldiers. They will keep their asses planted right here behind the unbreakable walls of Duskthorne during all of this. *So what does she mean....?*

-*Four...interesting...*- Soren rumbles and I quirk a brow, the tone in his voice making it seem as if he knows something we don't. He doesn't seem inclined to share though, watching Yara intently, tail swishing lazily behind him.

"I am meant to do this," she says. "I must walk my path and as you must walk yours."

"But we can find a different way, we can—"

"You cannot focus on all that you must if fear for those you love consumes part of your heart. The choice is made, the doorway waiting. We only need to walk through it."

I turn to Killian, not knowing what to do. He looks resigned. He'd explained that Yara's Gift is great, but takes a great toll as well. She hasn't used it in years for fear of it being too much for her, for pushing her to the Brink.

And now she's offering to use it, risking all—for me.

"If you want them safe—and quickly—then this is the only way. Yara is right, Thea. Your heart is torn with worry for them, and we need it whole for what's to come."

Killian shares a look with Yara.

"I told you, Beinmor" she tells him with a smug smile, winking. Killian sinks to one knee beside her chair.

"Beinmor?" I ask.

"It means *little mountain* in old Northlandish," Killian tells me. "It's what she's called me since I was a child."

"Because the mountain does not falter, no matter the hardships, no matter the assault thrust upon it by the winds and the snows. It stands tall and true." She reaches out and places a wrinkled hand on his cheek. "And it always will."

My heart twists then, knowing that she must be talking about Dorian and the abuse he rained down upon his son. But even as a child, Killian stood strong and true. He could have turned as bitter as his father, could have taken all of that hurt and hate and turned it outward against others, but he didn't. He chose a different path. He chose to help and protect, to punish those who prey on the weak and think to take what they want by force. I think to Turner and his men, cast out into the cold to die for trying to attack me.

And just like that, I fall even more in love with this man. My mountain. My heart. My king.

"Are you sure?" Killian asks Yara softly.

"I am. And who knows, perhaps this will not be the day I meet Noxum. Perhaps I shall keep him waiting a bit longer." She winks and Killian laughs. "I told you long ago that you would come to me when you needed your family whole. You should know by now that I am always right, Beinmor."

Your family. My chest clenches. Because Math and Cece are now his family too because of the love he has for me. I want to protest. I want to fight this, but it seems as if she is set on this path and it would be a great disrespect to try to sway her when she's offering me this gift. The gift of my family—*our* family—safe and by my side once more after all these months and with a war coming for us all.

I swallow hard, but nod when Yara asks me if I'm ready.

-Breathe, Thea,- Soren reminds me and I inhale deeply in response. -*Rumors are true then. You like obeying commands*-

My eyes widen and I whip my head to the big cat.

-What!?-

-Animals talk- is all he says in response and my cheeks feel like they're on fire. Killian tilts his head in concern but I wave him off.

-I cannot believe you talk about my sex life,- I hiss inside Soren's mind.

-I don't choose to hear about it, believe me. But you two are not subtle and, as I said, animals talk.- I feel the smug smile through the pathway between us and realize that he's succeeded in helping me to calm, to take my mind from what's about to happen, at least for a moment. Though I don't love that all of the animals in the kingdom apparently know about my bedroom preferences, I do appreciate his efforts to make this easier.

"I can hold the door open for twenty minutes, maybe a few more," Yara says, pulling me back into the fold.

"I'll be done in ten," I promise. Maybe if I don't take too long, the surge of power won't be too much for her, it won't push her to the Brink...

I clear my throat. "How...what do I do, exactly?"

"Think of the place you want to go. Picture it in your mind as clearly as you can, imagine yourself in it."

I do as she says, thinking of the tavern, of the hours upon hours spent there chatting with patrons and laughing with Cece, singing with Math—horrifically off-key—cleaning and swearing and cursing the hard work at times. I think of the smell of wood polish and spilled ale and the meat pies that Cece makes with her grandmam's recipe; I think of the sounds of the sailors singing their sea songs of distant shores and sirens, the clinking of glasses, the meaty thuds and grunts of pain as fists met flesh, and the grumbling of muttered apologies afterwards when it was that or be tossed out on their asses. I can see it all so clearly and my eyes prick with tears at the longing for it, for *them*.

I gasp when the air in front of us shivers and shimmers before splintering, as if someone put their fist into a mirror. The broken lines grow longer, thicker, until the entire large oval of space in front of me is black...but no. Not black. A faint, dark shimmering that grows brighter and brighter as shapes seem to appear and grow sharper...

A heartbeat later, I take a staggering step backward because I'm staring *at the tavern*, just as I left it all those months ago. It's as if I'm standing right there, in the far corner beside the fireplace instead of in Duskthorne, the entire continent separating us. It's blissfully empty—I'll admit I should have probably thought of the area behind the tavern instead just in case it wasn't.

"Great fucking Makers," I whisper and hear Killian chuckle low. "This is *extraordinary*." I can't quite make myself believe that it's truly a doorway, that I could actually step within it and be inside the walls of the first place where I truly felt safe, that in seconds, I can have Cece and Math in my arms. Yara's Gift is one of the most prolific I've ever seen...and I thank every fucking Maker that's ever blessed this earth that she's been here, safe in Duskthorne all this time. I shudder to think of what Barony would do with a power like this at his disposal.

"Quickly, Red," Killian says softly and I cut my gaze to Yara. Her face has already paled, though she's smiling at me encouragingly. *Fuck.* I can't let her push herself too far for me, I won't. *Just hold on*, I plead silently.

I nod and hesitate for a heartbeat, the idea of stepping through this doorway sending a skittering of unease up my spine, but I force myself forward. I hold my breath as I take a step, gasping when I feel the shift of air around me from cool with the bite of winter in the air, even indoors, to the stifling heat of Helios. The smells of the tavern slam into me, so different than those of Yara's small home, and it's jarring to say the least. Soren comes through behind me, and though I can tell it's hard for him to remain, even with me just a few feet away, Killian stays beside Yara, just to be safe.

"Makers..." I whisper, turning to look back through the doorway, convinced for a moment that it must have disappeared behind me, but there it stands, and I can see Yara rigid with concentration and Killian beside her, looking worried. I hear the door to the kitchen creak open but before I can even turn, I hear the scream.

"FUCK THE MAKERS' FUCKING MOTHER RIGHT IN THE ASS!!"

I hear a crash of breaking glasses and turn to find Math gaping and gasping, wheeling backwards until his back hits the wall, a shower of glass at his feet. His gaze is trained on Soren, eyes wide and chest rising and falling in shallow bursts. I should have realized that a giant frost cat in the middle of a tavern in Helios would be the first thing to draw the eye, not me.

"Math," I whisper, half laughing, half sobbing, just as Cece yells "Matthais!" from the back.

Math blinks and yanks his gaze from Soren to me, his jaw going slack at the sight.

"Thea??" he breathes. And then I'm running, sprinting across the room to throw my arms around his neck, tears sliding down my cheeks.

"Math!! Oh, great Makers, Math! I've missed you so much. I'm so glad you're alright."

"Thea, fucking hells, how are you—"

"Math, what was that racket?? I swear if you broke another round of glasses, I'll tan your hide...THEA!?!"

Cece stops dead halfway through the doorway, hands wrapped in her apron. She's frozen for a heartbeat but then flies at me, sobbing and pulling me into the world's tightest hug. I know we need to hurry, but I allow myself a moment, just a moment, to embrace my friend, my true sister—not by blood, but by love. I feel Math wrap his arms around us both, and I feel like my heart is finally complete.

-*We must hurry, daska.*-

I disentangle myself and scrub at my eyes.

"I don't have much time to explain, but you have to come with me."

"Come with you? What do you...holy fucking Makers what is that?!" Cece's eyes finally take in Soren and the doorway behind him, Killian watching with that intense blue-gray stare.

"The frost cat or the doorway...or the very large—and handsome," I add with a quick smile at Killian, "man?"

"A-all of them?" Math says, eyes darting nervously from Soren to Killian, to the edge of the doorway, then back to Soren.

"I'll explain it all later, I promise, but we have to leave. *Now*. Helios will fall soon and I can't have you here when it does."

"I know," Cece says, looking to Math. "We've been trying to find a way to get out, but we're all but surrounded now."

"Well, you aren't anymore. Gather your things, quickly as you can." Cece looks behind me again, worrying at her bottom lip. "Cece, I need you to trust me, ok? And I need you to hurry."

She looks back to me and nods, complete trust in her eyes, before turning to her husband.

"Come on, Math, you heard her. Hurry."

I motion to Killian for just a few more moments and rush upstairs on their heels.

"We've had everything packed for days, just in case. Randolph has been trying to secure passage out of one of the smaller, more treacherous bays to the east," Cece explains as she grabs up the smaller of the three bags, Math hefting the other two. She shoves a few more things into her bag before looking around, looking torn.

"We'll come back," I promise her. "Once it's safe, we'll come back." She nods and we head back out into the hallway. I eye my old room, debating on grabbing a few things, but turn away and run down the stairs with Cece and Math.

I have everything I need.

My heart stutters when I look across the main room of the tavern to the doorway and see Yara's small body trembling, sweating beading on her forehead.

"Thea. Now!" Killian yells.

"Go!" I cry, pushing Cece forward. Makers bless her, she doesn't hesitate. She runs for the doorway and leaps through it. Math's breath hitches as he watches his wife sail into the strange unknown, but he follows just after, trusting in me completely—though he does give Soren as wide a berth as possible as he sprints after Cece.

I'm just behind them one hand tangled in the fur at Soren's back as we jump through the doorway. Yara lets out a gasping breath, slumping in her chair and I turn and watch in awe as the doorway seems to shrink inward until it disappears completely and only Yara's sitting room remains, the fire burning and popping in the hearth.

"Yara!" I cry, running to her side. Killian is there, gripping her shoulders and putting two fingers against her throat, checking for her pulse. "Please, please, please," I whisper, tears welling once more as I gently grasp the old woman's hand. "Not yet. Not yet, Noxum, please..."

"She's alive!" Killian cries, eyes sliding closed in relief. I send up a prayer of thanks to all of the Makers. "We should get Copeland, just to be safe."

I turn to Soren and he nods before turning and leaping to the open window beside the fireplace. Cece gasps and I see Math yank her to his side out of the corner of my eye. I brush Yara's sweat-soaked silver hair from her brow and Killian lifts her from the chair and she looks like a child compared to his massive frame. He takes her from the room, and I assume, to her bed.

I lean my forehead against the arm of her chair and take a deep, shuddering breath.

"Sooo...what in the actual fuck just happened?" Math asks after a few beats of silence, jovial as ever but I can tell he's nervous, and a laugh bubbles up from my throat. Lightly at first, but all of these months of fear and worry and missing them, of the unknown if I'd ever see them again, the still unknown of this war and who will come out alive, all come together in what becomes a fit of laughter so ridiculous that soon Math and Cece have joined in and the three of us collapse into a heap on the floor. Killian comes back into the room, dark brows quirking up at the three of us, tears streaming and bellies aching, but his lips curl into a slow smile when I meet his gaze.

I know what he's asking without him having to use words.

Are you happy, love?

I grin at him, the sheer joy of having everyone I love together and safe within the walls of my kingdom—because yes, Duskthorne is mine. It's where I've always belonged and if the man I love is its king, then by the fucking Makers, I'll be its queen—fills my heart so fully that I think it might burst.

I nod to him and his smiles widely, the smile he reserves only for me.

I'm happy.

CHAPTER TWENTY-FIVE
TESNI

I take a few deep breaths, preparing myself for my next performance. Isn't that what all of my life is? Simply performance after performance, playing different parts. Sometimes the doting Gifted and ward; sometimes the cold fire bitch who would burn an entire village to the ground without a second thought; sometimes the lovesick woman who only wants a life of safety with the man she loves. I'm not sure which is the real me anymore. Maybe all of them. Maybe none of them.

Today, I'm playing the role of escaped prisoner of a madman who fought for her life to return to the place she truly belongs: Barony's side.

"Here we go," I whisper inside the carriage I flagged down just outside the city.

I open the door and step down just as the footmen come rushing forward.

"Lady Tesni!" one man cries in alarm. I have no idea what his name might be, though I know I've seen his face many times. I allow my knees to buckle and fall into his waiting arms. He catches me easily and I clutch at his shoulders, a shudder racking through my body. I need to play this just right, the correct mix of vulnerability and strength, of fear and vengeance. "Great Makers, what's happened to you?"

"Barony," I croak, clearing my throat before shifting my shoulders back and adding. "I need the king. Now."

"Yes, yes of course, my Lady." My Lady. Not my Queen. *Not yet*, I think sharply. Soon, though, if this all goes according to plan. My schemes usually do, save this ransom fiasco with Hastings, though I'll blame Thea for that. My darling fucking sister. I'm not sure how I feel about her ruining that particular plan. Part of me actually respects her for standing up for herself finally, for taking charge of her own life. But the other part vows to burn her to ash. As much as this new plan to become queen entices me, I would have been happier to leave all of this behind, to live out my days in luxury on an island where the sun and heat would ease the never-ending ache in my chest. I imagine that's how Thea felt all those years down in Helios, an intense longing for the cold and snow. I suppose she'll get what she longed for now that she'll be a prisoner of Dorian—at least until we're able to take Duskthorne ourselves.

So, yes, becoming queen will suffice as a second option, but Makers I do not want to deal with the bullshit of war and battle and Barony's little experiments. I hadn't lied when I told Thea that there will be no winners. My only hope is that Barony will agree to my terms that my Gift will not be touched. *Ever*.

The rest of the Gifteds are on their own. As long as I'm whole and safe and reigning, I don't really care what happens to everyone else. I know that I should, but that part of me is just...broken. Or at the very least, lost far too deeply in the darkness to make a difference. At least I know that I'm a monster, that my soul is twisted and I'm not quite...right. I admit it freely and openly to myself. People like Barony are the real monsters, the ones who think they're normal, good, decent people, justifying all of their horrible acts for this reason or that and never admitting what they truly are.

The man helps me inside, telling the other to fetch the king immediately. He leads me to Barony's personal study, looking entirely uncertain of how to assist, taking in the blood, the ripped clothes, the marks on my wrists where I was so clearly restrained. It had taken a while and quite a bit of pain to inflict all of these horrors upon myself, but it had to be done. It is all part of the plan.

"Should I fetch Gilda? Some towels and hot water, and some bandages, or—"

"I just want Barony," I say quietly, voice hard, but trembling ever so slightly. I need him to see me like this before Gilda cleans me up. I worked far too hard on this costume, as it were.

"Yes, my Lady. Of course. He'll be here soon. I'll have some food and water brought in immediately. Perhaps some wine, as well." I give him a small, grateful smile, and though he blinks in surprise for a moment, his lips curl in response before he bows his head and leaves me alone. A few moments later, the doors burst open and Barony barrels inside.

"Tesni, I—oh great Makers," he whispers when I turn and his eyes travel the length of my body. Ripped dress; blood covering the side of my face, my cheek swollen and black; the red, raw marks around each wrist where the rope cut into my skin and burned my flesh. They settle on my throat, on the collar fastened there. Tears well but I shift my shoulders back. "What happened to you?" he demands as he strides forward.

"He *took* me," I spit, but let fear and anger and pain all shine through. Perhaps I should have joined the playhouse. I would have been a star.

"Who? Who took you? What happened?" He reaches out one hand toward my face and I flinch back. He presses his lips into a hard line, but reaches forward again, slowly, and I let him run his fingers gently over my bruised cheek. I wince and inhale sharply, and he searches my eyes. To his credit, his black depths are filled with concern and confusion and fury. Oh yes, there's plenty of fury. Though he gave me away like I was nothing more than a piece of jewelry, in his mind I will always belong to him, and someone has taken—and damaged—what is his. He does not take kindly to such slights.

He leads me to the velvet sofa and eases me down beside him. Gilda comes in then with a tray of soup, bread, cheese, fruit, water, and wine. She gasps quietly as she sets it down.

"Oh, my Lady," she whispers, voice quavering. "Shall I bring the healing supplies?"

"Yes," Barony says at the same time as I say, "Not yet." He frowns at me and Gilda waits, looking between the two of us.

"I...I need to discuss this with you now." I swallow hard and let my strong facade crack just a bit as I add softly, "If I don't do it now, I'm afraid I'll never be able to speak of it."

His eyes soften and he nods.

"Give us a bit of time to talk, Gilda. I'll send for you when we're ready."

She inclines her head and leaves the room.

"Tell me."

"Hastings," I say, shuddering in a combination of fear and revulsion. "Hastings orchestrated some sort of scheme to have me kidnapped on the way to Marrowood and then steal the ransom. Except...well, it wasn't *me* headed to Marrowood. He...Makers, he found *Thea*, Your Majesty. You might have guessed that's who killed all of Amon's army—Hastings told me that they were encased in ice—but he told me that he fabricated that body all those years ago, making some beggar girl look like Thea, but really, she escaped. I don't know how or where she's been—maybe he's had her locked away all these years, I'm not sure. But he put her in the carriage to Marrowood in my place and let the route and time be leaked to Hunters, knowing it would be ambushed and lead to a kidnapping, and that you would pay whatever ransom was demanded in order to keep the alliance with Marrowood in place."

His brow furrows as he thinks through everything I've said, filling in the gaps, figuring it all out. He isn't the smartest man in Hypathia, but he can put this together, at least.

"He was going to steal the ransom when he went to deliver it for your supposed safe return and take it and you...where?"

"One of the islands, I think. He wouldn't tell me the exact location. He said that I belonged to him. He was a madman, delusional. He acted as if we were in love, that I shared his feelings and would be happy about being taken and chained up like a dog. He said he was going to make me his wife and keep me locked away forever...collared forever." I run my fingers along the metal.

Barony's jaw clenches.

"Did he..." His throat bobs as he swallows, trying to figure out how to ask the question.

"No," I tell him, letting out a relieved breath and Barony relaxes a fraction. "No," I continue, "he said he was saving that for our wedding night, thank the Makers." I clear my throat lightly before continuing. "I...I couldn't fight back against him, not with this on." I cast my eyes downward and Barony clenches his fists. I suppress a smile before looking up to meet his eyes again.

"Oh Makers, Tesni, I'm so sorry. It's my fault. I never should have trusted that bastard, I never should have put that collar on you..." He clenches his jaw. "I never should have sold you for the alliance. I could have made King Tybalt join another way, I never should have given into his demands. I was going to get you back afterwards, of course—there was already a plan in place, don't worry—but I shouldn't have risked it. You belong with *me*. You are *mine*, you always have been." That greed and fury blazes in his eyes, just as I knew it would when someone threatened to take what was his, take his power, in any form. Men are nothing if not predictable.

"He took me to a house out past the farmlands and I've been there all this time. Thea was taken in my place and told to pretend to be me to secure the ransom, but...well, he came back two days ago after you learned of Amon's forces being destroyed, and he was like a madman, his plan unraveling before his eyes. I managed to finally saw through the ropes with a nail that I pried from a floorboard, and I...I attacked him." I let out a long, shuddering breath, reaching my fingers to my battered and bloody face. "I should have known better. Without my Gift, I'm nothing. He fought back and I thought he was going to kill me, but I managed to get a knife and...and..."

Barony grips my chin and holds my gaze. I let a single tear slip from my eye, my lip trembling ever so gently. *A playhouse star, indeed.*

"You did what you had to do. What I am proud of you for doing." He studies me for a long moment. "It was different," he says, understanding my feigned fear and confusion. It was different killing with my hands than with my Gift, something I've done time and time ago without a second thought.

I nod and wipe my eyes with the back of my hand.

"He said that Tybalt planned to marry me so that you couldn't take me back, that he was aware of your plan and that your people there had been...compromised." I see the gears inside his mind turning, putting the pieces together. This part is actually true. Tybalt did plan to marry me and the men Barony had in place within Marrowood to help get me back had been found out and thrown in the dungeons. But it only helps in my plan.

"Because if you were Queen of Marrowood, you'd have to remain there. I couldn't bring you back here." He shakes his head. "It's smart, actually. I'll give that to the old bastard. But you won't be going there at all now."

"Well, what if we let him do it?"

"What?" His brows draw down and he shifts to face me fully. "What do you mean?"

"I mean..." I take a deep breath and shift my shoulders back. "What if you send me to him, he marries me, making me queen of Marrowood—and then we take Tybalt out of the equation altogether." I give him a moment to think it through, to understand what I'm saying before I push a little harder. "We would only need to swap out this collar for a fake..." I can see the idea taking shape in his mind, the merits of it, what it could mean for him. "I haven't been in the thick of this Alliance business, the coming war, but Hastings made me want to be. I don't *want* to be watching from the side, helpless, any longer. I don't want to be a pawn or a bargaining chip. I want to be part of this, Barony. I *should* be a part of this. You need me, you need my power. And, if I marry Marrowood..."

His eyes alight with that dark amusement that always endeared him to me. His darkness doesn't reach my own, but he has moments when it gets close.

"If you marry Marrowood, I shall need your kingdom...Your Highness." His lips curl as he bows his head. He would never give me the title of his queen, would never share his own kingdom, but if I can give him another to control, that changes things. His greed for more, always more, will outweigh his worry for sharing with me.

"Once I have Marrowood, you and I will marry and you'll rule *two* kingdoms." He quirks a brow. "I know you never wanted to marry me before, but this is different. It will gain you an entire kingdom. And why should we stop there? Between my power and what you'll have soon from the Gifteds—I assume Hastings was correct that the experiments are almost ready for you to reap the benefits yourself?"

"Yes, that's right." He has that calculating look in his eyes, the one that tells me he's taking this all seriously, that I've got him inside the trap. I just have to wait for the perfect moment to pull the noose tight...

"So, between the two kingdoms and all of our power, we can take the entire empire. We can—"

He laughs lightly, interrupting me, but I can tell he's intrigued. "You've got quite a plan already set out in that beautiful head of yours, don't you?" I smile at him, the wicked, dark smile that he's always been drawn to. "My cunning little ember," he says softly, pride shining in his black eyes.

"I want you to have *everything*, Barony. The entire empire, and I want to be by your side when you take it. My only request—" I barely keep my lip from curling in disgust at having to use the word *request* instead of *demand*, but I know I must continue to play the part of submissive, doting Gifted, "—is that my Gift remains mine. I will burn all of our enemies to the ground with it, I promise you, and I will bring you every damned Gifted within Duskthorne if that's what you desire. You will have all of their power soon enough. But my Gift remains with me."

His eyes narrow ever so slightly, and I can see the greed for what I have, but he smiles and nods.

"Of course, my dear. You will remain the Flame of Lyanna, always."

My lips curl upward. He leans in to kiss my forehead, tapping me gently on the end of my nose with his fingertip as he pulls away. His next words make my smile falter and a cold, hollow feeling settle in my chest.

"Besides, now that I've seen what your sister is capable of—*that's* the power I want for my own."

CHAPTER TWENTY-SIX
KILLIAN

My queen is happy. My people are safe behind my walls. My army is training harder than ever. Thea's Gift reaches new heights every day as she works to hone and control her power.

And yet.

Unease lives inside my chest like a serpent, slick and cold and coiling. Something is wrong. Something is coming. Something is missing.

That's the part that worries me the most. Missing. I'm missing something important. I'm not seeing something I should and it could mean the end of everything. I pour over the maps and correspondence, reports of Barony's abominations, of the army's movements.

"What the fuck am I missing?" I growl to myself, running a hand roughly through my hair and taking a long drink of my whisky. It burns in a comforting, familiar way, the same way Thea's skin does when she comes apart from my touch. Hers is a cold burn, of course, but a burn all the same. I don't think she even realizes that it happens and I've never told her. It's a secret touch meant only for me, a hidden language between the two of us. My lips curl at the thought of it happening just an hour ago, the cold burning my palms as my fingers clenched around her waist, pulling her down hard atop me over and over, her hands bound behind her back...

"Missing?" she asks sleepily from the doorway. I look up to find her leaning against the wooden frame, thin silk nightgown hiding little. Heat stirs and my cock takes immediate notice as it always does when I gaze upon her. Gorgeous. Perfect. Mine.

She strides inside and hops atop my war table, heedless of my papers, and I smile. She kisses me soft but deep, and puts her hand over my chest.

"What's wrong?"

I exhale roughly. Having someone to share these troubles with is novel, but something I can never thank the Makers enough for. I have Frederick. I have Dessa. I have my advisors and officers. But none of them are Thea. None of them know my heart and mind and soul the way she does.

"Something's...off, and I can't pinpoint why. I feel like I'm missing something important, forgetting some detail or...fuck, I don't know." I shake my head in frustration. "It feels as if I'm constantly running, my heart never slowing, my blood always pumping, always on edge and ready for something, but I have no idea what."

"You don't think it's just because of the coming battles?"

"No, this is different." I can't quite explain why, but it is.

"We'll figure it out, Killian. I know it." I lean my forehead against hers, taking the strength she gives me with one touch, the buoy in the stormy seas I can cling to. If I have her, I have everything. I can do anything. "Speaking of battles, I have two questions on that front."

I pull back and brush fiery locks from her forehead before kissing it and quirking a brow.

"Just two?"

"For tonight." I huff out a laugh but nod for her to continue. "One: when do you think the first fight will happen? Dessa said that there's a group moving across the northern edge of The Perilous. Will we meet them?"

"I think so." I try to find the best way to phrase what I want to say, pursing my lips. "It will be a good...practice ground for you." The contingent isn't small, but it isn't overly large. Ryker's ravens have heard that Barony is sending some of his abominations and I believe that he, too, is using this as a test of sorts. "We'll leave end of the week."

She takes a deep breath but nods. I know that she's nervous, but I can also see the fire in those emerald eyes, the warrior in her standing up and readying to fight.

"Well that brings me to question number two: if I'm to ride into battle as the Ice Queen of Duskthorne, shouldn't I actually *be* the queen of Duskthorne...?"

My eyes fly wide. I haven't pushed the idea of marriage, or her taking the smaller throne that could sit beside mine, that will only ever be meant for her. If she never wanted it, that was fine with me. I'd never given two fucks about royal business and royal lines and royal bullshit, so if she simply wanted to be together without marriage and titles, I was ok with that. But a part of me did long for it for reasons I can't even quite explain. Whether I wanted it or not, I am the King of Duskthorne, and having Thea choose to be my queen in truth, to watch over and protect my people by my side, to want to be tied to me in all of the ways both man and Makers have designed...

"Are you saying...?"

She wraps her arms around my neck, fingers sifting through the hair at my nape the way that I love. Such a casual, familiar touch, but one that makes my chest tighten.

"I'm saying that I am yours, Killian. I am yours in every way and that includes being by your side as your queen. This place is my home and it somehow always has been. Your people are my people." She kisses me then, just a quick brush of lips before she pulls back enough to add, "Plus, I think Tesni may very well die at the thought of me being a queen."

I laugh at that and kiss her fiercely, pouring every word I can't say into it, letting my body tell her everything my heart longs to. Within moments the ember becomes a full flame, and both of us burn out of control. Bodies clash, tongues dance, nails scratch, and oh does the ice burn.

My war table has never been in such shambles, but I don't think I've ever been happier.

"Does it feel different?" Dessa asks Thea as we make camp. The Alliance's forces are half a day's journey away and we'll meet them tomorrow. Thanks to Thea's Gift, we were able to make the trek from Duskthorne in half the time, even with stopping in Tithmoore to pick up some of their troops to bolster our numbers and to visit with Ryker. He and Thea have had a strange connection since the moment they met, and it's only grown since then. Neither of them can explain why, but the two of them act almost like...I shake myself, deciding to think on that after we've won this battle and are safely back home.

"May I present Queen Thea Blackheart," I'd said when we entered Ryker's throne room, making Thea roll her eyes but her smile only grew wider. We'd married the night after she'd decided she wanted to take up the crown, in a small ceremony—though Cece and Dessa both insist on a full week-long celebration once the war has been won. Cece and Dessa melded together immediately, and I could practically see the joy in Thea's heart at the sight of her old life and her new one coming together so perfectly. Mia had remained behind with Cece and Math looking after her and I know that Dessa is happy for it. As much as she loved having her sister near during the last campaign, I know she feels safer with her behind Duskthorne's walls now.

Thea had insisted on taking my mother's surname, deciding that the new line of Duskthorne royals should have nothing to do with my father. I agreed, not having realized how much I hated having to use his name as king, even as sparsely as I did.

"Besides," she'd said, "soon you won't have to hide who you are and the truth of this place. Soon Gifteds will be safe and Barony will be a pile of ash—er, well, a block of ice, technically."

"Does what feel different?" Thea responds now, pulling me back from my thoughts.

"Riding into camp as one of us instead of a prisoner?"

"Oh, I don't know, I do kind of miss the ropes," she says thoughtfully, but she shoots me a pointed look, that wicked gleam in her eye. I'd had her tied to our bed just a few days past, tethered and squirming and desperate as I brought her to the edge over and over, never letting her fall until she was nearly feral with need...I clear my throat and she laughs.

"And not just as one of us, but as our *queen*," Dessa sighs. "I never would have thought..." She shakes her head, a fond smile on her lips. I know she's happy because she loves Thea, but even more so because she never thought I'd find anyone to share this life with, these burdens. "I cannot wait until you let us celebrate properly."

Thea rolls her eyes but smiles, and they start to talk dresses and balls and parades, and I try to envision it all, but my mind keeps being pulled away by that uneasy feeling, stronger now. I keep telling myself that it's simply fear for my wife—*my wife*. Makers, I'll never tire of those words—being in battle for the first time, but I know there's more to it than that. Something is wrong. Something is coming.

The words echo inside my mind over and over until I grit my teeth, wanting to pull my hair out to make them stop.

We make camp and settle into our tent for the evening. Soren goes out to hunt and spy, and as soon as he slips away, a current of desperation charges the air around us. Tomorrow we fight and though we are well prepared—I can block any Gifts and Thea is nearly unstoppable, though she is insistent that she doesn't want a repeat performance of what happened on the tundra—there is always a chance that one of us may not walk off of the killing field.

"Killian," she whispers, and that's all it takes. A heartbeat later, she's in my arms, fingers clawing, fabric ripping, lips seeking and finding. Despite the desperation and fear, we move together slowly, deeply, savoring every moment, every touch and taste and sound. She breaks apart beneath me, clutching me close until I join her, whispering her name into the crook of her neck over and over.

She is my peace. She is my home.

And she will survive. I vow it to all the Makers. No matter what, my wife, my queen, my soul *will* survive.

WE'RE QUIET AS WE READY FOR BATTLE. I DON MY ARMOR AND HELP THEA DO the same, the act strangely sensual and intimate. I sweep her three warriors' braids over her shoulder so that I can buckle her breastplate across her shoulders, smiling at the style that she and Dessa now share. Sisters in battle and love. I finish and place a kiss at her nape before I pull the braids back, letting them fall down her back in fiery ribbons. She turns to face me, and I suck in a sharp breath.

"What?" she asks, running her hands self-consciously over the form-fitting armor, made of a mix of iron and dragon scales—some of the last in existence. My mother had several gowns made of them and we repurposed them for Thea and Soren's armor. Dragon scales are nearly impenetrable and though Thea protested when I'd first told the smith to have the dresses stripped, I told her that I'd have nothing less protecting my wife and her familiar on the battlefield.

"Is it not right?" she asks, worry in her voice. "Dessa said—"

"It's perfect," I whisper, the urge to drop to my knees and worship the Maker in disguise she surely is nearly overwhelming me. My throat goes dry and, damn me, my cock shoots hard. She looks... sexy. Great fucking Makers, she looks sexier than I've ever seen. The black scales shimmering ever so slightly, hair bright as fire, eyes burning with fierce determination. A true warrior queen. *My* warrior queen.

"You look...fiercely alluring." She rolls her eyes, but I pinch her chin, tilting her head back until she meets my gaze. "I am in no way joking, Thea." I grab her wrist and guide her hand to my aching cock, helping her to palm me through my leathers. "Feel that? Harder than any ice you can conjure, love. Hard as fucking stone from one look at you in this armor."

She swallows hard and bites her lip.

"Let's make short work of this," she says, voice breathy and rough. "I have many, many things I'd like to do to you this evening, Commander..."

I nearly growl at the thought, of celebrating a victory with her this eve in so many deliciously wicked ways...

"As my queen commands." I kiss her swiftly and step away before I lose all power to walk out of this tent. She gasps quietly and I know that she's realizing how many times I said the words even before she knew the truth of who I was, that I was calling her my queen as a true king, that I was already hers in so many ways. I give her a knowing smile and kiss her softly before turning to gather my weapons.

We ride to a clearing where we'll meet the Alliance's forces. We leave the horses and walk the last few hundred yards, but when we step out into the field and I see them across the expanse, I stutter step, momentarily stunned by what I'm feeling.

"Killian?"

"Something's...wrong with them, with their stolen Gifts." I can feel them, but their energies feel dark and twisted. Angry. It's as if the Gifts know that they've been stolen and are fighting against their captors. I feel as if I'm tainting my own soul just by sensing them, my own Gift recoiling as if to get away from the sick, unnatural imposters. "The energy feels..." I trail off, shaking my head and gritting my teeth. I can see Dessa give me a worried glance from the corner of my eye, and then share a look with Thea.

"Are you alright?" Thea asks.

"Yes," I assure her. "Yes, I'm fine. Let's get this done, shall we?" I send up a quick prayer to Brienne as is customary before every battle, but I beg the Maker of war for extra protection and swiftness today, to let our arrows fly true and our blades strike home. Dessa barks out orders to the men and they fall into formation like the well-oiled killing machine they are. She nods to me and nocks an arrow, waiting for my command to raise her bow and let her arrow fly with the other archers.

She's nervous about what she will witness here today—what she will do. She took life on the tundra, but this will be far, far different and we both know it. That was a desperate act of defiance and love. This is planned, deliberate killing.

This is war.

"Steady, love," I say quietly. "Steady."

"You can't think of them as people," Dessa tells her softly. "I know that sounds cold, but it's the best way to get past what you must do. You must only think of them as the enemy. Think of the evil they serve and the harm they may cause. You mustn't think of each individual soul, but the whole of the army as a beast to be slain." She hikes a shoulder.

Thea lets out a long, slow breath, and though I know how hard doing that will be for her, she nods. A moment later, ice erupts from her palm, taking the shape of a hilt and cross guard, lengthening into a thick, wickedly sharp blade. I quirk a dark brow when I spy the dragon carved on the pommel, wings outstretched: a perfect match of my own, sculpted in ice.

"I've been practicing." She shrugs and winks at me.

We stand for a few moments, the sound of a thousand soldiers waiting to see if Noxum comes for them this day echoing around us. Low breathing; the shuffling of feet; the metallic ringing of steel pulling free from scabbards. The snow is thick beneath my boots, great drifts of it piled around the clearing, and icicles hang from the trees like crystals. Thea inhales deeply, and I can see how calming the winter makes her, how it calls to her. I glance upward.

"Looks like snow."

"Not until after the battle," she says, and I can feel her Gift surging and swelling, moving through the gate in my walls that I always keep open for her now. She's keeping the storm at bay to aid us, and doing it as almost an afterthought. *This woman is fucking incredible.*

I shift on the small rise of packed snow that Thea created for us to watch and assist from until we're needed in the thick of the battle. I'm normally on the front lines, despite much grumbling from, well, practically everyone, really, but today I agreed to remain back with Thea. The first true battle for any warrior is a difficult thing, and I'll be by my wife's side to help her face it however she needs.

"So...does someone sound a horn or bang a drum signaling us to begin or...?"

I chuckle low at that and meet Dessa's eyes.

"The mountains do not move."

She nods and grins. "And the dragons do not yield."

Thea quirks a brow.

"Well, isn't that just adorable..."

"Fly!" Dessa yells, giving the order for her archers to make the first strike.

They raise their bows in perfect unison and loose their arrows. As they sail toward their targets, I roar to the men and the lines of Duskthorne and Tithmoore soldiers rush forward together, blades and axes and war hammers drawn and ready. The other side runs to meet them, their own cries and cheers joining the sounds of stomping boots and crunching snow.

Thea stares, wide eyed and frozen, and I can only imagine what it must look like to her. Chaos. Terror. A bit of excitement.

Soren shifts beside her, leaning his body against hers and I see her swallow hard, relaxing and pulling strength from her familiar. I send a silent thanks to the cat and watch as our arrows rain down, hitting targets. Screams ripple through the field and though Thea winces, she stands tall and strong. The white snow is soon painted red with blood as the first lines clash in a brutal collision that seems to echo through the entire world. The ringing of metal upon metal fills my mind as swords meet, screams and cries of pain and anger and fear, and the sounds of ripping flesh and crunching bone join the cacophony: the sounds of battle.

A line of their own archers fires back and Dessa cries warning, the same warning echoing throughout the ranks. Those that carry shields raise them, the others putting their faith in the Makers to keep them safe as they continue on, keeping both hands free for fighting.

Thea throws her free hand upward and a wave of ice strikes their arrows, not thick enough to encase them like at the tundra, but enough to knock them from their paths, all of them flying harmlessly into the woods as she sweeps the wave to the side.

Soren gives a chuff of what I believe to be approval, his icy blue eyes watching intently, the gold ring seeming to shine like the sun as he scans the battle for any signs of danger to his bonded. That feeling of unease and wrongness suddenly flares in my chest as I feel one of the abomination's twisted Gifts rise. I tense, readying myself for that awful, stolen power to touch my own, wondering if it might make me physically ill. My stomach roils as the power meets my wall —and sails right fucking through it.

"No," I gasp, blinking in shock as I see roots surge upward, bursting free from the earth below my men in a spray of snow and dirt and blood. Screams of pain and surprise and fear ring out as more roots break through the frozen earth, hurtling bodies across the field as if they're nothing more than pebbles.

"What the hells?" Thea whips her head to me, worry and confusion in her eyes. "Killian!? How...?"

"I can't block them," I grate, putting all of my power into fortifying my wall, on somehow stopping these twisted Gifts from getting by. I can see the one who wielded the roots, standing behind a group of what are most assuredly guards, there to protect him from the battle so he can attack with his power. My stomach sinks when I see two more standing beside him. "Their stolen Gifts are so twisted that my own can't block them."

"Oh fuck," Dessa grits, nocking another arrow and letting it fly.

"The ones behind the guards," I yell. "Get to the ones behind the guards!" I point to two men and one woman standing behind a line of soldiers, their skin nearly as white as the snow around them, dark circles beneath their eyes. Do their bodies not take well to the stolen power? The order to go after the abominations rushes through the lines of my men, mixing with the clashing of blades and screams of pain. The smell of blood permeates the air and Thea watches, eyes still wide and shoulders tense. Her eyes scan the lines and then her sword disappears, seeming to fold in upon itself before daggers of ice form in its place. She closes her eyes for a heartbeat before opening them, a fiery determination burning there as she sends them flying across the field, the speed unbelievable, her precision uncanny. They slide into enemy necks and eyes, into gaps in golden armor to stick between ribs. Bodies fall and she continues her attacks, but I'm mostly useless. There are a few true Gifteds among them, and I keep them blocked for all I'm worth, but these abominations…

Thea sends larger blades sailing over the heads of the soldiers towards the abominations, but they hit some kind of invisible wall, bouncing off and sailing back into the fray.

"One of them has some kind of shielding in place," she pants, sweat sheening her brow. I grind my teeth, fury rising. I'll shred the shield with cold steel if I have to.

"Stay here!" I call and take off into the melee, praying to Brienne for safety and telling Noxum to fuck right off.

CHAPTER TWENTY-SEVEN
TESNI

"Your Majesty," I say as I curtsey deeply, my gold and crimson gown falling out around me like the petals of a rose.

"Better late than never, I suppose," King Tybalt grumbles, voice reedy and thin. I grit my teeth but smile at him as I rise.

"Yes, Your Majesty. We do apologize for the delay." As far as the old prick—and every other royal in the Alliance—knows, I escaped the Hunters who were taking me to Duskthorne before a ransom could be negotiated, and fought my way back to Barony in hopes to keep our alliance with Marrowood in place. So, he's truly letting me apologize for being kidnapped. *The sooner I can render him to ash, the better.*

We spread the word of my miraculous return and waited for the first batch of battle-ready rats from the laboratories to make their way to The Perilous to meet Blackheart's forces before I made my way to Marrowood. With any luck, they'll defeat Blackheart easily enough and we'll be one step closer to taking Duskthorne and the entire empire. I wonder if Thea will be with them. Would Dorian force her to fight for him instead of keeping her in the cages? If what they say about Amon's army on the tundra is true...well, she's powerful enough that Dorian could surely see that having her on the battlefield would be the better choice. I'll admit that even I wouldn't wish life under that monster on anyone, but especially not my sister. I don't hate Thea. I never did, despite what she might think. I do love her, as much as I can love anyone, I think, but given a choice between her or me, I choose me. What's so wrong with that?

Even so, I do hope that Dorian isn't torturing her—or worse. I've heard the stories of that place, the way Dorian keeps female Gifteds to breed with in hopes of keeping the lines going. I shudder at the thought. I wouldn't want that for Thea, not when her only sin is being my twin—well, that and ruining my plans, though I can't truly fault her for that.

But will she be fighting with them? By force...or by choice? Would she really turn against the rest of the empire? It's possible, after the things I've done to her. She could hate me that much. And I couldn't blame her.

I suppose I'll find out soon enough. Barony has promised that we are partners in this now, that he will keep me apprised of what's happening with this war and his plans. I barely stop myself from looking to him now. He insisted on delivering me to Tybalt himself, to ensure that nothing went amiss this time and to solidify their alliance.

Tybalt's entire court is present, watching eagerly as he receives his gift. I feel as if I'm on display, one of the living statues that Barony used to bring in for his balls—the men and women painted gold and forced to remain standing and still for hours upon hours. They were quite lovely, come to think of it. Perhaps I'll demand that we bring them back for our wedding ceremony.

But first I must get through this one.

I wait as King Tybalt looks me over, taking in every inch of me in a way that makes my skin crawl. He's older than I am by at least forty years, much older than Barony, and the thought of consummating a marriage with him makes bile rise in my throat. Fortunately, that won't be necessary. We only need to wed in front of witnesses, mark the marriage decree in blood, and then it is done. I am officially his queen. The consummation rights are simply a perk—and obligation, for the woman—of marriage, not a requirement.

"Even prettier in person, little ember," he rasps, leering with his gray teeth on full display. I keep my face blank, my smile genial, just as a good little Gifted would for her king.

"Thank you, Your Majesty."

I can hear the courtiers whispering, some in awe, some in disgust—I do have quite a reputation, after all—all in wonder of what might happen next. They must know as well as I that Tybalt has something else planned. He wouldn't have gathered the entire court, all of his highest-ranking officials and houses, simply to receive his promised payment for joining the Alliance.

Tybalt finally shifts his gaze from me to the rest of his court, looking down on them from the head table atop the raised dais. Everyone else is seated at the numerous long tables set in neat rows on either side of the wide aisle running the length of the feasting chamber. It's grand, though not nearly as opulent as anything in Castle Lyanna, adorned with crystal chandeliers and sconces, and deep purple tapestries hanging from the high ceilings, the three-headed serpent sigil of Marrowood emblazoned upon each.

"What do you say to a little demonstration?" he asks the room loudly. "We've all heard the rumors, of course. The great Flame of Lyanna—Flame of Marrowood, now," he says, grinning directly at Barony. I can practically feel his fury, but I know that he's playing his role behind me, inclining his head to Tybalt in acknowledgment, allowing for the change of ownership. "But I, for one, would like to see it in person. What say you?"

The court claps and cheers for their king. He turns his gaze back to me and I incline my head.

"Of course, Your Majesty. Whatever you desire. Shall I light some candles? Spell words in flames across the air? The court at Lyanna particularly enjoy that one, or—"

He cuts me off. "I think something a little more...substantial, if you please." He gestures over my shoulder and I turn as the doors on the far end of the room open. Guards march in, shoving a group of four people before them. They're in rags and filthy, clearly prisoners. I glance quickly to Barony who gives me the tiniest nod of his head, telling me to keep to the plan, no matter what.

"These prisoners have been sentenced to death. You will carry out the execution."

A young man, early twenties, trembles, but keeps his shoulders back. The older man, the faintest of gray streaking his black hair, stands stoic and strong as he reaches to clasp the hand of the woman next to him, the shackles around their wrists clanking quietly. The woman squeezes his hand back and raises her eyes to meet mine. A single tear streams down her cheek as she grabs the other woman's hand with her free one. No, not woman, I realize. Girl. She can't be more than thirteen or fourteen, and she looks to the woman who is obviously her mother, swallowing hard as her lip trembles.

My stomach roils ever so slightly. I've killed before, countless times. I've burned villages and front lines of armies. But this feels…different. I've never looked anyone in the eye before I took their lives. I've never seen the accusation and the horror and the fear.

I clear my throat lightly. "What are their crimes, your majesty?"

"Nothing!" the mother cries, fire in her eyes. "Nothing more than demand money owed for food the palace stole from us!"

"SILENCE!" Tybalt roars, spittle flying.

Guards step closer to the family, threat clear and the woman presses her lips into a hard line, pulling her daughter closer. This family has been sentenced to death because they asked for what was theirs? My stomach roils ever so slightly, a tiny ripple in the darkness.

"It doesn't matter. You will do as you are told," Tybalt spits at me, voice harsh and grating as he rises from the table and comes to stand before me. I make a show of flinching away from him, acting afraid. "You are now my flame to wield, girl." He unlocks my collar with the small iron key and pulls the metal away. "Now fucking obey."

"Yes, Your Majesty," I say quietly, bowing my head and turning back to the group. The guards have moved away now, leaving the prisoners standing alone in the middle of the aisle. I don't want to meet her eye, but my gaze fixes on the mother's all the same. She juts her chin, and squeezes her daughter and husband's hands.

"Mama?" the girl whispers, voice shaking. The woman casts me one more disgusted, defiant look and turns to face her daughter. She pulls the girl close and tucks her face into her chest.

"It will be ok, Clara. Everything will be ok."

I don't like the pain that slices through me, the disgust at myself. I let the flames loose and screaming fills the feasting chamber with the smell of charred flesh. The courtiers gasp and shrink away, some people crying, some people shielding their eyes or covering their ears. I will the fire hotter, ending it as quickly as possible. Something about the woman's gaze unnerved me as nothing ever has. The screams die almost as soon as they began, the bodies crumbling and falling away. When I pull the fire back, only piles of ash and bits of charred bone remain.

The entire room goes silent and I blink at the spot where the mother and daughter stood moments ago. I don't...I don't like this feeling. I blink again, willing it to go away, willing the typical cold indifference I feel to settle over me.

After what feels like an eternity, Tybalt laughs loudly, clapping as if a jester just performed a particularly entertaining trick juggling fruits and knives. The rest of the court joins in uneasily, and a moment later, I feel the collar being snapped back into place around my throat.

"Well done!" Tybalt exclaims, still laughing. "I see why you've kept her under such lock and key all these years, Barony. She is quite the little toy, is she not?"

He raises his glass to Barony before taking a long sip. We're still standing before the head table on the dais, looking out over the room, the sea of people. I feel...odd. Uneasy. My eyes water and my throat feels tight. Makers, is this guilt? Regret? Disgust? I try desperately to force the feeling away, to focus on what I know will come next.

"I know what you had planned, Barony. How you planted spies in my midst, ready to kill me and take your precious Fire Bitch back with you, putting someone of your choosing on the throne and keeping the alliance with Marrowood in place." Barony makes a show of paling, body tensing, and Tybalt grins, looking supremely satisfied with himself. "Nothing happens in my kingdom that I don't know about, boy. I've been on this throne longer than you've been alive. Now, I am a man of my word, so I will keep up my end of the bargain. I pledge Marrowood to the Alliance and will supply your army with as weapons as you need. But you will not be taking her back. In fact, she is going to marry me, here, tonight, and become queen of Marrowood. She will never leave this kingdom again," he sneers.

"What? But I—" I allow panic to seep into my voice, let it show in my eyes when I meet Tybalt's gaze. I swallow hard, pretending to fear whatever it is I see there, and bow my head. "Yes, Your Majesty," I whisper. I glance to Barony and see him clenching and unclenching his fists at his sides, two guards in purple uniforms flanking him now.

"As it please you, Your Majesty," he finally grits out, inclining his head and admitting defeat. Tybalt grins again, throwing out an arm.

"High Priest Aquilar, if you please."

Another old man approaches, his gray beard nearly reaching the floor. He recites some words that I barely pay attention to, some nonsense about marriage being blessed by the Makers, invites any of the witnesses to object if they see fit—no one does, of course, many still cutting uneasy glances to the pile of ash and bone in the center of the room—and presents a scroll for us to seal our union.

The last step.

A golden needle pricks each of our fingers in turn and I press my bloody fingertip to the parchment. Tybalt does the same and the High Priest dusts both spots of blood with white sand, sealing our bond forever.

"Is…is that it?" I whisper quietly. "We're married? I'm…I'm Queen of Marrowood?"

"The fun part will come after dinner, my little fire cunt, when I take you in front of the entire court so all will know who you belong to," he says, voice thick with promised pain, "but yes, in the eyes of the High Priests, the Makers themselves, and the laws of Hypathia, we are wed and you are queen."

I sigh and turn my face up to his, reaching out to place a hand on his chest. His wicked smile falters at the touch, then disappears completely when he sees a smile of my own curling my lips, mine far more sinister and twisted than his could ever hope to be.

"That's so lovely to hear."

His eyes fly wide as a gaping, fiery hole appears in his chest, right over his heart. He gasps and writhes, but to his credit, he doesn't scream.

"Your…collar…" he pants, eyes filled with pain as he falls to his knees. I keep a hold on his chest, burning through skin and muscle and bone.

"This old thing?" I ask, waving to the metal about my throat that is no more than a necklace. "Beautiful, isn't it? It was a gift from my future husband, King Barony."

I glance to Barony now, splattered in crimson, bloody knife in his hand and two dead guards behind him. He slowly backs towards me, keeping the knife out as he eyes the other guards. The room is staring in stunned silence, but I can feel the chaos about to erupt. I send a ring of fire around the perimeter, keeping everyone in place.

"I am your queen," I call. "You will obey or you will burn. The choice is yours." Tybalt slumps to the ground, a smoking hole through his chest, a crumbling, charred lump of meat where his heart should be. I turn to face the gathered court—*my* court now—blood mixing with the flames dancing across my palm. "*Kneel.*"

A power like I've never known fills me as one by one, every person in the room sinks to their knees before me. I grin, the uneasy feeling from before all but burned away to nothing, disappearing like smoke on the wind. What was one little family compared to *this*??

I meet Barony's eyes and he smiles widely. I finally understand him. I finally understand my true destiny.

They will *all* kneel before me.

CHAPTER TWENTY-EIGHT

THEA

This is unlike anything I could have imagined. This battle is intense and chaotic and awful, but a part of me that I never truly knew existed until recently rises up, a sense of purpose that I've always longed for burning brightly through my veins and making my blood sing. I may be scared shitless and worried beyond measure for my family and all of our men, but I am also exactly where I'm meant to be. I'm meant to do this. I'm meant to fight and protect, just like Killian.

I know that this isn't even a large battle—a "wee skirmish" Tristan had called it, actually—not compared to what we might face soon enough, so I try to let this serve as a lesson and prepare myself for what's to come. It was an onslaught at first, sending my senses into overdrive. The screams and the clashing metal, the smell of blood as the white quickly—too quickly—became stained with scarlet. As horrible as I felt about it, I'd taken Dessa's advice. I had stopped thinking of the army across from me as people. If I hadn't, I never would have been able to do what had to be done. I sent those daggers of ice soaring through the air, saw the blood spurt as they found their targets, saw the bodies fall.

This is war, I keep telling myself. It's war and it's messy and everything is gray. But I will do whatever it takes to keep the people I care about safe, to stop the horrors that Barony is raining down on his people, the horrors he hopes to spread through the whole of the empire.

I'm doing my best to keep the snow at bay and protect our people, but I know I can't help everyone at once.

-*You are doing well, daska. Keep going,*- Soren says encouragingly, though the big cat is on edge, has been since this morning. When I asked him if it was just the coming battle, he said that there were rumblings among the animals, rumblings that made him uneasy. Not uneasy enough to share with me, though. Stubborn damned feline.

-*Stay beside me.*-

-*Always,*- he promises.

Killian being unable to block the power of the abominations is...troubling to say the least, but we'll deal with that later. For now, we need to make it out of this alive. What was supposed to be a small skirmish is becoming a losing battle. The roots are ripping through the army, tossing men about as if they're dolls, and one of the abominations, though I can't tell which, has some sort of shielding ability.

"Stay here!" Killian roars and leaps from the small rise. I don't try to stop him, knowing this is what he needs to do. He'll do anything for his people, and right now, anything means somehow getting those guards out of the way and that shield gone. So, I call to him to be safe and keep my eyes on every fucking step he takes. Anyone who nears him is met with a dagger of ice before Killian can even swing his great sword. He casts a glance over his shoulder and winks, smiling in the middle of the bloodbath.

More roots burst through the ground as he turns to keep making his way through the melee, desperate to get to that shield. I gasp when I see them *reach* for the soldiers now, impaling and grabbing, like gnarled fingers.

"Great fucking Makers," Odessa grates from beside me, letting arrow after arrow fly. Her aim is impeccable and I watch enemy after enemy fall. Enemies only. Not people. I keep having to remind myself over and over as the bodies litter the field.

I watch, eyes narrowed. One abomination has the power to control the trees, or the very least the roots beneath the field, and the other has this shielding. I spare a quick glance back to the group being guarded. There's one more.

"So what the hells can the other do?"

"I don't think we want to—" Dessa cuts off as a great wind sweeps through the field, sending soldiers sprawling, others managing to hold their positions by digging swords or fingers into the bloody ground. It isn't precise or targeted, the Alliance's own men being thrown along with ours, but the power is undeniable. "Wind," she finishes as I see one of the male abominations sag, apparently worn out quickly from the use of power. "Fucking wind."

I send another assault of icy blades sailing across the field, hammering against the shield and...

"Did you see that?" I yell.

"See what?!" Dessa shouts back.

"Watch the shield!"

I send another volley, putting more power behind them, leaning into Soren and pulling from his strength. *Come on...I know I saw it...yes!*

"There!!" When the blades strike this time, I see the shield ripple and then splinter, like the surface of a frozen pond. Just tiny cracks, but cracks all the same. "It can be destroyed physically!"

I shift my gaze back to Killian, wondering if he saw, and watch in awe as he cuts a bloody swath through the field. He's magnificent, spinning and slicing through the men as if they were parchment. He twists and parries and bends in the most beautiful, lethal ballet. How a man that big can move his body like that is beyond me.

"Incredibly sexy, isn't it?" Dessa says from beside me. I fling another volley of ice into the shield and the splinters grow. The abomination shakes violently, holding out her hands trying to keep the shield in place. I wonder if these abominations can reach the Brink as we can? Can they feel it coming, or will they simply...expire when it becomes too much with no warning?

I force those thoughts away and focus on what Dessa just said, turning to look at her incredulously.

"Not him in particular," she amends, rolling her eyes, "but the skill itself is incredibly sexy. That kind of deadly grace is...mmmm. Just watch Jonathan, *great Makers* that man can wield that sword..."

"Are you...are you really talking about how arousing these men are fighting right now? In the middle of a battle?" It's taking everything I have not to have a complete breakdown here on this field, the screams and the blood and the death all lashing at me like a whip.

"Why not?" she shrugs. "It helps me stay calm."

I blink at that, supposing that it makes a sort of sense. Keeping things light in the face of death could be a good way to keep yourself from spiraling into panic. As if hearing our conversation, Tristan parries and spins, driving his twin short swords into a man's chest, and then turns towards the rise with a grin.

"Dessa!"

"What!?"

"Marry me!"

I huff out a laugh, despite the situation. She grins widely and lets another arrow fly.

"I'm a bit busy at the moment, but I'm happy to oblige when we finish this battle!"

He blows her a kiss and turns back, charging forward to find another foe.

"Did you...did you just become betrothed in the middle of a battle??"

"I think I did," she says with a shrug and a laugh.

I turn my gaze back to Killian, sending a star of ice into a soldier on his right as the Commander quickly decapitates two others in quick succession. He turns to glance at me over his shoulder again and I can't help but smile—and alright, yes, agree with Dessa: it's intensely attractive, the blood and dirt splattered across his neck and face making it more so. Makers, don't ask me to explain it.

But all of those thoughts melt from my mind as a root the size of a sapling surges from the earth just beneath him, flinging him skyward. Spindly branches reach out like fingers and grab him, slamming him back to the ground as a scream tears free from my throat. I send a surge of ice forward, coating the limb, but the fingers of that hells-birthed hand keep squeezing Killian, pressing him deeper into the earth. I grit my teeth, about to encase the entire thing in a block of ice so thick it would take years to dig it out, but I stop myself as the power surges within me. I can't be sure that I won't hurt Killian in the process, the limb too intertwined with him to be sure I'd only coat the wood.

"Killian!" I scream as I dash forward. Dessa tries to grab at my arm but I'm too quick, spinning out of her grasp and sprinting down the rise, Soren beside me. I may not be able to freeze the thing, but I can sure as hells chop it to bits. Fury and rage and a strange calm all settle over me as I throw myself into the fray. I form my sword of ice again, thick and sharp and ready to taste blood. Soren shifts as we run and I'm tossed into the air and settled on his back in one quick, practiced movement. I curl my fingers into the small notch in his armor, put there for this very reason, and he sprints through the throng. I swing out with my blade as we speed by soldiers, not able to see where they fall or in how many pieces, but then Soren falters, shaking his head as if something's wrong.

-Something is coming. Something...big.-

-What? Another abomination?- I send waves of ice forward, tossing soldiers aside like ragdolls as it clears a path for us. We can't move fast enough cleaving one at a time with my sword, drenched in blood as it is. I send silent apologies to our men who are tossed aside as well and hope none of them are hurt too badly in the process.

-Um, not quite...-

And then the air shifts overhead, a strange, immense pressure, and then the sound, almost like the beating of...wings?

The first scream rings out, followed by hundreds of others. Soren digs his claws into the churned earth, a mix of blood and melted snow and mud, sliding to a stop, and we both crane our heads upward.

"*Makers*," I whisper, reeling backward.

CHAPTER TWENTY-NINE

KILLIAN

This cannot be how it ends. Strangled by a fucking tree? No. I refuse. But try as I might, I can't get free. The finger-like branches squeeze tighter the more I struggle, like a great serpent constricting its prey, and press me deeper into the earth, the cold seeping into my bones.

I hear Thea scream and grit my teeth, renewing my fight. I will get back to her. I will not die this day. I claw at the branches and see my sword lying just out of reach in the snow to my right. I strain, screaming through clenched teeth. My shoulder feels like it might be torn from its socket, but I keep reaching, fingers finally scrabbling on the very edge of the pommel.

"Come on, damnit!!" I reach farther still and feel something tear and pain lace through my body, but it's enough. My fingers close around the grip and I yank it towards me, stabbing and cleaving, desperate to escape. My vision starts to darken around the edges as the branches continue to squeeze, squeeze, squeeze...

"Thea," I whisper as the darkness starts to overtake me, but then something welcoming settles over me. Accepting death? No, that isn't it...but that feeling of wrongness that's been plaguing me these weeks, that feeling that I'm missing something fades away as something bright flares inside of my chest, hot as fire, but it doesn't burn. No, it *forges*, solidifying some connection that reaches out for—

Screams erupt across the field and the ground shakes as thunder cracks. No, not thunder. The sound of something *giant* landing just beside me. A moment later the tree is ripped away and I'm staring up at—

Great. Fucking. Makers.

-Hello, Killian Blackheart,- a voice whispers inside my mind. I blink, unable to move or breathe or think. The voice is warm and soft. Welcoming. A piece of me. Somehow she's always been a part of me, a missing part of my soul now made whole again. Thea was the first piece to be found. She is the second.

I understand then, what's happened, what this means.

I've bonded. I have a familiar.

And she's a fucking *dragon*.

-Are you going to just lie there all day? We've a battle to win.- she says inside my mind again, staring at me with those strange golden eyes, ringed in ice blue—a mirror image of Soren's, I realize. I can feel the amusement in her voice and I wonder idly how long it took Thea to get used to this.

-I am Isolde.-

"It-it's nice to make your acquaintance," I manage to say, voice barely more than a whisper. I clear my throat and wince, fire flaring up my side. Broken ribs. At least three. I push the pain away to be dealt with later and manage to get to my feet as she...fucking *winks* at me and turns towards field.

A dragon.

Just winked at me.

In the middle of a battle.

Is this real? This can't possibly be real. Perhaps I did die on this field under that damned tree and this is Noxum's strange idea of a joke.

I stare in utter wonder at her. She's magnificent, standing at least twelve feet tall, maybe more, with deep gray scales, so dark they're nearly black, that shimmer faintly in the sunlight, and spiked ridges down her spine and curling back from the sides of her head. She spreads her dark wings outward, the undersides a deep crimson in the sunlight. She turns towards the Alliance's forces and lowers her head and lets out a roar so loud that I barely stop myself from clamping my hands over my ears. I turn to see Thea standing a few feet away doing just that, eyes wide and jaw slack, Dessa beside her looking like she might cry from the sheer awe of what she's seeing. We've both dreamed of this day since we were children, hoping and praying that the dragons would return to us one day, pretending for countless hours that we were chasing them or fighting with them or, hells, even *were* them, flying high above the kingdom, free from everything else.

Isolde turns her head back over her shoulder, looking directly at Thea for a heartbeat before she turns to the army once more. She roars again, the earth shaking and ice raining down from the trees around us, tinkling melodically. The guards surrounding the abominations look as if they might have pissed themselves, their line falling apart as half of them turn and run. The abominations themselves don't look much better, their pallid skin draining of what little color they had.

The dragon inhales, her massive chest expanding and wings flaring again, and without knowing how, exactly, I know what's going to happen next. I run to Thea. I know that she's in no danger, but I can only imagine what she must be thinking, and I need my hands on her. It had been far too close, that darkness creeping in...

I reach her side and she grabs for me, clutching at my arm without ever taking her eyes off of the dragon. A second later blue fire erupts from Isolde's throat. It's unlike any fire I've ever seen, azure flames scorching everything in their path as they roil forward. Ear-piercing screams of agony ring out but don't last long as the wave of fire drowns them all. When the fire dissipates, nothing but a field of death remains. I swallow hard as my gaze skirts over mangled bodies, some still with bits of burned flesh attached, others just piles of charred bones.

"Great fucking Makers," Thea whispers beside me, clenching my arm harder, her other hand clutching Soren's fur. The remaining members of the Alliance's forces that were on *this* side of Isolde, fighting against our soldiers immediately throw down their weapons and surrender, dropping to their knees and begging for forgiveness and protection. We all stand there in stunned silence for what feels like an eternity, watching as the dragon huffs, wisps of blue-gray smoke curling from her nostrils before she turns to face me once more.

She sits in front of us, spiked tail curling around her front feet and giant talons digging into the earth. She waits patiently, tilting her head as she studies the line of us.

Before anyone can say a word, Dessa drops to one knee and bows her head.

"What are you doing?" Thea whispers from the corner of her mouth, keeping one eye on the admittedly terrifying creature in front of her. Beautiful to be sure, but terrifying all the same. Isolde peels her lips back ever so slightly, letting us get a glimpse of those massive, razor-sharp fangs, and Thea tenses. I swear I feel amusement from the dragon whispering in my mind. *Wait.* Had she *heard* my thoughts?

-*Yes, I did. You'll learn to control them. Look for the doorway in your mind, the pathway between us.*- I don't really understand what she could mean, but I take a deep breath and do as she says, looking within my mind, the same way I do with my Gift. It takes a moment, but a shimmering golden doorway seems to appear. It beckons, feeling like the road home.

-*Um...can you hear me?*-

-*Very good.*-

All of this takes seconds, and in the span of these few heartbeats, soldiers across the field join Odessa, kneeling in the bloody, muddy snow, and Thea finally tears her gaze away from Isolde to look at the spectacle.

"What's happening?" she whispers.

"We revere dragons, Red. In Duskthorne legends, dragons were once the form Makers took to walk among mortals and are therefore blessed for all eternity. They used to roam all over our kingdom, living in peace with us, protecting us. It's why Duskthorne's sigil is a dragon."

Isolde notices what's happening and huffs out a soft breath, the air clouding in front of her nose. She...bows in return, head sinking down so low that her chin touches the snow.

I step forward and tentatively hold out a hand towards her snout. She lifts her face once more, easing forward until she—

A strangled scream tears from Thea's throat as Isolde opens her massive jaws, truly revealing those gleaming fangs, and snapping them shut an inch from my hand. I rear back, slipping on the snow and landing firmly on my ass. Thea lunges forward, but freezes when the dragon...laughs? Her lips curl up in the corners and her shoulders and chest shake with the rumbling sound, reminding me a bit of Soren's chuffing.

I blink and then throw my head back, laughing so hard that my ribs scream in agony, but I can't stop. Thea looks between me, Isolde, and Soren, who I assume is joining in our laughter inside her mind, shaking her head as if we're all insane.

"Did that dragon just...play a joke on the Commander?" I hear Tristan ask in shock as he comes to stand beside Dessa, who's now back on her feet and looking torn between laughter and tears of joy.

"Yes, yes she did," I say, wiping tears from my eyes.

-*A good one, I think,*- Isolde adds, a smile in her voice.

-*Makers, I have so many questions.*-

-*All in time.*- She cuts her eyes back towards the field, the aftermath of the battle. -*Perhaps after we finish this.*-

She's right, of course. Though she took care of most of the Alliance's forces, we have at least two hundred who have surrendered, and our own wounded and dead to collect and handle. I incline my head to her, a thousand things running through my mind.

First and foremost, though, I need to greet my wife properly.

CHAPTER
THIRTY
THEA

In the words of Matthais: holy ruddy fucking fuck. Far too much has happened in a span of a few minutes, and I can barely wrap my head around a damn bit of it.

We fought against the abominations.

Dessa was betrothed in the heat of battle.

We learned that the abominations can't be blocked by Killian's Gift.

Killian almost died.

Dragons are real.

One showed up.

And bonded with Killian.

Holy. Ruddy. Fucking. Fuck.

-Indeed,- Soren says, laughing inside my mind.

-Is this what the rumblings you mentioned earlier were about?-

-Yes, but nothing was certain until she arrived.-

And what an arrival it was. I can't stop replaying it over and over again in my mind, her landing in the clearing with such force that the ground shook, the sunlight glinting off of her shimmering gray-black scales, the sleek, fluid movements as she turned to face our enemies—and utterly destroyed them with one breath. Her fire is beautiful and terrifying, reminding me for a heartbeat of my sister. But Tesni's fire has always seemed…angry to me. Wicked. Evil. The dragon's fire felt pure, called forth from a place of love and protection.

Makers I sound like a lunatic.

So, Killian's familiar is not only a creature of legend, thought to be gone from this world entirely, she is also beautiful and deadly—and apparently blessed with a sense of humor.

I shake my head and huff out a laugh, unbelieving that any of this can possibly be real. Killian turns then and meets my gaze, and the look in them has me leaping into his open arms. Soon, I will sort through everything that happened this day, all of the lives I took, all of the blood spilled, and what everything we've learned about the abominations could mean. Soon. Right now, I need my arms around my husband. I need to know that he's alright and safe and still here with me.

I wrap my arms around his neck and hold him so tightly I don't know if I'll ever be able to let go, squeezing my eyes shut. He grunts quietly, but circles his arms around me, holding me to him and I know he's feeling all of the same things I am. The worry and the fear and the unknown all melting away, at least for a few precious moments. Right now, all I feel is love and joy, and I send up thanks to all of the Makers for keeping Killian safe, for sending him this dragon that saved him. Saved all of us.

Killian sets me down and cradles my face between his big, scarred hands, holding my gaze.

"You're alright?"

"Yes, I'm fine, but I wasn't the one attacked by a fucking tree, Killian. Are *you* ok??"

He huffs out a laugh, that slow smile curling his lips, the most gorgeous thing I've ever seen. His thumbs gently trace over my cheekbones, the touch so tender and out of place on a battlefield surrounded by blood and gore and piles of ash.

"Yes, I'm fine. A cracked rib or five, but nothing that Copeland can't heal."

"Makers, why didn't you say that?! I shouldn't have jumped on you like that, I—" He silences my objections with a kiss, a firm, unyielding kiss that has me melting in his arms. He pulls back and my cheeks heat, realizing that a few hundred people, plus a dragon and a frost cat, are staring.

"I don't care how many bones are broken within this body, Red. If you don't hug me like that after every battle, I will be highly offended." I laugh and kiss him again, softly, reaching up to run my palm over his stubbled cheek.

"You're truly alright?"

"Yes, love. I'm fine."

I exhale, long and slow, the knot in my chest unraveling now that I know he's ok. I glance up at the dragon, her golden eyes staring inquisitively. There's a ring of ice blue around the gold—the opposite of Soren's. I wonder if all familiars have a combination of the two colors or if it's merely coincidence. These days, I don't believe for a second that any damned thing is coincidence.

"So, um...care to introduce me?"

"Still can't believe this is truly happening," he murmurs, "but Thea, allow me to present—"

-*Isolde*- the soft, feminine voice echoes inside my mind. I reel back and Killian whips his head to look at the dragon before cutting his gaze back to me.

"Did she just..."

"Uh huh," I say, barely able to get the words out. I know I'm staring, gaping like a fish out of water, but I can't help it.

"Have you been able to speak to me this whole time and just chose *not* to?" Killian shoots at Soren, accusation in his eyes. I almost laugh and Soren rolls his eyes, letting out an annoyed huff.

-*No need for hurt feelings,*- she says, and Killian starts to protest that he had no such things, but she continues on, a smile in her voice. -*Bonded Gifteds and familiars can speak this way to each other or other bondeds. Or to those like your King Ryker, who has a Gift for speaking with animalkind,-* she adds thoughtfully.

She's right. Inside my mind, I see new glowing doorways now. Neither are as strong as Soren's, but they're there, open to me should I choose to use them. I understand without knowing how that I can choose to use a single pathway, or multiple at once.

Holy. Fuck.

I swallow hard and try. Pushing my thoughts toward what I know is Killian's pathway, silver and shining like starlight, I say, -*Can...can you hear me?-*

"Holy fucking Makers," he says, blinking rapidly and reeling back as if I slapped him. I huff out a strained, almost hysterical laugh.

-*This is...interesting,-* Soren says to all three of us, testing out the new ability.

-*Hello, frost cat,-* Isolde says, lips curling again. I never knew that dragons could smile. I never knew they existed at all, to be fair, but still, a smiling dragon is almost too much.

-*Hello, ice dragon,-* he says casually.

I tilt my head, wondering why they're called ice dragons if they don't, well, look like ice. I imagined the creatures being white, or even light blue perhaps, spewing ice or snow or frost instead of fire. I'll add it to my now never-ending list of questions I have after this day.

"Ok, can someone please tell us what the fuck is going on here?" Kendall breaks in finally, pulling the four of us from our strange conversation. Jonathan elbows him in the ribs and he grunts. "What?! It's a valid question. They're all just standing around staring at each other when we just had a battle with abominations with stolen Gifts that the Commander couldn't block, and, oh yeah, THERE'S A FUCKING DRAGON SITTING HERE!" he hisses throwing out a hand at Isolde. His eyes go wide and he quickly turns to the dragon. "All due respect, of course, your grace. No, wait. Your...lady?"

Jonathan snorts.

"Your lady? Do you mean *my* lady?"

"Yes." He shakes his head, sweat beading on his brow. "I mean no. I know that's not what I would call her...I mean, I *think* she's a her? Oh fuck, please don't eat me if you aren't a her and that's offensive..." He glances around at the rest of us, panic in his eyes. "For the love of all the Makers, would someone make me stop fucking talking?!"

I can feel Isolde laugh inside my mind and Killian's smile widens. Dessa still seems to be in a bit of shock, just...starting, but Tristan steps up then and clamps a hand over Kendall's mouth. He bows to Isolde.

"Excuse him. He's an idiot. There's no other real explanation."

Isolde nods, huffing a bit of smoke from her nostrils as if in agreement, and Tristan grins. He turns to Killian.

"Sir, we've rounded up those who surrendered."

That seems to bring Killian back to the matters at hand and he nods to Tristan.

"Very good." He slips back into Commander Blackheart and starts issuing orders to the soldiers. Some are assigned to help the wounded back to camp immediately to see Copeland and the other healers, others are to gather the bodies and prepare them for the funeral pyre. He quirks a brow at me, making sure I'm alright if he goes about his duties and I nod, telling him I'm fine. He strides off, Isolde following, her spiked tail swishing back and forth behind her as she watches over Killian protectively.

-*Magnificent*,- Soren purrs inside my mind only.

-*That they are*,- I agree.

Dessa finally seems to get over the shock of seeing a dragon appear on the battlefield and turns to me.

"You're alright?" She looks me over for injuries. "You went off into the melee like a fool and I wasn't sure—"

"I'm alright," I promise her. "Are *you* ok? You seem a little...shaken."

She lets out a long breath. "It's a dragon, Thea. A fucking *dragon*. After all these years! And she's his. He's hers." I knew she would figure out that Killian and Isolde had bonded. She shakes her head. "It's just...I can't explain it, I just feel the divinity in it all, the Makers' hands guiding everything, leading us to the path that will end Barony's terror and somehow fix the entire empire." I blink at that, but I can feel the truth in her words, see exactly what she means. I feel it in my bones that we are all headed for something important, something so important the Makers themselves have intervened to make sure we're all ready.

I give Dessa a smile before Tristan grabs her and pulls her face to his for a deep, searing kiss that makes me look away, still smiling. I avoid looking at the bodies and the blood, the carnage left behind from this day, and frown when I realize that I don't see Lucinda. She's normally not far from Kendall and Jonathan, the three of them nearly joined at the hip most days and almost always assigned to the same details.

"Where's Lucinda?" I ask, though a part of me already knows, that cold sinking feeling dragging my stomach down, down, down. Jonathan tears his gaze away from the dragon walking across the field and casts his eyes downward, shaking his head.

"What?" I whisper as my heart goes cold. No, this can't be right. She can't be...

"She died a warrior's death," Kendall says, looking stoic for the first time since I met him. They each place their right fist over their heart, some sign of respect for the fallen, I assume. I blink rapidly to try to clear the tears blurring my vision. Lucinda and I weren't exactly close, but I'd consider her a friend. And now she's just...gone. Fallen on this very field while I'm able to walk away without a scratch.

Odessa places a hand on my shoulder, squeezing gently.

"This is the life we chose, princess. She died honorably fighting for her kingdom. Fighting for what's right. Take comfort in knowing that it's how she wanted to meet Noxum."

I nod, trying to take comfort in that, but none can be found, at least not now. I knew that we were riding into battle, that lives would be lost, that I would take life myself, but it didn't truly feel real until this moment. I push the sorrow away, adding it to the things that I'll deal with later, and distract myself by helping to bandage wounds enough to hold until we get back to camp.

Eventually Killian returns to my side and we make our way back to our temporary home, a dragon keeping watch overhead.

CHAPTER THIRTY-ONE
KILLIAN

It's been a week since that fateful day and I can still scarcely wrap my mind around...well, much of anything, truthfully. Knowing that dragons aren't gone from this world is mind boggling enough, but to be *bonded* to one? Why would the Makers bless me so? It's still so hard to believe and yet I feel as if Isolde has been a part of me for my entire life. She was the thing I was missing, the reason for that uneasy feeling that wouldn't let up. I was waiting for her, feeling her imminent arrival somewhere deep inside my bones.

Having a familiar is difficult to explain and I'm so thankful I have Thea to understand the things I can't put into words. The fact that she went through it alone, on top of trying to keep her identity a secret and fearing for what might happen to her once we reached Duskthorne, makes my respect for my wife grow more each day.

Isolde made quite the impression on the kingdom, soaring overhead as we rode through the city, the crowds staring up in awe and wonder, cheering louder than I've ever heard. Many wept with joy, dropping to their knees and raising their hands to the sky. She made a show of swooping low over the crowd gathered in the square before soaring straight into the air like a shooting star, flipping over and sending a spray of blue fire through the late afternoon sky.

She has a flair for the dramatic, to be honest, but I couldn't help but smile as I watched. I could see it as she flew over my people, the hope rising within them all, lifting them up and giving them faith that things would turn out ok, that this war would end, these horrors would be stopped, and our revered dragons would come back to us once more.

I'd asked Isolde why they'd left Duskthorne all those years ago.

-It was foretold in our histories that we would retreat into our ancestral lands beyond the mountains until the awaited came to end the darkness spreading across this world-

I'd frowned. "The awaited...You mean *Thea*?"

-Yes, your beautiful queen was written into our tapestry long, long ago,- Isolde had said with a soft smile in her voice. She adores Thea and Soren both.

Many in Hypathia mock Duskthorne's reverence for the dragons and our beliefs in the lore of their power, their connection to the earth and the Makers. My father never cared much for the legends or believed in the old magiks of the dragons, but my mother did and she'd passed that respect and belief onto me. I can only imagine the way her heart would soar to know that her own son's familiar would be one of these blessed creatures.

-So, we did as our ancestors bid and waited. We grew our strength and numbers, but kept watch over our kingdom from the shadows.-

I'd blinked at that.

"You've been watching?"

-Of course we have. The warrior caste patrol the mountains regularly, keeping a close eye on things.-

She preened at that, holding her head high. I've learned that the dragons are broken out into castes, each one having different skills and responsibilities. She is a warrior, and a fierce one at that as that scorched battlefield and fallen foes can attest, but she's also gentle and kind, and I find that though her warrior side calls to me, it's her other facets that complement and calm me, balancing out the ferocity inside my soul. I've learned that many of the dragons can shift the coloring of their scales to blend into the skies when needed. We'd only have seen them if we'd been actively looking. I wonder how many times I've stared at the sky and there's been a silent protector looking back.

She told me that though she didn't know it true until the day she came to my aid on the battlefield, she'd been drawn to me since I was born, often perching on the peak of the mountain that overlooked my wing of the palace, her scales blending in perfectly to the stones. She's been watching over me my whole life and I never knew.

-I'm sorry I couldn't intervene when your father hurt you the way he did, when he hurt all of those people,- she'd told me, voice both sorrowful and furious. *-I was told I could watch but not interfere, not until the Makers declared it time for our bond-*

"It's alright," I'd told her. "You're here now when I truly need you the most."

She'd huffed at that, tiny blue flames licking the air in front of her snout, but I could feel her joy.

Bonding with her has not only mended the last broken piece of me left from the years of torment and loneliness and fear, but the power of my Gift has grown so much I wonder sometimes if I can truly hold it all within myself. I feel as if there's no limit to it now—and though I have an inkling of how that new strength might be used, a whisper in the back of my mind telling me this is possible, today is the first day I've finally relented and agreed to try.

I'm taut as a bow string as we enter The Seventh, a group of Gifteds waiting. Isolde insisted on being nearby, so the entire east wall has been opened, the panels folding into themselves to fully open the building to the field beyond. The dragon settles to the ground just outside, wings tucked against her sides, Soren watching as Mia clambers up the dragon's leg and across her back, shimmying up her neck until the girl settles just behind Isolde's head. Mia props her elbows on Isolde's skull and settles her chin into her upturned hands, looking on expectantly as if she's watching a play in the town square.

Mia's affinity for animals unsurprisingly included the massive dragon and the two of them and Soren have become a nearly inseparable trio. Thea snorts in laughter as Soren begins to chase the small licks of blue fire that Isolde breathes into the field in front of her. Mia giggles and points at the small bundles of fire.

"There! Over there, Soren! Now there!"

"I've never seen her so happy," Dessa says, watching fondly. "At least not since mum and da..." I squeeze her shoulder and she meets my gaze. Her icy blue eyes are glassy but she nods in silent thanks. She shakes herself and smiles. "I still can't believe she's here, that dragons still exist. *Hundreds* of them, all out there, waiting." She looks to the mountains beyond the palace, those wilds where the rest of the dragons apparently wait and watch over us still. She toys with the troth ring on her finger and I smile at her.

"Can't believe you married that dolt."

"He's a truly adorable dolt though. And the things he can do with this tongue—"

I immediately throw up my hands to halt her. "Stop. Stop right now, I don't want to hear it."

"Oh sod off. I have to hear about your exploits and expertise in songs in the tavern for fuck's sake."

"That's not my doing! And most of it's bullshit anyway."

"I'd disagree with that. That trick with your fingers is quite nice."

I shoot Thea a glare and she smiles sweetly at me while Dessa chokes on her laughter. My bride goes up onto her toes to kiss me softly.

"You'll pay for that later, Red," I mutter against her lips, putting all the wicked promises in the words, pitching my voice low and rough just the way she likes it. I grin when a gentle shiver runs through her body.

"I'm counting on it," she whispers back before pulling away and turning to watch Mia and the two familiars. "The three of them really are ridiculous," she says with a fond smile on her lips. She sighs and turns back to me. "Do you really think this could work?"

I let out a long exhale. "I suppose we'll see."

I don't love the idea of trying this on my own people, but there's no other choice in truth, and everyone here volunteered happily, even knowing the possible outcome. Thea has told me over and over that this is nothing like what Barony is doing, but a part of me still recoils at the thought that I'm doing anything close to what that monster is. Yara had attempted to volunteer and I'd firmly declined her offer. She'd nearly died using her Gift to help us get Math and Cece to safety, I won't let her give anything else. She'd tried to protest, but I'd planned a distraction at that precise moment and though she knew damn well what I was doing, she let it slide as her eyes welled with tears at the sight of Isolde landing in her front yard and bowing low.

"I've waited so long to see one of your kind once more," the old woman had whispered, lowering her head and putting her closed fist over her heart. Not for the first time, I wondered how old Yara truly was, but she'd never given me a straight answer before in my life and I didn't envision her starting then, so I kept my question to myself.

Cece and Math join us then, Math out of breath and Cece trying her best to act like she isn't.

"How...in the bloody hells...do you people...breathe up here?" Math pants and Thea laughs. I can tell that he barely stops himself from bowing to me or calling me Majesty. I'd put a stop to that almost immediately. I've always hated being treated like a fucking king.

"You'll get used to it," I assure him. I can't imagine the difficulty of coming from Helios, with its warm, soft breezes, to the thin, painfully cold air of the Obsidians. "Copeland and the healers can help. I believe there are herbs that can aid your lungs with processing the air here differently."

"Or you could just not be a baby about it," Thea offers. Math's mouth pops open and he glares at her.

"Have you always been this rude, or is this something that came with the title of queen?"

"Oh, she's always been that rude," Cece assures him, smiling widely at Thea's quirked brow and mock-outraged expression.

"Why are we friends with her then?" Math puts his hands on his head, grimacing as he tries to get his breathing regulated.

"Because you love me and your life would be entirely boring without me."

"Nah, I think it's because you have a frost cat familiar which makes you somewhat interesting."

"That's it," Thea says, frost forming over her hands and I try to hide my smile as she starts pelting both of them with balls of soft snow. Mia cheers from atop Isolde, Cece screams and hides behind her husband, Dessa grins, and a feeling I've never had before settles over me like a soft, comforting blanket. Is this what it's like to have a true family? To be surrounded by love and joy instead of fear and anger and hatred? I rub the heel of my hand against my chest. This is what life should be, what it could be once we finish this war.

Though I'd be more than happy to watch this all day, we're here for a reason, so I clear my throat pointedly. Thea stops her assault and Math shakes snow from his hair like a hound. She comes over to me, the mood shifting subtly as she reads my emotions so clearly. My stomach starts churning and twisting, worry worming its way through my veins. She places her palm against my chest, just over my racing heart.

"Calm, Killian. Everything will be alright."

I try to listen but...

"What if—"

"Those here know the risks, but believe in you, in this cause, enough to pay whatever the price may be. Trust in their belief."

I close my eyes and exhale roughly, thanking the Makers all over again for bringing this woman into my life. I open them again and she smiles. I return it, put my hand over hers where it still rests on my chest, and nod. We head towards the group that's gathered.

"Your Majesty," the first volunteer says with a bow. My close friends obey my request to drop the titles, but the rest of the kingdom doesn't seem inclined to do so.

"Aaron," I nod. "Thank you for being here. For..." I trail off, not quite sure how to word what we're attempting. I don't want to call it an experiment as it brings to mind the horrors that Barony and his alchemists have brought down on Gifteds all these years, but in truth, this *will* be an experiment of sorts. I have no true idea of how to do what I believe I can save a whisper in my mind and my heart telling me to try.

-Have faith,- Isolde tells me and I glance her way, our connection bolstering my wavering conviction. Mia is weaving flowers around her horns and Soren is keeping a watchful eye on everyone. Aaron smiles. He's of middle-age and works on one of the goat farms, hand-delivers milk and cheese to the palace every few weeks. His Gift calls out to me now, and while I've always been able to sense a Gifted by the energy they give off, like a faint aura inside my mind, now I can truly *see* it. I can see the true nature of the Gifts, their strength and power, how they might be used. Thea had laughed when I'd first told her how my power had shifted since bonding.

"Well, it's a good thing that Isolde didn't decide to find you *before* you kidnapped me—I would have been fucked well and good."

"Fucked well and good, you say...I can arrange that..." I'd rasped, making her squeal as I chased her around the room before catching her, tossing her on the bed, and doing just that. But she was right, of course. If I'd been able to see the Gifts clearly when we'd first found her, I'm not sure what I would have done. There would have been no real reason to keep her knowing she wasn't Barony's Gifted, no ransom to be had, but I like to believe that our love was blessed by the Makers, that they put each of us on our paths in life long ago so that we would find each other, and so one way or another, we would have fallen.

"Aaron, I don't know..." I clear my throat and then sigh. "I have no fucking clue what I'm doing," I tell him honestly and he huffs out a laugh, smiling wide.

"My Gift is not much use to me now, Your Majesty. If it should be gone…" He hikes a shoulder as if to say that wouldn't upset him.

I swallow hard. "And if…it does more than take the Gift?"

His smile turns bittersweet.

"I lost my wife recently. My son as well. If I should join them in hereafter in the pursuit of stopping a monster like Barony, then I would be honored. My cousin can run the farm now."

I don't have anything to say to that, so I simply nod in thanks.

-Now what?- I ask Isolde, my palms sweating.

-You act as if I've done this before.-

-I thought a sage, centuries-old dragon might have some fucking insight to share.-

-I am *quite sage, thank you for noticing.*- I turn and narrow my eyes at the dragon and she meets my gaze, huffing out tiny blue flames from her nostrils and quirking the ridged line of scales above her eye that serves as a brow. -*Let your Gift guide you,*- she adds, more seriously this time.

So, I do. I turn back to Aaron, ask him if he's ready, and begin. I let my Gift lead me, let it reach out to Aaron's own.

-*Unclench your jaw, Killian, you'll crack your teeth,*- Thea whispers inside my mind, the presence a warm, crimson glow. -*This is nothing like Barony,*- she adds, knowing exactly why I'm holding back, apparently trying to grind my damned teeth to dust. I make an effort to do as she asks and unclench my jaw.

-*As my queen commands,*- I whisper back and I can feel her smile in my head.

I'm not like Barony. I'm not taking what does not belong to me. I'm not reaching for Aaron's Gift with malice in my heart or ill intent. I know this is different and let myself relax. I'm still worried about what might happen, of course, but I'm able to let my Gift fully explore this new facet now. My power wraps around Aaron's, almost in greeting, and his responds, glowing brighter, welcoming. A surge of power sparks through my chest, and then Aaron's Gift...joins my own, the two of them existing side by side within me. I inhale sharply at the same time Aaron gasps quietly.

"Are you alright? Is this hurting you?" I ask urgently, keeping his Gift steady beside my own. It's strange, going from feeling the energy or essence or whatever you want to call it *outside*, to feeling inside my own body, to have it greet me like an old friend and open itself to me.

"No, not at all, Majesty. I can just feel your Gift...asking mine for access?" He huffs out a laugh. "That sounds ridiculous, apologies."

"No, no, it doesn't. I understand what you mean, I think. I...hells, I think it worked?"

Aaron blinks at me, excitement and intrigue dancing in his eyes. "One way to find out, I suppose."

I take a deep breath and turn from Aaron towards the wall of weapons to our left. I let his Gift rise, not quite sure how to—

"Holy fucking Makers!" Thea and Math both say at the exact same moment as one of the swords comes flying across the space into my waiting hand, slamming into my palm as if...

"Magnetism," I whisper and Aaron inclines his head, a warm smile curling his lips.

"Yes, Majesty. I can call metal objects to me as if I'm magnetic. Mostly small things, but I've been able to get the plow out of a ditch a time or two over the years with it."

"And can you still wield it? I didn't...I didn't *take* it from you?"

He purses his lips, looking contemplative. "I don't believe so...surely I would feel it if it was taken? But let's see..." He looks to the wall and a small war hammer sails to him, admittedly more gracefully than my sword had come to me. "Looks like everything is in working order." He smiles widely. "Well done, Majesty."

Thea runs up and throws her arms around me.

"I knew it! I knew you could do it and see—absolutely nothing to worry about, right, Aaron?"

"Right, Your Majesty." His eyes go wide in surprise when she throws her arms around him as well, but he quickly recovers and gives her a gentle squeeze back.

"How does it feel?" she asks me after she releases Aaron.

"Strange," I tell her honestly. "But...good."

"Do you know how long you'll be able to hold it?"

"No fucking clue, but I guess we'll find out."

"What if...well, what if they stay forever? What if you can just collect Gifts like Ryker collects crystal sculptures of winged horses." I quirk a brow and she winces. "And that was not something I was supposed to share, so erase it from your memory immediately." I laugh at that and she smiles, but presses on. "I'm serious. What if you could have multiple Gifts, Killian? What if that's the reason that the Makers made your father the way they did, collecting all of these Gifteds here within these walls? So that you would have some of the most powerful Gifts in the empire here to...not take, that's not the right word really, is it? Copy? It doesn't matter—but *what if?*"

I can see the excitement churning inside her, the possibilities of what this could mean for the coming war.

"Let's not get ahead of ourselves, love. We need to take this one step at a time. Let's just see how long I can hold onto Aaron's contribution first, make sure he doesn't suffer any ill effects, and then we'll go from there."

She rolls her eyes, but agrees.

I turn to the other volunteers. "If you would all be so kind as to come back in...I don't know, let's say three days. I think we'll be ready to try another test by then."

They all agree without question, excitement and wonder in their eyes. There's never been any Gifted like this in all of Hypathia, at least not that I've seen record or heard tale of. I try not to let Thea's excitement fill my own heart, but if this works, if I can replicate some of their Gifts and keep them, at least for a time, this could change the tide of battle entirely. This, plus a fucking dragon? Barony and his Alliance will be crushed beneath our might.

Everyone starts to leave The Seventh, our small group remaining. Thea waggles her fingers at me.

"Sure you aren't ready to try ice?"

She knows damn well that I won't be touching her Gift until we know for sure that she won't be harmed or affected in any way. I won't allow her to be hurt or her Gift diminished in any fucking way, not for this, not for me. I know she would be willing to do whatever was necessary to end this war and stop Barony, but I'm not willing to let her.

Just as I'm about to tell her that myself, Alexi caws loudly as he soars towards the open doors of The Seventh. Isolde tilts her head as the raven flies past her and I swear she licks her lips.

-*Not on the menu,*- I warn.

-*I promise not to eat the messenger. But she did pique my appetite—I'm going to hunt with Soren.*-

"Mia! Unless you want to be Isolde's dinner, time to disembark."

She sighs but scrambles off of Isolde's head and slides down her leg, boots crunching in the snow as she lands lithely. She's been training with her sister, it seems.

"She would never eat me," she tells me, hands on her hips.

"You're probably right. Too scrawny. Probably taste awful too," Dessa calls. Mia narrows her eyes at her sister and begins scooping up handfuls of snow and forming them into balls as Isolde stands, stretching her long body and flaring her wings. She bumps Mia gently in the back in goodbye and takes to the sky. Soren licks Mia's face, making her giggle and wipe the slobber from her cheek with her shoulder, still packing the snow into her arsenal as the frost cat streaks off after the dragon.

Dessa winks at me before sprinting for her sister, making her scream. She tries to throw the balls of snow, but she's not nearly fast enough. Dessa is quick as hells. While the two of them chase each other around, Thea takes the message from Alexi's leg, rubbing the bird's head and neck lovingly before handing the envelope to me. Cece and Math join us.

"He's beautiful," Math says, reaching a tentative hand toward the raven. Alexi tilts his head at him, but eventually decides that he's worthy of showering the bird with affection, and hops closer to him. "I like you much better than that terrifying bastard that came from Lyanna all those months ago," he tells the bird. Alexi caws in agreement, nuzzling his head beneath Math's fingers in clear agreement.

I chuckle and tear open the envelope, my blood going cold as my eyes scan the words, then scan them again to be sure I'm reading them correctly.

"Fuck," I whisper and Thea tenses, immediately on alert.

"What's happened?"

Cece puts a hand on her arm, reassuring and calm. Not for the first time, I'm so happy that Thea found this woman, found them both all those years ago. They're two of the best people I've ever met, truly good to their cores, and Cece treats Thea the way her own sister should have. I know that a part of Thea's heart will always be broken from the loss of her twin, from the betrayal and the hurt and what should have been, but I pray that Cece's love helps to make that fracture easier to bear.

"Your sister...Makers, she's the queen of Marrowood now—*and* Lyanna."

"What??" Thea barks, yanking the letter from my hand and reading the words herself, beginning to pace. My lips quirk ever so slightly: it's a habit we both share.

"What the fucking hells do you mean she's the queen of two fucking kingdoms??" Math asks me.

"Their plan fell apart when you learned the truth about me," Thea says, wide eyes meeting mine. "She must have gone back to Barony—killed Hastings, I'd wager, blamed everything on him—and they took her to Marrowood to keep them in the Alliance." Her eyes go back to the letter again, shaking her head, and I continue explaining what happened to the others.

"Apparently once there, Tybalt forced a marriage, probably to taunt Barony, but once the decree was signed, she burned him to death, taking control of the kingdom and uniting it with Lyanna by then marrying Barony."

"Holy fucking Makers, that's…diabolical."

"My sister has always been cunning, that's for fucking sure. The rest of the Alliance is terrified of them now, of what they're capable of," Thea says, eyes still on the letter. "And it's believed that Barony is ready to take Gifts himself." She crumbles the paper in her fist, fire in her eyes. The temperature drops around us, frost coating her hands and neck and lips. "Fuck, fuck, fuck," she hisses between clenched teeth.

"It's alright, love," I assure her. "We'll stop them."

She meets my gaze. "But how many more people will they hurt before we do? How many more kingdoms will they take? How many more Gifteds will they destroy?"

I stride forward, pinching her chin and lifting it so she meets my eyes.

"They will pay for every soul they hurt, I promise you. Every. Single. One. But we must wait until we are ready to face them. We need more time." I run the pad of my thumb over her bottom lip, the frost cool and tempting. She shivers, the fire in her eyes shifting to a different kind entirely. "Patience, Red," I whisper. "We will make this right, but you must have patience."

She takes a deep breath before letting it out slowly. "I know," she whispers. "I just hate this. I hate her out there, hurting people and taking power. I know her—I know them both—this taste of it will only make them savage for more. They won't stop."

"*We* will stop them," I promise her.

"I know." She sighs, nodding. She turns her head and places a soft kiss on the pad of my thumb, before biting it gently and sending a ripple of desire through my body, directly to my cock. She meets my gaze again, that wicked fire dancing within the emerald. "Until then, I have ideas of ways for you to teach me patience…"

CHAPTER
THIRTY-TWO
TESNI

Word has spread of my queendom, of what transpired in Marrowood—every single detail. Everyone in Hypathia should know what I am capable of, what will come for them should they resist or try to fight back. Barony is practically frothing at the mouth like a rabid hound with all of the power within his grasp, both in the empire and from the alchemists. He's finally ready to attempt the experiment on himself, despite what happened to his first set of rats against Duskthorne's forces. We don't know what, exactly, transpired, only that my damned sister sent a missive to me herself.

> YOUR ABOMINATIONS ARE NO MATCH FOR US. GIVE UP NOW AND PERHAPS I'LL LET YOU LIVE.
> I WILL NOT OFFER AGAIN.
> —T

No one has heard a word from the cadre that was sent into that battle, no trace of them left on the killing field. Granted, it was covered in ten feet of snow by the time scouts arrived to investigate.

There were no storms reported in that area, at least none so strong as to lead to that much snow. Thea had buried all traces of the battle. Was it a message? That she could—and would—bury us all?...Or was there something she was hiding? I can't imagine what she would want to hide on a battlefield. Maybe just that there weren't many bodies remaining, showing that they'd actually captured most of the soldiers and taken them back to Duskthorne?

I rub my temples now, thinking on it giving me a headache as it has these past few weeks every time I try to figure out what she's up to. It probably means nothing, and she did it just because she could. Or perhaps, she didn't even mean to cover the field. Her power was never reliable all those years ago. Sure, she's gotten stronger since then, but what if that showing on the tundra was just a fluke, something brought on by fear for her life or some other heightened emotion. Maybe Blackheart was torturing her, demanding that she use her Gift to fight against Amon's forces—expecting fire, of course, thinking she was me.

None of it matters, not really. I'm a queen of two kingdoms. I'm the most powerful Gifted in all of Hypathia. And soon, I'll be nearly unstoppable. But first, I have to let Barony and the others have their fun, let them believe that they're in charge of all of this.

"Are you ready?" I ask him. The invitation had been sent a week ago, telling all royals in the Alliance that the time had come to claim their power, should they wish to. Only three accepted: Queen Nicolette of Karthania, King William of Nocadia, and Queen Ruby of Enola. Queen Pheobe of Abrasia and King Decosta of Helios had no interest in partaking in these "blasphemous experiments" as they'd called them, and though they pledged fealty to the Alliance, they did so out of fear, not out of lust for power.

"I am," he says, voice even and sure, but I can see the tick in his jaw, the bead of sweat at his temple. I don't blame him for being nervous, but we know that the process has been perfected, enhanced even since the rats met Blackheart in battle. Their bodies tired too easily, the Gifts taking too much, but the alchemists have worked nonstop for these last weeks to find a way to correct that. The last round of rats were far superior, their power impressing even me.

No match for us, indeed, I sneer silently at my sister.

She will learn.

She will pay.

She will fucking kneel.

The other royals look on as Barony settles into his chair beside the iron table. The other royals, understandably skeptical, insisted that Barony receive his Gift first and once he survived and proved his power, they would accept their own. Being the only naturally Gifted among them, it was agreed that I would wait until they had undergone the process before I was given an additional Gift.

I agreed.

What's another week in the grand scheme of this plan?

The lead alchemist, Klaus, meets my gaze for a heartbeat before nodding to one of his assistants. A moment later, a young man is dragged into the room. He's been given some sort of drug to keep him subdued by the way his head lulls, barely aware of what's going on. They hoist him onto the table and secure him with leather straps around his wrists, ankles, chest, and thighs. Makers, is all of that truly necessary? I notice the dark, rust-colored stains marring the iron table and tilt my head. Just how bad will this be?

Klaus explains the process for everyone, how it's a mixture of elixirs and very old alchemy, and using star opals to hold and transfer the power of the Gift. I don't particularly care about the hows of it, so I don't pay much attention, instead going through my plans over and over in my mind, making sure I've covered every detail, that I have everything in place and contingencies should anything go awry. My mind drifts to what it might be like when I meet Thea again, assuming she makes it through the battle and actually faces me, that is. Will she cower once she sees what I've become? Beg for mercy? Kneel and accept my power and position?

And what will I do?

I...don't know. Let her live, I think. As a prisoner, a permanent collar around that pretty little neck of hers, but I don't think I like the thought of killing her. I will if it comes down to that, but I don't think it would bring me joy.

The screams of agony tear me from my thoughts and I blink, focusing on what's happening in front of me. The Gifted strains against the straps holding him to the table, against Klaus' hand on his chest, thrashing and crying and screaming. Makers, the *screaming*. It sounds like the man's very soul is being ripped from his body. It is, I realize then. By taking his Gift, we're taking his soul, his essence, his very being from him. Bile rises in my throat at the thought, that small part of me that isn't completely cold and unfeeling recoiling from what's happening in front of me, screaming to stop it, that it isn't right. That part has never been strong enough to overtake the rest though, and it remains that way. It quietly fades to the background as the star opal in Klaus' other hand begins to glow. Faintly at first, the tiniest shimmering gold, but it grows as the power fills it, the power of the Gift tearing free from the man on the table.

His wrists bleed as he thrashes, more blood flowing from his nose and ears, and soon his screams become garbled as he chokes on the blood pouring from his lips.

Queen Nicolette turns away and vomits quietly behind her chair and I turn to the others, quirking a brow. They've paled, but their lunches remain firmly in their stomachs thankfully. I turn back and see that the opal is glowing so brightly now that I have to squint against the light. The man on the table screams and bucks one last time before his body goes still. Klaus turns from the man who looks so much more like a boy now, young and frail in death, without so much as a glance.

Barony is practically salivating as Klaus brings the opal closer.

"Drink the elixir now," he tells Barony. He takes the stoppered vial from the table to his left and tosses the blue liquid back in one gulp. He makes a face and I wonder what it might taste like, but I suppose I'll find out for myself soon enough. Klaus waits a few heartbeats and then nods. "Are you ready?"

Barony takes a deep breath and clenches his jaw. He casts one quick look to King William, then to me, and then looks back to Klaus.

"Yes, I'm ready."

Klaus places his free hand against Barony's chest, just as he had the Gifted. Barony closes his eyes and the star opal flares once before the light slowly starts to dim as the power is transferred from the stone—into Barony. He gasps and clutches the armrests, but remains steady. We all watch in silent fascination as the light leaves the star opal and seems to fill Barony, a faint glowing beneath his skin, until finally the stone goes dull once more and Barony sucks in a sharp inhale, his body bowing from the chair before slumping.

He sucks in ragged breaths and King William and I rush forward at the same time. We exchange a quick glance, understanding passing between us, and I give him a subtle nod. There are no laws against a man marrying another man in Hypathia, but William's father had arranged a marriage for him, and he'd had no choice but to go through with it. That's the only reason he and Barony didn't join the kingdoms long ago, marrying each other. If it were me, I'd simply have killed the queen and married whomever I pleased. But I suppose murder isn't most people's first thought in these situations.

Barony lifts his head as we reach him, William and I both dropping to our knees in front of the chair. His forehead is covered in sweat, his head still bowed as he tries to slow his breathing.

"Barony?? Barony are you alright?" William asks, urgency and worry clear and sharp in his deep voice.

"Y-yes," he gasps. "Yes, I'm...I'm fine...Great Makers, I can *feel* it..." He lifts his head to meet Williams' eyes, then mine, and puts a hand to his chest. "I can feel it inside me...spreading through my body, becoming a part of me..."

"That will last for a few minutes more as the power adjusts to its new home," Klaus tells him. "Drink this—it will help as the Gift begins to take root. It can be...uncomfortable." He hands Barony another stoppered vial, this one filled with red liquid, and Barony again drinks it in one swallow. It must taste worse than the last by the face he makes and William huffs out a quiet laugh. Barony glares at him but his lips curl before his face twists into a grimace of pain, his teeth bared and clenched.

"Barony??" William says, clearly worried.

"This is perfectly normal," Klaus assures everyone. The other royals have drifted over now, Queen Nicolette primly wiping her mouth with a silk handkerchief. Barony takes sawing breaths through his nostrils, tendons straining in his neck as he fights to hold himself as still as possible as the power fills him. I imagine the Gift searching for a way out, fighting its new enclosure as a trapped animal might fight a cage, clawing at every inch trying to find a weak point. Once it finds none, it will settle into submission, but the fight always comes first. "It will only last a few minutes."

We wait, the minutes slowly ticking by, until Barony begins to relax, the tension easing out of him.

"Great fucking Makers," he gasps, eyes flying wide, utter exaltation shining within the black.

I smile at him, sharing in this lust and love of power.

"Well," I tell him, "let us see what you can do, Your Majesty."

I can't help but laugh indulgently as Barony once again lifts a vase from the table and sets it back again. It's all he can do for now, but it's only been a few days. He will learn to grow and use the full potential of the Gift, as all of us do: in time.

Well, in theory.

"It's incredible. The power brimming inside, the potential I know I possess. It's still...fighting is the best way to describe it, but it will submit completely soon, I'm sure. I can only imagine what it will be like when I take another. And another. And—"

"Don't get too ahead of yourself," I tell him with a laugh. "Klaus has said you should wait before you try to take another Gift—though I know you don't plan to," I add before he can interrupt to say the same thing. "But the most anyone has been given is three."

"I intend to be the first to take more," he says simply, grinning at me. It actually makes my chest clench, his joy infectious. My eyes burn and I force the ridiculous tears away.

"Let us begin with two and see where it leads us, shall we?"

He leans in and kisses me on the cheek, absolutely nothing romantic in the gesture which is fine by me, before holding out a hand to help me from the chair and lead me from the room. We make our way back down to the transfer chamber. The other royals are there already, waiting anxiously. Additional tables and chairs have been added, set up the same way as Barony's had been before. Klaus' acolytes stand at the ready, trained in the procedure by the master himself. Despite my Gift, I've always been a little jealous of the alchemists—the *true* alchemists.

There are many who study the art, as I did long ago, and call themselves alchemists, but true alchemy can only be done by those with special blood. *Magik* they used to call it when Hypathia was still in its infancy, kingdoms nothing more than mounds of dirt. Similar to Gifts, but instead of one particular power or talent, those with magik could do all manner of things. It's been lost over the centuries, turned into what we know now as alchemy, a mixture of the tiny amount of magik left in their blood and tonics and potions and the interaction of metals and herbs.

"Do it again," Queen Ruby says, pale blue eyes alight. "Show us, Barony."

Barony laughs, grinning like a showman at the theater as he raises his hand and lifts one of the straps from the table beside her, waving it in the air before letting it flop back to the table. She titters like a child, nearly squealing and I barely stop myself from rolling my eyes, keeping my doting smile plastered on my lips. Lifting a strap from a table? Please. It's little more than a party trick. None of them know anything about real power, none of them can instill fear into the hearts of everyone around them with the mere mention of their name.

But I can.

Klaus and the others come in, the acolytes dragging more incapacitated Gifteds along and depositing them on the awaiting tables. William embraces Barony, squeezing him hard before pulling away and cupping his cheek lovingly. The two queens don't act as if anything is amiss and I realize that all of the other royals must already know the truth about William and Barony's relationship, of their true feelings. I watch as they share a look, one of those looks that has always mystified me. How can a simple look convey so much power, such emotion? The look says *I am yours and you are mine and as long as we're together, anything is possible.*

This is how I know that Barony could never match my darkness. He's capable of looks like that. I never will be. My chest tightens again, that small voice whispering in the back of my mind, begging...

I silence it, gritting my teeth and shifting my shoulders back.

They all settle into their chairs, preparing themselves for what's to come. Klaus meets my eyes, the question clear, and I give him an almost imperceptible nod.

"Drink your first elixir now," he instructs and all of the royals take up their vials. Queen Ruby raises hers, laughing, and the others do the same, toasting to their first step in gaining ultimate power. They all drink and that little voice inside me, the one shred of goodness that remains, demands enough attention to make me avert my gaze from Barony and William as the poison takes hold, as they reach for each other before toppling, blood dripping from their eyes and their throats starting to smoke as the acid eats through their flesh.

CHAPTER
THIRTY-THREE
KILLIAN

"I would die for you, Killian. I would die for you, kill for you, and everything in between. But this—*this*—I will not fucking do!"

"Oh, come on," I taunt from atop Isolde's back, settled just between her shoulders. The ridges of scales seem to be made specifically for a person to sit—or two people, if someone's wife would stop being such a damned sissy. "It's amazing!"

I could spend the rest of my life soaring through the skies with the dragon. I've never felt so free, so close to the Makers and my kingdom, to *myself*, as I do flying so high that even the clouds can't touch us.

"Absolutely. Fucking. Not," she says through gritted teeth.

-I promise I won't drop you,- Isolde teases.

-You are acting like a child,- Soren adds. -Actually, the child loves flying with the dragon, so you are acting even worse than that.-

It's true: Mia may love flying even more than I do, begging to be taken up as often as possible. It's become a nice way to ensure she completes her chores, according to Dessa. Everything Mia is responsible for is done by mid-morning in hopes of getting to go out with Isolde in the afternoon. Soren allowed Isolde to grasp him in her talons and take him high up into the mountains to hunt game he'd never seen before. Dessa and Tristan, Yara, hells, even Jonathan took a flight around the kingdom and he's terrified of heights. He came back looking a bit green, but he still admitted that it had been exhilarating. Thea is the only one who refuses.

She crosses her arms over her chest, jutting her chin. The very picture of stubborn.

"We could make the journey in a few days if you'd agree to fly," I remind her, hoping that perhaps the idea of cutting the length of our trip considerably will entice her—and actually allow us to fly there. We've decided not to wait for the Alliance to come to us. We're taking the battle to them. We leave tomorrow to meet Ryker and his forces in Tithmoore, and then we march for Lyanna where Barony and the Alliance are mustering their own armies. The reports from Ryker's ravens are saying that Barony, Tesni, and a handful of others have holed themselves up within Castle Lyanna. We assume it's because they've gone through with taking Gifts upon themselves and are learning to handle that in private. I can only imagine what the process might be, how their bodies might react when trying to adjust to all of that unnatural power thrust inside them. I don't know what Gifts they might have stolen or if they'll use them in battle against us—most of the royals don't seem like the type to *actually* fight—but whatever is waiting for us, we'll be ready to face it.

"I'm perfectly happy to endure a sore ass and chapped thighs from weeks upon Zaro, thank you very much." Knowing I won't sway her tonight, I shift objectives and slide from Isolde's back, landing on the balcony attached to our bed chamber and stalking towards her.

-I know that look. I'll be in the caves, far, far away from here,- Isolde says, sounding amused.

-For the love of all the Great Makers, take me with you,- Soren begs, wholly *un*amused, jumping lithely up onto the stone railing lining the balcony. They've only spoken to me, so Thea watches the silent exchange with a quirked brow, her fiery hair blowing about her in

the crisp wind. Isolde chuckles inside our minds and blue flames spark from her nostrils. She launches into the air without warning and Thea gasps, eyes following the dragon up, up, up. She makes a wide arch from the balcony and circles back, grabbing Soren from the ledge as she glides past as if they've done the maneuver a thousand times.

"And where are they off to in such a hurry?" Thea asks, eyes sparking with the knowledge of exactly why they've escaped. She takes slow steps backwards as I keep advancing, through the doors from the balcony into our chambers.

"A sore ass and chapped thighs, you say...I think I can arrange that..." My voice is low, gruff, desire coursing through me like the lava deep within the mountains around us. She swallows hard but her lips curl upward and she gives me that challenging look that sets my blood afire.

"Promises, promises..."

She keeps backing away across the room towards the bed. I tug my shirt off and throw it aside as I follow. Her eyes widen as they rove over my bare chest, the tattoos that she has an affinity for tracing with her tongue. Her teeth dig into her bottom lip as her gaze dips lower. The muscles in my stomach flex in response, her gaze whispering over my body like the softest caress, memories of her trailing soft kisses down my torso just this morning, lower, her tongue running teasingly along the crown of my cock as it strained toward her greedy little mouth, desperate. A low growl rumbles through my chest and her eyes meet mine, sparking with amusement, knowing exactly what I was recalling.

I smirk and as she takes another step backwards, she freezes. She gasps quietly and tries to move again, but she's stuck, held fast by this mirrored Gifted. That's what Thea has come to call them: mirrored Gifts. I'm not *taking* them, only borrowing them for a time, reflecting them back to the world.

"Thought this one had left you already," she says softly, watching me as I stalk closer, circling her as she remains held steadfast, imagining all the things I have planned for this last night in our home for a while. It could be our last night here...ever.

I try not to let that thought creep in, but we both know it's true. We're riding into a battle unlike anything either of us has ever seen, up against things we've never even dreamed of facing. Our eyes meet and the unspoken understanding passes between us. We know what this night might mean, and we plan to make the most of it.

I stop circling, stepping up behind her and gripping her hips. I shift my own against her ass, showing her just how ready I am. She moans softly and then gasps when I move my hands to the collar of her tunic and rip, tearing the soft wool in two and letting the pieces fall to the floor, her corset following a heartbeat later. I lean down and kiss her now bare shoulder and she tilts her head, giving me all the access I want. I smile against her skin, so soft beneath my lips.

"Not gone quite yet," I murmur, planting another kiss to the side of her throat while I palm her breast with one hand, kneading as I run the pad of my thumb over her nipple, already pebbled and desperate for my touch, my tongue, my teeth. I trail the other hand downward, tunneling my fingers beneath her silk panties and making her groan and buck as much as she's able while still held fast by my power. I massage her clit. Slow. Torturous. And trail open-mouthed kisses up and down her throat.

"Killian," she pants, the word a plea and a curse and a prayer. I chuckle darkly against her skin before pressing two fingers deep inside. She moans loudly and I ease the hold off of her enough that she can grind her ass against my cock, her pussy against my hand. "Don't stop," she begs, arching and desperate. "Fucking hells, don't stop."

"I mirrored another Gift today," I tell her low in her ear, keeping up the slow thrusts of my fingers, the light pinching of her nipple. She trembles and pants, still rocking her hips, still chasing her release that I won't let her reach. Not yet. "A man named Harlon has the Gift of incredible *stamina*." I bite at her ear as the word sinks in.

She inhales sharply and snakes one hand up behind her to tunnel in my hair.

"You were already fairly gifted in that regard," she says, voice shaky, chest rising and falling quicker and quicker, anticipation thick and sparking in the air.

"You aren't wrong there, love," I agree with a smile.

Inside her mind, I purr, -*But Harlon...well, he can do extremely demanding physical activity for days without tiring...*-

"Days," Thea repeats out loud, voice choked with shock and anticipation and maybe even a bit of concern. I shift my hand from her breast to pinch her chin between my thumb and forefinger, pulling back as I tilt her head up to meet my gaze. Her eyes are blazing, her pupils blown.

"I'm going to fuck my queen until the sun comes up," I promise her. "I'm going to make you scream so loudly that you won't be able to speak for days, Thea. I'm going to make you come so hard and so many times that you forget your own name. I'm going to kiss and lick every inch of you, fuck this smart mouth, this perfect pussy, and this magnificent ass, and worship you until even the Makers are jealous." She shudders at my words and I curl my fingers inside her on my next thrust, making her gasp and moan. "And then, when you think you can't possibly take any more—I'm going to do it all again, love."

"Makers," she whispers, rocking her hips into my hand again, desperate.

-*Is that a promise, Your Majesty?*-

I barely stifle a shudder, the feel of her voice inside my mind like the softest, most sensual touch. My blood sings at that challenge, the sexy curl of her lips, that intense look in her eyes telling me that not only does she accept, but she plans to meet me each step of the way, giving as good as she gets, doing this together. Always together. No matter what.

"It's a fucking vow, Red."

CHAPTER
THIRTY-FOUR
THEA

I've done everything I can to prepare. I've trained until my fingers bled and I nearly passed out from exhaustion; I've practiced for hours upon hours, pushing my Gift as hard as I dare, finding every facet within it that might be of use; I've studied battle healing and strategy; I've learned to fight in tandem with Soren and the others should I find myself in the heart of the battle this time.

No, not should. *When.*

I will not remain on some safe island behind the real fighting this time, watching and using my power from afar. I will be there with my people. I will bleed beside them. I will send up the final goodbye and prayer to Noxum should they fall beside me. I will battle back against the evil of this empire next to the man that I love. My king. My heart. My soul.

And he isn't trying to stop me. I know that he worries, of course, and the thought of me in the fray terrifies him, but Killian understands the warrior spirit inside of me, the one that calls to his own. He knows how important this fight is, not just for Hypathia, but for me. It's *my* sister on the other side of those battle lines, *my* former home. I know deep in my heart that I'm meant to be in this fight, that I'm meant to face my sister.

And I'm ready.

The journey has taken us two weeks since I refused to make it atop the damned dragon's back. Just the thought of soaring through the air, with nothing between us and the ground so far, far, *far* below, makes my stomach turn flips and sweat break out across the back of my neck. So, we rode with the rest of the army as we'd done all those months before—though this time the numbers in our party are staggering. They go on for miles and miles, horses and carriages and soldiers. So many soldiers. I pray to Brienne for their safety, for our victory so that most of these men and women will return to their homes and loved ones. I know not all will, and I pray to Noxum to care for their souls.

I made the trip quicker than it would normally have been, keeping the worst of the storms away from our path and clearing the snow as much as possible, so I'd call that a good compromise.

Now, the time has come. There's a strange energy within the camp as we ready ourselves for battle. Tense. Excited. Calm. Afraid. A mixture that sends a soft fire through my veins. Yes, there is fear, but there is also an overwhelming sense of purpose.

I watch as Killian dons his armor, the black shining like Isolde's scales, the emblazoned dragon head proud and watchful on his chest. He is war personified, that quiet, steel-hard determination, calculation, and, when necessary, brutality all simmering in those stormy eyes. He doesn't turn as he straps weapons to his thighs and chest, but addresses me anyway, knowing damned well I was admiring the view.

"Like what you see, Red?"

"Always," I breathe as I start to strap on my own armor.

"Always, huh?" he asks, turning finally and striding over to help me strap on my chest plate, as he did the last time we rode into a fight together. I turn my back to him and he shifts my braids over one shoulder. He runs a finger down the back of my neck, over the newly-inked tattoo there, making me shiver. He's taken every opportunity to touch me over these last two weeks, even the tiniest whispers of fingertips as he passes by. I know why. The same reason I've been doing the same to him. In case we fall today. If that is what the Makers have planned, then we've both wanted to take advantage of every single minute that we've had left.

"Just because you were a pretentious, overbearing prick who was delivering me to my doom—or so I thought—when I first met you, doesn't mean my eyesight was hindered."

"Pretentious, overbearing prick? How you wound me, my love."

I laugh and he chuckles low in return, buckling my armor tightly. He places a kiss at my nape and then I turn, wrapping my arms around his neck and pressing my lips to his. It isn't frenzied or desperate. It's deep and unyielding, a kiss that conveys all that I am, all that I've ever been and ever will be: his. I am his and he is mine.

"I love you, Killian Blackheart."

"And I you, Thea Blackheart."

"If...if things don't go..." He silences me with a kiss.

"No," he says simply as he pulls away and I know what he's saying: no goodbyes. No final declarations, just in case. He smiles softly, running the backs of his knuckles gently over my cheek, and I smile back and nod. No goodbyes. There are no goodbyes for us, no matter what happens on that field. There are no goodbyes when you are one soul split into two bodies.

He leans his forehead against mine, eyes sliding closed. He stays that way for five long heartbeats and then sighs, pulling back to kiss the place his brow just was, and finally stepping away. He slides his sword into the scabbard at his back and we leave our tent.

The army is ready, all gathered at the east side of the camp to make our final march on Lyanna. We're facing them at the castle itself, away from the city, which I see as a good thing—at least it keeps the citizens far away from the fighting—but Killian isn't so sure.

Dessa joins us, Mia hugging her side as they walk together. Cece and Math arrive next and I have to fight to swallow past the lump in my throat at the sight of Math in armor. He'd insisted back at Duskthorne, saying that this was his fight too and he couldn't stand by and watch. I'd gasped, tears immediately filling my eyes when Cece, tears in her own, had taken his hands and placed them on her belly.

"You fight for what's right and make your son or daughter proud." Math's eyes had gone wide and though anyone wouldn't blame him for changing his mind in that instant, it only hardened his resolve. He trained harder than anyone in those few weeks, becoming one hells of a soldier in my humble opinion.

"Look at you," I say now, watching him stroll over in his armor, a war hammer resting on his hip and a short sword strapped to his back.

"I look fucking fantastic, I know," he says, preening. "This one couldn't keep her hands off of me." He jerks a thumb at Cece. "This is the third time I've dressed, she kept—ow!" Cece grabs his ear and tugs, but brings his face to hers for a kiss.

"You're a damned fool," she tells him, but smiles fondly and winks at me when she turns away. All around me, soldiers ready themselves. Some quiet and contemplative, others loud and boisterous; some praying, some drinking, some stoic.

Cece comes forward and wraps her arms around me.

"Are you sure you're ready?" she whispers as she hugs me tightly. I know she doesn't mean for battle. Am I ready to face my sister, to do what needs to be done.

"I am."

She looks saddened but she knows now what my twin is truly capable of, the darkness inside of her that's destroyed all that I used to love. I would not have been ready to kill Tess, the other part of me, the girl who protected me and laughed with me and made up silly stories about the stars to make me smile. But I am ready to kill Tesni, the girl who betrayed me, the woman who did it yet again; the woman who has done unspeakable things and let unspeakable things be done without lifting a finger to stop them.

Cece pulls away and cradles my cheek with one hand, the other going to her belly. "He or she will want their aunt back in one piece." I smile, kiss her cheek, give Mia a big hug, and then turn and walk away without another word. If I don't, if I try to find the words to say goodbye, I'll never leave.

Dessa, Tristan, Math, and Killian follow a moment later, and they all know me well enough not to ask if I'm alright, not to try to hug me or make this better. My heart just needs a moment to allow the breaking. The breaking that will hopefully mend itself once we all come out of this safely, but it breaks all the same as I walk away from my true sister, the one I chose for myself and the one that has loved me unconditionally since the moment I met her; as I walk away from the girl who stole my heart and made me find light in those first awful weeks of terror and darkness after I'd been taken; as I walk away from my family.

I'm leaving part of my family behind.

But the rest is with me, walking into battle beside me—or flying overhead. I look up and, squinting, I can make out the faint rippling in the air as Isolde flies above us. She's camouflaged herself, as the warrior caste of dragons is able to do, though only for short amounts of time. To our knowledge, the Alliance knows nothing of her existence, let alone that she's bonded with the Commander of the whole fucking army. My lips curl, imagining Tesni and Barony's reactions to that little surprise we have waiting for them.

-*I'd very much like to rip Barony's throat out myself,*- Soren purrs inside my mind, bounding out from the tree line as we mount our horses.

-*I'll fight you for him, cat,*- Killian replies, fury blazing in his eyes. He will hate Barony forever for what he'd done to me all those years ago, forcing us to choose. Forcing Tesni to show her true colors and break my heart in two.

Soren bares his fangs at Killian astride his giant Northland, and Killian bares his teeth right back, making all of us laugh.

-*Ready, love?*- my husband asks.

I take one more big breath in and hold it for a long moment before letting it out slowly.

-I'm ready.-

With that, we ride.

"Great," I say.

"Fucking," Math adds.

"Makers," Dessa and Tristan finish as one.

The chosen battlefield is the wide expanse of fields and the frozen lake that lie just outside the castle's northern edge, and it is filled with soldiers. Tens of thousands, hundreds of thousands, so many I can't possibly wrap my head around it. We have an impressive number of our own forces, of course, but seeing the Alliance's army in lines spread out before us, a sea of armor and weapons and bodies, is truly something to behold.

"Is the lake solid?" Killian asks, his mind working as he wonders the same thing I do: why here?

I reach out with my Gift and nod. "Frozen completely. It can hold the weight of our men."

He's mirrored my Gift, but he can't do nearly as much with it as I can, not yet. Killian nods and scans the battlements and ramparts, archers lining them with bows at the ready. They can't possibly reach our men from there, but once we get closer, they'll rain those arrows down upon us like a summer storm.

-They'll try,- Killian tells me. Between my ice, Isolde, and all of the Gifts Killian is mirroring, the arrows won't get near our lines. I smile at him and the twisting unease in my chest eases a bit. We have more power than they could possibly imagine.

"How many Gifteds among them? How many abominations?" Dessa asks, her voice hard and calculating, the voice not of my friend who likes to steal my clothes and likes Abrasian chocolate as much as I do, but the battle-hardened Captain and famed archer of Duskthorne. The sun glints off of the silver medallions woven into her warrior brads, the rings in her brows and ears.

"A handful of Gifteds. I can block them, no problem." His lip curls in disgust. "A good many more abominations."

I recoil, bile rising in my throat. They've stolen Gifts from that many people? I thought—hoped—it would only be a few, that the process would be too difficult or too demanding. But apparently not. And how many of them have more than one stolen Gift? How many Gifteds have died because of them??

The bile recedes as white-hot fury rises, filling every inch of me. Frost covers my skin, the temperature dropping around us, and Killian gives me a look that's part pride and part feral lust.

-*My warrior queen,*- he rasps inside my mind, reverent and desirous and so incredibly sexy that I have to fight to keep my expression even. -*The things I'm going to do to you when we finish this...*-

-*You'll want to borrow from Harlon again for the things I have in store for you, Commander, I promise you that...*-

He makes a low growling sound and I try to hide my smile.

"We all know when you're saying filthy things to each other inside your minds, just so you're aware," Math informs us and I whirl to him, gaping. He shrugs and everyone around us bursts into laughing fits.

"I should have left you in Helios," I grumble, but can't fight my own smile. I shake my head and turn back to the awaiting army in front of us, scanning the lines for flaming red hair. No, she would never be down in the trenches with the soldiers, I remind myself, so I shift my gaze upward to the ramparts. She'll want to watch, I know it, but she'll be somewhere completely fortified. I look to the north tower, the slitted windows overlooking the lake and the grounds, and I swear I see a flash of red.

We have a quick discussion laying out our plans and then, we ready ourselves.

"I still say there should be a horn or something to signal—"

A battle cry ripples through the Alliance's army and then they're charging forward. We'll have to make it through the fields before we reach the lake, and then the castle walls. I steady myself, knowing it's going to be a long, long day, and call up my power, my palms tingling as ice coats them, ready and waiting.

"Hold!" Killian roars, holding our men in place all around us. As much as I want to be on the front lines, I'm farther back for now, upon another rise of my own making so that I can assist in these first waves of attack. Then, we'll join the real battle.

Soren shifts beside me, fangs and claws bared. Watchful. Ready.

"Almost..." Killian says, watching. "Almost..." He wants to let the first of their lines make it across the field before I stop them, something about too many bodies crammed in the back of the fight and bottlenecking and other things I didn't understand. "Now, Thea!" he yells and I unleash my Gift. A wave of ice rears up in front of the lines advancing towards us, soaring forward and sending them sprawling and tumbling. I don't encase them like I did on the tundra, but they crumple and scream as the force of running into a solid wall of ice destroys them.

"Forward!" Killian yells and our lines rush onward behind my wave of ice. It wipes through hundreds of men before I have to let it turn to powder and fall harmlessly to the ground, but our men are there in its wake, swords and axes and hammers drawn and raining down blows on the stunned army.

Just as it had the first time we faced the abominations, the battle turns into pure chaos and I can't seem to see enough of it, my eyes darting too many places too quickly. Storm clouds form overhead, blocking out the sun, and thunder rumbles ominously. Lightning streaks downward, the ground exploding in sprays of snow and dirt and blood, screams ringing out as soldiers are burned or thrown aside from the blast. Again and again.

"Fucking abomination," Killian growls, narrowing his eyes. He uses his mirrored telekinesis to throw the woman aside. He may not be able to block them, but he can still feel them, still pinpoint where and who they are. I send a wall of snow onto the soldiers at the far left flank, Killian flings more soldiers, and Dessa and the archers let arrows fly. Just when I think that things might be easier than I thought, things turn from chaos to pure insanity.

More abominations let lose their stolen Gifts and I can't keep track of everything happening. The ground beneath us shakes violently, opening up in some places; more lightning rains down; violent winds thrash; pelting rain joins the lightning; soldiers in our lines *turn to fucking stone.*

"Fucking hells!" Math yells. I turn to Killian, eyes wide and heart hammering.

"What do we do?" I ask over the din.

"We fight," he says, jaw set and sword singing as he unsheathes it from his back. I nod and he rushes for me, pressing his lips to mine in a rough, soul searing kiss, before pulling away, waiting. Despite everything I smile, knowing this is going to be something for the ages.

An unholy screeching roar fills the air, making almost all of the soldiers cower, looking to the skies in confusion and terror. A moment later, Isolde sheds her camouflage, her black scales shining in the dark skies as lightning flashes again. Cries ring out as she soars over the battle, screams of terror and shock and panic. Some of the Alliance's forces actually flee, breaking ranks and running in all directions. Isolde circles back to us, tucking her wings and dropping like a stone towards Killian. She flares them again and levels out just as she passes over our heads and Killian leaps. She catches him in her talons in a graceful, fluid movement—one they've practiced for countless hours over the last few weeks—and tosses him upward. He flips in the air and lands on her back, clutching her ridges and settling into the spot between her shoulders made for him.

"Holy fucking hells, that was the most amazing thing I've ever seen!" Tristan calls out, whooping, and I see Jonathan and Kendall hoist their weapons upward in triumph. All of our soldiers roar in delight, their king and commander and the symbol of their kingdom soaring into battle above them. I can practically feel the burst of strength it gives them, bolstering their resolve. They continue their war cries, sprinting forward into the fray with a new vigor.

-*Showoff*,- I say through the connection to all four of us.

-*Jealous!*- Killian calls back, and I can hear the utter excitement and joy in his voice. They soar closer to the castle, and I brace as Isolde inhales deeply, a stream of blue fire erupting from her gaping maw and incinerating hundreds of the enemy within seconds. She must rest between bursts of fire, otherwise I'm sure she would gladly lay the entire battlefield to waste in a matter of minutes and we could call this day done.

More of their forces turn and flee, desperate to escape that azure inferno, that death carried on sleek, midnight wings. *Beautiful.*

Tristan turns to me now. "Shall we?" he asks and I nod, ready to truly join the fight. I form my sword of ice in one hand, my other palm ready to wield my Gift.

"The mountains do not move!" Dessa calls, nocking another arrow and readying to cover us as we enter the fray.

"And the dragons do not yield!" I yell back, finishing the battle cry she and Killian made up when they were children.

She grins and winks, blows a kiss to Tristan, and then I'm running and everything is a blur. I don't think as I throw myself into the melee, don't think as I plunge my sword through a man in forest green armor, don't think as I do it again, and again, and again. I slash and parry and block blows, just as I was taught in The Seventh. I spin and throw blades of ice, my blood singing and burning in my veins. I duck as Soren leaps over me to sink his claws into a man's chest, cutting through his armor and leaving it in silvery ribbons coated with blood.

I have no idea how to know whether we're winning or losing or gaining any ground. Isolde lets more fire burn, but I know that will stop soon, once our forces get closer to the castle. Killian won't risk us getting caught in the flames. We fight and fight and fight, everything becoming a dull ringing in my ears as my soul soars and instincts I didn't know I had take over. I remember everything Killian and Dessa taught me, every lesson given to me by Kendall and Jonathan and Tristan, the other lessons from long ago that still serve me, the ones given to me by the first person in this world to truly love me. Tobias' voice sounds through my mind as I whirl and kicking one man on my left while plunging my sword into another on my right. *You are meant for greatness, sparrow. Never stop fighting.*

The abominations are still wielding their stolen Gifts but we're doing our best to combat them. I reach into the clouds above with my own Gift and turn the rain to snow and divert the flakes away from the fight and over the castle instead.

"Much obliged!" Kendall calls as he buries an axe into a man's throat. "I hate fighting in the damned rain!" He's off then, after another enemy. Over and over, the dance continues.

My arms are screaming after what feels like it must be hours later, though I'm sure it hasn't been very long at all. Isolde has taken to the ground, she and Killian are ripping through the Alliance on the lake. It's difficult to see much of anything, a wall of bodies surrounding me on all sides, but Isolde towers high above everything, her fangs bared, jaws snapping, arrows bouncing harmlessly off of her scales. Some of the abominations are still wielding, but many of them seem to have stopped. Thankfully someone was able to take out whichever one was somehow turning people to stone without touching them. Great fucking Makers. I wish I could see them all like Killian can, know who to target, but I don't want to distract him by asking him to point them out.

More blood coats my blade. More bodies fall. Soren roars and rips a woman's arm off before she can stab Math in the back.

-*Thank you,*- I breathe, heart in my throat.

-*Your family is my family, daska. I will defend them with my last breath.*-

Math meets my eyes and nods, and we keep pushing forward amid the chaos.

"Are you having fun yet, princess?!" Dessa calls from behind me now. I glance over my shoulder and see that she's exchanged her bow for sword with gleaming stars etched down the blade. Her braids are coated with blood, her face and neck splattered with it, but I don't think any of it is hers.

"Oh, a jolly fucking—" I scream when I'm hit in the chest by a war hammer, so hard I go sailing backwards. I can barely breathe, the air ripped from my lungs. My armor holds, thank the Makers, but fucking hells does it hurt. My chest burns and I think a rib or two might be cracked, and my head swims for a moment from the pain.

"Thea!" Dessa yells, battling a man and a woman in crimson armor as she tries to get to me.

I blink as the man above me raises his hammer again. I throw out a hand and a heartbeat later he's frozen solid—just before Soren clamps his jaws around his neck and tears his head free. His frozen body remains upright, thick, sludge-like blood oozing slowly down his gaping neck.

-*Are you alright??*- Soren demands.

-*What the fuck is happening over there?!*- Killian barks through all of our minds. I gasp for breath, my ribs burning, but the pain is manageable.

-*I'm...fine,*- I grit.

Dessa is there a moment later, yanking me to my feet none too gently. I clench my teeth, but nod, telling her I'm alright. That's all we have time for, pushing forward once more. The abominations Gifts slowly stop working and I assume that Killian and Isolde are responsible. Though I can't see him, I know he's using his mirrored Gifts: speeding through the ranks faster than any other human can possibly run; pulling weapons from hands with the magnetic ability; throwing opponents aside with his telekinesis. I smile, knowing in my heart that we can do this, we can win.

That's when a wall of orange fire engulfs our entire right flank.

CHAPTER
THIRTY-FIVE
KILLIAN

My heart stops as fire erupts out of nowhere and devours a good portion of our forces—Alliance forces as well. *No. Makers please don't let it be where Thea was...*

-*THEA!*-

Isolde roars, spraying her own blue fire again and lashing out with talons and her spiked tail as I cut through any Alliance forces who approach us. We were making real progress, culling their numbers and ending their abominations' threats, and I guess that was finally enough for Barony. He sicced his fucking fire bitch on us.

-*Fine! We're fine!*- she assures us back, but I can hear the fear in her voice. The flames are snuffed out quickly, smothered in a heap of ice and snow. *That's my girl.*

-*Soren get her out of there!*-

-*Trying,*- he growls.

I'm just about to send Isolde to go pick all of them up when the ice beneath us begins to crack. I lose my balance for a moment before righting myself. I frown realizing that the ground beneath my boots is...wet.

Oh fuck.

Isolde flares her wings, readying to lift us into the air but I tell her to hold. We need this position. We cannot lose the ground we've gained here.

But the lake is fucking melting.

CHAPTER
THIRTY-SIX
THEA

I cut my eyes to the ramparts, knowing what I'll see before I spy it: flaming red hair blowing in the wind. She sends balls of fire soaring through the air, flaming death raining down all around us. I blast as many as I can with ice, freezing them before they can strike but fucking hells how is she sending so many?? I see more ice joining my own and smile savagely: Killian. Him using my mirrored Gift sends a thrill through me that I can't understand or explain.

-*Thea! The lake!*-

I whip my head towards them. I can't see Killian of course, but I see Isolde, looking uneasy, wings flaring and smoke and fire roiling from his nostrils.

-*She's melting the fucking lake!*-

Fuck.

I send power surging towards the lake, shoring up the ice, making it as solid as fucking steel. Killian can wield my Gift, but not as powerfully as I can. He won't be able to fight *and* keep the lake solid beneath them all *and* wield all his mirrored gifts, and he knows it. If that ice breaks, hundreds of soldiers could drown, pulled to the depths by their heavy armor.

-*I've got you,*- I promise, charging towards the lake, determined to cut down every fucking soldier in my path. Fury gives me a flare of strength. Tesni made a mistake by showing herself, by burning my men and trying to melt that lake. I slash and stab and send waves of ice sailing across the field as I run, but more of those balls of fire rain overhead, more pillars of it flaring up all around. Our people are falling. Our soldiers burning and screaming. I freeze the fires with Killian's help, but there are so fucking many of them, I can't keep up.

-*Thea, the lake!*- Soren reminds me.

I grit my teeth, sweat beading my brow as I reinforce the ice in the lake again. I can't keep up. I can't...oh Makers, I can't beat her. I look up and I swear, even from this distance, I can see her smirking, as if she can read my thoughts. That smirk does it. Rage roils, love and anger and the need to protect my people all filling my chest like Tesni's own fire. I'm done with this.

It's time to face my fucking sister.

Though I feel physically ill about what's about to happen, I know it's the only way.

-*Isolde! Get me up there!*- I yell through the bond. I don't put my plan into words, exactly, too focused on keeping the lake solid and putting out as many fires as I can while still slashing out with my blade, Tristan and Dessa and Math beside me, Jonathan and Kendall just ahead, but push my intentions through the doorways and I see her launch into the air a moment later.

-*Come back to me, Red,*- Killian says, not trying to stop me and my love for him grows ever deeper. He trusts me to do this, trusts that this is what I think is right and will follow me no matter where I lead.

-*Always.*-

"Get to Killian!" I yell to Dessa and the others, shoving Math towards Tristan and nodding at him in thanks, knowing he'll keep my friend safe. I try to keep it inside, but the scream rips from my throat as Isolde's claws wrap around me, surprisingly gently, and she launches us skyward. My heart leaps directly into my throat, all air leaving my lungs, and I'm honestly surprised that I don't piss myself from fear as I see the battlefield below me, the soldiers looking like ants scrambling around a kicked-over hill.

"Fuck, fuck, fuck!!" I scream, clutching her claws, desperate to hold on.

-*I promised I wouldn't drop you,*- she reminds me, a bit of humor in her voice despite everything. She lets out a spray of fire and I squeeze my eyes closed, the heat rushing over my skin even from this height. Soren, clutched in her other set of claws, roars loudly, clearly enjoying himself. I'm doing all I can not to vomit all over the battle below and pray that this will be over soon. Why Killian loves this so much is something I will never, ever understand.

The flight only takes seconds but it feels like a fucking eternity.

-*Brace yourself,*- Isolde finally warns and pry my eyes open. We're almost to the ramparts and I can see Tesni clearly now, eyes wide despite herself as she spies a fucking dragon coming for her. She staggers back, clearly afraid, and a twisted flash of satisfaction rushes through me. Good. She should be afraid.

Isolde roars and Tesni cowers. It distracts my sister enough that I can drop from Isolde's claws and land on the battlements, the impact jarring, but I bend my knees and roll as Tobias taught me all those years ago. Soren lands lithely beside me and I spare a second to be annoyed with the cat. It really isn't fair that he can be so damned nimble.

-*Go!*- I tell Isolde. -*Protect them!*-

She roars again and flies straight up into the air, flipping backwards to make her way back to Killian and, Makers willing, the rest of my family. I rise slowly, Soren snarling by my side, and Tesni turns to face me. She can't quite hide the awe and fear in her eyes as she watches Isolde fly back into the fray, and her eyes widen even more when she sees Soren. She actually takes a step back from the frost cat, but as a rush of soldiers floods up from the stairs a few yards behind me, Soren growls, flashing his fangs at my twin once more for good measure before turning and bounding towards the men coming for my back. Tesni composes herself and her lips curl into that cold, wicked smile.

"Good to see you, sister. Care to watch all of your little friends drown?" She flicks her fingers towards the lake, but I send a surge of power into the water, making it completely solid once more before clenching my teeth and throwing up a dome of ice around us. She quirks a brow and I can feel when she tries to push her Gift past it. It holds strong. Now it's my turn to smile.

"It's just you and me now, Tesni," I spit, tensing my muscles, preparing for whatever she has planned.

She narrows her eyes. "The cat is your familiar," she says, quickly assessing everything she's seeing. "And the fucking dragon??" she asks through clenched teeth, clearly angry but unable to stop herself from asking the question.

"The Commander's."

Fury blazes in her eyes and fire dances along her knuckles. "*You get a familiar. You and that bastard's lapdog both??*" She screeches some intelligible sound of rage and a wall of fire hurdles towards me.

-*Thea!*- Soren roars. He won't be happy when he realizes that the dome around Tesni and me has him firmly locked *out*. I throw up a wall of ice and the flames crash against it, sizzling as they die out.

"You're strong now, Thea, I'll give you that much. But you're no match for me, you never were." There's a maniacal look in her eyes, something that was never there before. I wonder if it's this taste of power she's gotten now that she's a queen, igniting a thirst that she'll die trying to quench.

"I won't let your Alliance do this, Tesni."

Another round of flames soars towards me, the stone beneath my boots suddenly hot as lava, and though my dome holds, the entirety of the area above us becomes a ceiling of fire. *Great fucking Makers.* I cool the stone, force the icy dome to grow thicker, and stop the fire coming for me again. Sweat drips, stinging my eyes, but I don't dare let up.

-*Keep fighting,*- I tell Killian. I need them to win the battle outside, or at least hold until I find a way to finish this with Tesni.

-*Always,*- Killian assures me. -*Always, Red.*-

I attack this time, sending spikes of ice flying towards Tesni. She melts them easily.

"Tell Barony to stop this!" I yell, panting.

She throws her head back and laughs, sounding truly crazed.

"Barony is *dead*," she sneers, baring her teeth. I blink at that. "They're all dead. Barony, Nicolette, William, Ruby. All gone, by *my* doing. I rule their kingdoms now. Half of Hypathia is *mine*."

"Dead? You...murdered Barony? Murdered four other fucking royals??" *Makers*.

"Technically, the alchemist did before they attempted the procedure to take Gifts, but it was my plan, yes. Klaus was more than happy to assist when I promised him a fortune bigger than all of Enola. Assist in...many ways." Her lips curl, her eyes sparking like living flames. I take a step backwards as realization sinks in.

"Makers, you've done it, haven't you? You've taken Gifts. That's how you're so much stronger now."

She grins, a wicked slash of wine-red lips against porcelain skin.

"I did. They didn't give me new Gifts. Klaus had never tried the procedure on someone who already possessed a Gift, so we weren't exactly sure what might happen. Isn't the irony so fucking disgusting? A normal, insignificant human can steal as many Gifts as they wish, have as many powers as their puny bodies can withstand, but a blessed Gifted can only become stronger, gain nothing new?" She curls her lip but shakes herself. "No new Gift for me, still only fire, but *great Makers* the new power roiling through my veins..." She shudders. Feeling the need to demonstrate apparently, two giant pillars of fire spring from her upturned palms, soaring thirty feet over our heads. They shift and writhe until they join and become—

"Holy fucking fuck," I gasp, stumbling backwards several steps. A great serpent of fire soars over us now, coiling its flaming body before rearing back and striking at my dome of ice. It holds, thank the Makers, but I force my power into it, reinforcing the walls until they're a foot thick. I can hardly take my eyes from the display, the power of it staggering, but I hear Tesni panting. I cut my gaze away from the snake and narrow my eyes at her. She's sweating and pale, teeth gritted as she keeps the fiery serpent coiling and striking above us.

"The extra Gifts are fighting you, aren't they?" She all but snarls at me, the look dark and killing, and I know that I'm right. "They are! They know that they don't belong to you, they know that you stole them like a fucking coward!"

"They are MINE! They are ALL MINE! The power. The Gifts. This entire empire!! They will all kneel before me. I am a queen!" she shrieks. That serpent slithers from the top of the dome, rearing up behind Tesni before bounding over her shoulder for me. Ice explodes from my palms, but the snake attacks with so much force that I'm shoved backwards, boots sliding over the slick stone. I grit my teeth as the fire pushes, harder and harder, the heat of it unreal.

-*Thea!*- Killian roars in my mind.

This is it.

I reach deep down within myself, pulling up as much of my power as I can. I can feel her fire burning outward now too, pushing against the dome. If it falters, if that fire breaks free, it will destroy everyone outside the walls of the castle. The people that I love.

No. I will not fail them.

-*Daska,*- Soren warns, knowing my mind better than anyone else, so much a part of me, and I can feel him clawing at the ice behind me, desperate to make his way inside the dome. -*Daska, you will not!*-

I put everything I have into the ice, stepping forward, the cold over taking the flames inch by inch, step by step. Sweat pours down my face and neck, my muscles trembling from the strain, but I don't stop. I will never fucking stop. Tesni grits her teeth, screaming in defiance as she tries to overtake me, her flames burning hotter and brighter, but she can't. She might have stolen power in her veins, but I have the power given to me by the Makers, a familiar chosen for me by fate, a love bigger than the endless sky. I pull on all of it now, pushing back those fucking flames, inching closer and closer to my sister.

"So. Am. I," I grit. Another inch. Another step.

"What?" she hisses, eyes wide but hard as stone.

"I am Thea Blackheart, Queen of Duskthorne." I press my shoulders back, proud and sure. A crown of ice appears, the sharp edges looking like the Obsidians that have always been home. Our beloved dragon's head is carved in the center, cold eyes staring at Tesni as if daring her to try to refute it. "I am a queen of this empire and I will not let you continue to hurt my people."

I keep pushing, willing the ice to overtake the flames.

"You...you married that monster, Dorian?? Even I wouldn't be that desperate," she spits.

"No," I say easily and tilt my head towards the battle outside, towards Killian and Isolde laying waste to the Alliance's forces. "I married Dorian Killian Elvania—*the second*," I add, my lips curling remembering how hastily Killian had added that bit in when Frederick had first introduced him in the throne room, when I'd first learned the whole truth. "King of Duskthorne, High Commander, and my husband."

Tesni stares, brow furrowing as she looks from Killian to me, as realization sinks in. Pure fury fills her face, all traces of confusion gone in an instant.

"No!" she screams. "No! You cannot be! You don't deserve to be a queen, you don't deserve a familiar, you don't deserve *any* of it!" A surge of power flares with her rage, pushing back against my ice, sending me sliding backwards again. I can hear the others screaming down the pathway between us, but I don't let them in. I can't let them in. "You were the weak one, the pathetic excuse for a Gifted. You didn't see it for the truth that it was: we should be worshipped for what we are, Thea. We are the real Makers. They should all kneel before us in fear."

"No," I tell her, looking at her with nothing but pity now. "No one should kneel in fear."

I open the pathway long enough to tell them one more thing before the end:

-I love you all.-

-THEA!!- Killian roars and I can feel Isolde's fire trying to burn through my dome to get to me. I won't let that happen. I feel Soren's frantic clawing at the ice, feel him putting as much of his strength into our bond as he possibly can.

I can see the Brink in my mind, a dark abyss on the horizon, but I keep pushing against my sister, her fanatical belief and anger making her power surge even higher. I push harder.

Another inch.

Another step.

Closer.

Closer.

I'm close enough now that I can see the fear in Tesni's eyes, only a foot of fire standing between her and my ice.

"No," she whispers. "No..."

"Goodbye, Tess," I say, tears in my eyes. I will not shed any for Tesni, but I will let them fall for the sister I lost, the one that I think might still be buried somewhere inside this monster before me, so deep that I'll never find her again. I reach the Brink and careen over it, tumbling into oblivion as the cold explodes from my body, dousing every fire within the dome, the fire within Tesni's veins.

She screams in agony and defiance, and I think perhaps a tiny shred of sorrow, and then I'm falling into nothingness.

CHAPTER THIRTY-SEVEN
TESNI

No! No, this cannot be happening. I can't...lose. I can't fall to my sister. She was the weaker one, she was the one to be thrown away. I was the one raised up and feared and revered throughout the empire. I am the queen of five kingdoms!

And yet, she's stronger than me. I feel it, the moment I've lost. That small voice inside myself, the last bit of light, sighs—in relief. Happy for it to be over. Happy to not be a prisoner inside this darkness any longer.

But Thea is reaching the Brink now. I see it, can almost feel it as if it's happening to me. I guess some of the strange connection between us as twins remains, even after all this time, after all the hurt and betrayal.

She screams as a cold so deep that it burns explodes from her, extinguishing my fires, nearly freezing me completely, but I hold onto the knowledge that she's gone. She's used every bit of strength she has left and if I can just hold on for a few more seconds, I'll have won. Yes. Yes, I deserve to win. I deserve everything!!

So I hold on, digging deep inside of myself, gripping my own Gift and the ones that I've taken and hold steadfast, refusing to give up. A tiny flame flickers inside my chest, remaining alight against the cold, but it's enough.

Thea drops to her knees, the Brink destroying her body from the inside out, the power overtaking her. Blood pours from her nose and she bows her head, her body sagging as it gives its last. The cold recedes and I take a few ragged, gasping breaths. I was nearly gone. But I was stronger, just like I've always known that I was.

I look to my sister, the blood dripping to the dark stone of the ramparts. The tiny voice that I thought was gone forever, silenced by the impenetrable darkness that overtook everything when I'd orchestrated the deaths of Barony and the others, manages to claw its way through. It recoils at what I've done, feels such much pain at the loss of my sister that my heart actually splinters.

You were supposed to love her. You were supposed to protect her, it hisses, accusing and full of grief.

But it can only stay afloat for so long, swallowed up again all too quickly by the darkness that's dancing with glee. I've won. I smile in triumph, taking a staggering step forward towards my sister's body.

Searing pain explodes through my chest, hot and angry and burning.

I look down to see a sword through my heart.

A sword of ice.

CHAPTER THIRTY-EIGHT
THEA

Tesni stares down at the blade in her chest, frowning. Blood pours, soaking her front, but she still just stares.

"How..." She falls to her knees and gasps, the sound wet and sticky. "How...did you survive...the Brink. I...saw you...I saw you reach it. I *felt* it." A part of my heart clenches at that, knowing that the connection between us that I had always thought made us so special still remained, despite everything.

"I did reach it, but my own power isn't all that resides within me."

Just as I'd reached the Brink, that oddly beautiful end to my story, I felt them all grab me, clutching me and pulling me back. The tattoo on my neck is an ancient troth rune, one from the days of magik, according to Duskthorne legend. Killian and I were bound by love and the laws of Hypathia, but this tattoo—and his matching one—bind us in old, lost ways. Ways that connect us, twining our lives and our powers together on a level I can't even fully understand.

But that connection also gave me a line to his power, along with a certain dragon's.

Soren's power held me aloft from that churning endless sea of the Brink. Isolde's hauled me back up that never-ending trench, closer and closer to the light. And Killian's had hurled me back into myself, telling me in no uncertain terms that I would *not* be leaving his side. Not today. Not ever.

Of course, when I'd found the symbol in an old tome in the library, I hadn't had any idea this is what it would mean. It just called to me, and since I'd always admired his tattoos, I'd told Killian I wanted to have one as well. I'd shown him the ancient symbol of love and devotion and eternal connection, and he'd immediately agreed—and had touched and kissed and licked the swirling knot any chance he got since it had been inked there, saying that it was his new favorite thing on this earth.

Again, I feel the Makers' hands in all of this. They led me to that book, that symbol, knowing it would save my life and end this war.

Tesni coughs, blood bubbling over her lips and dripping down her chin. She meets my gaze then, her emerald eyes, an exact reflection of my own, softening for the first time in nearly sixteen years. Her lips curl into a surprised, but real smile.

"I'm sorry...I turned out...so wrong. I did love you...Tee. I really did."

Tears burn my eyes.

"I loved you too, Tess," I whisper as a tear slides free and freezes on my cheek. She smiles wider, blood staining her teeth, and then collapses back, the blade sliding free from her chest. I try to ignore the way it grinds against her bones on the way out, the way the blood drips onto the stone beneath me, the way Tesni finally looks like the sister I'd known again, that cold sharpness gone in death.

I drop to my knees beside her and let the dome around us fall away. The blade falls to the stone and slowly melts, the water mixing with the blood. If the battle still rages on below, I don't hear it. Soren is at my back a second later and Killian drops to the rampart beside me a heartbeat after that. Isolde lands a few feet away, claws digging into the stone.

Killian falls to his knees beside me, cupping my face gently.

"Thea? Thea, love, are you alright?"

After a moment, I lift my gaze to his, letting the tears fall freely.

"No," I tell him honestly, and he pulls me into his chest, letting me fall apart inside the safety of his arms. He strokes the back of my head as I cry, letting everything that's happened wash through me.

We fought a battle.

We lost thousands of our people.

We killed thousands more of theirs.

I killed a true monster.

I killed my sister.

"It's alright, love. It's alright." Killian rocks me gently and I feel Soren's forehead against my back, giving me even more of his strength, just in a different way now.

-*You did well, Daska. I am proud to call you mine.*-

I can't speak but I send as much love as I can to him through our pathway. I clutch at Killian for what feels like hours, but I finally pull away, sniffling. He cradles my face again, brushing away tears and blood with his thumbs.

"There you are," he whispers, his smile so heartbreakingly beautiful.

"What happened?" I ask, voice rough. I jerk my head toward the lake and field beyond. "Down there?"

"Once you contained your sister, we were able to overtake the rest of their forces. Most of them cowered and surrendered before Isolde, truth be told."

-*I am quite fearsome, in case you've forgotten,*- she adds, a smile in her voice. I huff out a laugh, scrubbing at my eyes.

"She killed Barony. The others, too. Or had them killed anyway."

Killian blinks at that, brow furrowing.

"That means..." He lets the unspoken words hang in the air. We all know what it means, but I'm in no state to truly think about that now. "Later," he says and I squeeze his hand gratefully.

Apparently Dessa and the others are securing the rest of the castle now, rounding up the alchemists and freeing the Gifteds from the dungeons.

"So...it's over?" I ask.

"It's over," Killian confirms, arms still wrapped around me. I know there is so much more left to do, so many things to figure out to try to fix this ruined empire, but for now, there's only one thing I want to do.

"Let's go home."

He smiles, kisses me softly, that touch of his lips like oxygen bringing me back to life.

"Home it is."

"From an orphan on the road alone, to a tavern owner and Gifted in hiding, to an imposter prisoner, to the queen of *six* kingdoms," Ryker shakes his head. "That is quite a life, my dear."

I laugh. "You're telling me." I still can't quite wrap my head around everything that's happened, what killing Tesni and ending this war really meant. The alchemists were all imprisoned for their crimes, the Gifteds being held in the dungeons in Lyanna all released and healed and offered homes in any kingdom they wished across the empire. All Hunting and slaving has been outlawed, allowing Gifteds throughout Hypathia to feel safe for the first time in centuries. King Decosta and Queen Pheobe were more than happy to agree to our terms after hearing of the fall of Barony and Tesni. Neither of them wanted anything to do with the Alliance to begin with and neither of them had wanted to take Gifts like the others.

Decosta just wanted to go back to living his life mostly separate from the rest of Hypathia, which wasn't surprising, but Phoebe had some really intriguing ideas of creating a council of sorts for the empire, a place where representatives, not just the royals, from each kingdom come together to discuss the wellbeing of everyone in

Hypathia, making decisions together that keep everyone safe and happy.

She and Killian have been corresponding nonstop about the plans, the idea of it making excitement dance in his eyes any time we discuss it.

"A queen to six kingdoms..." Ryker continues, clearing his throat lightly, "and an heir to a seventh, it would seem."

I frown. "Heir...?"

"I've had my scholars combing through records over these months since I first met you, and they finally found the records to prove it: you are my niece."

"Niece?" I breathe. My mind reeling, my heart swelling.

"My brother, Edmund, was your father. You have his eyes," he says with a sad smile.

"But...but how?"

"Edmund had a wild and restless heart—a good heart, mind you, but wild and restless all the same. He never had interest in court or politics or the life of a royal. He wanted to travel, to see everything the empire had to offer. So that's what he did. He loved every second of it, especially when he reached Lyanna. He met your mother, they fell in love. They had plans to travel together, explore the islands, but he fell ill. He died before he even knew your mother was pregnant." I blink, unsure how to process all of this, but a strange, profound sorrow fills my heart for the stranger who was my father.

"I believe that Barony knew Edmund was your father. The two of them had dealings when he was in Lyanna, so it stands to reason that he might have known about his personal relationships and that's why he took the opportunity to adopt you when your mother died. He knew that Edmund was Gifted—he could turn any object to silver with a touch—and hoped that his children would be as well."

I'm silent for a long time, trying to process everything. I've never known a single thing about my father, and all we'd been told of my mother was that she'd died alone. To know that she had been loved, that she was happy and had plans to explore this world with the man she loved, makes something deep inside me heal, something I didn't even truly realize was broken until now.

"I don't mean to have upset you, I just thought—"

I smile at him. I wish I could explain how this makes me feel, that though I have so many people that I love beyond measure, who are my family down to my soul, having someone of my blood here with me after I thought Tesni was the last means so much. With the way he smiles back, I think perhaps he doesn't need me to explain it. He understands.

I throw my arms around him and he hugs me tightly.

"I can tell you all about him."

Through tears, I tell him, "I'd like that very much."

CHAPTER
THIRTY-NINE
KILLIAN

My kingdom is safe. The empire is healing. Gifteds are free. My familiar makes me stronger every day. Dragons have returned to our lands. The family I never thought I'd be lucky enough to have seems to grow every single day: a frost cat, Tristan, Cece, Math, and their unborn daughter all a part of it now. My heart is so full it could fucking burst.

And my wife is happy and whole and safe in my arms.

It's been a few months since the Battle of Fire and Ice as the bards have dubbed it, singing songs about it in taverns across the empire, and though there is still much to do, I can see the world we're making taking shape. A better world for everyone.

More familiars are bonding with Gifteds everyday, as if the Makers are blessing us once more, rewarding all of us for stopping the darkness. Cece and Math decided to go back to Helios to raise their daughter in the home they built there—not the *physical* home above the tavern since a certain Ice Queen insisted on building them an entirely new one right on the beach, big enough for them to add at least ten more to their brood should they wish to—but now that we know for sure mirroring a Gift causes no harm to the bearer, I'm able to borrow from Yara as often as I like, opening doorways between the two kingdoms as easy as breathing so visits happen nearly every day.

Thea stirs as I run a finger down her spine, along all of the new ink there. Ancient runes that had called to her from the old magikal texts: strength; courage; family; love; loyalty; bread-making. That particular one she and Dessa had gotten together when they'd been completely drunk on sweet ale from Sol. I probably should have talked them out of it, but it was too funny not to let them continue. I can see her lips curl upward, but her eyes remain closed as I trace the lines of my favorite one of all: the troth rune. The one that we share. The one that saved her life that day.

The one that saves my life every day.

"That one's my favorite too," she says softly, eyes still closed. I frown wondering if I'd said the words through the pathway without realizing it. She cracks one eye open, her grin widening. "No, you didn't, but I still know your mind, Killian Blackheart."

I lean down and kiss her softly.

"That you do, love."

She sighs and shifts enough that she can face me as I lie on the pillow next to her.

"Do you think they were steering it all, knowing how this would all end?" I know who she means. The Makers.

"I think they set us on paths that would lead us to each other, and then the rest was up to us." I do think that Thea and I were destined for each other, that we were meant to be together and find our familiars and end this war and the atrocities Barony and the Alliance were committing against Gifteds, but I don't think we had no choices of our own to make. We had to find our own way to love, had to learn how much we could trust and mean to each other.

"Well, it's a good thing I refused to accept that pathetic excuse for a kiss that night then," she says with a sleepy grin.

"Pathetic excuse for a kiss," I repeat, shaking my head, remembering that night so clearly, every detail seared into my memory forever. "I proved you wrong there, Red."

"Hmm...did you? I can't recall..."

That spark of mischief shines in those emerald eyes, and she squeals when I move, twisting and pulling her beneath me. She giggles, but there's fire in her gaze when I grip her wrists, moving them slowly above her head, and pinning them there.

"Do you need a reminder?" I purr, leaning down and putting my lips a hairsbreadth from hers.

"Always," she breathes.

I smile, my whole world shrinking to this room, this bed, this moment with the woman I love.

"As my queen commands."

ACKNOWLEDGMENTS

As usual, I have so many people to thank:

- My husband for always supporting this weird little hobby and snoring beside me like a champ while I wrote this book.
- The Book Babes (no, Timmy, you still can't join). Lexie, Kayleigh, and Kala, I love y'all so hard. Thank you for being my literal nonstop cheerleaders, fangirls, bullies, and sounding boards. I wouldn't be able to function or put a single damn book out without y'all.
- Lexie. My bestie, ride or die, alpha reader, beta reader, editor, legal counsel, business advisor, therapist, and a thousand other titles that could never all fit on a business card. I love you. None of this would happen without you.
- My amazing PA, Nancy. You are the literal best.
- Tyler for creating the most epic art of these characters and for putting up with my nonstop shenanigans. You're officially in the Cool Kids Club (but only if you bring Morgan, because she's cooler than you).
- Tess for reading my garbage first draft and still believing I should be allowed to write books. Also for not taking it personally that the bitch twin shared your name - I SWEAR it was an accident!
- My awesome Street Team and ARC Readers!
- Every single person who took a chance and picked up this book. THANK YOU!

ALSO BY K. D. MILLER

ADULT ROMANTASY & PARANORMAL ROMANCE

- Veracity of the Gods series:
    - Dark Burning
    - Sweet Tempest
    - Untamed Fate
- Red
- Vows Forged in Blood
- Wrong Place, Wrong Time, Right Viscount

ADULT CONTEMPORARY ROMANCE

- Vipers Sin Bin series:
    - Puck the Holidays
    - Puck of the Irish
- Carpe F*cking Diem
- The Pieces You Kept

ADULT DYSTOPIAN ROMANCE

- Worth the Ruin

UPPER YA SCI-FI AND FANTASY

- Outliers Series
    - Titan Rising
    - Titan Unleashed
    - Titan Reckoning
- Evansfire